RISE
OF THE
RAINBOW
TRIBE

JANNEL MOHAMMED

Published by The Morado Group Inc.
First edition, October 2020

Library and Archives Canada Cataloguing in Publication
Mohammed, Jannel
Rise of the Rainbow Tribe: a novel/Jannel Mohammed. – 1st ed.

ISBN 978-1-7771999-0-6 (paperback)
ISBN 978-1-7771999-1-3 (ebook)
ISBN 978-1-7771999-2-0 (hardcover)

Cover Art by Pintado
Layout Design: James Mensidor
Editors: Pam Elise Harris, Sarah Khan

www.jannelmohammed.com

THE MORADO
GROUP

For my husband, Ryan, and my big sister, Juliet.
Thank you for indulging my creative whims
with enthusiastic cheer and thought-provoking critique.
You read it first and loved it first.
Thank you.

RISE OF THE RAINBOW TRIBE

JANNEL MOHAMMED

'The beginning is near. When the Earth is ravaged, and the animals are dying, a new tribe of people shall come unto the Earth from many colours, classes, creeds, and who by their actions and deeds shall make the Earth green again. They will be known as the Warriors of the Rainbow.'

- Native American Prophecy

CONTENTS

Chapter 1   Mini-Mansion 1

Chapter 2   Keep the Secret 9

Chapter 3   The Clans 20

Chapter 4   New Neighbours 31

Chapter 5   A Surprise in the Woods 44

Chapter 6   Tour Guide 49

Chapter 7   A Parade for Shakti 56

Chapter 8   The Pyramid...70

Chapter 9   The Visitors 84

Chapter 10 The Garden Club 96

Chapter 11 The White Light of Protection............................103

Chapter 12 A Party for Winston 109

Chapter 13 May the Best Nerd Win 126

Chapter 14 The Harder You Work...138

Chapter 15 Paris 150

Chapter 16 Hurricane Kali...164

Chapter 17 The Science Conference 177

Chapter 18 Home 188

Chapter 19 Earning Lights... 200

Chapter 20 Watch This..211

Chapter 21 Magical Mary 215

Chapter 22 First Day, Last Year.. 224

Chapter 23 First, November.. 234

Chapter 24 Run, Shakti, Run...247

Chapter 25 Iris Pavlopoulos 261

Chapter 26 Follow Me...273

Chapter 27 What Lies Beneath 289

Chapter 28 You and Me 301

CHAPTER 1

MINI-
MANSION

G ayatri laid on her bed, facing the open balcony door. The sky was slowly fading to dusk outside, and the thought of mosquitoes coming in did not bother her. It was too beautiful an evening to worry about trivial matters. She welcomed the cool breeze after a brazen summer. Fall was in the air. Toronto was not known for pleasant weather, but a beautiful evening in the city meant just that. Torontonians relished their summer days, but winding down to fall was welcomed by many.

The curtains blew subtly at the side of the door. A fading orange sky appeared as a canvas behind swaying mature trees. A perfect moment in time, Gayatri realized. She wanted to be as present as she could be. She gently rubbed her baby bump and felt hopeful for the future. She knew her baby would have a better childhood than she ever did. Gayatri had grown up in an orphanage. Her parents had died in a car crash when she was five years old, but even though she had been young, she remembered them clearly.

She had no other family willing to take her in because her parents had gotten married against her mom's family's wishes. Her dad was the only child of Trinidadian parents. Her mother, an Indian woman, was estranged from her family. The details were unclear to Gayatri, but she didn't care. Their love story made her happy. She remembered her dad making snorting sounds in the morning time when she woke up. Then, she would run up to him, and he would dramatically catch her. She also remembered her mom making aloo-parathas for dinner that she served with yogurt. In Gayatri's mind, it was still the most delicious meal.

Despite Gayatri's harsh start to life, she excelled at most things. With little to no friends, she immersed herself in her studies. Eventually, Gayatri won a scholarship to the University of Toronto, where she studied biochemistry. She would later go on to get her Ph.D. at the university. She dabbled in research and working for the government. However, she loved her alma mater and landed a professorship at the local St. George Campus of U of T. Her success did not escape her. She appreciated her unique story. It gave her strength when she had no one. Quite often, she was alone. Therefore, evenings like this special one gave her the solace she was quite familiar with.

Gayatri positioned her head on the pillow, took deep bated breaths, and started blinking slowly. She had earned an evening nap after being on her feet all day teaching at the campus. Her husband, Harrison, was in Montreal for a few days to attend a trade show. Gayatri was all alone in their beautiful home in Swansea, Toronto. Swansea was located in the west of the city and had a mixture of older homes along with newer grand ones. Real estate in Toronto was exorbitant. Therefore, neighbourhoods like Swansea would see their share of little homes being bought over and replaced with mini-mansions. Older folks made a fortune selling their modest homes.

Gayatri's home was a midsize detached house. Harrison had inherited an older home from his parents. It was a small house on a large lot that needed a lot of work. They decided to break it down and build a modern two-story house. She loved her home. It was just what she dreamt of. The property was surrounded by tall mature trees and backed onto a forested area. This was extremely rare in Toronto. To say the least, their home was quite special indeed.

As she slipped deeper into slumber, something most peculiar happened. The roof of her mini-mansion disappeared. She froze in time, staring up at the dusky sky, but she was good. After all, she must be dreaming. She did not fight it. She wanted to be entertained.

As she lay there, staring, she caught a glimpse of a spark of light way up in the sky. She kept her eye on it. At first, it looked like a tiny golden light. It appeared to be falling fast and getting larger and larger as it approached her. She was still calm and reflective of her wondrous mind conjuring what seemed to be a fantastic dream. The light quickly started to take a human shape, that of a tall man with broad shoulders. She squinted a bit as if she was studying for an exam, and this motion would better help her understand what she was seeing. However, because she thought it was a dream, she felt there was no need to analyze it.

She saw the full shape of the man as he was almost right above the house and about to enter her room. She could clearly see his face. The safety of her dream world kept her collected.

The strange man slowed down as he entered the house and landed with a thunderous roar, on one bended knee. The floor cracked, and light spilled out beneath it. Gayatri's heart jumped. She grabbed her belly as if to protect her unborn child. She immediately calmed down.

It's a dream, she reminded herself. The man straightened his posture and stood upright. As he lifted his head to make eye contact with her, the ground seemed to mend itself, and the light faded away. He hadn't actually cracked open the espresso hardwood floor. No, this was an energetic surface just above the bedroom floor.

As he gazed upon sleepy Gayatri on the bed, she immediately noticed his gentle face. He was dressed in a white robe held together with a golden rope at the waist. He wore sandals, unlike anything she had ever seen before. His hair was past shoulder-length and golden brown. He was unnaturally tall and robust. By all standards, he was striking and most attractive. An unusual copper aura surrounded his upper body. It reminded Gayatri of her rose gold watch for some reason.

He smiled at her gently. Now disarmed and curious, she wondered what a heavenly creature like him was doing in her Swansea residence. A large translucent structure stood firmly at his back, but Gayatri did not recognize it.

"Peace be unto you, Gayatri," he said with a deep and steady voice. The echo in his voice startled her a bit. His eyes lit rose gold from within.

"Umm, hello. Who are you?" Gayatri replied with a soft voice.

"I am Gabriel." He smiled kindly.

"I am Gayatri." She felt stupid saying that because he addressed her by name, but continued, "How can I help you?"

He grinned at her question. Gabriel respectfully answered, "I am here to deliver a message to you, Gayatri. It is of great importance, and you must listen carefully and remember what I say."

Gayatri wondered if she really was dreaming. She sat up in the bed with little difficulty, holding her belly. She stared right at him attentively and replied, "Okay, Gabriel, I'll do my best."

"You are about to give birth to a beautiful baby girl," he started.

"Oh my, I didn't know that. I deliberately didn't find out," she said excitedly. She didn't care that the surprise was ruined for her. The thought of a baby girl elated her heart.

"You will have a difficult labour, but you and your child will be happy and healthy." He glowed radiantly.

"Okay," she muttered under her breath, with her heart thumping out of her chest. She anticipated that Gabriel did not descend from heaven to tell her that her baby would be happy.

"What I am here to tell you is that your baby will grow up to be an important influencer. She will possess the ability to change the trajectory of humanity on Earth," Gabriel said, staring straight into her eyes.

Gayatri squinted her eyes in confusion. "What do you mean, Gabriel?"

"My message is more about you, Gayatri. You will raise her with love and compassion in her heart, and protect her from all those who try to hurt her and sway her into darkness."

"What? Do you mean she will be in danger?" Gayatri's voice elevated.

"Yes, Gayatri. Just as we know she is special, there are dark forces that will come to know this, too. They do not want her to become the person she is destined to be."

Breathing heavily, tears rolled down her cheeks and fear set in hard.

"Gayatri, you are not alone in this. We, the Angels of Light, are here with you. However, we are restricted from intervening. The most we can do is guide you. You cannot tell anyone about this. Not even your husband," Gabriel warned. "Not yet. I will reveal more to you in time."

"This is too much for me," Gayatri said in distress. "Why would you come here and drop this on me? I can't do this."

"Yes, you can, Gayatri. You've been preparing for this your whole life." Gabriel smiled gently. "I must go now, for I am needed elsewhere."

"Please don't go. What do I do with this information?" she cried out to him.

"Nothing right now. More will come in time," he assured her.

Gabriel smiled once more and rested his large hand on her head. She closed her teary eyes in a state of confusion. When she opened her eyes, he was gone. The room returned to its form, roof and all. She sat up quickly with her feet on the ground and felt her face. It was wet with tears. She wiped them with her hands and got up quickly and closed the balcony door.

Gayatri stood for a few seconds, wondering if that had been, in fact, a dream. It felt so real. Perhaps she was more tired than she realized. Her attention was broken when her stomach growled. "Right, dinner."

The next morning, Gayatri woke up early. She couldn't take her mind off her dream. Was it a dream? She felt ridiculous thinking it was not. She thought about Gabriel's face and how gentle he was. Gayatri wondered what the tall structure behind him was, as she tossed and turned in bed. She figured since it was a dream, she would tell Harrison all about it when he got home that day. Then she felt she should not because Gabriel asked her not to.

"It's a dream, Gayatri!" she said out loud. She buried her head into her pillow.

Gayatri was an early bird. She hopped out of bed and made it nicely with her poofy pillows. She rolled out her yoga mat and performed maternity yoga. While in her closing pose, Savasana, she thought about the message Gabriel had given to her. Her heart started to beat faster. The thought of her child being in danger plagued her. She prayed that it was a dream, and none of it was true.

Harrison would be home around lunchtime, Gayatri estimated. She wanted to have a delicious meal prepared for him when he arrived. She made pesto pasta, stuffed chicken breast, and a garden salad for lunch. At 12:40 pm, Harrison rang the doorbell. He had a key, but he loved her coming to the door to greet him with a huge smile and kiss. She did just that. He washed up and sat at the table. They enjoyed their meal and talked about the week gone by.

Harrison Clairemont was a French-Canadian businessman who manufactured refined cooking oils. He was a soft-spoken gentleman. He adored his wife and thought she was the cleverest person he had ever met. Harrison attended Ryerson University for Business. Many years ago, while they were both in university, Gayatri had attended an event at Ryerson University one evening. She was introduced to Harrison by mutual friends. They had been inseparable ever since. Like Gayatri, Harrison lost his parents early in life, although it was while he was in university. He was an only child. Harrison's street-savvy smarts allowed him to negotiate brilliantly. That hustle in his character got him into his current business.

"Honey, you look a little off today. Are you tired?" Harrison inquired

Little did Harrison know that Gayatri was fighting every urge to tell him about her encounter with Gabriel. "Yes, I'm tired. I had a long week, and I picked up an extra class because one of our faculty members fell ill."

"I hope it's not too serious," he said with concern. "But why did you pick it up? You're almost eight months pregnant."

"I know, but I'm already teaching the same course. It made sense for me to take it on," she replied.

"I see. Try to take it easy, though. Your health and the baby's health are more important than anything." He smiled and rubbed her belly gently. "I'm exhausted today. I think I'll have a nap."

"Yes, you do that. I'm going to water the garden, and then I'll join you," Gayatri said.

"You know, you really shouldn't water the garden in the middle of the day," Harrison advised.

"I know, but I haven't done it in four or five days, and the flowers look sad," she said with a smile.

He laughed with an exaggerated tone. "Oh, really? Well, that makes perfect sense!"

Harrison got up from their repurposed wooden table and stretched his arms over his head. He picked up their plates and glasses and made his way to the kitchen. He loaded the dishwasher and covered the remainder of the food.

Gayatri sat a bit longer. After a few minutes, she made her way to their mudroom, replaced her house shoes for old sneakers, pulled a garden apron over her head, and wore a giant garden hat. She looked back at him to see his reaction as always.

He stared and had a chuckle. "You're the cutest pregnant gardener in the whole wide world."

"I know," Gayatri said confidently and carried on to the garden.

As she stood in the garden watering the plants, against Harrison's advice, she noticed someone approaching with a stroller. Always a polite neighbour, Gayatri shut off the water and turned around to get a better look at who it was.

"Dr. Akiyama! How are you?" Gayatri was pleasantly happy to see the nicest neighbour on the street.

"Please call me Kira. I'm good. Tired, but good," Dr. Akiyama replied.

"Of course, you just gave birth, Kira. How is the baby? Can I see him?" she asked, holding her hands together.

"Of course. I just got him to sleep, but have a peek," Kira lifted the blanket ever so slightly, so Gayatri could look inside.

"He's perfect! What's his name?" Gayatri inquired.

"His name is Hikaru Akiyama." Kira glowed, saying his name with love and pride.

"Oh! That's beautiful." Gayatri bent down further and whispered to the baby, "I'm pleased to meet you, Hikaru." She looked up at Kira. "What does the name mean?"

"It means shining light," Kira explained. "When are you due, Gayatri?"

"In approximately six weeks. I can't wait. I've been so tired lately."

"Yes, it's expected. Get as much rest as you can. Because when your baby comes, then you'll get no sleep." Kira laughed

"So I've heard." Gayatri giggled along.

"Well, I better be off. Have a good day. You know," Kira paused, "I'm right here if you need someone to talk to about the pregnancy or babies." She gestured at her home three houses away, "Come over or call me anytime."

"Thank you so much, Kira," Gayatri felt herself getting a little emotional. She was not used to anyone helping her other than Harrison.

CHAPTER 2

KEEP THE SECRET

FIVE WEEKS LATER

Over the last few days of October, Gayatri taught her last set of classes. She had just over one week to prepare for her baby's arrival. Harrison was over the moon happy and could not wait to smoke his celebratory cigar, given to him by one of his clients. Gayatri and Harrison worked together to put the finishing touches on their baby's yellow nursery. They wanted the gender of the baby to be a surprise. Gayatri had a hunch that it would be a girl. Harrison didn't have a preference. However, the thought of taking his son to basketball games excited him.

"Harry, do you want to join me in the garden for tea?" Gayatri hollered at him from their bedroom. "It's not too cool out."

They were both in a great mood. Harry peeked out of the nursery. "That sounds great, G. Can you give me about twenty minutes? I need to email a distributor."

"Sure, meet me when you can," Gayatri replied.

She made her way down to their backyard, with her tea in one hand and a knitted throw in the other. This was her favourite part of their home. Every inch of their backyard, they completed on their own. It was wide and led up to a forested area. The end of the yard and through the forest led into the bank of Grenadier Pond. There was no fence separating their yard and the woods, just a fence separating their yard from their neighbours. They liked it like that. Most of the neighbours had a fence enclosing their backyards.

Harrison and Gayatri's backyard oasis included a vegetable garden and a stone patio that they painstakingly installed themselves. Strings of dimmable lights ran from side fence to side fence. The trees were tall and beautiful. The garden was rarely quiet. Gayatri hung a small bamboo wind chime on one of the trees. She read somewhere that it was feng shui. All this added to their perfectly Zen space. Gayatri never had a backyard prior to this house, so this was truly a heavenly place for her.

She sat on their loveseat swing set with her tea. The loveseat swayed softly with her legs dangling. Her stomach was huge now, so she rested the teacup and saucer on top of her belly. She rather enjoyed doing this, and she wouldn't be able to do it much longer. Gayatri looked around her garden with appreciation. She smiled from within, being present to take it in again.

Immersed in her sanctuary, Gayatri didn't notice the atmosphere changing around her. Suddenly, the air became still, and the towering trees seemed to sway slower. Time felt like it slowed to a halt. She picked up her teacup and sipped it slowly when she realized the bamboo chime stopped making noise. She recognized the energy around her. It was light and fragrant.

"Is that you, Gabriel?" Gayatri said softly. She surprised herself with her candour.

Sitting next to her on the swing, Gabriel appeared, as striking as he was gentle. "Yes, Gayatri. I am here." He looked at her like an old friend. She didn't reciprocate. She could not hide behind a dream this time. It was real and happening before her eyes.

"I recognized the feeling." Her eyes teared up. "I always knew that vision was real. I didn't want to admit it because it would mean coming to terms with my child being in danger." She moved the teacup and saucer off her tabletop belly and set them down next to her. Her heart sank into her stomach, and she placed her hands over her face. Gayatri's method of dealing with stress over the years was taking three deep breaths. However, this time she was not able to get her breaths deep enough. It was too much to bear.

"Gayatri, you can handle the task ahead of you," Gabriel said with conviction. "Look at the life you created in spite of a tragic start. You did this." He gestured at her home as a reflection of her life.

"I'm not strong enough for this," she cried. "Please, please, choose someone else. I want a normal life for my child."

"It does not work like that," Gabriel said, looking into her eyes. "We've been with you from the beginning. We know you are capable of mothering a leader the world needs. It is much bigger than you can understand."

"You ask too much of me, and yet you don't want me to share it with my Harry. It's his child, too! I can't!" Gayatri wept. "It's too heavy a burden to carry alone."

"You will be able to tell your husband about it one day. Not now. It's for both you and the baby's protection," Gabriel warned. "Keep the secret. For now, do not speak of it out loud to anyone."

This information should have scared Gayatri more, but the seriousness of Gabriel's message somehow gave her strength. Feeling defeated, she said, "Okay, Gabriel. I'm trusting you. I'm not a religious person, and I'm not aware of your role here, but I'm allowing you to guide me through this." Gayatri meant business.

"Thank you, Gayatri," Gabriel said. His eyes were a colour she has never seen before on any human. They appeared hazel at first, but upon looking directly at him, she saw they were a bright copper tone. Almost too intense to look at. He continued, "I have another important message for you today."

Exhausted from the crying, Gayatri said, "Go on." She wondered how he could upset her further.

"My message today is to tell you about guardian angels. Every human being has a beautiful angel with them at all times."

"Guardian angels?" Gayatri, the academic, tried to keep an open mind. She figured Gabriel, the Angel, deserved more respect than lacing her question with sarcasm.

"Yes." He smiled. "It is imperative you teach your daughter about guardian angels as she grows up. It will help her immensely one day."

"I see." Gayatri thought she knew nothing about guardian angels, but she would do it anyway.

"Every human born on Earth has a guardian angel with them."

"All humans? Even the bad ones?" Gayatri inquired.

"Yes, even the bad ones. Humans do not always listen to their angels," Gabriel said with a sad look on his face. "Mankind has free will. We cannot intervene when they go astray. We can only influence."

"I see," she said genuinely. "That must be difficult to stand by and watch us ruin ourselves."

"Yes, it is." Gabriel laughed subtly.

"I have a question for you, Gabriel." Gayatri turned herself to face him slightly.

"Sure, one question today," he said.

"You said humans have a guardian angel and angels to influence them. Is there anything out there to influence them into doing wrong?" Gayatri, always a critical thinker and believer in balance, knew she was setting up her question to answer other questions.

"Yes, there is, Gayatri. There are several influencers out there who are trying to win the attention of humans. Some are of the light, and some are of the dark side. This is why your role is so important. Your daughter must have the tools to make decisions to better humanity." Gabriel's answer was short and to the point. Gayatri felt satisfied with his reply.

"Thank you, Gabriel. I have so many more questions for you, but I cannot seem to think right now."

"We will have many more opportunities to talk," he said. "For now, I must go. Your beloved is on his way to you. Dry your eyes and receive him with love." He placed his hands over her forehead and disappeared once more.

Gayatri did not know how to feel. Although she felt pretty beat up after talking to Gabriel, she also started to put the pieces together. It was becoming clearer to her that her child needed to be surrounded by love and be selfless. Gayatri thought this was precisely how she would raise her child anyway. Perhaps, she could be successful by Gabriel's standards. How hard could it be?

"Boo!" Harrison, always the joker, tried lamely to scare her, but not too much because of her advanced stage of pregnancy.

"Honey, it's going to take a lot more than that to scare me tonight," Gayatri said, placing the teacup and saucer back on her belly top.

"Huh?" Harrison asked, confused.

"Never mind. How about that tea, my love?" Gayatri smiled.

"Thank you, honey. I'll have whatever you're having," he said.

"Chamomile?"

"Anything but that." He laughed.

"Holy Basil?"

"Yes, perfect."

They sat for a while, talking about the backyard and improvements they would like to make. Gayatri felt her recovery from her conversation with Gabriel was stellar. It must mean she was stronger than she thought.

* * *

Later that night, to their surprise, Gayatri went into labour. Harrison ran around the house like a headless chicken trying to find their bags for the hospital. Gayatri already had the bags packed and waiting by the door. He wore mismatched socks and his shirt inside out, which Gayatri pointed out to him.

She took a moment to calm him down and assured him he had it under control. She remembered Gabriel's message of having a difficult labour and wanted to prepare Harrison for it.

"Harry, come sit with me for one minute," Gayatri said softly.

"G, we gotta go," Harrison said with concern.

"We can take a minute. Trust me." She smiled.

"Okay." He held her hand.

"Whatever happens in the next few hours or days, I want you to know we will make it through together." Her eyes teared up as she spoke.

"You're scaring me, G," said Harrison, also tearing up.

"Don't be scared. Labour is difficult, but it will be worth it," she assured him. "I need you to be strong and keep it together for me."

"You and our baby are all I have in this world." Harrison started to weep. "Is there something you're not telling me?"

"And you are all I have, too." She smiled, tears rolling down her cheeks, avoiding his question. "Remember what I said, no matter what, the baby and I will be fine."

"Yes, my love. I know you will be. You're the strongest person I know. Our baby is so lucky." Harrison ended on that note and jumped up to grab the bags. He came back to help Gayatri to their SUV, buckled her up and off they went to Mount Sinai Hospital.

* * *

The next few days were harrowing for Harrison, Gayatri, and their baby. The labour was long and difficult. There were many scares for both Gayatri and the baby. Harrison held true to his word and kept it together when Gayatri started to fall apart. He held her hand, calmed her down, and conferred with the medical staff.

After some thirty-odd hours of labour, they informed Gayatri and Harrison that they needed to do a C-section because the baby's heart rate had dropped to a dangerous level. Harrison looked at Gayatri with pure terror in his eyes. He remembered what she said, though.

Like a prophecy, he thought.

Suddenly, a strength came over him, and he agreed to the C-section and signed the necessary paperwork.

"G, you got this," Harry whispered in her ear.

Not herself from the pain and exhaustion, Gayatri said, "You remembered." She managed to smile at him. Feeling overwhelmed, Gayatri noticed Harrison's green eyes had turned a shade of dark brown. She tried to pull herself together in case it was the last time they spoke.

The nurses entered the room to wheel Gayatri away. Harrison kissed his wife on her forehead and held her hand. "I'll be right here. I love you."

"I love you, too," Gayatri replied as they took her away.

Harrison watched as they ran Gayatri down the brightly lit hallway, disappearing behind swinging double doors. His heart beating rapidly and stomach involuntarily concaved, he fell to his knees. Harrison needed to fall apart for a moment and let it out. He covered his face with his hands and cried profusely. No one could hear his muffled wail or experience his version of hell. He leaned his head on the wall and wept for many minutes. His breathing became shallow, and he could feel his face puffing up.

He wished he had a larger family to be there to support him. He thought about calling his friends to come to the hospital, but he was frozen. The wall was the only support he had at that moment. Just as Harrison was deep into the scariest moment of his life, he felt a small hand on his shoulder. He looked up and saw an older woman looking at him. Her face was gentle and disarming. She smiled at him and took him by his hands, standing him up to her level. Harrison followed her lead as if he were a child. She wrapped her hands around his tall frame and hugged him tightly. He buried his face into her shoulders and cried a bit more.

No words were exchanged, just the kindness of a stranger seeing someone in distress. To his surprise, Harrison felt better, and his strength came rushing back to him. After about thirty seconds, they detangled and looked at each other. She simply smiled and patted him on the hands. Then, she turned around and left. Harrison couldn't thank her in time. No words left his lips. He sat down in the chair slowly. He glanced down the hall to get one more look at the nice lady who took the time to hug him. She was not there, but he didn't think about it much. He felt grateful for her kindness.

Harrison waited and waited. Each minute felt like an hour. A nurse passing by approached him. "Mr. Clairemont, your wife will be fine. C-sections are routine procedures." This did wonders for Harrison. Then, he thought about the baby's heartbeat dropping.

He replied to the nurse, "Thank you, but I'm also worried about the baby."

"I understand. Soon you will hear from the doctor." She smiled. "Do you have someone you can call to be with you?"

"I'm okay for now. Thank you." He forced a smile to assure her.

Harrison closed his eyes and laid his head back onto the wall. He took deep breaths and tried to be positive. He took comfort, holding onto the words "routine procedure."

As he was nursing himself back to good mental health, he heard a whisper ever so softly. "They are both doing well."

Harrison opened his eyes quickly, raised his head, and looked around. There was no one there.

"Hello?" Was his mind playing tricks on him? Perhaps. His stress level was unlike anything he had experienced before.

At that moment, the double doors swung open, and the doctor came walking down the hall. He locked eyes with Harrison, who was sprinting towards him.

"Congratulations, Mr. Clairemont. You have a healthy baby girl," the doctor gleefully shared.

"Oh my God!" Harrison shouted on a high. "Thank you! How is my wife?".

"She's doing well. She needs some time to heal, but by all accounts, she's great."

"Thank you so much, Doctor!" Harrison felt the weight of the world fall off his shoulders. "I'm a dad!"

"You sure are, sir." The doctor patted him on the shoulder. "You can go see them both right now."

Harrison was led down the hall by a nurse and into the post-operative room. There, he saw his wife holding their daughter wrapped in the hospital's blanket. Gayatri looked up at him and smiled.

"Come meet your daughter," Gayatri said with an exhausted smile.

"You did so great, G. She's absolutely perfect." Harrison marvelled at his daughter with tears in his eyes. Gayatri handed the baby over to him. Harrison looked at her, and all his stress seemed to dissipate. He lifted her closer to him and examined her little cherub face. Black spiky hair pointed in every direction. "Happy birthday, little one. We will celebrate November first as the best day of our lives."

Gayatri said, "Stay with her. I need to rest."

"I'll be right here." Harrison meant it. The nurses attended to Gayatri while Harrison sat holding his daughter.

The next morning came quickly. Harrison could not stop staring at his new daughter. She was perfect in his eyes. He felt something switch inside of him. His world had expanded to include his daughter, along with Gayatri. It was indeed a blissful moment for the new dad.

Gayatri struggled with her C-section recovery. The pain was intense. She asked Harrison to get her something delicious to eat. He placed the baby next to her, and off he went down the busy University Avenue to find food.

*   *   *

Alone with the baby for the first time, Gayatri forgot about her pain and stared at the infant for some time. She watched her yawn and wrinkled her little nose. Gayatri was most entertained by her offspring. She checked to make sure they were alone, and she whispered, "Hi, little one. Mom is here. I want you to know I love you. I don't know what the world has planned for us, but I will always be with you."

As Gayatri looked on at her baby, she noticed someone walk in. To her surprise, it was Angel Gabriel. This time Gayatri was pleased to see the heavenly creature. She smiled at him and gestured at the baby.

Gabriel stepped forward and admired the little one. He smiled gently while his eyes glowed brightly. Gabriel then placed his large hands over the baby's head and touched her forehead with his index finger and said, "Sight," out loud. His finger glowed as he came into contact with her little forehead.

Gayatri looked up at him and asked. "What does 'sight' mean?"

"I granted your baby a gift that would help her in her life. We, the Angels of Light, are allowed to grant these gifts to certain individuals," Gabriel explained. "She will need it to help her see behind the veil."

"The veil? See what?" Gayatri asked, exhausted.

"You will see in time," Gabriel said. "But first, I have a gift for you, Gayatri." He lifted his hands and pointed to the left side of the room. Standing on the other side of the bed were two people, a man and a woman. They looked like they were in their mid-thirties. The woman wore a white sari with gold embroidery, and the man wore a black collared three button shirt and white pants. They looked at Gayatri and smiled.

"Mom? Dad?" Gayatri said in utter disbelief. Her eyes were wide open, and her mouth dropped.

"Yes, my love." Gayatri's mother replied. She clasped her hands together in front of her.

Her dad stepped forward and said, "Sweetheart, I see you have your beautiful daughter in your arms. We met her already. She is a lot like you at that age." He smiled with that winsome smile Gayatri knew so well. "I want you to know we were always with you, Gayatri."

"Yes, we were. From the day we left, we've been by your side." Gayatri's mom added.

Gayatri's heart was thumping out of her chest. She not only received the greatest gift of her life, a healthy baby girl, but she also found out her prayers were answered. Every night Gayatri had spent in the orphanage, she had prayed that her parents would be with her.

"Thank you, Mom and Dad. I miss you so much. I will love you forever," Gayatri said with tears rolling down her cheeks and her lip curling.

"We love you, too. Take good care of our granddaughter," her dad said, bidding farewell and waving at Gabriel. Then they disappeared.

Gayatri looked over to Gabriel. She wanted to thank him for this wondrous gift, but he too was gone. She said out loud, "Thank you, Gabriel." Then she hugged her baby tightly and kissed her gently.

About an hour after the miraculous encounter with her parents, Harrison walked into the room with bags and bags of food.

Gayatri laughed. "What did you do? I hope you left food for other hungry Torontonians."

"I wasn't sure what you wanted, so I grabbed an Uber and bought you food from Thai King, Souvlaki House, and cheesecake from Big Fat Cheesecake," he admitted.

Gayatri had a good laugh and thought how lucky she was. "Thank you, honey. I'll nurse the baby first, and then I'll eat."

"How long are we going to call her the *baby*"? Harrison inquired.

"Right. I'm glad you brought that up," Gayatri said. "I know we discussed some beautiful names for a girl. Lily, Emily, Sarah."

"Yes, I liked all of those names, but we have to decide on one," he stated.

"Well, I was thinking, how would you feel about the name Shakti Devi?"

Harrison looked up immediately. "After your mom?"

"Yes, but only if you love it." Gayatri wanted them to make this decision together.

"Shakti Devi Clairemont." He smiled. "I love it. A name as unique as our family and story."

"Are you sure?" Gayatri inquired. "I know I sprung this on you."

"I really love it, Gayatri. How long have you been thinking about this?"

"Just in the last hour. I was inspired." Gayatri beamed, looking at her baby while thinking of her beautiful mother.

"Well, it's settled then." Harrison clapped his hands quietly. "Shakti, Shak, Shak-attack, Shak-Shak. This is the best name ever!" Harrison was off in his mind thinking up fun nicknames. "Shake Shak!"

Gayatri stared at her baby, feeling wonderful about their decision. "Hello, Shakti. I hope you love your name as much as we do."

CHAPTER 3

THE CLANS

A t the age of two, Gayatri noticed Shakti loved to play outside in their backyard. She would often talk to the flowers and seemed intrigued by the vegetable garden. Harrison adored his daughter. He came home as early as he could every day and ran to the backyard to play with her. As she got older and was able to speak clearly, she would tell her dad of fantastical stories of her imaginary friends in the backyard. She called them, the Clans. There were fairies, angels, trolls, and she once even saw a salamander. Harrison loved these stories. He kept track of them, too. He knew she loved the fairies and angels, but she said the trolls were grumpy little men. Harrison had a great laugh whenever she spoke about them. He adored her profound imagination.

One evening, after Gayatri tucked the then six-year-old Shakti into bed, Harrison sat at the kitchen table waiting to have their ritual tea time together. Gayatri had her usual chamomile tea and Harrison, a holy basil tea.

"Shaks sure has a fantastic imagination," Harrison said.

"Why do you say so?" Gayatri asked.

"Oh, she tells me all these stories of her friends in the garden."

"What friends? I mean, I see her talking to herself a lot out there, but she never told me about her friends." Gayatri said.

"She tells me all about her fairy and angel friends," Harrison said as he sipped his tea.

"Angels?" Gayatri said.

"Yes, angels. Very tall angels."

"Do they have names?"

"She told me their names, but I don't quite remember," Harrison recalled. "I think one was Michael."

"Michael? Hmmm…never heard of him before," Gayatri stated.

"As opposed to all the other angels you're familiar with, G?" Harrison laughed.

Gayatri had to chuckle. "I guess our Shakti Devi has quite an active imagination."

These stories continued for years to come. Harrison was fully invested in the storyline as well. There was a lot of politics between the fairies and trolls. Gnomes were introduced to the story later on because they were great at hiding, and they contributed significantly to the growing tensions between the fairies and trolls. Gnomes also were major troublemakers.

According to ten-year-old Shakti, each clan had its own responsibilities. Fairies took care of flowers, and trolls cared for trees. She was still unsure what the gnomes did besides make trouble. Shakti spoke about the angels that visited her with love and admiration. She explained they didn't talk much. They would just appear and smile at her. She felt safe around them.

Shakti even started talking to her mom about her nature friends. Gayatri was not sure how to respond to these stories. Based on her experiences, Gayatri knew better than to react with doubt.

One day she asked Shakti, "Shaks, do you actually see these wonderful creatures in our garden?"

"Yes, Mom. You don't see them?" Shakti asked.

"No, sweetheart, I don't. Maybe I'm not as cool as you." Gayatri laughed in response to lighten the conversation.

"I guess so," she naughtily replied.

"I believe you one hundred percent, but if you were to tell anyone outside of home, they may not. So, can we keep this in our family? Don't tell anyone else about your nature friends." Gayatri's sincerity came across to Shakti.

"Yes, Mom. I know now."

"What do you know?"

"I know that I'm the only one who can see the Clans."

Gayatri laughed heartily at Shakti, referring to her friends as the Clans. She composed herself and positioned her body to come face to face with Shakti. "Shaks, don't forget, your guardian angel is always with you. If you are ever in trouble, ask for help."

Shakti stared at Gayatri with her deep brown eyes, wide and full of wonder, "I know, Mom." She smiled. "Can I go outside now? I'm all done with my homework."

"Sure," Gayatri kissed her forehead. She needed to be alone to think.

She expected that Shakti might come into contact with angels, but what on Earth were these other creatures? Gayatri knew her daughter was telling the truth. Shakti did not lie. It had been years of her telling these stories, and it all tracked with no inconsistencies. She wondered if the gift of *Sight* granted by Gabriel was the cause of this. She made a mental note to ask Gabriel all about it when she saw him next.

Over the next few years, Shakti enjoyed a beautiful home life. She was blessed with two attentive parents that spent a great deal of time showering her with love. Gayatri did her best to bring Shakti up with love, compassion, and lessons on guardian angels, as she promised she would. Shakti demonstrated clear qualities of an extraordinarily caring child. Gayatri filled her young life with trips to the homeless shelter to volunteer, yoga camp for kids, and countless visits to Sick Kids Hospital. Gayatri figured it was important for her to be aware of what was most important in life, helping others.

* * *

Gayatri and Harrison noticed that Shakti did not have many friends. Her only human friend was the neighbour's son, Hikaru Akiyama. It concerned her parents that Shakti did not want to make new friends. There was never any talk about her friends at school or playdates or even kids she didn't like. Shakti kept to herself and was perfectly happy that way. Harrison figured if his daughter was happy and progressing well, why worry? She did exceptionally well at school and basketball. She also played the piano beautifully.

Hikaru and Shakti ended up as friends largely because they were both socially awkward, and they lived on the same street. When they hung out together, they could just be themselves. Hikaru was in the gifted class. He excelled in math and science, but he was awful at gym and art. His parents did not mind that at all.

Hikaru Akiyama grew to become a whip-thin teenager with glasses. He had perfectly straight black hair that he kept a few inches long because it would spike up when it was too short. He played the violin and loved singing to Bruno Mars when he was all alone. He adored Shakti. She was the only person outside his family he would let his guard down around.

They would often hang out in Shakti's backyard. When no one was looking, they would escape to the forest for countless evenings of adventure and exploring the woods. In fact, they enjoyed each other's company so much that they had no intention of expanding their friendship circle.

During one summer break, Shakti and Hikaru decided to expand Gayatri's vegetable garden. They grew tomatoes, zucchini, spinach, strawberries, peppers, and much more. It became a project for them. They did extensive research on how to get the best results and often asked Harrison to drive them to the local gardening shop. Harrison happily obliged. He was proud of them for doing this. Many times, he called Hikaru's father, Shinzo, to come to his house to see how the vegetable garden was progressing. Both fathers would pick the ripe fruits and vegetables. They would divide the produce amongst their homes and discuss making elaborate smoothies, which rarely happened.

Unfortunately, when they started high school at age fourteen, Hikaru became the subject of much bullying. Every day he was picked on by a group of vicious boys. Hikaru went home every day and cried. During this time, Shakti truly found her voice. And did she ever. It started off by putting her arm around Hikaru's shoulders and walking away with him, but this quickly became a scandal. The boys would taunt Hikaru by saying, "Is that your girlfriend?" and "You need your girlfriend to save you?"

They ignored the taunts for the most part. Sometimes Shakti would stand up to them and argue. But Hikaru never said anything. He tried to be as inconspicuous as possible, hoping it would stop one day for good behaviour.

This did not hinder their friendship in any way. They played together after school every day. What had started with tag, moved on to high-tech inventions and research about gardening. They were both brilliant kids. In the next two years, Hikaru was a permanent fixture at Shakti's house. It worked well for him because both his parents were doctors and worked long hours. His baby brother, Ki, stayed at home often with a babysitter and his maternal grandmother.

One Friday after school, Hikaru and Shakti were sitting in the park talking to each other. The boys from school approached and yanked Hikaru's Raptors cap off his head. Hikaru loved that cap, and he was a huge Toronto Raptors fan. He got up, and for the first time and yelled, "Give it back."

The boys laughed and pointed at him. "Come and get it."

Shakti sat still watching the commotion. She felt her rage bubbling as the boys tossed the cap back and forth, while Hikaru chased after it. The leader of the group was a burly boy named Travis. When the hat got to Travis, Hikaru reached up to grab it from him. Travis placed his foot behind himself to brace his stance and forcefully pushed Hikaru down. Poor Hikaru went flying back, landing on his back and slamming his head on the concrete.

This was all too much for Shakti. The sight of Hikaru's skinny frame lying on the ground, grasping his head, was overwhelming.

She turned around slowly with a slightly hunched back and glared at Travis.

"Hey, jerk!" She picked up her reusable metal water bottle and whipped it with precision and force at Travis's face. It made contact with an incredibly distressing thud. Travis's head snapped back, and he stood for a second, holding his face.

He dropped to the ground, with a line of blood leaking down his nose, onto his T-shirt and jeans. His friends ran towards him. Shakti expeditiously grabbed the Raptor's cap and ran towards Hikaru. She pulled him up with one solid jolt. Holding his head at first, Hikaru looked unsteady. Shakti held his hand, and they sprinted towards home. As they were bolting towards their street, Shakti looked back and saw the most unusual sight, tall, dark human-like figures hovering over the boys. She didn't have time to look further into it, they were running for their lives. They ran straight to Hikaru's house and told his mother what had happened.

Kira immediately called Gayatri to tell her what had happened. Gayatri came running over and asked if they were okay. Then she scolded Shakti for acting out violently.

Kira intervened, "Gayatri, they pushed Hikaru, and he fell and hit his head. Shakti was protecting him!" Kira's eyes were welling.

"I know, Kira." Gayatri softened. "My concern is if the boys in the group retaliated, they would beat the two of them up. They were heavily outnumbered. I'm more scared than mad. Sometimes these school fights escalate, and we are not always there to protect them."

"I agree," Kira said sadly. "I will inform the principal."

"Good idea," Gayatri agreed. They had a plan to stick together.

* * *

On Monday morning, Gayatri and Kira went to school to speak with the principal, Mr. Edgar. They both demanded that Travis's parents be informed of their son's history of bullying. Mr. Edgar explained to the parents that Travis Nickels has had many infractions within the school. However, his father, Mr. Nickels, was an influential lawyer who also sat on the school board and kept getting Travis back into the school. This made Kira and Gayatri nervous. Clearly, they were dealing with a troubled boy with no consequences for his actions.

"We will do what it takes to protect our children, Mr. Edgar," Gayatri said firmly, as she stood up to leave his office. Gayatri was a soft-spoken woman, but she radiated confidence.

"We most definitely will," Kira agreed. They both shook Mr. Edgar's hand.

"I will inform the teachers of Hikaru's situation, and we will keep an eye out." Mr. Edgar tried to be supportive.

Given Travis's history of violence in school, Shakti did not get into much trouble this time. She had never had a violent incident before. But Mr. Edgar gave her a stiff warning. She told him he should do a better job of protecting Hikaru. Mr. Edgar was not impressed at all.

Kira drove home with Gayatri in silence. They were both deeply troubled by the situation their kids were in. As they turned down their street and approached Kira's house, which was three houses before Gayatri's house, they noticed two large black SUVs on Gayatri's driveway. They looked at each other, sensing it was not good.

"Were you expecting someone?" Kira inquired.

"No, but Harry is home. I wonder who is visiting," Gayatri replied, already on edge.

"Would you like me to come with you?" Kira offered.

"Sure." Gayatri jumped out of Kira's car and waited for Kira to gather her things.

They walked over to Gayatri's house like a team. Gayatri took her keys out and opened the door. She could hear Harrison approach the door as she did.

"Hi, honey. Hi, Kira," Harrison greeted the two. "We have company."

"So, I see," Gayatri said.

Gayatri and Kira placed their purses on the front hall credenza and walked into the living room. Sitting properly were two people, a man and a woman. The man stood up, revealing his slender frame and offered his hand for shaking. The woman continued to sit. She looked displeased to be there and barely made eye contact with Kira and Gayatri.

"Mrs. Clairemont, Dr. Akiyama, I'm assuming. I am Travis's father, Alan Nickels, and this is my wife, Gretchen," Mr. Nickels introduced. They shook hands with him.

Gayatri shook his hand firmly. "It's a pleasure to meet you," Gayatri lied.

"Nice to meet you," Kira lied, too.

Harrison tried to break the tension by offering everyone something to drink. They declined abruptly.

"How can I help you, Mr. Nickels?" Gayatri started, firmly.

Gretchen looked surprised by Gayatri's lack of remorse and smirked. Alan looked at his wife and gestured for her to calm down. She rolled her eyes and folded her arms.

"Right to it. Are you aware that your child broke our son's nose?" Alan asked.

"Yes, I'm fully aware," Gayatri quickly replied. "However, I don't think you and your wife are striking the proper tone here."

"Oh? How is that?" Alan's raised his eyebrows and dropped his lower lip in surprise.

"Your son, Travis, has been tormenting Dr. Akiyama's son for many months. Were you aware of that fact?" Gayatri didn't give them a second to answer her question. "No! I bet you are also unaware that your son is a well-known bully." Gayatri was on a roll. "Tell me, Mr. Nickels, how can you stand here in my house and start this conversation with what my daughter did to your son?"

Harrison touched his wife softly on the back, "Honey, let's calm down and keep the conversation civil."

"I'm not done," Gayatri announced, her index finger in the air. "Yes, to answer your question, I am fully aware that my daughter threw a water bottle at Travis's face and broke his nose. For that, I am sorry. Travis is a kid. However, I am not sorry for her protecting her friend." Gayatri never once broke eye contact with Nr. Nickels.

27

Kira came in hot at this point, "Your bully son pushed my son so hard, he fell back and hit his head on the concrete floor. He had a bump on his head for days! Tell me, what do you have to say about that, Mr. and Mrs. Nickels? Shame on you!" Her voice was screechy and elevated.

Alan looked at the lot of them. "Perhaps Hike-ah-row should learn to defend himself."

"Perhaps you should do a better job parenting because clearly, Travis gets no attention at home!" Kira snapped back.

"All right, all right," Harrison, the unintentional mediator. "This is getting out of control."

"How dare you speak of my son like that," Gretchen broke her silence. "You're lucky we don't sue you."

"Go right ahead! Travis has a history of violence and bullying at school. We can lawyer up, too," Gayatri popped off.

Alan and Gretchen got up and looked at Gayatri. "Keep your wretched little child away from Travis," Alan snarled.

This statement took Harrison by surprise. Gayatri looked over and noticed Harrison's face became beet-red, and his shoulders tensed up.

Harrison stood up, pointed at the door and all diplomacy to the wind, "Get out of my house, now!" His tone startled Gayatri. She stood next to him, facing them and held his arm.

"Yes, please leave," Gayatri asked calmly. "You didn't come here to make peace, but rather seeking an undeserving apology."

"You will regret this!" Alan threatened and stormed out. Gretchen followed closely behind. Alan and Gretchen climbed into the back seat of their separate SUVs, and their drivers took off.

"I guess they both need two vehicles to carry all that ego," Kira remarked. "Anyway, I need to tell Shinzo what is going on. He should be home from the hospital by now. We will talk about everything tomorrow. I'm exhausted from all of this."

"No problem, Kira." Gayatri stretched her arms out to hug Kira. They embraced as friends do, and Kira left.

Harrison and Gayatri sat down at the kitchen table to discuss what happened.

"Gayatri, that escalated too quickly," Harrison said with a worried tone.

"I agree," Gayatri replied. "I just hated how smug they were. What did they expect, for me to get on bended knees and beg for their forgiveness?"

"That's exactly what they wanted." Harrison was annoyed at the whole situation. "Do you wish Shakti had not gotten involved?".

"No, she did the right thing by helping Hikaru. I wished she didn't throw the bottle, though."

"I was thinking the same thing. It's out of character." Harrison looked deeply sad. He quickly became angry when he recalled Alan referring to his child as wretched. "Well, I'm not entirely mad about that.

"He's a kid, Harry. A horrible kid, but a kid nonetheless."

"I guess. Let's not mention the Nickels' visit to Shaks."

"Definitely," Gayatri agreed.

Shakti and Hikaru came bursting through the door, laughing and talking as Gayatri and Harrison were finishing up their conversation at the table. They quickly switched gears to welcome their daughter and Hikaru. Shakti smiled and ran into her dad's arms and then turned around to kiss her mom on the cheek.

"How was your day?" Harrison asked, looking at the two of them.

"It was okay." Hikaru smiled and looked at Shakti

"Yeah," Shakti said. "Everyone was staring and whispering about Karu and me all day."

"I guess they all know about Travis?" Gayatri inquired.

"Yes, but he was not in school today," Shakti replied to her mom.

"How's your head, Karu?" Gayatri asked with concern.

"It's okay. The bump is still there, but it doesn't hurt as much anymore," Hikaru touched the back of his head. "Mrs. Clairemont?"

"Yes," Gayatri looked up.

"And Mr. Clairemont. I'm really sorry Shakti had to get involved," he said, looking at his feet. "I'm more sorry I wasn't strong enough to deal with them myself." His sincerity surprised Harrison, Gayatri, and, most of all, Shakti.

Harrison stood up and walked over to Hikaru and held his shoulder as a father would, "Karu, please don't apologize. Not fighting back is not a sign of weakness." He smiled and then looked at Shakti and said, "And, fighting back with violence is not a sign of strength."

"Karu, you are not weak. You both were heavily outnumbered," Gayatri interjected. "You didn't ask for this. Shakti reacted to the situation as any good friend would."

Hikaru replied, "Thank you, Mrs. Clairemont. I would do the same for her."

At that moment, it occurred to Shakti just how much the incident affected Hikaru.

"Listen to me, the both of you," Gayatri started. "It's very important you let us know if any other incidents happen with Travis or the other boys."

They both nodded their heads in agreement.

"Okay, Mom. We don't have any homework. Can we go in the back?"

"Both of you, wash your hands and get something to eat first. There is food in the fridge. Then you can go back."

"Okay, Mom," Shakti said, and she and Hikaru took off.

CHAPTER 4

NEW NEIGHBOURS

The school year continued as usual. Travis returned to school and was quite embarrassed that he sustained a broken nose from Shakti. He avoided contact with Hikaru and Shakti. The boys in his group followed suit. Shakti and Hikaru spent a lot of time together studying, gardening, researching almost anything they could, and exploring the forest behind their homes.

They were particularly happy when Shakti's grumpy next-door neighbours put their house up for sale. It took three days for the house to sell at a record price on their street, Grand Heights Avenue. All the neighbours buzzed about the value of their homes. Toronto's real estate market seemed to be booming.

Three months later, grumpy Mr. and Mrs. Johnson moved out. No one moved in for almost two months. The new neighbours had the house gutted and redone. Shakti and Hikaru would sneak into the yard and peek through the windows to see the progress. The entire house was decorated with a white and grey palette. The kitchen showcased towering white cabinets and expensive-looking stone counters. There was wainscoting throughout the house, most notably up the staircase. The ongoing construction made the neighbours even more curious about who had bought the house and renovated it so beautifully.

Shakti and Hikaru would report the progress to their parents. After their parents' intrigued wowing, Shakti and Hikaru would get into trouble for sneaking into someone's private property. When the garden was landscaped and the new stone driveway was installed, Shakti and Hikaru figured the new owners must be close to moving in. The entire neighbourhood waited to meet their fancy new neighbours. This fascination quickly turned into gasps and ogles.

The new neighbours were an unconventional family compared to the otherwise stush neighbours. After the movers delivered their belongings and set them all up, the family finally arrived a few days later. They pulled up to the street in a roaring Porsche Cayenne Turbo and out climbed a man, woman, and two teenagers. The father was a huge Jamaican man with knee-length dreadlocks. He had a cloth wrapped around his head that matched his white T-shirt with a picture of Bob Marley. He wore skinny jeans and red kicks. His wife was a beautiful petite European woman with shoulder-length blond hair. She wore fashionably ripped jeans with high heeled boots and a large scarf wrapped around her neck. Her designer sunglasses were tucked neatly in her hair.

Shakti and Hikaru were plastered to the second-floor front window of Shakti's house. They stood on chairs or whatever they could to stare from one of the spare bedrooms. They were intrigued by the new family, but more than anything, they wanted to see who the kids were. The family stood around, observing the house and making comments about the garden. Finally, the kids came into clear view, which was great for Shakti and Hikaru because they were about to fall out of the window straining to see them.

The older teenager was a handsome boy, about eighteen years old, Shakti estimated. He was dressed similarly to his dad with short brown hair. He, too, was tall and athletic-looking. The younger teenager was a girl around Shakti and Hikaru's age. She was petite like her mom. Her long curly hair fell gracefully around her small frame. She was dressed in tracks, a crop top, and matching kicks. She walked around with her arms folded and observed the grounds of the house. From their hand gestures, the parents and son seemed excited to see their new house, but not so much the girl. Eventually, they made their way inside their move-in ready home.

"What's their story?" Hikaru asked out loud.

"I would love to know," said Shakti, still trying to see what's going on inside.

"Our neighbours are so rude. Look at them outside, staring with their mouths open," Hikaru complained.

"And what exactly are we doing?" Shakti pointed out.

Hikaru laughed and said, "We're inside staring with our mouths open. However, unlike them, we like what we see."

Shakti agreed, "Yeah! Did you see the son?"

"Did you see the daughter?" Hikaru and Shakti grinned and high fived each other. Both of them knowing deep down, they lacked any game.

"They sure beat grumpy Mr. Johnson," Shakti said.

* * *

While the pair were upstairs checking out the new neighbours, Gayatri and Harrison were downstairs doing the same. They were having a good laugh watching the other neighbours react to the new unconventional family. They knew that feeling. They, too, were a mixed-race family who had moved into the neighbourhood many years before.

"We should invite them over for dinner," Gayatri said, staring out the window.

"That's a good idea," Harrison noted.

After a full week passed, Gayatri and Harrison decided to walk over to the neighbours one evening and welcome them to the neighbourhood. They carried a bouquet of beautiful flowers and a chocolate bunt cake. Gayatri made sure she wore lipstick and a pair of high heels. She also made Harrison change his shoes to look cooler.

They walked over hand in hand, entered the property, and rang the doorbell.

Ding dong. After a few seconds, the lady opened the door. She was even more beautiful up close.

"Hi there." Gayatri flashed a big smile. "My name is Gayatri, and this is my husband, Harrison," Gayatri said softly.

"Hello, I am Agnes," she said with a distinct Swedish accent, squinting from the sun hitting her sparkling green eyes.

"We wanted to welcome you to the neighbourhood. We live right next to you." Gayatri pointed at her house. She handed the flowers to her, and Harrison offered the cake.

"Oh my God! That's great! Thank you so much," Agnes said enthusiastically.

"You're most welcome," said Gayatri, pleased with her reaction.

"If you need to know anything about the neighbourhood, please feel free to ask us," Harrison said kindly.

"That would be great. Thank you. Would you like to come in?" Agnes gestured inside.

"Oh no, we don't want to intrude. We just wanted to introduce ourselves and welcome you," Gayatri said.

"No! No intrusion! I would love to talk to you. I wish my husband was home, too," Agnes said.

"We would love to chat with you too, and meet your husband. If you are free next Saturday, we would like to invite you and your family to our place for dinner," Gayatri said.

"Oh, that would be awesome!" Agnes clearly was open to making friends. "Let me check with my husband. He has a very busy schedule, and I'll confirm with you tomorrow."

"Of course, of course." Harrison smiled.

"Well, it was great to meet you, and I look forward to having you and your family over." Gayatri waved and walked away.

"Thank you! Goodbye." Agnes was smiling from ear to ear and waved back

The very next day, Agnes knocked on Gayatri's door and confirmed plans for Saturday. Gayatri was excited to have the family over. Agnes mentioned her husband was vegan, but she emphasized that the rest of the family were not. They had a quick conversation, and Agnes left.

Gayatri and Harrison wanted to make a lovely dinner for the new family.

"The father is vegan, Harrison," Gayatri mentioned while clearing the table.

"That's fine. I can look up some vegan recipes, and then we can also make salmon or chicken for the rest of us."

"Sounds good. I wish it was summertime. We could have used Shaks and Karu's produce from our garden," Gayatri wishfully said, thinking it would be a wonderful conversation piece.

"There are still a few vegetables: broccoli, cauliflower, onions, beets. We can use them," Harrison noted.

"I'm excited. The only neighbours we get along with are the Akiyamas," Gayatri noted.

Saturday came quickly. Gayatri invited the Akiyamas too, but they were unable to make it as it was Hikaru's grandmother's birthday, and they were taking her to the CN Tower for dinner. Hikaru would have traded that evening to spend it with Shakti and meet the new neighbours, but he was not allowed to.

Gayatri and Harrison prepared the house beautifully, accented with aromatic candles and fresh flowers. They made several vegan dishes that included dhal soup, broccoli and cauliflower in a garlic sauce, balsamic tomato bruschetta, roast potatoes and pasta in an olive oil and pesto sauce. Shakti baked a delicious artisan bread while Harrison made his famous roast chicken.

Shakti set the table formally for seven with the nice dishes and fancy wine glasses. The only people they ever had over for dinner were Hikaru and his family and a few family friends. The Clairemonts were dressed trendy but casual.

Right at 7:00 pm, the doorbell rang. Shakti, Gayatri, and Harrison assembled quickly in the foyer and answered the door together.

"Hello! Welcome, welcome!" Harrison shouted with a huge smile. The new neighbours stood at the door with a huge basket of assorted fruits and packs of coffee and treats, all wrapped in plastic with a dramatic bow at the top. Harrison stepped back to allow the family to come in. The father entered first. He was a towering man with broad shoulders. He appeared even larger because his dreadlocks were wrapped precisely in a cloth on top of his head. Shakti bent her neck all the way back to see his full height with his dreadlock crown.

Agnes entered the house with their genetically blessed kids. They all removed their shoes. It took a few seconds for Shakti to realize that there were, in fact, three kids. The handsome boy, his sister, and another girl who looked about ten years old.

"Hello, I am Gayatri, and this is my husband, Harrison and our daughter, Shakti." She stretched her hand out to shake the man's hand.

"Nice to meet you. I am Winston Sutherland." His voice was deep, and his Jamaican accent friendly. "I know you've already met my wife, Agnes." He gestured at his wife and then his kids. "This is Mark, Zoe, and Mary."

"It is such a pleasure to meet you all," Gayatri said.

"Thank you for having us over," Winston said with a smile. "We brought some local fruits and treats from Jamaica." He handed the giant basket to Harrison.

"Wow! It's heavy! Thank you so much!" Harrison said, looking at the contents with excitement.

*   *   *

Shakti made eye contact with all the kids and smiled. The older kids smiled at her and nodded. Mary hid behind her mom, not letting go of her hand. Shakti immediately remembered she set the table for seven instead of eight. Amid this thought, she noticed a colourful light around Mary's body. She didn't think anything of this as seeing weird lights and figures around people was not unusual for Shakti.

They all made their way to the family room. Everyone was in a great mood, but the kids were quiet at first. Harrison made delicious hand-blended fruit drinks. He asked Winston if he wanted something harder to drink, Winston graciously declined. Harrison decided he would have fruit juice instead, while the women had white wine.

Shakti said to the kids, "Would you like to go outside to see my garden?"

"Sure!" Mark said, and he and Zoe got up and followed Shakti to the beautifully lit garden.

"My parents and I built this entire garden ourselves," Shakti said proudly.

"Wow! It's really beautiful," Zoe said for the first time. She appeared shy at first, but Shakti managed to get her talking. "I love the hanging lights."

"Yes, it's really nice," Mark said with a striking smile.

He could be the poster boy for a toothpaste commercial, Shakti thought.

"Doesn't your little sister want to come, too?" Shakti inquired.

"No, she's really shy and doesn't talk that much to strangers," Mark said. "But she's really cute when you get to know her."

"Oh, that's so nice," Shakti said, "Maybe we can get her to come out later."

They sat on the swings talking for a while. Mark and Zoe told Shakti all about their old school and how much they missed their friends. Mark started Guelph University in September. He was home only for the weekend. Zoe was starting Shakti's school on Monday.

"Awesome! I'll be happy to show you around," Shakti declared.

"That would be great!" Zoe said.

"You have to meet my best friend, Karu. He lives just a few houses down," Shakti said

"Zoe, that's awesome," Mark said. "You already have friends. See? You were worried for nothing."

Shakti thought that Mark seemed like an awesome big brother.

"That's right!" Shakti was elated. She figured she and Hikaru could use another member of their group, and Zoe seemed friendly enough.

*   *   *

Inside, the conversation with the adults was coming along swimmingly. Agnes complimented their house and made comments about the beautiful modern rustic look. Then she got up and went to the back door and called out to Mark to come to take his little sister to be with them. He got up right away and took her by the hand and walked her over to Zoe and Shakti. Agnes wanted a moment to tell Harrison and Gayatri about Mary.

"Our little Mary has a form of Asperger's Syndrome," Agnes explained, "That's why she is so shy."

"I see," Gayatri said with empathy. "She is absolutely lovely."

"Thank you. She went to public school with Zoe until Zoe started high school, but she has special help at the school when needed," Agnes said.

Winston added proudly, "She's the joy of our family, and she makes us proud every day. She's even in the chess club at school and loves to be outside."

"I'm sure she is," Harrison said. "Is she communicative?

"Yes, but it's limited around strangers," Winston noted. "At home, she talks a lot."

"Mark and Zoe are so great with her. They protect her and make sure she feels included," Agnes said like a proud mom.

"That has to be a direct result of excellent parenting," Gayatri complimented. "I've had students with Asperger's in my classes."

"Thank you," Agnes blushed, looking at Winston.

Harrison pointed outdoors to Winston to go outside, "I have some Cuban cigars. Want to have one with me?

"Nah, man, I have my own stuff. I'll come with you, though." Winston stood up.

Both men went out on the deck where they could see the kids on the lower level playing on the swings, laughing and talking.

"How did you and Agnes meet?" Harrison asked.

"We met while I was selling fruits at the local farmers' market, and she was a cashier at a nearby store. She would come by every week to buy vegetables from me, and I finally asked her out."

"That's awesome, man."

"Harrison, your home and family are beautiful. Thanks for inviting us over, man. We got a lot of weird looks from the neighbours when we moved in."

"Never mind them. We did too when Gayatri and I moved in many years ago. They don't mean any harm."

"That's good to hear. Since Agnes and I got married, we've been dealing with this," said Winston.

"That must be difficult."

"It was at first, but then my business took off, and I didn't have time to think about it anymore. It bothers Agnes, though."

"I see. It's better that way. Don't think about it. What business do you do?" Harrison inquired.

"I import fruits, vegetables and assorted products like coffee and cocoa from Jamaica and other Caribbean Islands."

"Wow, that's awesome! I'm in the food business as well. I manufacture and export cooking oils."

"Very good. Well, you must have done great to live in this neighbourhood." Winston smiled.

"I could say the same about you, my friend." Harrison laughed and offered his fist for a bounce.

Winston laughed out loud and reciprocated.

Harrison lit his cigar during their conversation. Soon after, Winston pulled a joint out of this pocket and asked, "Do you mind?"

"No, of course not. Please go ahead," Harrison said confidently.

"You want one? I have a lot," Winston said with a smirk.

"No, thanks. I haven't had one since my university days."

"I try to consume all-natural products," Winston explained, "I try to get my kids and Agnes on my vegan way of life, but they're not having it." Winston laughed, "Maybe in time. Lead by example. But I insist on Mary having a natural diet with little meat and absolutely no preservatives."

Harrison nodded. "That's awesome, man. It is certainly kinder and better for the environment as well."

"Yes, those are the main benefits of it," Winston agreed. "What it does for our body is the cherry on top. I've been vegan for fifteen years."

"Wow, that's a long time," said Harrison with surprise.

*   *   *

Meanwhile, Mary sat quietly while the kids laughed and talked. She held Mark's hand the whole time. Then, she got up and walked over to the vegetable garden and looked at it. Shakti could not help but notice how vivid the colours of her aura were. They seemed to dance around her and left a trail behind her as she walked. In the past, Shakti saw auras as a mist of calm colours around a person's head and body. But for Mary, it was a performance of vivid colours. It swirled and twirled around her like a frilled dress. Shakti looked on in awe of its vibrant energy.

Shakti got up from the swing and walked over to Mary and stood next to her. Mary stopped and stared at Shakti. Shakti smiled gently and asked her, "Do you like my garden?"

Mary didn't answer. She just continued looking at the garden intensely. She paused, then pointed at the garden and looked at Shakti. Mary said, "Fairy."

Shakti's eyes went wide, and her mouth dropped. She felt her neck getting warmer. Shakti thought her knees would knock loud enough for the kids to hear. She gasped and said quietly to her, "You see a fairy?"

Mary smiled and nodded. Mark and Zoe were talking to each other too far away to hear any of this conversation.

"Little man," Mary spoke again.

"Yes, yes, little man! They're called trolls," Shakti said excitedly, yet she felt like she wanted to cry.

"Bad?" Mary asked.

"No, not bad, just grumpy." Shakti laughed, and to her pleasant surprise, Mary laughed, too.

Mary's laughter made Zoe and Mark stop cold in their conversation to watch their sister. Mark got up and walked over to them. Shakti stopped laughing and became nervous.

"Mary, you are laughing with Shakti? Good for you!" Mark said. "It usually takes much longer for her to warm up to anyone." He looked at Shakti.

"She is so cute!" Shakti said, feeling relieved.

"Fairy," Mary said once more, this time to Mark.

"Yes, fairy. You love fairies. We know," Mark said, patting her awkwardly on the head. He then turned to Shakti and said, "It's not that she doesn't talk. She just doesn't talk to people she doesn't know. So, it's really surprising she spoke to you."

"I see. Well, I feel extra special then." Shakti smiled.

"You should!" Mark laughed out.

Just then, Harrison shouted from the deck, "Dinner time!"

The kids all ran up to the house, washed their hands, and made their way to the table. Shakti quickly set one extra spot at the table for Mary.

Dinner was enjoyable. It was very loud because everyone was laughing and talking. Winston and Agnes were impressed at the effort made to accommodate Winston's vegan diet. The kids looked pleased that their dad was happy. The evening ended with orange sorbet for Winston and a delicious chocolate truffle cake for everyone else. Shakti was distracted for the rest of the night. She couldn't take her mind off Mary seeing the fairies and trolls. She wondered how only she and Mary could see them. She thought about every time she wanted to tell Hikaru about the Clans but refrained because of the warning her mom had given her. Now, there was finally someone she could talk to about it.

The Clairemonts and the Sutherlands hung out late into the night. Agnes, Mark, Shakti, and Gayatri cleared the dishes and packed away the food in the kitchen, despite protests from Gayatri. After everyone said their goodbyes, Agnes and Winston with their kids walked home.

Gayatri, Harrison, and Shakti sat at their table to recap the night. "He imports products from Jamaica," Harrison said excitedly. "The basket is filled with the products he sells."

"Isn't that an amazing story?" Gayatri asked, "To start off selling in a farmers' market to wholesaling to the largest grocery stores in the GTA. Amazing really. I enjoyed their company."

"They're a great family," Harrison agreed. "Winston seems like a nice family man."

"Mom, Dad," Shakti said softly. "You know Mary?"

"Yes, Shaks. Did they explain to you about her?" Gayatri asked.

"Yes, they did," Shakti said. "She's very sweet. But Mary was with me in the garden, and she pointed at it and said she saw fairies and trolls."

Harrison's face showed genuine surprise, and Gayatri's mouth dropped.

"Are you serious?" Gayatri said, "How?"

"Well, at first, I noticed a colourful light around her," Shakti said. "I didn't think anything of it, and then she said she saw the fairies and trolls."

"Wait, wait, wait! Girls, the fairies and trolls are just imaginary friends you made up as a child," Harrison stated. "Right?"

"Harry, Shakti still sees her nature friends, and so did Mary," Gayatri hinted at Harrison, careful not to break her promise to Gabriel.

"I'm confused." Harrison scratched his head. "Should we be seeking counselling here?"

"No, Dad!" Shakti said loudly and then went back to speaking softly, "I know what I see, and I just got confirmation that someone else sees it. Does this mean I have Asperger's, too?"

"No, honey, that's not how it works," Gayatri said, "Perhaps Mary is gifted with Sight as you are."

"Sight?" Harrison said, holding his forehead.

"Yes, Harry. Do you, at all, believe in the unseen world? Spirituality?"

"I haven't given much thought to it, but yes, I do think it exists. Do you, G?"

"Yes, I have seen it in my life, but I'll talk about that another time," Gayatri said.

Already bored with the conversation, Shakti said, "I'm tired. I think I'll go to bed now. I'm showing Zoe around the school on Monday."

"That's so great, Shaks. Maybe you and Karu can include her in your group," Gayatri said.

"For sure. She's super nice." Shakti kissed her mom and dad and went off to bed.

CHAPTER 5

A SURPRISE
IN THE
WOODS

Shakti could not wait to tell Hikaru about the new family. She woke up extra early the next morning, slipped out the house quietly and marched over to Hikaru's house. She knew his Grandma would be up, so she did not hesitate to knock on the door. Sure enough, his Grandma Hoshi answered it, and Shakti popped in.

"Hi, Grams. Happy belated birthday! Is Hikaru up?"

"No, he's sleeping," Grams said.

"That's okay. I'll wake him up," Shakti said and proceeded upstairs before Grams could have a chance to react.

"Uhh…okay." Grams appeared not to have the energy to run after her.

As Shakti hit the landing, she beelined straight for his door. She didn't knock or even wobble the knob an extra second. She entered his room and went for the blinds. Hikaru was fast asleep.

"Karu, wake up," Shakti demanded.

Hikaru woke up, silly, "Huh?"

"Wake up! I need to talk to you," Shakti said in a bossy tone.

"Shakti! Why are you in my room, dude?" Hikaru said, reaching for his glasses. "It's six o'clock in the morning!"

"Why not? I'm always in your room."

"It's not appropriate for you to come into my room unannounced!" he grumbled.

"Why?"

"What if I was naked?" Hikaru argued as he held the glasses in his hand.

"Why would you be naked first thing in the morning, you weirdo?" Shakti said.

"Okay, okay. What do you have to talk to me about?" Hikaru surrendered.

"So!" Shakti started. "We had the new neighbours over for dinner last night!"

"Oh yeah!" Hikaru, showing interest, sat up to hear her better. "How did it go?"

"Amazing! They are the nicest people ever!" Shakti said excitedly.

"Oh, really?"

"Yes, and they have three kids! Not two."

"Wait, what? We only saw two."

"I know," Shakti agreed. "There is one son, Mark. He's eighteen, dreamy, and in Guelph University. Then there is Zoe. She's sixteen and starting school with us on Monday!"

"No way!"

"Yes. She's beautiful! We are showing her around school," she said with two thumbs up for Hikaru.

"Oh my God."

"She's really nice. Then, there is a ten-year-old sister, Mary. They told me she has Asperger's. She is super-duper sweet but shy."

"Oh, man, I wish I was there."

"Yeah, me too. They are a very interesting family. Oh! And they're loaded." Shakti and Hikaru hadn't been this excited about anything since they picked their first set of strawberries.

Shakti decided to leave and let Hikaru go back to sleep. She figured it was early in the morning, so she would go in the backyard and watch the Clans. She went down to the swings and sat carefree, swinging back and forth. She noticed over the years that she was able to see the fairies and other Clans much more around sunrise and sunset. They were usually out in groves at this time. As she sat, she saw them bustling around her doing their work. The trolls, grumpy as ever, looked like she bothered them by just sitting there.

She wondered how she had been able to keep this a secret for so long, especially from Hikaru. He didn't know she loved going into the forest mostly to see it come alive with creatures only she could see. Shakti decided to get up and walk into the woods. She was not afraid since she had done it several times before.

She approached the woods slowly and entered. She loved the smell of the woods in the morning. The trees were particularly gorgeous that day as the sun peeked through from the east. It was quiet, other than Gayatri's bamboo chime. Shakti saw a multitude of colours on the ground moving about. There was a communion of trolls and gnomes gathered around. She walked up to them and stood watching. They all stopped and turned around and watched her for a second. She was pretty sure she saw some of the trolls roll their eyes and continue on.

The gnomes were up to no good as usual. It appeared they were getting an earful from the trolls. Then a few fairies came buzzing around Shakti. They were always lovely and playful. Shakti smiled at them. Three fairies flew around her and through her long hair, causing her to lift her arms and giggle.

In the distance, closer to Hikaru's house, she thought she saw a moving white light. It was hard to say. It just flashed by. Shakti knew better than to ignore it. It meant something. She made her way in that direction. She looked at the fairies.

"Come with me, please," Shakti said under her voice, wanting their protection. She didn't know for sure if they would understand her, but they did. Five fairies flew around her as she walked north towards Hikaru's house.

Shakti got a glimpse of the light again and went running towards it. It looked human. But she wasn't sure. As she approached the light, it seemed to take the shape of a girl, but she could see through it. Shakti approached the light slowly. She should have been scared, but the light appeared too playful and happy.

The girl-shaped light finally turned around. Shakti put her hands over her mouth and screamed. It was Mary!

"Mary! Is that you?" Shakti feared the absolute worst. "What happened?" Tears formed in the corner of her eyes. The only explanation she could come up with was that Mary had passed away.

"Hi, Shakti. I'm playing with the fairies," the Mary-shaped light said. "Don't be scared. I'm just asleep."

"Oh, thank God!" Shakti said with a sigh of relief. She immediately noted a maturity in her voice. "How are you talking so well?"

"My body holds me back sometimes." Mary smiled. "But my light body is free to play and be myself."

"That's so great, Mary. How long have you been out here?" Shakti inquired.

"Just a few minutes. I'll be up soon."

"Do you only come out of your body to play in the morning?"

"I do mostly in the morning. I don't like the tall dark men. They are out mostly at night."

"What tall dark men?" Shakti immediately remembers seeing a tall dark figure over Travis after she threw the water bottle.

"I feel angry and sad around them," Mary said. "Okay, I'm leaving now. I'm about to wake up."

"Mary! Wait! Will you remember we met?"

"Yes, but I won't be able to talk about it. Sometimes I think it's just a dream."

"I see." Shakti was very confused. "Goodbye!"

Mary's astral body flew up to her house and entered through a window. Shakti was in shock, watching her defy gravity. She turned around and walked towards her house slowly, the fairies still buzzing around her. She said, "Can you believe that?"

The fairies nodded their heads in agreement. Shakti did not understand any of it, but she was determined to get answers.

Shakti went into her home and ran up to her bedroom. She grabbed her laptop and got comfortable on her bed.

"What do I search?" Shakti wondered out loud. "Creepy astral projection? No! Just astral projection."

She went right to the search and typed in *astral projection*. She read a few articles and was not satisfied with what she found. So, she tried many other possible word combinations.

Visiting fairies, children leave body asleep, gifted kids, trolls, fairies, gnomes, forest people, nature friends.

This went on for a while. She read for a few hours. Her parents were up and doing their thing. They checked on her a few times.

Shakti spent all day educating herself on the topic. She read many fascinating stories of people who watched themselves while they slept and walked around outside. The more she read, the more she was introduced to new topics that related to her. There was an entire community of people out there who claimed they saw the Clans. They called them elementals. This made her very excited, and she felt a bit more normal. The search ended when Shakti read there was a meeting and meditation session on Friday at 6:00 pm for people who had these experiences. It was free and mediated by a woman named Vidia. Shakti quickly grabbed a pen and wrote down the location and time of the meeting. It was at a townhouse, close to the intersection of College and Bathurst. It was not too far from her, but she thought it would be best not to go alone.

She wondered how she would get Hikaru to come with her. She would have to tell him all about the Clans. That thought scared Shakti, as she couldn't afford to lose her only friend. Then she thought she was his only friend too, and he would believe her after some convincing. It was all too overwhelming for Shakti. She needed a break from the topic. She got up and went to hang out with her parents.

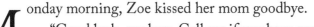

CHAPTER 6

TOUR
GUIDE

Monday morning, Zoe kissed her mom goodbye.

"Good luck, my love. Call me if you have any trouble." Agnes hugged her daughter as tight as she could.

"Thanks, Mom." Zoe smiled nervously.

"Okay, have some fruit and get ready to leave. Big day for my pickney." Winston smiled and gave his daughter a pat on the head.

Winston drove her to school. He got out of the fancy SUV to walk her into the office. All eyes were fixated on the huge Rastafarian walking Zoe in. They looked at Zoe and then Winston back and forth. Zoe's anxiety started creeping into her stomach.

"Don't worry, Zoe. We always get a lot of stares wherever we go," Winston assured his daughter. "Then they get to know you and love you. We're a modern family," he said jokingly.

"I know. I'm very proud of you, Daddy. I don't like it when they look at you this way."

"Guess what? I don't care. Promise," Winston said. "Also, they're not looking because they don't like me. They're looking because I'm different. That's okay."

After they made introductions to the office staff, Winston held Zoe by the shoulders. "Jah bless." He kissed her on the forehead.

"Thanks, Dad. I'm going to call Shakti."

"Good idea."

Winston left with all eyes on him once more.

Zoe followed the office's directions to her locker. On her way, she called Shakti.

"Hi, Zoe!" Shakti answered enthusiastically.

"Hi, Shakti," Zoe meekly replied. "I'm at school and on my way to my locker."

"Where is that?"

"Level two, locker two zero four zero."

"We will meet you there."

Sure enough, by the time Zoe located her locker, Shakti and Hikaru were there. She greeted Shakti with a smile. Hikaru stood by awkwardly.

"Zoe, this is my best friend, Karu," Shakti introduced.

"Nice to meet you, Karu," Zoe said softly.

"What up?" Hikaru raised his fist for a fist pump. Zoe reciprocated, and Hikaru missed the mark upon contact. He felt silly but recovered quickly. "So, did you find your way around?"

Watching the train wreck that was Hikaru, Zoe smiled. "So far, so good," She seemed a little more at ease.

Shakti intervened. "We have about fifteen minutes before the first bell. Let's show you around."

They would spend the rest of the day between classes together. Zoe felt deeply grateful for her friends. She was a beautiful girl and gained a lot of attention immediately.

*　*　*

Shakti's mind was preoccupied all day. She had to figure out a way to get to the meditation group without alarming her parents. She thought the responsible thing to do would be to take Hikaru, but that would involve telling him everything. She wondered if she should do it on her own. When she was alone between classes, she pulled out the piece of paper and called Vidia's number. A man answered, and she put her name in for the meditation session. She couldn't help but feel it was a big risk, going alone to a private townhouse for a meditation group she found online. She decided to tell Hikaru. She picked up her phone and texted him.

Shakti: *Karu, I need a favour.*
Hikaru: *Sure, what?*
Shakti: *You have to keep it a secret.*
Hikaru: *Ummm. No.*
Shakti: *I'm serious!*
Hikaru: *Obviously! Who would I tell? My other friends?*
Shakti: *Can you come with me to something on Friday evening?*
Hikaru: *Come to what?*
Shakti: *A meditation group*
Hikaru: *A what??????*
Shakti: *Please, Karu. I need you to trust me and not ask too many questions about it.*
Hikaru: *Geez. Why the sudden interest in meditation?*
Shakti: *I wanted to talk to the instructor. Please don't ask anything else. I would go alone, but it's at someone's house*
Hikaru: *Are you crazy?? DO NOT GO ALONE! I'll go with you*
Shakti: *Thanks, Karu! You're the best. One more thing.*
Hikaru: *Yessssss.*
Shakti: *We can't tell our parents.*
Hikaru: *Ya think?*

* * *

On Wednesdays, Gayatri got home early, around 1:00 pm. She looked forward to it. That Wednesday, she came home, kicked her shoes off, and plopped herself on the sofa. She estimated Harrison would be home around 6:00 pm. She had lots of time to figure out dinner. She thought she might surprise Shakti and pick her up after school. As she was sitting there, feeling relaxed, she immediately noticed the air change. Angel Gabriel appeared.

"Gabriel!" She smiled and lit up like she saw her oldest friend.

"Peace be unto you, Gayatri." Gabriel smiled with his brilliant copper aura.

"And with you, Gabriel."

"How your mood towards me has changed over the years," Gabriel observed.

"It's true." Gayatri giggled, "I'm no longer scared as I was before. In my defence, you did give me a lot of information to process in a short time."

"Agreed," Gabriel smiled. "But, you handled it beautifully."

"I hope I did well by your standards."

"Yes, you did, Gayatri. So did Harrison. He is a most caring father. We've been watching," Gabriel noted.

"He really is." Gayatri blushed. "It's been years since you last visited me. To what do I owe this honour?"

"I only come when I have a message to deliver or when needed," Gabriel softly said.

"I know."

"Shakti is about to enter into a new phase of her life."

"Oh?" Gayatri was at full attention on her feet.

"A new world is about to open to her, and the veil lifted." Gabriel stood tall as if delivering a sermon. "She has seen behind this veil many times in the garden and forest."

"So, the Clans are real?" Gayatri noted.

"Yes, they are real." Gabriel smiled. "They are wonderful creatures, although eccentric."

"Apparently." Gayatri chuckled. "But, what do you mean a veil is to be lifted?"

"Shakti has only seen a small glimpse into this world. She is about to seek out methods that would lift the veil completely." Gabriel walked up to Gayatri and stared down at her from his towering height. "Gayatri, it is most important that you do not stop her."

"How or why would I do that?"

"As a mother, you may try to protect her. What she is about to find out will be a tool for her in the future. It will ultimately protect her. Give her the necessary freedom she needs."

"I see. As long as she is being safe," Gayatri reluctantly said, "Do you think I should talk to her about all of this?"

"Not now. She needs to come about this information at her own pace."

"Yes, true," Gayatri agreed.

Gayatri sat back down on the sofa, contemplating what Gabriel told her once again.

"Gayatri, it is time for you to tell Harrison about us."

Gayatri looked up at Gabriel in shock, "Are you sure?"

Gabriel smiled. "He earned this respect, don't you agree?"

"Definitely!" Gayatri was excited. She dreamt of this day. "I have no idea how I will do it but thank you. Should I be concerned for him?"

"In the past, it was best to keep him out of it. The situation is about to change. Shakti will need protection and guidance she does not know she needs."

"Okay." Gayatri became worried.

"You will know when the time comes. I must leave you now," Gabriel said gently. Again, Gayatri noticed a large structure that followed him. She thought it best not to ask.

"Goodbye, Gabriel. Until we meet again."

"Peace be unto you, Gayatri." He placed his hands over her head and disappeared.

Gayatri laid down slowly on the sofa. She placed her arm over her eyes as if to deepen her concentration. She thought about Shakti entering this journey and how it hurt that she couldn't guide her more. How would she react the day she found out that her mother knew all along? Had she given her the tools to survive the life she would lead? Did she have the level of compassion the world required? The questions swirled around her head like a tornado. It was enough to make her panic. She took deep breaths and decided that she would guide Shakti from afar. As she was coming to grips with her situation, she thought about Harrison. This was a much smaller mountain to climb, but a task anyway. She figured she would simply lay it out on the table.

While Gayatri was pondering her situation, she heard the keys turn in the lock and in bounced Shakti.

"Hi, Mom!" Shakti greeted enthusiastically.

"Hi, Shaks. You're home early."

"No, it's four pm. I'm actually late." Shakti laughed. "I was at Karu's house doing homework."

"Oh my! I must have been lying here for hours, thinking!" Gayatri didn't realize that time escaped her.

"Thinking about what?"

"Oh! I have a lot on my mind. How about we go out for dinner?" Gayatri smiled.

"Ramen noodles?" Shakti said with clasped hands.

"Yes! We haven't had Ramen in forever." Gayatri felt at ease again. "Can you text Dad to meet us there?"

Shakti and Gayatri left after an hour to meet Harrison at a nearby ramen restaurant. Gayatri let Shakti decide the place and time. Harrison was to meet them fifteen minutes after they arrived. Gayatri wanted to enjoy the time with her daughter.

"So, what's new with you, Shaks?" Gayatri inquired.

"Not much. School is great. Zoe hangs out with Karu and I. She's been awesome."

"I'm really proud of you, Shaks. Without hesitation, you showed Zoe around school and made her feel welcomed. Her parents are grateful for this. I spoke to Agnes yesterday, and she was raving about you."

Shakti blushed. "I was happy to. Zoe is great. She's smart and friendly."

"That was really nice of you. Also, I know it's out of your comfort zone to make new friends."

"Tell me about it." Shakti laughed. "Mom, are you working on Friday evening?"

"Yes, until eight pm," Gayatri said nonchalantly, then clued in. "Why? Do you need something that day?"

"No, no, I wanted to go out with Karu. We were thinking of biking farther into the city."

Here was Gayatri's moment of truth. She needed to fight every urge to not go into mother mode and ask about Shakti's whereabouts and when and why and how long and how late.

Instead, she said, "Bike? Why bike? Download the Uber app on your phone, and I'll put my credit card on it. You can use it to get around easier, or you can take the bus or subway. Only use the bike for shorter distances."

Stunned for a few seconds, Shakti responded, "Umm, okay. But bikes are safe too and more environmentally friendly."

"This is true." Gayatri nodded her head in agreement. She felt her emotions creeping in and her eyes tearing up. "Shakti, your safety is all that matters to me." A tear escaped.

"Mom, what's wrong?" Shakti touched her mom's hand.

"Nothing. Nothing at all. You're just so grown up. I forget sometimes."

Shakti smiled. "I'll always be safe, Mom."

"I know. It's important to explore your world, but you must always be careful." Gayatri held her daughter's hands firmly and looked into her eyes and said, "Shakti, I want you to know one thing."

Shakti took a deep breath. "Yes?"

"If you ever need us, we will come running to you. Don't worry about getting into trouble. The most you'll get is a good yelling, and that's nothing. No one will look after your interests more than Dad and me."

"I know, Mom," Shakti said with a somber look in her face.

"Anytime, anywhere," Gayatri continued.

"I promise, Mom." Gayatri could tell that Shakti meant it.

Gayatri wiped her eyes. She then picked up the menu, and the evening carried on as normal. Harrison joined them soon after, and the Clairemonts had a lovely family dinner together.

CHAPTER 7

A PARADE FOR SHAKTI

Friday came quickly.

Shakti had been quiet all week. She had a lot on her mind, and her mom's emotional conversation made her reflect. She wondered why Gayatri didn't ask where she and Hikaru would be going. She didn't even ask what time they would be back. This was most unlike her protective mom. However, Shakti was grateful that she didn't need to lie.

That evening, Shakti and Hikaru went to their respective homes. They made a plan to meet at 5:00 pm in front of her house. Shakti went home and had something to eat and got ready. She heard her phone vibrate. It was a text from Zoe.

Zoe: *Hi, Shaks. What are you up to this evening?*

Oh no, Shakti thought. She forgot all about what she would say to Zoe. Both she and Hikaru would be gone, and they did not think about Zoe asking questions. Shakti called Hikaru.

"Karu, Zoe is asking what we're up to," Shakti said.

"Oh no," Hikaru replied, "Should we include her?"

"No way," Shakti said. "This is top secret. You don't even know what we're doing!"

"True."

"Okay. I'll text her and tell her we will hang out tomorrow."

Shakti: *Hi, Zoe. I'm busy this evening. Let's hang out tomorrow with Karu.*

Zoe: *Sounds good.*

As Gayatri suggested, Shakti called an Uber. She texted Hikaru to be there in five minutes. As she pulled on her jacket, she glimpsed over at Zoe's house. She could see Zoe sitting at the table talking to Mark. Then she looked at the second-floor front window and saw Mary looking at her. She waved at Mary, and she waved back and smiled. She adored Mary. Something about her was warm and welcoming, completely nonthreatening.

Hikaru came walking over just as the Uber arrived. They both jumped in the Honda, and off they went.

"Are you sure about this?" Hikaru asked.

"Yes, don't worry. It's just a meditation group and meeting of like-minded people," Shakti reassured Hikaru. She made a decision to get right into it. "I always thought I was different. These people seem to have a lot in common with me."

"Different how?"

"Well, since I was little, I could see other beings." Shakti avoided eye contact with him.

"Beings? Like ghosts?" Hikaru glanced over at the driver when he said it. Thankfully, the driver was singing along to his music.

"Not ghosts, but other beings, and I always wanted an explanation for it." She briefly glanced at him.

"Why didn't you tell me?" Hikaru asked with a surprised look on his face.

Shakti looked at Hikaru, her eyes glazed. "I always wanted to, but I was afraid I'd lose you because you would think I was a freak." The sides of her mouth drooped, and a tear escaped her eyes. "You're my only friend."

Hikaru took one of her hands and said, "I would have believed you, Shaks. You will never lose me. You've been my only friend, too."

"Thanks, Karu. But before you say you believe me, you should know what I'm talking about. I'll tell you all about it in time. You should know my parents know about it. They believe me."

"Well, that's great. So, the point of today is to meet other people like yourself?"

"Yes, apparently there's a lot of people like this. One more thing, Zoe's sister, Mary, is like me, too."

"What?"

"Yes, we have communicated about it. I'll tell you all about it one day," Shakti promised.

"Okay, one reveal at a time. My stomach can't handle it." Hikaru propped his forehead on the front headrest.

Toronto's traffic was crawling, as always. The Uber seemed to move five feet every minute. However, it gave Shakti and Hikaru enough time to talk.

After thirty minutes, the Uber pulled up into the street, close to the intersection of College and Bathurst. The driver stopped in front of a very old row of townhomes, all of which looked distinctly different. Shakti and Hikaru jumped out of the Uber and thanked the driver. Shakti had a backpack with a notebook and pen, two water bottles, a small towel, and two yoga mats. She showed Hikaru what she brought along, and he laughed. It was clear that Shakti wanted to be prepared for her meditation session. She assumed it was just like yoga class.

Shakti located number thirty-four. They walked up to the front door and rang the doorbell. Hikaru touched Shakti's hand and said, "Be cool."

"I know," Shakti replied, understanding that Hikaru was more nervous than she was for some reason. Perhaps he felt responsible for her.

After a few seconds, they heard quick footsteps. The door opened, and they were greeted by a short man with a huge smile, "Hello," he said.

"Umm...Hi. I am Shakti, and this is Karu." Shakti reciprocated a huge smile. Hikaru raised his hand briefly and did a one-second smile.

"Welcome. Are you here for the meditation class? I guess it's your first time," the short man said. "I am Martinez, but you can call me Marty." All the while, he maintained his impressive smile. "Please come in." Marty stepped to the side and allowed them enough room to enter.

Although the house was old from the outside, the inside was beautiful with all-white walls and chestnut wood floors. The foyer ceiling was high and welcoming. The townhouse was long and narrow, and so were all the rooms. Shakti almost had to turn sideways to walk next to someone in the foyer. Marty motioned at their shoes. Hikaru and Shakti removed them and placed them neatly on the shoe stand along with many other pairs of shoes.

Shakti gathered her stuff and stood up straight. Her eyes immediately fell on a giant statue of a winged angel. It was almost as tall as Hikaru. By the time she stepped one step forward, she could see into the living and dining room. There were many bookshelves and glass cases. Books stacked from the floor to the ceiling. Some books looked very old, some new. The glass cases housed hundreds of statues of angels, fairies, and other little creatures she didn't recognize from where she was standing. She knew right away she was in the right place.

"Vidia will join us in the basement for the session," Marty said, leading the way to the basement staircase. Shakti and Hikaru looked at each other briefly and descended the carpeted steps. The stairs curved down to reveal a large open space at the bottom of the staircase. It did not feel like a basement at all. There were over twenty people sitting cross-legged on the carpet facing the front of the room.

Shakti and Hikaru found a spot together on the carpet. As they got comfortable, Shakti made eye contact with some people around her. There were all different kinds of people: young, old, black, white, Asian, tattooed. One man looked like a dad from her school. They all seemed friendly. Hikaru couldn't seem to find a comfortable position on the carpet. One lady stared in their direction and smiled. Shakti's first thought she was smiling at her, so she smiled back. She soon realized she was looking right above her. Shakti tried to follow her line of sight over her head. There was nothing there. The lady continued to stare intensely. At some point, her eyes wandered around like she was watching a movie right over Shakti's head. She was most entertained by it.

A few minutes after, Marty reappeared in the basement with his smile. He walked over to the side of the room and reached out for the lights. He said, "Let us begin," as he dimmed the lights to an ambient glow. The lowered lights made Hikaru fidget even more. Shakti touched his leg to calm him down. By this time, a lady had started walking up to the front, through the crowd. She wore a kimono-type dress with huge cape-like sleeves that connected to the knee area. Her hair was raven black and rolled in a French twist. She was petite and slender. Shakti assumed this was Vidia. She appeared to be of East Asian descent, but she couldn't quite tell which nationality she was.

"Good evening," she charismatically said while she clasped her hands. "Namaste. Shalom. Konnichiwa. Guten tag. Nin hao. Asalaam Alaikum. Bonjour. Hola." She glowed.

The crowd reacted favourably to her gesture with subtle laughs, and a blend of answers ensued. This immediately broke the tension for Shakti and Hikaru. Shakti noticed Hikaru holding back a smile because the lady had said Konnichiwa.

The lady continued, "For those of you that are new to the class, I am Vidia." She locked eyes with Shakti and smiled like a friendly principal on the first day of school. "Let us begin. If you would like to talk to me, meet me after class." Her eyes still locked on Shakti.

"What do we do?" Hikaru whispered to Shakti.

"Follow the instructions, I guess," Shakti whispered back.

"Get into your comfortable position," Vidia started. Almost everyone changed their position. Some of the class laid down on their backs, some on their sides, a few people straightened their posture, and others slouched. Marty was fiddling with a remote in the background and turned on a most peculiar-sounding drum sound. It sounded like the ocean, but no rhythm to it.

Vidia then went through step-by-step instructions. It included imagining grounding yourself into the Earth and then connecting with your ethereal light. Shakti and Hikaru followed these steps. To Shakti's surprise, she was quite into the meditation. The images of swaying in thin air came quite naturally for her. Hikaru appeared relaxed as well. The hour flew by quickly. Vidia's soft rhythmic voice was comforting. She was excellent at narrating the experience. She closed off the meditation by bringing everyone's mind back down to Earth.

At the end of the session, Marty made his way over to the lights and brightened the room.

Hikaru leaned over to Shakti and said, "That was amazing!"

Shakti replied, "I know. I'm surprised you liked it."

"I did. Who knew?"

"I did something like this in yoga before but never so deep."

Some people were talking in the corner. Vidia walked up to Shakti and greeted her.

"Hello, Shakti. Thank you for coming to our meditation class."

"Thank you. It was amazing." Shakti smiled. "How do you know my name?"

"Well, you called in earlier this week to book a spot. So, it was either you or him." She giggled, gesturing at Hikaru.

Shakti laughed and said, "That makes sense. This is my friend, Karu."

"Nice to meet you."

On his feet now, Hikaru extended his hand to shake Vidia's. She ignored his hand and opened her arms for a hug. He awkwardly hugged her with a little double tap on her back. Then, she looked at Shakti and hugged her, too.

"I'm guessing you came to talk to me," Vidia said to Shakti while holding the sides of her arms.

"Yes, I would like that very much. Can we chat in private?"

"Of course. Give me a few minutes to say goodbye to my class."

"Sure, take your time," Shakti said.

Vidia went over to the group chatting in the corner. They stood there for a few minutes, talking and laughing. Just then, the lady who was staring over Shakti's head came up to her.

"Hi there," she said. "I am Jennifer."

"Hi, I'm Shakti, and this is Karu."

"I must apologize to you. I didn't mean to stare earlier." Jennifer's admittance surprised Shakti.

"Oh no, no, it's not a problem. I was wondering what you were looking at, though."

"Since you walked into the room, there was an entire parade behind you." Jennifer laughed. Shakti's mouth fell open a bit.

"A p...p...parade?" Shakti stammered.

"Yes, a huge parade of people dressed in red. It looked like quite the party," Jennifer spoke about it like it was normal.

"What does that mean?" Shakti felt uneasy.

"Who knows?" Jennifer said with her shoulders up and hands extended, "But I've never seen a parade before."

"I see. Okay. Thanks." Shakti wondered if Jennifer was off the rocker. But felt she was a hypocrite because she had seen all kinds of crazy things before, too. Maybe she should keep an open mind. Her tone changed. "Thank you for letting me know, Jennifer. I wish I saw it, too."

"Oh, you will. You'll see it all one day." Jennifer then turned on her heel and walked away.

"Okay, that was weird," Hikaru chimed in.

"It's all good."

"Hmm."

"I'm going to talk to Vidia after in private. Do you mind waiting for me?"

"No problem. I'll chat with my good friend, Marty."

Shakti laughed. "He seems friendly enough."

"Yeah. I'll be fine. Will you be fine?"

"Yes, this is what I came for," Shakti assured him.

About ten minutes after, the room cleared out, and the last person left. Marty instructed Hikaru and Shakti to join him upstairs. He led them back up the stairs and made them wait in the angel-themed living room. The room looked posh with neutral walls and plush cool-tone pillows on a beige sofa. Angel statues from different parts of the world surrounded them. They varied in sizes, textures, and colours. Some looked expensive, made of marble and exotic stones. Some statues and figurines appeared to come from artisan markets from Marty and Vidia's travels. An oversized coffee table with a giant black obsidian rock placed on a deliberate angle centred the room.

"Would you kids like some hot chocolate?" Marty offered.

Hikaru answered first, "Yes, please!"

Shakti was about to say no thanks, then quickly changed to, "Yes, please," with a big smile.

"Alrighty." Marty was most pleased. He ran into the kitchen and got started.

Vidia came up from the basement and turned the lights off behind her. She smiled at the pair and said, "Let me guess, Marty is making you hot chocolate."

"Yes, he is," Hikaru said with a smile.

"He prides himself on making the world's best hot chocolate." Vidia chuckled.

"I can't wait to try it," Hikaru replied. Shakti was pleasantly surprised to see how vocal and comfortable Hikaru was being around these people.

Vidia sat next to them. Marty popped in and asked if she wanted hot chocolate, too. She declined.

"We will go upstairs to my office after you get your hot chocolate." Vidia smiled. "How long have you two been friends?"

"We grew up on the same street, three houses away since we were born," Shakti explained.

"Ah, friends by default," Vidia joked.

"Yes, I guess." Shakti laughed, too. Hikaru was preoccupied, looking at all the angels.

He said, "You really like angels, don't you?"

"Yes, very much. They always appear when I need them," Vidia said seriously.

"That's nice," Hikaru replied while tapping his thumbs together.

A few minutes passed, and Marty came into the room with a fancy tray with two giant cups of hot chocolate.

"Thank you, Marty," Shakti and Hikaru said in unison.

"You're very welcome." Marty looked more excited than they did.

Vidia got up and asked Shakti to join her upstairs. Shakti picked up her hot chocolate and followed Vidia up the stairs. Hikaru and Marty were already in conversation as Shakti ascended the stairs.

Vidia led her into a room with a desk in the middle. Unlike the rest of the house, this room was filled with warm, colourful tones. Three of the room's walls were flanked with giant bookcases filled with books.

Vidia must love to read, Shakti thought.

Vidia gestured to Shakti to sit on the chair while she went around the other side of the table to sit. Shakti felt like it was an interview. Except she was here for clarity.

Vidia noticed Shakti was intrigued by all the books. "Seek knowledge from the cradle to the grave." Vidia smiled. "Prophet Mohammed."

"Yes, I see you live by this." Shakti gestured to the books.

"I do. I'm a student of the light," Vidia explained. "I've been doing this a long time."

"Doing what, exactly?"

"I've been studying the spirit world and transcendental energies. My area of expertise is shamanism and Vedic astrology."

"I see." Shakti had no idea what that meant.

"I've been advised by my spirit guides that I would have a visitor who would come to me for help," Vidia said. "I didn't realize you would be so young. Tell me, how old are you?"

"I'm sixteen."

"Oh, you're a baby." She giggled. "Tell me all about what you've been seeing your whole life."

Shakti was surprised that Vidia was spot on. "Well, since I was a little kid, I've been seeing creatures and beings around me. At first, I thought everyone could see them, but then I realized it was just me."

"Specifically, what type of creatures?" Vidia asked.

"Fairies, gnomes, trolls." Shakti counted on her fingers.

"So, the elementals."

"That's what I understand they are called. I call them the Clans."

Vidia looked up at Shakti, "Clans?" She laughed.

"Yes," Shakti said, feeling a little embarrassed.

"That's absolutely precious! Do you see anything else?"

"Yes, I've seen angels. They usually don't talk much. They stand around and pretty much smile at me. Once, one of them told me his name."

"What was his name?"

"Michael."

"Ahhh…Michael! He's very special indeed. He's an Archangel."

"You know of him?"

"Yes, of course, he's the angel of protection. I'm guessing you have had no religious upbringing?"

"No. My family and I believe in God, but we don't follow any religion." Shakti wasn't sure how Vidia would react to that. She moved on. "From a distance, I've also seen tall, dark creatures hanging around people."

"Would you say they are good creatures or bad?" Vidia asked.

"Bad, definitely bad."

"That's what I thought. They are evil Jinns." She paused. "They whisper into the ears of men, influencing them to do cruel things."

"That makes so much sense," Shakti recalled Travis taunting Hikaru.

Vidia leaned over a bit and looked at Shakti. "Tell me, Shakti, how would you like me to help you?"

"I don't know, to be honest," Shakti said. "I want an explanation for what this is."

"I see. The only way to explain this to you is for you to jump right in and pursue it," Vidia explained. "All our gifts are different, given to us for one purpose or another. You have to make a decision whether you want to truly find out where this leads you, or if you want to shut it off and carry on with your life in blissful ignorance."

Shakti didn't know what she wanted. She thought she should honour her gift and find out what it was. However, did she want to be one of those people? Someone who lived between worlds and not fully present in either. What would it mean to turn it off? Would she never see the Clans again? No. She picked up her hot chocolate and gulped it. It was delicious, she noted, looking into the cup.

"I think I owe it to myself to open my eyes to this world," Shakti said honestly.

"Interesting choice of words, Shakti," Vidia pointed out. "That's exactly what you will be doing. Opening your third eye. It will open the spirit world to you."

"That sounds terrifying," Shakti admitted.

"It could be if you don't protect yourself. I will teach you how to do that."

"I don't mean to be rude, but what is in it for you? I'm just a student. I don't have money to pay you."

"Look around you. I'm doing okay," Vidia said, referring to her home in a boujee part of Toronto, "It's my duty to guide Rainbow Children.

"What are Rainbow Children?"

"You are what we call a Rainbow Child. These are children born during and after the year two thousand who have gifts of being able to see into the spirit world."

"Okay, I guess I would qualify as a Rainbow Child then."

"It's more than that. They are born with a sense of responsibility to Mother Earth and the need to save her. More and more Rainbow Children are popping up around the world. I suspect it's because the world is in such turmoil. Also, they possess qualities of kindness, tolerance, and they love very deeply. They often get hurt easily. Some are born with gifts, some develop them over time, and some never do. They all have a fondness of nature."

"I see."

"I've met several Rainbow Children over the years. It is prophesied that a great Warrior will emerge from them. No one knows who this child will be." She leaned forward. "There are many Rainbow Children around the world. They will be game-changers in the future. So much so that the dark side are terrified of them."

"Why is that? Who is the dark side?"

"Oh, the dark side are the Jinns and people they influence. They essentially rule the world right now." Vidia looked frustrated. "They are people surrounded by evil Jinns and seek fortune and power with no consequence. They are all about power and control. This is what is ruining our planet today. They, too, are aware of the prophecy. They will do anything in the world to stop the Rainbow Tribe and, most of all, the Warrior."

"When will this Warrior emerge?" Shakti made air quotes when she said *Warrior*.

"No one knows. There have been signs that he or she is already born."

"Signs like what?"

"They said a lot of natural disasters would take place like the melting of the polar ice caps and the burning of the Amazon rainforest due to global warming. Basically, the need to save the world will become urgent. This is all unverified, of course, folktales," Vidia said.

"Is there a difference between the Rainbow Children and the Rainbow Tribe?"

"They are pretty much one and the same. But Rainbow Children are already born into this purpose. The Rainbow Tribe will be activated somehow by the Warrior. They will all be called the Rainbow Tribe. That's all I know about it," Vidia declared. "But, Shakti, let's get back to you. There is lots of time to talk about the Rainbow Tribe. You have a decision to make."

"I know what I need to do. I'm scared, though. I know it's a lot to ask of you, and you barely know me. But, would you guide me?"

Vidia didn't need to think about it. "Yes, I will. But you will require many teachers, not just me."

"I don't know where to start to find these people."

"You start right here." Vidia smiled caringly. "I know many excellent spiritual teachers. Many of whom are willing to impart their knowledge onto the Rainbow Tribe of the world." Her tone suddenly changed. "It is dangerous work, though."

"Dangerous, how?" Shakti became nervous.

"Well, we started to keep a book of the Rainbow Children that sought us out. But we had to destroy it because a group from a secret society called the King's Guard started looking for it. We feared for the children's safety."

"Oh no. That's scary," Shakti said.

"It was scary. They entered many of the teacher's homes and offices and trashed them, looking for the list. Luckily, they never found it." Vidia's forehead became tense. "It's an extremely serious situation, Shakti. I don't want to mislead you in any way. You should know what you are getting yourself into. You will be a keeper of secrets."

"I see." Shakti thought this decision would impact her life, her parents, her friends. But what choice did she have? "Where and how do I start?"

Vidia's forehead started to uncrunch slowly. It was evident that the time of the King's Guard affected her. "I am meeting with a friend tomorrow for breakfast. He is a brilliant author and was heavily involved with the Rainbow Children before it came to an abrupt stop. I will talk to him about you."

"Thank you, Vidia. Here is my number." Shakti wrote her cell phone number on a writing pad on top of Vidia's desk. "Please call me when you decide how we will do this."

"Please give me some time. Some of the teachers are scared to get back into their work with the Rainbow Tribe. I need to remind them it is for a much greater good than us," Vidia said. "You will be the first child we're taking back on."

"I see." Shakti was confused and wanted to leave. "I better be off."

"Okay, Shakti." Vidia smiled as she rose from her seat. "It was my genuine pleasure to meet you."

"It was an honour to meet you, Vidia. Thank you for answering these questions I've had all my life."

"I know you still have many questions, but I think that's a lot of information for now."

"It is." Shakti giggled.

The two made their way down the stairs and heard Marty and Hikaru talking passionately about something.

"Marty, that was the best tasting hot chocolate I've ever had." Shakti lifted her cup at Marty.

Marty's face lit up. "I'm glad you loved it. Please come back for more."

"We will," Hikaru said.

Vidia and Marty walked the pair to the door and gave them both a huge warm hug. Shakti managed to turn around and looked at Vidia one more time. They locked eyes, and Vidia smiled with confidence. Shakti felt deeply connected to her.

Shakti called an Uber again. On the way home, she told Hikaru all about the conversation. He seemed deeply enthralled by what he heard. Shakti's head was exploding with information and new questions. She needed to get home and to bed to relax and take it all in. She did just that.

CHAPTER 8

THE
PYRAMID

arrison woke up early Saturday morning to watch the
basketball game he had recorded the night before. As he
was making waffles for the family, Shakti came downstairs
around 6:30 am. Her hair was a mess, and she looked like she had
rolled out of bed and down the stairs.

"*Wow*! Rough night?" Harrison said too loudly for such an early
hour, "If I didn't know better, I'd think you were hungover."

"Shhhhh." Shakti placed her fingers over her lips while shushing
him kindly. "Not hungover, obviously. I didn't sleep great. I have a
lot on my mind, Dad."

"Hmm. Anything you want to talk to me about?" Harrison said
in a much softer tone.

"Thanks, Dad, but I don't think you can help me this time."
Shakti looked sad as she glanced up at him.

"Try me." Harrison reached for the remote to lower the volume of
the TV. "You can tell me anything. No judgment." He held his hand
up for scout's honour.

"You're going to think I'm crazy, Dad. I think I'm crazy!" She pouted and sat at the breakfast bar.

"Hey! I will never think that." Harrison felt his heart rate increasing. He spun around to the fridge and grabbed a container of strawberries.

"Okay, let's see." Shakti started. "Dad, since I was little, I used to talk to you about the Clans, remember?"

"Yes, I do. I loved those stories."

"Well, what if I told you, it was all real? What if I told you I also saw angels and wanted to find out why?"

"I would believe you." Harrison had already been eased into the conversation by Gayatri telling him the Clans were real, "Both you and Mom said Mary also saw them in our backyard."

"Oh yes, we did," Shakti remembered. "What do you think about that?"

"It's weird but awesome," Harrison said. "At first, I was confused. Then I researched it and saw there are a number of people that see all kinds of creatures."

"You did?" Shakti was fully awake now. "Why didn't you tell me?"

Harrison said, "Because, my love, I knew you would figure it out. Some journeys in your life, you have to make on your own."

"I see," Shakti said suspiciously and giggled.

"I want to be clear about one thing, though."

"Okay," Shakti answered attentively.

"Your academic studies should be your number one priority. If you can promise me that, I would support you in any way I can for you to figure out what this is all about."

"Thank you, Dad." Shakti went up to her dad and hugged him around his waist tightly. "I promise school first and everything else after that."

Harrison hugged Shakti back around her shoulders. He rested his cheek on top of her head, emphasizing their height difference. He saw Shakti getting emotional, and he was surprised it meant so much to her.

"I don't know how Mom will react to this," Shakti whispered.

"Oh, Mom is the easy one," Harrison said. "She's totally into this stuff. She told me yesterday she has seen angels and had conversations with them."

"Really?"

"Yes, and you know what?" Harrison held her by the arms.

"What?"

"I believe her one hundred percent. She also told me that you are gifted with Sight."

"Sight? Right, she did mention that before. Interesting," Shakti said.

"She's the smartest person I know," Harrison said, "There is no hiding anything from her."

"Yes, I agree. The nerd gene is strong in this family."

Harrison burst out laughing. "It sure is. I couldn't be prouder of my girls."

"Okay, Dad, good talk. I'm going back to sleep after I devour this waffle."

"Good girl, but please brush your hair. You're scaring me," Harrison cracked himself up.

*   *   *

The annual science competition was to be hosted by their school this year. It was a competition that included other schools in the West Toronto area. Shakti and Hikaru had entered it in the past. They placed third last year for building a water filtration system using common household items. They were happy with third place, but this year they had their heart set on placing first, largely because the grand prize was a trip to Paris to attend the Paris Science Conference. For them, this was the equivalent of winning a trip to Disney World for most kids their age. A place they could geek out freely.

Hikaru sent a text to Zoe and Shakti to meet at lunch to brainstorm ideas for the science competition. Zoe was pumped and ready to prove her worthiness to her new friends. They all came up with great ideas. They wrestled with electrical inventions, creating wind energy, vegetable battery power, how to build a model bridge applying engineering principles, etcetera. One brilliant idea after the other. Their heads were spinning as they tried to decide what to do.

Zoe stood up twenty minutes into the conversation. "Guys, we're overthinking it." Her hands wafted in the air. "Everyone is going to have similar brilliant science ideas. We need to be completely different and stand out from the herd of nerds."

"Yes, that's true, Zoe. But what?" Hikaru said.

"Think, Karu, Shakti. What is it that you both are great at?"

"Studying?" Shakti scratched her head.

"No, girl. You're both amazing at gardening!" Zoe said loudly, a hint of frustration apparent.

"Gardening?" Shakti said, "How will that help us?"

"It's obvious! Plant a fruit and vegetable garden and apply scientific principles to it. Perhaps use recycled materials you find right here at school or document the environmental impact of having a green space. You guys can figure that part out."

"Zoe," Hikaru stood up. "I think that's absolutely brilliant!"

"Zoe, you're a genius." Shakti jumped up and hugged her. "I bet Mr. Edgar would let us use a part of the school grounds. We can donate the fresh produce to the school cafeteria, free for the students of Swansea District High."

"We have to angle the project from a highly technical and scientific perspective," Hikaru added.

"That's the easy part," Shakti said. "We've been training for this for years." She put her both palms up and double high fived Zoe and Hikaru.

"We can leave it for other students to take over in the future. Make it a permanent part of the landscape," Zoe said with confidence.

"Wow, Zoe, you're quite the businesswoman." Shakti looked at Zoe proudly.

"I got it from my dad." Zoe received her compliment with a twinkle in her eye. "You two take care of the scientific aspect of it.

I'll market it and get other students involved. It sounds like it's a lot of physical work."

"On this scale, it will be," Hikaru said.

"I'll talk to teachers and the student body president to get kids involved," Zoe said, "Also, we should all schedule time towards it."

"Zoe, I think you should be the project manager. Karu and I will plan the layout and payoff of the garden," Shakti said, thinking out loud.

"Sounds good." Zoe smiled.

"Okay, it's settled then!" Hikaru grabbed his backpack. "Let's get to class."

The trio scattered and went off in their respective directions.

*   *   *

As Thursday evening rolled around, Shakti missed a call from Vidia. She called her back right after school was out. Vidia told her she would like to meet her again on Friday evening after the meditation. Vidia planned to introduce her to a friend. Shakti agreed to attend the class. As she ended the conversation, she called Hikaru and told him she was meeting Vidia again on Friday. Hikaru was excited and wanted to join her for the meditation, but he had promised his mom he would watch his baby brother, Ki, that evening. Shakti reassured him she would be fine. Hikaru felt good about it too.

On Friday after school, Shakti ran home and showered, ate dinner, and bolted out the house by 5:00 pm. She called an Uber and got dropped off at Vidia's house on time. Almost the same group of people were there. Most smiled at Shakti, perhaps happy to see her. Jennifer was there again. She didn't stare this time, just nodded at Shakti and moved on. Shakti wondered if there was no parade over her head today. It didn't bother her. She got into a position to meditate.

Marty came downstairs at 6:00 pm and dimmed the lights. This time he lit incense, and Shakti recognized the smell of sage right away. Her mom burned sage at home to get rid of *negative energies*. Shakti giggled to herself, thinking of her mom's neurosis. Vidia followed Marty and made her way to the front. Shakti felt more ready for the meditation this week than last. She was relaxed and readied herself to be swept away by Vidia's soothing voice.

"Let us begin." Vidia raised both hands. She did a different meditation this time. It entailed imagining themselves walking along a beach towards a giant pyramid with a diamond tip. She asked them to enter the pyramid, sit there, and wait for someone special to enter. The room was perfectly silent. No drums this week, just perfect stillness. Shakti sank deep into the meditation.

As she was instructed, Shakti imagined herself walking along the beach at first. She was dressed in a flowing red gown with a train. Shakti touched her head, sitting on top was a flower crown.

How pretty I must look, she thought.

As she walked along the bay, the warm blue water touched her feet playfully. The sand was soft and a beautiful shade of beige. She walked along the stunning crescent-shaped beach until the end. Shakti wandered around the corner of the crescent, standing in the distance was a colossal pyramid, just like Vidia promised. She picked up her pace and hastened towards the structure.

As she arrived at the base of the pyramid, she noticed a huge diamond tip at the very top. She walked around the base to look for an entrance. Sure enough, she found one. The doorway was thin and tall.

She thought, *What a fascinating imagination I must have.*

She pushed the tall doors open with little effort, as if they were expecting her. Quietly, it swung open, and she entered the triangular space. It was a bright, open space. The single source of light came from the diamond ceiling at the very top. It looked like an ancient contraption that harnessed sunlight to create a never-ending mirror effect. Shakti squinted and covered her eyes with her arms. She gave herself a second for her eyes to adjust. Then she looked around to see what was before her.

A single tall stool with a plush purple cushion and gold legs stood solemnly, close to the furthest wall from the door. Shakti reluctantly walked up to the stool and sat down cautiously. She could no longer hear Vidia's voice giving instructions. This made her nervous at first, then she thought the logical reason was Vidia deliberately stopped talking to allow them to have their own experience.

Shakti sat and looked around. She took a second to look at her dress. As she admired her clothes and wondered if her mind designed the dress, she felt a faint vibration. Something was happening. The vibration was soothing and non-threatening, even as it increased in intensity. The light in the pyramid transformed uniformly, much like a kaleidoscope. She looked up. The diamond top of the pyramid started to shift away. It didn't open by collapsing backwards. It simply moved aside. This changed the light in the room dramatically. From being a well-lit triangular space, the light became a focus pin drop down the centre of the pyramid. Shakti was sure the sun was right above the enormous structure. The diamond was no longer visible to her. As her eyes focused on the opening of the ceiling at the very top, she felt herself become flustered with fear. She reminded herself, this is a meditation, go with it.

As she continued to concentrate on the opening, she saw a gold light flicker. The gold transitioned to an effervescent blue sparkle. Enter, a beautiful being so brilliant and bright, she again covered her eyes with her arms. She tried not to look away, it was so stunning and heavenly, and she did not want to miss a second of it.

First, she saw a pair of feet in metal boots, followed by a male body dressed in an armoured suit. The ceiling was far above her. She couldn't see his face very well. He descended slowly while spinning around. As he got closer, Shakti noticed his eyes were closed. He turned around about five more times while floating to the ground. As he touched the ground, he did so with a deafening thunderous roar. The sound made Shakti scream. She held her mouth quickly. The ground beneath him cracked, and gold light spilled out, it mended quickly and the light beneath faded away.

He landed on both feet, facing her direction. The brilliant being opened his eyes, and electric blue sparks twinkled outwards, a blue flame burning within. His dark hair appeared like he was floating on water. It did not fall to his shoulders like long hair normally would. On his right hip, sat a luminous sword as tall as she was. The energy around him pulsed like a heartbeat. Shakti felt every beat go through her soul.

Only heaven could produce this manner of being, Shakti thought. The being looked at her with no expression at all. Now that he stopped moving, she could get a proper look at him and size him up.

Shakti removed her hands from her mouth slowly and stood up. He looked at her intensely. She took three steps toward him. He was still far away because the room was huge, but she thought it was close enough. Shakti immediately noticed the obvious. He was a giant. She guessed about twenty feet tall. His armour covered up to his knees, and Shakti looked at his muscular physique. She thought his calves had to be bigger than her head, for sure. He was breathtakingly striking. Shakti stood in complete awe.

Standing tall behind him was a translucent structure that was even taller than he was. Still, he had not acknowledged her. Shakti felt like she met this angelic creature before, multiple times. He seemed to be present somewhere in a distant memory.

She stood more confidently and said, "Angel Michael?"

His eyes filled with expression, and his lips lifted. Her voice seemed to have activated him. "Peace be unto you, Shakti." His voice reverberated across the room.

Her heart raced. "Same to you, Angel Michael. I now remember you so clearly," Shakti recalled. "You came to visit me so many times in my backyard. Then, one day you stopped coming."

"Yes, Shakti, I visited you and your friends," Michael said with a soothing but deep tone. "My presence was to let you know I was with you."

"Thank you." Shakti didn't know what to think about that. "May I ask why?"

"Yes, you may," Michael said, quite literally.

Shakti didn't catch on immediately that she actually had to ask the question. "Uhh…umm, why did you want me to know you were around?"

"Shakti, you will be in need of our protection in the future. You have a most important task ahead of you. One that will put you in danger. The angels are here to help you with that task," Angel Michael explained.

Shakti wished she hadn't asked. "Me? Danger?" She stumbled through her words. "What task?"

"The task will unfold before you as time goes on." Michael smiled to comfort her. "I am Angel Michael, the Protector. I am here for you. You must understand I can guide you, but the laws of your world apply first."

"I'm sorry. I don't understand. Please explain further, Angel Michael."

"Your world has laws. If you were to leap off a bridge, the laws of gravity would pull you to the ground. I could not help you in that case. Our help is of spiritual guidance and gifts I can provide you. We can protect you from the dark side."

"I see, so don't jump off a bridge," Shakti said, feeling overwhelmed. "Why would the dark side try to hurt me?"

"Your decisions and actions will change the trajectory of the world. The dark side wants the world to proceed on its current path. When humans perish by their own hands, Jinns will inherit the world for their kind." Michael explained. "Shakti, you are stronger than you understand at this time. We, the angels, believe in humankind."

"I see, Michael. I mean Angel Michael." Shakti seemed to compress the information and swallow it like a pill. "Why me?"

"We chose you," Michael walked closer to her, his armour made a delicate tune as he moved elegantly. Shakti raised her head to maintain eye contact with him. She was hoping for more of an explanation.

"If I am in trouble, how do I get to you?"

"You need only ask, Shakti," Michael said. "I must go now, so must you. Retrace your steps and re-enter your state of consciousness."

"Thank you for coming to see me, Angel Michael." Shakti's eyes welled with gratitude and confusion.

"Little Warrior," Michael bent his knees to come face to face with her, "it is you who came to see me." He smiled and touched her shoulder gently. Michael's feet lifted, and he ascended with a sparkling blue aura surrounding him. Shakti admired the glorious angel as he exited the ceiling and disappeared. The diamond tip came back in place, and the light danced around until it stopped moving. The pyramid was well lit again.

Shakti headed for the door and ran back to the crescent-shaped beach. She jogged along her previous footsteps. She could not fully comprehend the enormity of meeting a divine creature such as Angel Michael. She only knew she was forever changed. As she reached halfway down the bay, she could hear Vidia's voice again.

Vidia's voice elevated, and she instructed everyone to come back to their earthly conscience and wake up.

Just like that, Shakti was in the room again. Her eyes opened, and she smelled the sage. She grasped her chest and whispered, "Oh my God. What an experience!"

The meditation class was buzzing about who entered the pyramid to talk to them. The visitors ranged vastly, dead grandmothers, spouses, their higher self, a brother from a past life, and many more. No one spoke of angels and definitely not Archangels. Shakti didn't offer any clues about who came to her. She just listened and nodded and smiled. She was trying to be social when she wanted to scream and run around the neighbourhood. Jennifer smiled at her longer than she was comfortable with. It was like she knew something special happened, but she said nothing to Shakti about it. Shakti thought she better not ask.

Vidia walked up to Shakti and touched her hand. "Hello, my dear."

"Hi, Vidia." Shakti straightened her back and came out of her meditation position.

"You were having fun during this meditation." Vidia smiled.

"Why do you say that?" Shakti wondered if Vidia knew about her vision.

"Because during the meditation, your aura was dancing around you. More so than anyone else in the class," Vidia explained. "Seeing auras is one of my gifts."

"Really? I sometimes see auras, too. I had the most vivid vision."

"Don't tell me about it right now." Vidia looked around and whispered in her ear, "Don't tell anyone about it."

"Not even you?"

"I'll leave that up to you." Vidia smiled. "You don't have to if you want to keep it to yourself. I have someone I'd like to introduce you to soon. He is a wonderful spiritual teacher and well-versed in the Rainbow Tribe." She patted her back and walked away.

"Thank you, Vidia. I can't wait to meet him," Shakti said.

Shakti waited about a half-hour for everyone to leave. She followed Marty up to the angel living room. As she sat there, her eyes fell on a painting of a dramatic scene of an angel with one foot perched on top of a devil lying on the ground. The angel held a sword that pierced the heart of the devil. She looked at the inscription below, and it read, *Saint Archangel Michael defeats Lucifer.*

She got up and walked over to the painting and had a good look at it. "He looks nothing like that," she said under her breath. Shakti thought Angel Michael was a million times more glorious than the illustration, but how would anyone know this? They clearly were painting this from their perception of him. Shakti realized how privileged she was for seeing such a heavenly creature. She reflected on that until she was interrupted by Marty.

"Shakti, would you like some hot chocolate?" Marty said with his glowing smile.

"If you're having some, I'll have some, too." Shakti was shy when she didn't have Hikaru there to yell yes at him.

"I'll have some, too." Marty turned on the ball of his foot and went to the kitchen.

"Thank you!" Shakti shouted out to him.

Vidia came up the basement staircase and closed the lights behind her. She said to Shakti, "He will be here soon. He's running a little late." She closed the basement door and came to sit on the adjacent sofa.

"Okay, great. Marty is making hot chocolate," Shakti said excitedly.

"Oh great. I think I'll have some, too."

Marty poked his head in, and she told him as such. He nodded and left the room with a cheery grin.

"So, tell me, how did you like today's meditation?"

"Oh, Vidia. It was incredible!"

"Remember, you are obligated to no one to tell them about your visions. Some people rather keep it to themselves."

"I know, but I'd like to share it with you," Shakti said. "I'm here to learn."

"Okay, Shakti," said Vidia.

"So, I went through your steps and walked along the beach and went into the pyramid," Shakti started. "There, I was visited by Archangel Michael."

"My God!" Vidia held her chest. "What a gift!"

"He was truly spectacular. I realized he visited me throughout my childhood."

"Shakti, stop right there. This is amazing, but do not tell me any more."

Shakti was surprised and a little hurt. "But, why?"

"Because I don't know who or what is around listening," Vidia said as she came over to her sofa. "I first have to make sure the room is protected from Jinns. They are invisible to most people."

"I see. You're right. I have seen them around before."

"Yes, but you won't always know when they are around. They are crafty. Also, Angel Michael will only come to you if it was of utmost importance. When my friend arrives, do not say anything about your vision to him," Vidia instructed.

"We can't trust him?" Shakti inquired.

"No, of course, that's not it. We can trust him. It's just that some things can only be said under the right conditions. It's not the time.

Remember, I told you, pursuing this life means you will be a keeper of secrets."

"Yes, I understand. Thank you for looking out for me."

"It's my pleasure. Shakti, I think you came to me for a reason that is much bigger than we know right now. Only time will tell. For now, my job is to educate you and guide you. It is of utmost importance that you are protected. I should thank you, Shakti."

"Me? Why? You're helping me."

"You have reignited my love for the Rainbow Tribe. After we had to shut down all operations with the children, we were all broken-hearted. You can't help but love the children like your own."

"The teachers closed the operations only because the King's Guard was looking for the book?"

"No, Shakti, it was more than that." Vidia's sadness washed over her like a mist. Shakti noticed Vidia's aura changed from a vivid halo of colours on top her head to a swampy brown cloud. It drifted low around her shoulders. "Something terrible happened."

"Please, tell me," Shakti pleaded.

"We had an extremely gifted student, James. Oh, I loved him like a son." Vidia shook her head side to side, and tears rolled down her cheeks. "James was incredibly gifted, but he did not take the time to protect himself, and the gifts turned out to be a curse for him. He opened himself up to the spiritual world recklessly."

"What happened to him?" Shakti asked bravely.

"The Jinns tormented him day and night. I begged him to ask Angel Michael for help. He didn't." She wept. "James became a recluse, which is the worst thing you can do in that situation. The Jinns had him all to themselves. We were cut off from him. Just over a year ago," Vidia took a deep breath and said, "James took his life."

Vidia put her hands over her face and leaned forward onto her lap and wept. Shakti rested both her arms over Vidia and hugged her.

"There was nothing you could have done, Vidia." It seemed like the right thing for Shakti to say.

"Yes, there was. I could have gone to his house and broke down that door." Vidia screeched, "I knew he was in trouble. But dealing with the Rainbow Tribe is new to every spiritual teacher in the world. There is no handbook."

"That's right. So, don't blame yourself."

"We have learnt our lesson. We start with protection first. The Jinns are ruthless beings. Their mission is to prevent the Rainbow Tribe from changing the world."

"We will not let them win. We will protect every child from them." Shakti seemed to have gone into business mode. She meant every word she said. From that moment on, Shakti's perspective on her spiritual education had changed from being about her to being a part of a bigger network, the Rainbow Tribe.

CHAPTER 9

THE
VISITORS

Ding dong.

"Ah! It's Bill." Vidia got up and walked quickly to the door, not before drying her eyes and straightening her kimono-style dress. "Welcome, welcome." They both laughed and embraced.

"I'm so sorry I'm late," said a soft-spoken jolly gentleman, "I lost track of time while I was at the library. I wanted to refresh my memory since we spoke last."

"Oh, don't worry. Let me take your coat and umbrella." Vidia spoke to him like he was her oldest friend. "Come into the living room."

They both walked into the living room, and Shakti stood up to meet Bill. He was an older gentleman of average height. His hair and beard were a perfect proportion of black and white. He was dressed elegantly in grey dockers and a blue blazer. A red pocket square peeked out. He also had on funky patterned socks and thick-framed glasses. Vidia brought him closer to Shakti, and he raised both hands to shake hers.

"Shakti, this is my dear friend, William." Vidia introduced him like she was proud of him. "But we call him Bill."

"It is my distinct pleasure to meet you, my dear." Bill shook her hand gently with a glint in his eye.

"It's a pleasure to meet you too, sir," Shakti said respectfully.

Bill reached into the zippered part of his briefcase and pulled out a beautiful red rose wrapped in plastic. There was a little plastic water container at the end of it. He looked at Shakti sweetly and handed it to her.

"For you, my dear."

"Thank you, sir!" Shakti accepted the rose with genuine surprise. She brought it up to her face and took a whiff.

"Come sit. I'll call Marty." Vidia took off into the kitchen. "Marty! Bill is here!"

Marty came running into the living room and straight for Bill. He lifted Bill off the floor, hugging him.

"Bill, my buddy! It's been too long!"

"Marty! I think you're ageing backwards, my friend."

"Ah, well, Vidia makes me eat healthy, so I lost a lot of weight" Marty proceeded to turn around to show off his new body.

"Maybe, I should do the same. It seems the weight you lost, I found!" Bill said, tapping his ample round stomach. They all erupted in laughter. Shakti haha-ed along with them awkwardly, trying not to be the only kid in the room amongst an adult conversation.

"You hungry, Bill? Vidia made a great dinner."

"No, no. I ate dinner already."

"Sorry I couldn't join you and Vidia last week for breakfast. I had the flu."

"No worries. I knew I'd see you soon."

"Hot chocolate? I just made a pot," Marty offered.

"Your hot chocolate? How could I refuse your hot chocolate?" Bill seemed to be in the loop about Marty's delicious hot chocolate.

Marty took off to the kitchen again. Vidia sat on the opposite sofa, and Bill sat next to Shakti. Shakti was getting tired of smiling so much, although she liked their friendly banter. She imagined that was what it would be like in the future for her and Karu, and now Zoe. The thought of her friends warmed her heart.

"So, Shakti," Bill started. "Vidia tells me you're a Rainbow Child."

"Umm, yes. Apparently." Shakti chuckled.

"Right. I'm guessing all of this is new to you," Bill inquired.

"Yes." Shakti looked uncertain. "I'm not sure how I feel about it at this point."

"That's perfectly understandable," Bill said sincerely. "Did Vidia explain to you the characteristics of Rainbow Children?"

"Yes, she did." She glanced over to Vidia and smiled. "She's been great. I understand that most of the kids are born after the year two thousand. They are caring, kind, and compassionate. They also have a deep love for the planet. Am I missing anything?"

"That is basically it in a nutshell. However, you're missing one important factor." Bill adjusted his glasses. "Many of the children possess gifts of extrasensory perception."

"Ah, yes. Vidia did say that. So, some of the children are psychic?"

"Well, I don't like to use the term psychic in this case because it's not about predicting a possible outcome. It's about using different methods to tap into a higher frequency." Bill's explanation reduced some of the mystery. He was more technical than Vidia. Shakti wondered if they argued about such matters.

"Do they all have the same gifts?" Shakti inquired.

"Good question. No, they vary vastly. In fact, they rarely have the same cocktail of abilities." Bill turned directly towards Shakti, with one foot bent on the sofa and his arm resting on the backrest. "Some kids could see entities that lived around us, not visible to a regular person's eye. Yet, there were detailed consistencies with their descriptions of such entities. How is this possible? These are untapped and unexplored areas in science," Bill said excitedly. "Shakti, I have been a man of science for my entire life. But I started studying these wonderful children, and now, I'm a believer."

"I can see beings around me that no one else I know can. What other gifts are there?"

"Some children can see auras. Some can communicate telepathically. Let's see, most kids were in tune with nature. The list goes on, but we are still discovering abilities."

Marty came into the room with the fancy tray and four large mugs of hot chocolate. Three of the mugs were matching with black and white stripes. The fourth was a pink mug with a painting of a unicorn with wings. He set the tray down and picked up the unicorn cup and handed it to Shakti. She was hoping the unicorn mug was for her. She admired it and then took a gulp of the hot chocolate.

"It's delicious, Marty. Thank you," Shakti said with a chocolate lip.

"I'm glad you love it." Marty glowed.

"It tastes a little different this time."

"Yes, I added nutmeg."

"Oh! Yummy!" Shakti was not trying to flatter Marty. She thought it was truly the best hot chocolate she had ever had.

"Shakti, the reason I wanted you to meet Bill was he has experience with the Rainbow Children, and he coordinated their education," Vidia explained.

"I see." Shakti put down her cup. "You mean their spiritual education?"

Bill turned to her again. "Yes, that's exactly right. You see, Rainbow Children needed more than traditional education to feed their minds. Otherwise, their gifts would go unchecked, and often they became quite depressed."

Vidia agreed, "Yes, imagine what it would feel like hearing voices, seeing beings, having unexplained feelings, and not being able to tell anyone about it."

"I don't need to imagine, I lived it. The only difference is, I was able to tell my parents, and they believed me." Shakti felt happy and sad at the same time, saying that.

"You're very lucky then," Bill said. "We created a safe space for the kids, and they were able to harness their energies and use them positively."

" For the Rainbow Children, what outcome had you hoped for?" Shakti inquired.

"Very intelligent, you are, my dear." Impressed, Bill glanced at Marty and Vidia. "We didn't have an outcome in mind. We simply wanted to observe and document. One day I was hoping to publish my findings, but that hope died quickly when the King's Guard started viciously tracking every move we made."

"What did you do with your findings and work on the Rainbow Tribe?" Shakti asked.

"Unfortunately, I, along with Vidia, Marty, and the rest of the teachers decided we would burn everything." Bill's face dropped. He removed his glasses and used one hand to rub his eyes. Vidia leaned over and touched Bill's shoulder.

Marty also reached over and patted Bill on the leg. "It's okay, Bill. Your hard work will not go in vain. Shakti found us, and she along with others, will benefit greatly from it."

"I know, Marty. Thank you." Bill cracked a smile. "This time, we will be more cautious, and I will coordinate the lessons in order of importance. We do it again for James."

"For James." Vidia raised her mug.

"For James." Marty raised his mug.

"For James." Shakti raised her unicorn mug. A pact was silently made.

Shakti was pleased to see the ball rolling. She glanced at the time, and it was 9:45 pm, "Oh my, it's getting late."

"Yes, my dear. You better head home. How are you getting home?" Marty inquired.

"I'll take an Uber."

"Good idea," Vidia said, "Can you send me a text when you arrive?"

"Yes, I will." Shakti grabbed her phone and requested an Uber. "Bill, it was an honour to meet you."

"The pleasure was all mine." Bill touched his chest with his left hand and shook Shakti's hand with his right.

Shakti blushed. "Thank you. And thank you for the world's best hot chocolate, Marty."

They all got up to see Shakti off.

"Shakti, keep this to yourself," Marty warned. "This time, we are taking extra precautions."

"I will, Marty. Bye, everyone."

Shakti waved and got into the Uber. She was excited and scared for her indoctrination into the spirit world. She thought about James and how scared he would have been. Shakti told herself if she ever felt overwhelmed, she would tell someone, her parents or Hikaru or Vidia. She would not let herself get to the point that James got to.

The Uber pulled up unto Shakti's driveway, and she jumped out. "Thank you! Good night."

"Good night, miss," the Uber driver replied.

Shakti stood there for a minute and watched him drive off. She raised her head, facing the dark sky and closed her eyes. It was a crisp Toronto night. She took a second to herself as a lot was happening quickly. While clutching the rose in one hand, Shakti inhaled the fresh cool air, filling her lungs to capacity. This was a trick her mom taught her to calm down. She used it mostly before an exam to centre herself. Feeling rejuvenated, she turned on her heel to walk towards the house. Shakti stopped, frozen. Her hands at her side and fingers stretched, frozen. Her mouth slightly open and eyes wide, frozen. The red rose dropped on the ground next to her feet.

Standing in front of her were five unnaturally tall male figures, dressed in dark flowy garb. She could not see their faces as they were covered in hooded cloaks with their heads tilted down. The tall figures swayed slightly back and forth in unison, as if to a rhythm only they heard. Their hands were clasped by the fingers in front of them. Shakti stood frozen. Jinns were here for her?

Four of the Jinns stood tall, lining the walkway to her house, the last Jinn blocked the front door. Shakti snapped out of her fear and came to her senses. She was cognizant that she was unlike most teenagers. The Jinns knew it. That was why they had come, and it was time she knew it, too. Bravery, whether false or real, washed over her.

As she walked closer, their swaying heads came to a sudden halt. Shakti's breath became short and shallow. In unison, the four Jinns lining the walkway unclasped their fingers and lifted their arms. Bony index fingers pointed in the direction of the Jinn standing at the door, a gesture that demanded an audience with Shakti.

She took a deep breath and walked down the path lined by Jinns to her front door, all the while reaching into her pockets to find her keys. The four Jinns hissed into her ears as she crossed their path, "Ssshhhhhhhaktii…Sssssshhhaktiiii…Sssshhaaaakkktii" Her name echoed and bounced off them. She continued to walk slowly.

Shakti made her way to the front door. With an effortful inhale, she said, "Get out of my way."

"Ssshhhhaaakkkttiiii, we are here to talk to you," the Jinn at the front door hissed. His voice sounded strained and low. He began to circle her slowly, round and round. She stood up straight and did not follow him.

"I want nothing to do with your kind." Shakti looked up at him, trying to see his eyes.

He stopped in front of her and raised his head to reveal his face. The Jinn's face was skeletal, revealing a sharp bone structure. Instead of eyes, a hollow space seemed to defy logic. Far into the distance of his eyes, a yellow fire burned low and slow.

"We know who you are now."

He grinned and unveiled his serpent tongue and blackened mouth. Shakti's heart skipped a beat. She glanced up at him nonchalantly.

"You just figured that out?" She smirked. "You're not very quick." Shakti's wit engaged. She realized this technique compensated for her thumping heart.

"We can give you everything your heart desires. Money, fame, a life many dream of." His mouth smelled of decay.

"At what cost? My soul?" Shakti said.

"No, Ssshhhaaaktiii. No cost. Join our ranks, and we will take you to the top. You will be at the King's side, a great honour bestowed unto you," the Jinn pleaded. "We've been looking for you." He raised his hands to draw her into his compelling offer.

"You're not listening, Jinn. I will never join you. I see what you do to people like Travis and James. You are evil, and I will always be on the path of light." Shakti's strength was palpable. She couldn't believe the words leaving her lips. "Now, get out of my way before I call on angels to remove you." An empty threat as she had no clue how to call on angels.

The four Jinns behind Shakti became visibly agitated. They barked at her for being rude to their own. They aimed distressing noises at her, like wolves cornering their prey. "Grrrrr."

The one on the far side howled, and it turned towards her like it was about to charge. At that very moment, the front door swung open. It was Gayatri! She stood there looking at the scene of Shakti surrounded by tall, darkly dressed figures.

Gayatri's hand left the door, she stepped through the talking Jinn and embraced Shakti.

Shakti feared for her mom immediately. "Mom, no!"

Gayatri looked at the Jinn, still standing at the front door, who she walked right through, straight into his eyes and said, "Leave my daughter alone, you bloodless demon!" Her stance, like a tiger above her cub. No fear in sight. Her words rippled like a stone landing on the surface of a calm lake. Only Shakti saw the waves of energy spread around them. A cracking sound ensued.

The Jinns stepped back and fully retreated while they hissed angrily. They were no match for Gayatri's maternal love. They glided towards the driveway in unison. Then they disappeared before they hit the street. Shakti looked at her mom in utter disbelief and in awe of her strength.

"Mom, how did you do that? How did you know?" Shakti hugged her mom tightly around the shoulders.

"Gabriel warned me. I came running." Gayatri burst into tears as she hugged her daughter.

"Mom, I'm okay. I was not scared."

"Baby, you should be. Don't trust those demons."

"I know. They are evil Jinns," Shakti explained.

"What? How do you know?" Gayatri said curiously.

"For the last two Fridays, I've been going to meditation classes, and the teacher has been telling me all about them. She is going to teach me to protect myself from them," Shakti spoke rapidly while trying to catch her breath.

"Let's go inside." Gayatri looked around one more time to make sure the Jinns were gone.

They stepped inside and locked the door behind them.

"Mom, it all makes sense now."

"I'm so confused." Gayatri walked over to the sofa and sat down and wept, "I'm so scared for you, Shaks. I want to be selfish and tell you to stop and just be our daughter and no one's hero, but Gabriel told me that could not be."

"Mom, who is this Gabriel you speak of?" Shakti sat next to her mom and held her hand.

"Gabriel is an Archangel. He's been in my life since before you were born." Gayatri wiped her eyes. "He's wonderful. He just came to me while I was having my tea and told me to run to the front door because you were in trouble. I ran as fast as I could, but the door seemed so far away." She placed her hands over her face.

"But you made it, Mom. Also, I was handling it myself. I'm not afraid of them. They are afraid of me, I think." Shakti scratched her forehead.

"Why do you think they are afraid of you, sweetheart?"

"Mom, just hear me out. Okay? I think I may be the Warrior they speak of in the prophecies." Shakti squeezed her mom's hand tightly.

"Shakti, tell me, why do you think this?"

"I get the feeling, I'm not sure, though."

"I see. Okay, my love." Gayatri's hands trembled, and her eyes flowed when she turned towards Shakti and looked into her eyes. "Shakti, hear me now. Don't tell anyone you think you are the Warrior."

"But, Mom, I am getting help from spiritual teachers to protect me."

"Then get the help you need. Don't mention it to them right now." Gayatri meant business. It was clear to Shakti she was not going to win this one.

"Okay, Mom. I won't tell anyone just yet."

"Thank you, Shaks." Gayatri hugged her daughter again. Shakti could feel her mom's body trembling with every breath. She was incredibly sad that her mom had to go through this torment.

"Where's Dad?" Shakti asked.

"He's in bed. He leaves for Montreal in the morning for a trade show." Gayatri let Shakti go. "Better that he does not know about tonight."

"Okay, Mom. The worst is over. At least for tonight," Shakti joked. "I need to get to bed. I have a ton of homework, and I'm meeting Zoe and Karu tomorrow evening to plan our vegetable garden for school."

Gayatri still visibly broken and scared, faked enthusiasm. "That's great, honey. I think it's a great idea for the science competition."

"Thanks, Mom. Good night. I love you to the moon and back." Shakti kissed her mom on the forehead and went upstairs.

"Love you too, Shaks."

Shakti thought about her strange family. They fight demons one minute and prepare for bed the next. She sat on her bed for a minute. She felt dirty after standing so close to the filthy demon. Every fibre of the Jinn felt impure and dark. She jumped up and grabbed her towel and ran into her washroom to shower. After a few minutes, her phone rang. She rushed back out to answer it. It was Vidia.

"Hi, Vidia," Shakti answered.

"Shakti, I was worried about you. You said you would text when you got home," Vidia scolded. "I got the worst feeling. Are you okay?"

"Yes, I'm fine. I'm sorry, Vidia." Shakti took a breath. "Something happened."

"Marty, I was right!" Vidia shouted to Marty then spoke softly, again. "What happened, my dear?"

"Five Jinns were waiting for me when I got home."

"Oh!" Vidia screamed out. "What did you do?"

"I basically told them to get out of here. Then my mom came and screamed at them. Then they left." Shakti didn't have the energy to explain what happened play by play.

"There's nothing more powerful than love, Shakti. In this case, a mother's love," Vidia said softly. "I can tell you're exhausted. Go get some rest, and we will talk tomorrow. We should bring the next class up earlier this week. You need to protect yourself sooner than I thought."

"Okay, good idea. Thank you. I am fine, and so is my mom." Shakti didn't want to worry Vidia.

"Okay, Shakti. Good night." Vidia's voice was heavy with worry. "Please know you can call me anytime for help."

"Thank you so much, Vidia. Good night."

Shakti dropped the phone on the bed, got dressed in her pyjamas, and brushed her teeth. She climbed into bed and opened the case to get her retainers out. She thought about the night's event. She wondered what the future held for her. Her strength in dealing with the Jinns surprised her deeply. Shakti decided the next few days she would take a break from all of this. Hikaru and Zoe were coming to her house, and that was exactly what she needed, normal teenage antics. With that, she reached her hand out and switched the bedside lamp off and went to sleep.

The sun peeked into Shakti's room around 6:30 am. She moved her legs closer to her to get warmer and adjusted her fluffy blanket. She woke up wondering if she had dreamt the previous night's events. Shakti glimpsed a light at the corner of her bed and turned around immediately to see what awaited her.

"Hi, Shakti," Mary's astral body sat on the bottom corner of her bed. Shakti jumped and then felt relieved it was Mary. Wonderful Mary. Shakti was almost brought to tears because there was no one she would rather see that morning than Mary.

"Hi, Mary," Shakti said with a broken sleepy voice. "What are you doing here?"

"Sorry to scare you." Mary smiled so beautifully, "I don't have much time because I'm about to wake up. But I need to tell you something that's very important, Shakti."

Shakti sat up and faced Mary. "What is it, Mary?"

"The tall men are all around your house. In the backyard and in the forest." Mary looked alarmed. "I don't want to go outside to play with the fairies anymore."

Shakti became visibly saddened for Mary more than for herself.

"I'm so sorry, Mary. They are here for me, not for you. They are called Jinns. I'm sorry you are scared to play with your friends."

"That's okay, Shakti. I know you are special to children like us," Mary said.

"Why do you say that?"

"Children like myself have a natural gift to read energies," Mary explained in a mature manner that was beyond her years. "Most people need to develop their gifts. We are born with them."

"Wow, I did not know that, Mary. Thank you."

"Anytime." Mary smiled like an angel, so pure. It warmed Shakti's heart.

"I'm not sure what to do about the Jinns," Shakti said.

"Do nothing. Ignore them. You only give them power when you are scared of them."

Shakti figured that Mary must be onto something. "Really? I didn't think about that."

"I gotta go now. I'm waking up."

"Mary, please visit me anytime." Shakti felt Mary was like a friend she could truly tell anything to. "I would really love that."

Mary giggled. "Okay, Shakti. I will. Bye!" Mary left the bed and leaped out Shakti's closed window and into her house.

CHAPTER 10

THE GARDEN CLUB

A gnes slipped on her fashionable winter boots and wrapped a giant scarf around her neck. She slipped out the front door and walked outside. Bracing the cold on that December morning, she scurried over to Gayatri's house and rang the doorbell. Gayatri answered, and she was delighted to see Agnes.

"Agnes! How are you?" Gayatri said in the most welcoming manner.

"Hi, Gayatri," Agnes leaned over and hugged her.

"Please, come in, come in. It's freezing."

"Oh, just for a minute," Agnes stepped in and closed the door behind her. "I wanted to invite you and your family over for a surprise birthday dinner for Winston."

"Oh, thank you. When is it?" Gayatri was happy for the invite.

"It's this Saturday at eight pm," Agnes said. "I'm sorry for the late invite, but Winston works all kinds of hours. I wanted to make sure he would be around this Saturday. Also, I've been meaning to invite you and Karu's family over since we moved in. Again, I was waiting to make sure Winston would be home."

"No worries! He's a busy man. What would you like me to bring?"

"Oh, nothing! Just yourselves." Agnes smiled. "I'm having it catered since most of the dishes are vegan. Thanks for offering."

"Sounds great," Gayatri seemed genuinely enthusiastic.

"I'm also inviting our friends and some of Winston's work colleagues," she said excitedly. "Okay. I'm heading over to the Akiyamas to invite them over, too. I don't want Winston to suspect a thing, so I sneaked out." Agnes laughed. "Okay. Bye!"

"Bye! Thank you for the invite. Can't wait."

*   *   *

The upcoming week had one purpose, for the trio of friends to get Mr. Edgar to agree to give them space on the school grounds for their vegetable garden. They knew they had to prove its extreme value and benefit to the school and its students for him to be on board. They already decided that Zoe would be the spokesperson for the group because she had the business savvy to pull it off, and Shakti and Hikaru didn't want to. They made an appointment at lunchtime on Tuesday to speak to him. Hikaru, Zoe, and Shakti rehearsed their lines, and Zoe made a list of points to talk about. They had a few months for the science competition, and the friends needed to plan it out.

On Tuesday morning, Gayatri agreed to drop Hikaru and Shakti at school early so they could get their final rehearsal in.

"Zoe will be here in a few minutes," Shakti said to Hikaru as they sat in the common area.

"Okay, let's make sure we've got our parts down." Hikaru pulled a large folding cardboard display out of a bag.

"I'll review my notes, too." Shakti took her notebook out.

"I hope Zoe turns up the charm," Hikaru said. "We can't pull this off on our own. Also, I don't think he's very fond of us after the Travis incident."

"And after my mom yelled at him." Shakti shook her head, "Yeah. The truth is, he knows what Travis is all about. Maybe he was secretly happy." Shakti laughed.

"It's true," Hikaru smirked. "Okay, let's focus."

Zoe arrived ten minutes after them. She walked in with her backpack and in a great mood.

"Hey, you two." She swung her arms.

"Hi, Zoe." Shakti smiled.

"Hey, Zoe," Hikaru replied. "Are you ready?"

"I sure am." Zoe showed no signs of anxiety, unlike Shakti and Hikaru.

"Do you want to go over your part one more time?" Hikaru asked.

"Nope! I got this." Zoe smiled brightly and sat next to them. Shakti glanced at Hikaru nervously. "What about you, guys? How do you feel about your part?"

"Nervous!" Shakti said with a half-laugh.

"Don't be! You two are absolutely brilliant. Don't worry about the delivery too much. It's just one person. However, speak loud and clear. We're asking to use school property for free for many months." The first school bell rang. "Let's meet in front of his office at lunch."

Off to class they went. Shakti felt less nervous about everything, but she was hiding something from her friends. Since her encounter with the Jinns on Friday night, she kept seeing them. They were around her house, lining the streets on the way to school and outside the school. However, they weren't around that morning. She took Mary's advice and tried to ignore them. She did not want them to intimidate her. They were there for her, to taunt and torture her. She pulled out her phone on the way to class and called Vidia. They made a plan to meet on Wednesday evening after school for Shakti's protection class.

At the lunch bell, the three walked hastily to Mr. Edgar's office. They met, out of breath, at the door.

"Calm down, guys," Zoe said. She turned to the secretary, "Good afternoon, Mrs. Muller. That blouse looks great on you."

"Well, thank you, Zoe." Mrs. Muller usually looked mean, but Zoe's compliment completely disarmed her. "How can I help you?"

"We have an appointment with Mr. Edgar."

"Let's see here." Mrs. Muller pulled up a calendar on her computer screen, "Ah, yes. You sure do. Have a seat, and I'll tell him you are here."

"Thank you, Mrs. Muller." Zoe turned and walked over to Hikaru and Shakti and sat between them.

"Geez, what did you have for breakfast?" Hikaru said. "A bowl of confidence?"

"Haha. It's part of my plan. We have to show we can pull this off."

"Awesome," said Hikaru.

Mrs. Muller returned and walked up to them. "He will see you now." She gestured to go inside.

They picked up their bags and walked nervously into the office.

"Welcome, kids," Mr. Edgar said loudly. "Have a seat" There were exactly three chairs, and they sat down.

"Good afternoon, Mr. Edgar," Zoe started with a giant smile. "I am Zoe, and this is Shakti and Karu."

"Very good. It's nice to see you three again. Tell me, how can I help you?"

Zoe stood up. "As you are aware, the science competition is in June again."

"Yes, that's right."

"We wanted to present a proposal for our entry into the competition."

"I see. You do know you don't need my permission."

"Yes, that's correct. But we would like your valuable opinion and direction."

Mr. Edgar appeared flattered. "I see. Well, then let's hear it."

Shakti and Hikaru glanced at each other. Zoe was on fire.

"The science competition is very important to us. Shakti and Hikaru are brilliant science students, and they have the technical and scientific expertise to do wondrous things. Our proposal for the science competition is to plant a sustainable fruit and vegetable garden, here on the school grounds." Zoe said in a single breath while maintaining eye contact with Mr. Edgar. "Our plan is for this project to become a part of the school's identity and commitment to a sustainable future. It will be a legacy for future students to maintain and enjoy."

"I see." Mr. Edgar leaned back and crossed his arms.

Shakti got up awkwardly and remembered to speak loudly and clearly. "Zoe is right. The competition is very important to us, but what's more important is for us to reduce our carbon footprint and encourage students to do the same. We want this experiment to be as self-sustainable as possible. Therefore, we will set up a rain collection system to water the garden and use the perishable waste from the cafeteria for compost and to eliminate the amount of waste the school produces. However, the best part of all is all the produce goes towards the students and staff of the school." Shakti had Mr. Edgar's attention fully. "Karu and I have had our own vegetable garden for three years. We grow a lot of fruits and vegetables, so much that we end up giving it away to neighbours and friends." Shakti was a lot more relaxed. "Karu will now explain the plans for the ideal location on the school grounds."

"Hi, Mr. Edgar." Hikaru pulled out his cardboard display, which featured an aerial view of the school. "This is our school grounds. If you notice, the west side is quite hilly and exposed to the road. The east side is flat, and parts are shaded with large trees. Also, it's closer to the back of the school and, for the most part, it's unused land. No one goes there. We figured, with your permission, we could use this piece of land outlined in red." Hikaru turned and made eye contact with Mr. Edgar. "It's an ideal location for the type of fruits and vegetables we would like to grow. Also, we can collect rainwater from the roof of the East building, and it will be in close proximity to the garden to carry the water."

Shakti interjected, "Mr. Edgar, please keep in mind this is a system we will set up to make it easy for future students to take over.

Students are always complaining they don't have anywhere to do their obligatory volunteer hours. This could be how they donate their time towards helping the school and the environment while getting the hours they need to graduate."

"Wow!" Mr. Edgar said abruptly. "This is quite an undertaking for just the three of you."

"Yes, sir. We thought so at first. But then we realized that we would get students involved because it is not just about winning the competition, it's about giving back to the school and the environment," Zoe explained.

"Yes, sir." Hikaru supported Zoe's point. "Picture walking into the cafeteria and seeing a giant bowl of organic fruits and vegetables waiting for students and staff to take for free."

"I do like the idea of being a health-conscious school," said Mr. Edgar. "It does sound amazing. However, how do you plan to fund this? It will cost a lot of money to buy supplies, seeds, plants, soil. The list goes on."

Shakti said, "We already have most of the equipment and supplies required. Karu and I have been gardening for years."

"I see." Mr. Edgar propped his chin up with his fingers and looked down at the desk. "Hmm...I am perhaps saying this way too early, but it sounds absolutely brilliant." He glanced up at them.

Shakti, Zoe, and Hikaru looked at each other. Then nodded their heads in agreement.

"You three did a superb job presenting this to me. I sincerely hope you can pull it off. I'll be even willing to roll my sleeves up and give you a hand with it."

"Thank you, Mr. Edgar!" Shakti said excitedly. "We don't need to start until spring, but we will start planning it out now. Call us, The Garden Club." All three of them nodded in unison and had smiles plastered on their faces.

"The Garden Club. I like it. We should outline the space you need. Karu, come with me and let's take a walk to the area. I'll get a spray can."

"Yes, sir." Hikaru jumped up and stuffed the cardboard into his bag. "I have the ideal dimensions here."

"Great. I'll get a measuring tape from Mr. Cooper. Great job, kids. You're dismissed."

Zoe and Shakti left with Hikaru and Mr. Edgar and walked in the opposite direction. They jumped and screamed and hugged each other.

"Zoe, you were amazing!" Shakti was genuinely impressed.

"Shaks, you were amazing, too!" said Zoe. "Let The Garden Club commence!"

CHAPTER 11

THE WHITE
LIGHT OF
PROTECTION

On Wednesday evening after school, Shakti made her way to Vidia's house. She was anxious to talk to her about many things.

"Shakti, welcome," Marty greeted her at the door.

"Hi, Marty! How are you?"

"I'm well. Come on in."

He took her coat from her, and she removed her shoes. Just then, Vidia came down the stairs, and Shakti went up to her for a hug.

"How are you, my darling?" Vidia hugged her tightly. Shakti knew Vidia was worried about her. It seemed that losing James had taken its toll on her, and she was desperate not to make the same mistake again.

"I'm okay." Shakti looked her in the eye. "I have so much to tell you."

"Do you want to go upstairs?" Vidia asked.

"No, I want Marty here, too."

They all walked over to the angel living room and sat down. Marty had a tray with hot chocolate already waiting for them. Shakti laughed when she saw it. He was pleased by her reaction and picked up the unicorn mug and handed it to her.

"Where do I start?" Shakti was eager to fill them in. "Jinns have been following me since last Friday. Mostly when I am alone, they are everywhere, around my house, on the streets, in front of my school."

"What did you do? You must have been scared," Vidia said with her hand over her mouth.

"I was at first. Then when my mom came outside and yelled at them, and I saw them run away. I realized they're scared of something, too."

"Yes, brilliant, Shakti! They only have power when you give it to them."

"I wish I could take the credit, but there is something else I have to tell you. But it stays between us." Shakti waited for them to agree.

"Of course. It will not leave this room," Vidia promised.

"I promise," Marty said.

"I have a friend who is ten years old. She is on the autism spectrum. She's very special, and I adore her. She has the ability to astral project while she's asleep. The morning after the Jinns, she came into my room in astral form, and she warned me that the Jinns were outside and all around the house."

"Hmm, I see," Vidia said.

"She also told me not to be afraid of them. She is wise beyond her years. She speaks like an old soul when she's in her astral form. I get the feeling she looks out for me."

"Oh, believe it, Shakti," Vidia said quickly. "Children like your friend are the most gifted in our world. They see almost all creatures around them, and they read energies better than anyone else."

"Wow, that's amazing. I adore Mary. There is a connection between her and me. I can't explain it."

Marty lifted his cup and sipped it slowly. "It sounds to me like she would be a great counsel to you in the future."

"Yes, Shakti. In the past, a lot of Rainbow Children told us they would have great conversations and receive advice from children with various disabilities. It turns out, these kids were very old souls. Wise beyond belief and highly favoured by the elementals and angels."

"Oh my, it makes so much sense. They sound like the ultimate Rainbow Children."

"They absolutely are, Shakti. You're lucky you have a friend like Mary."

"I'm beginning to see that now." Shakti sipped her chocolate. It was the perfect temperature, and she drank half the cup. "You should know too that I made a promise to my dad that I would put my schoolwork as a priority over everything else. Therefore, I will continue my spiritual studies, but it can't get in the way of my academics."

"Absolutely! Your spiritual education is the garnish on top of your conventional education. Also, if you are to change the world, you need to be a credible influencer," Vidia explained. "Most people tend to do this through education and career. Some take other paths and are successful, too."

"Thank you for being so understanding, Vidia. I didn't want you to think I wasn't serious."

Vidia smiled. "My dear, you are here of your own free will. I am here to assist you in any way I can. That being said, let's start today's lesson."

Shakti placed her empty cup on the tray. "Let's start."

"Follow me to the basement." Vidia led the way, and they both went to the basement while Marty took the tray to the kitchen.

Vidia turned on the lights and lit a beautiful-scented incense.

"What incense is that? It smells great."

"Ah, it's patchouli. I'll give you some to take home. Sit comfortably." Vidia sat on the floor in front of Shakti, facing her. "Do you remember when we did the first meditation, and I told you to connect with the ethereal light above you?"

"Yes, I do."

"That divine light is God's Light energy. It is the most powerful force in the universe. Some people call it Universal Light, Christ Light, Divine Light, White Light. It depends on their religious background, but it belongs to everyone," Vidia said happily.

"I see," Shakti recalled this fascinating energy and way she felt after the first meditation.

"We are going to connect to that source and bring it down to us. Then we are going to ask the Divine to put a White Light of Protection around us. It should appear like a bubble of protection because that's exactly what it is."

"Wow, that's amazing."

"Let us begin. Close your eyes and get into a comfortable position."

Shakti adjusted her posture down and placed her back against the wall next to her. "I'm ready."

Vidia went through the steps again. The first few minutes entailed getting their breath deep and slow. She instructed Shakti to feel the life energy run through her body and limbs. "Now, look up in your mind's eye and see the White Light above you."

Shakti didn't see the light at first, but she relaxed more into it and saw it.

Vidia said, "Enjoy the brilliance of the light and bathe in its warmth. Now, raise your arms and touch the white light."

Shakti raised her arms to touch the light. To her surprise, she felt her palms get warmer and warmer.

Vidia continued, "Now, take that light from the source and pull it around you. Let it go under your feet and over your head. Imagine the light encasing you in a bubble."

Both Vidia and Shakti were deep into their meditation. Shakti loved the idea of floating around in a bubble of protection.

"Feel free to stay in this form, and then open your eyes," Vidia said softly.

Shakti opened her eyes. For a split second, she saw the bubble around her. It faded as her eyes adjusted to the room. "Wow, that was great."

"This is how you protect yourself against most energetic forces. If you are ever scared or feel threatened, imagine the white light and pull the energy around you."

"Thank you for that." Shakti knew this was a most valuable lesson. "I wish I knew about this on Friday night."

Vidia laughed and said, "I know. So do I. That's why I insisted we bring the class up earlier in the week. The purpose of the White Light of Protection is to give you strength and to keep the Jinns at a distance. They will still be around you, but it's harder for them to find you. They are low vibrational beings, and this is a high vibrational encasement."

"I see. So, it's not full protection from them and the dark side?"

"I'm afraid not, Shakti. There isn't much that is. Jinns will always be around. This way of life is about managing, not avoiding. I want you to practice every night before you go to sleep."

"I will. It seems easy enough. Do you think Mary knows about this?"

"Most definitely. She would have known how to do it without anyone telling her." Vidia got up and turned the light on brighter. "Mary will know how to do a lot of this intuitively. You will have to learn."

"Wow, she's incredible." Shakti got up and gathered her things. "Vidia, thank you again for your time. I better be off. It's a school night."

"Ah yes, of course. Let me get some patchouli and sage incense for you. The Jinns hate the smell of it."

"Is that so?" Shakti asked, quite amused.

"Just light one or two at a time." Vidia laughed. "Get a small vase, and put loose rice grains in it, then stick the bottom of the incense into it. Be sure to put it on something that's not flammable."

"Will do." Shakti hugged Vidia. "Goodbye." Shakti left Vidia and Marty's house with a sense of confidence. She figured it would be easier to protect herself now, and she would not allow the Jinn to intimidate her.

CHAPTER 12

A PARTY
FOR
WINSTON

The days leading up to Winston's party, Agnes was busy. She wanted everything to be perfect. Zoe helped her arrange the house and menu for the party. She consulted Mark, while he was at university, on the guest list and DJ. Agnes wanted to keep the party small and intimate, but the list kept growing and growing. Mark was set to come home on Thursday to decorate the basement for dancing. Mary picked flowers from the garden and made bouquets around the house. Winston didn't notice any of it because they hid the evidence in the basement before he came home. Also, he was always tired after work and came home in time to shower, have dinner, read Mary a story, and sleep.

Zoe asked Shakti and Hikaru to accompany her to the city to order a birthday cake for her dad. They were happy to go because it involved cake tasting. Everything Zoe and her family did was posh. The three friends and Mary crammed into an Uber and made their way to the boutique-styled café downtown.

As they entered the extravagant café, their eyes were drawn to meticulously laid out desserts in rounded glass showcases. Industrial steel cappuccino machines sat shiny and clean behind the counter. The owner stood in front of the impressive display waiting for them. Kate, a middle-aged woman with round red glasses and a baker's coat and hat, addressed Zoe and Mary by name and hugged them. Shakti and Hikaru figured they were regular customers. Zoe introduced Shakti and Hikaru. Kate was as fancy as they came in terms of pastry chefs.

Kate directed the group to a beautifully set table with flowers and stem glasses. A waiter came from the back and filled the glasses with water. The chef spoke to Zoe about the party in detail, and she sounded most enthusiastic about it. Shakti figured out that Kate and her partner, Elise, were invited to the party, too. The same waiter came back with a huge tray balanced perfectly on one hand. He placed five rectangular plates with four cubes of cake in front of each of them. Each cube looked distinctly different and fancier than the next.

Kate walked them through the culinary intricacies of each piece of cake. "The first sample is our Pink Champagne. It is an exquisite blend of raspberry mousse and vanilla buttercream. The second is the delectable Ginger Fantasy, hand-blended with our secret spices and cream cheese frosting. The third is our famous Death by Chocolate, a divine trio of dark, milk, and white chocolate on a wafer base and topped with dollops of freshly whipped cream. Last but not least, our Grand Mariner, a citrus-flavoured cake soaked in fine brandy and paired with cognac frosting." Kate glowed as she talked about each flavour.

"Excuse me, Zoe," Shakti interrupted. "Isn't your dad vegan?"

"Yes, Kate will prepare a special vegan cake for him."

"Yes, my dear. Winston's favourite is my Vegan Earl Grey vanilla cake with lemon frosting. These cakes are for the guests."

It was time for the cake tasting. Hikaru went at it. Kate reminded him to clean his palette between each cake, while gesturing at the glass of water. All four samples were delicious. Mary often glanced at Shakti and smiled.

"Mary, which is your favourite?" Shakti asked. Mary pointed at the chocolate. "That's my favourite, too!" Shakti high fived her. Zoe glanced at her sister and Shakti and smiled.

Zoe asked, "Karu, which did you like the most?"

"Dude, they're all great." Hikaru cleaned his plate. "I can't choose."

"You're useless." Zoe laughed. "But he's right. They're all delicious. My favourite is Death by Chocolate, too."

"Ahh...chocolat is it!" Kate said in an exaggerated French accent. The group laughed with her.

Zoe started the order, "We will have a double tier of the Death by Chocolate, and the third tier will be my dad's vegan cake. Also, we would like an assortment of macaroons, perhaps four dozen and thirty pieces of biscotti for later in the night. Please include a number fifty ornament as the cake topper."

"Wow, Zoe. Your dad is fifty?" Hikaru asked. "He looks great!"

"I know! It must be his diet because he does not work out," Zoe said. "Also, he dresses very well."

"Must be," Hikaru replied.

"Oh, Kate, Mark will drop off the fruits tomorrow for the fruit tray." Zoe was insistent on having a fruit tray filled with Jamaican fruits at the party. She thought it would make her dad happy to have his heritage represented. Zoe got up and walked with Kate to the counter. She pulled out her wallet and paid for the order. Shakti and Hikaru noticed she paid Kate with several hundred-dollar bills.

Hikaru leaned over and whispered to Shakti, "That's a lot of dough for some chocolate cake."

"Be quiet," Shakti whispered back. "They can afford it."

"I'm kidding!" He put his hands up and giggled. "I'm kidding."

"I think I'm a little drunk after the Grand Mariner sample," Shakti admitted.

"I know! It was so boozy but yummy. That's pretty much a gateway cake." Hikaru laughed at his own joke. Shakti didn't get it. By then, Zoe was ready to leave. They said their goodbyes to Kate and left.

The girls spoke about what they should wear for the party. Hikaru didn't say much, but it got him thinking about his outfit. Upon hearing Mark's friends would be attending the party, Shakti decided she needed a new dress. She hustled home to ask Gayatri for a ride to Queen Street to buy a dress. Gayatri happily obliged because she needed a trendy dress as well. After all, the Sutherlands were not the average family. They had made the street cooler by just moving in.

Shakti went about her time, heavily ignoring the Jinns around her. She noticed they were only outside, which was good and bad because she could easily escape them, but it prevented her from checking in with the Clans. She hadn't seen them in a while and missed their shenanigans. She decided she would try to use the White Light of Protection and see her friends. After shopping with her mom, she went up to her room to admire her new dress one more time. She placed it in the closet and sat silently on her bed. Eyes closed and three deep inhales and exhales, she imagined the white light above her. It came quite easily to her. She followed the steps Vidia had given her and encased herself in a white bubble.

Shakti got up and made her way down to the backyard. Immediately, she spotted Jinns around. However, they were further away now. Shakti thought the White Light kept them away, or at least at a distance. She walked past them slowly with perfect posture, almost to taunt them. Some Jinns looked at her directly and snarled, their serpent tongues slithering in and out. Shakti was disgusted by their foul appearance and smell. Vidia and Mary were right, not showing fear took their power away. Then, like a bag of tricks, Shakti reached deep into her jacket pocket and pulled out a sage stick and lighter. She turned and wickedly looked at the Jinns, bent down and stuck it into the soil, then lit it. It was her little experiment to test Vidia's theory on Jinns hating the smell of incense. It turned out, Vidia was right. The Jinns scattered, moving further away from the house like it repulsed them. Shakti laughed out loud.

She wondered why it entertained her so. In the midst of her experiment, she glanced down and jumped. One of the trolls stood in front of her with his hands on his hips, staring blankly at her. She stopped laughing and got on her knees to see him better. He looked quite vexed. She wasn't sure why. The little troll looked right at her, lifted his index finger, and wagged it side to side along with his head.

"No?" Shakti asked. "No to what?"

Always annoyed by her, the troll, rolled his eyes at her and said, "No! Stupid girl!"

Shakti gasped. She could not believe he spoke. "You can talk!" she screeched. "Why are you saying no?"

"Because you stupid!" He covered his eyes with his hand. "You don't play with Jinns! They come back for you."

"I see. Thank you for telling me." Shakti was confused. "But I have my White Light of Protection. Can you see it?" Shakti showed off her new trick.

"So what, stupid?" the troll yelled. "The White Light will help you with the spirit world. They will go talk to humans to come for you now."

Shakti went from being in a good mood to being downright terrified. "Oh my God! I didn't know they could do that!"

"Because, you stupid," the troll said with zero expression on his face.

"What am I going to do?" Shakti placed her hands over her mouth.

"First, you stop being stupid," the troll put one finger in the air, "and then, you ask your guides and angels to help you." He put a second finger in the air. The troll clearly didn't have a wide vocabulary. A gnome was standing closely behind him the whole time listening to their conversation.

"Would they be able to help me against human beings?" Shakti's voice trembled.

"They can, by asking humans of light to help you or by warning you. Next time, don't provoke Jinns! They are very evil. Now, go away!"

"Thank you, Mr. Troll." Shakti felt a little better in spite of the troll repeatedly calling her stupid. "My name is Shakti."

"I don't care." The little troll turned the other direction and hustled off. As he walked past the gnome, he pushed him over by the face. The gnome rolled over and didn't get up for many seconds.

"What the heck!" Shakti whispered. She wasn't sure whether to be grateful or offended. She decided she was grateful. She got up and dusted her knees. Right now, she could worry about the Jinns' retaliation, or she could worry about looking fabulous for the party. She chose to focus on the party.

*　　*　　*

Kira started her Saturday morning frantically by looking through her closet for something interesting to wear. Her husband, Shinzo, avoided her at all cost because she was not in a good mood. Hikaru entered the room and looked at clothes flung all over the bed and floor.

"Mom, why are you freaking out? Haven't you been to a party before?" Hikaru said.

"Karu," she snapped, "don't start with me. Of course, I've been to many parties. In the nineties! I probably haven't shopped for clothes since then." She shrieked, "I have nothing to wear!" while standing next to a mountain of dresses.

Hikaru attempted to help the situation, "Let's go buy a dress for you," he suggested. "Shakti and her mom went to Queen Street to shop for the party."

"They did?" Kira's attention peaked. "Shinzooo!" She yelled, facing the bedroom doorway.

Shinzo jumped and whispered, "Dammit!" Then replied, "Yes, darling."

"Come with me. You're driving me to Queen Street to buy a dress. This way, I don't need to park."

"No problem, sweetheart!" Shinzo grabbed his keys, and iPad, anticipating a long wait in the car.

* * *

Over at the much calmer Clairemonts' house, Harrison and Gayatri sat with Shakti for breakfast. They spoke about the party, and Shakti told them all about the school's vegetable garden. Harrison was very impressed with their plans and offered to give them large barrels from his factory to collect the rainwater. Shakti was happy to hear that was one less thing they would need to buy.

Gayatri made hair appointments for both her and Shakti to have their hair blown out before the party. They came home in a great mood after their girls' day out with hair appointments, a trip to Starbucks, and a stop at the flower shop to accompany the gift they got for Winston. Shakti came up to her room and admired her hair. She emptied her makeup pouch on the bathroom counter and decided to get ready for the party. While she was applying her minimalist makeup look, she felt the air go still. There was an electrical undercurrent in the room. She immediately understood she was about to have a visitor. Whether it was good or bad, she didn't know just yet. She dropped her liquid liner on the counter and quickly pulled the White Light of Protection around her.

Shakti walked from her ensuite into the bedroom and stood at the bed. She saw the roof disappear and down floated Angel Michael, glorious and electric as her vision in the pyramid. The blue glow encased his muscular physique, and his eyes sparkled with blue fire.

"Peace be unto you, Little Warrior," Michael's voice was deep and smooth. His feet touched the ground and again cracked the energetic surface with a roar. Shakti thought she'd have to get used to that sound without jumping out of her skin.

"Peace be unto you, Angel Michael." Shakti was spellbound by his perfection. "I'm so happy, it's you. I've had awful visitors all week."

"I noticed. That's why I'm here." He smiled. "I see you've learnt about the White Light of Protection."

"Yes, I have," Shakti replied happily.

He walked towards her. His head was taller than her ceiling, but he was uninterrupted by it, as if the ceiling were not there. "Your spiritual development has rattled the world of demons."

Shakti's heart sank upon hearing this. "Demons? You mean the Jinns?"

"Yes, the Jinns that came to you are demons. Not all Jinns are demons, but all demons are Jinns. This race is known in our world as the Ifrit Jinns. They will try everything to stop you from reaching your potential."

"I don't even know what my potential or goal is at this point," Shakti said, confused.

"All in due time. The White Light of Protection will help you, and we, the angels, will come to your aid when you are in need of it." Michael's words were comforting. "Understand, your real fight is in the physical realm, against other humans and institutions. The Jinns are here to scare you, but their real power is in influencing others against you."

"I see. Can they influence anyone?"

"They try, but only humans with a dark purpose will listen." He bent down to her eye level. "You must find the strength and power within you to push through. Do you understand, Little Warrior?"

Shakti felt disoriented with the high energy in the room and said, "Yes, I do."

"Trust, you will know what to do when the time comes." Michael stood up and walked back to the centre of the room. "I must go now." His smile revealed perfect glowing white teeth. He lifted off with no effort and exited the room quickly. The ceiling of her room reappeared.

"Goodbye, Angel Michael," she whispered.

Harrison knocked on Shakti's door just then and startled her. "Come in."

He opened the door slowly and popped his head in, "We leave in fifteen minutes. We have a long drive." Harrison stood at the door with his *Daddy* robe on, which Shakti bought him when she was ten.

"Very funny, Dad." Shakti chuckled at her goofy dad.

Harrison walked into the room and looked at her carefully. "You only lined one eye. Is that a new style?"

"Oh! I almost forgot, and, no, it's not a new style."

"Okay, chop-chop. Wait till you see your mom! Ahh, woohoooo!" He gave her two thumbs up.

"Really? I can't wait to see her. Meet you downstairs."

"Okay, kid." Harrison sprinted out of the room to get dressed, too.

Harrison was downstairs as promised in fifteen minutes and hollering at the women to join him. They took an extra fifteen minutes to get downstairs. Gayatri came down the stairs, and Harrison held his chest and exaggerated his heart pumping with his hands. Gayatri looked beautiful in a flirty red dress with a low back and nude high heels. She boasted red lips with an exaggerated pout.

"Wow, G! You're breathtaking!" Harrison gushed and kissed her hand. "Daddy likes."

"Thank you, Mr. Clairemont, but I'm married." Gayatri pulled her hand away, playfully.

"Dammit!" Harrison winked. He looked up the stairs. "Shakti, we have to get there before the surprise."

Shakti came running down the stairs with her earrings in her hands. "*Wow*! Mom! You look stunning! The professor cleans up nice." She giggled.

Gayatri and Harrison stared at Shakti. They didn't say anything for a few seconds. She stood on the last stair, looking at them. Her parents were taken aback by their beautiful young lady adorned in a short sapphire blue dress centred by a tiny waist and romantic ruffles flowing over her hips. Her youthful flair indicative by contrasting red heels tied up around her ankles, voluminous long dark hair and subtle makeup. She was striking.

"What?" Shakti asked worriedly.

"Honey, you look absolutely beautiful! And so grown up," Gayatri finally said with a glint in her eye.

"Yes, I agree," said Harrison. "You definitely look like me!"

"Thanks, guys. How is my makeup?"

"Perfect! Your dress is lovely, too." Gayatri said.

"Ahemmm." Harrison cleared his throat dramatically and posed. "You look dashing too, Dad."

"Thank you! Now let's go. A lot of people are already there." Harrison grabbed his keys.

The Clairemonts locked their front door and made their way to the Sutherlands. Shakti looked around far and wide for Jinns. She didn't see any. It should have made her happy, but it worried her more. They rang the doorbell with Shakti standing behind them, fixing her dress one last time before entering.

Mark answered the door. "Hello, Clairemonts! Welcome, welcome. Please leave your shoes on."

"Hi, Mark. Thank you. Here is a gift for your dad," Gayatri said with a huge smile as she and Harrison stepped in.

"Thank y...*wow!*" Mark stopped cold upon seeing Shakti.

Shakti's face went red, and she handed him the flowers and blushed. "This is for your mom," Shakti mumbled. Gayatri and Harrison glanced at each other, watching the awkward exchange.

"Thank you, Shakti. I'll give it to her. You...you all look...umm... great." Mark closed the door behind them.

Mary came running around the corner and into Shakti for a hug. "Hi, Shakti," she said.

Shakti snapped out of her blushing trance. "Hi, Mary! You look so pretty!" She hugged her tightly.

Mary giggled and pulled her further into the house. It was Gayatri and Harrison's first time seeing the inside of the gorgeous house. It looked nothing like the previous neighbour's home. They made it look like something featured in an interior design magazine.

"Wowzers!" Harrison exclaimed.

They walked towards the family room, where there were a few people standing with Agnes. She made eye contact and walked up to them immediately. "Gayatri, Harrison, welcome!" Agnes looked like a model in a black lace dress with a daring nude mesh lining and super high red bottom shoes. "You guys look sensational."

"Thank you, Agnes. You look incredible!" said Gayatri.

"Thank you! Everything is set up in the basement, the food, drinks, music," Agnes said. "But first, have a look around at the renovations we made."

"Yes, I can't wait," Gayatri said.

"Shakti!" Agnes spotted her. "Wow! Look at you!" She then glanced at Harrison, shaking her head. "You're in so much trouble, Harrison. She is going to break a lot of hearts."

"Tell me about it. Mark couldn't speak a second ago." Harrison laughed.

"Dad!" Shakti said, annoyed.

Agnes took Shakti's hand and said, "At least I know my son has excellent taste." She winked.

"Thank you. Where's Zoe?" Shakti changed the topic swiftly.

"She's in the basement with Karu."

"Oh, yay! Karu's here already." Shakti made her way down to the basement with Mary holding her hand.

Shakti descended to the basement in awe. The walkout basement was as nice as the rest of the house with beautiful high ceilings, wainscoting, large windows and grey two-toned wood floors. Ambient lighting and tasteful decorations set the mood for a grown-up party.

There were a lot more people in the basement than Shakti anticipated. Shakti immediately noticed the food station, which was well lit and laid out in spectacular fashion. Each corner had little trees made of stacked pineapples and wrapped in lights. There were waiters dressed formally in white shirts, black bow ties, and black aprons tied neatly around their waists. They walked around the crowd with tiny foods and stemmed glasses filled with bubbly drinks. The floor was set for dancing with cocktail tables and soft seats lining the walls. A

DJ by the name Selector Bad Man was on an elevated stage next to the dance floor.

Zoe spotted her as she entered and came running up to her. She was dressed in a tuxedo-styled short pantsuit with funky stockings and black heels. She pulled it off seamlessly.

"Shakti!" Zoe hugged her. "That dress is amazing on you! And your hair! And makeup! Shaks!"

Shakti blushed again. "Thank you. You look awesome in that outfit!"

"Thanks, Shaks. Come see Karu."

Zoe held Shakti by her other hand and weaved her way through the crowd. They came up to Hikaru. He stood there, holding a drink and smiled at Zoe. Then he did a double-take when he saw Shakti.

"Shakti! Holy smokes! I almost didn't recognize you!" Hikaru shouted. "You look great."

"Thanks, Karu. So do you." Shakti was pleasantly happy to see Hikaru making an attempt to dress with some fashion sensibility. "What are you drinking?"

"It's called Guava Shandy," he said pretentiously. "It's delicious." Hikaru seemed impressed. "I'll get you one."

Zoe pulled Shakti closer and whispered, "There are a lot of hot guys here. It's going to be epic."

"I can tell." Shakti giggled, scanning the floor. "Where do you meet these people?"

"Some are Mark's friends, and some are my parents' friends' kids," Zoe explained. "Either way, prepare to have the best time ever."

"Oh, my God! I'm so excited!" Shakti exaggerated her voice and squeezed Zoe's arm.

"Let me introduce you to some people."

"Okay, let's wait on Karu."

Hikaru came around the corner and handed both Zoe and Shakti Guava Shandy drinks. He was not kidding, Shakti thought it was the best cold drink she'd ever had. Zoe held both their hands with Mary, still in tow, and made her way around the crowd introducing her friends. Everyone was friendly and shook their hands. Mark's friends were particularly attentive to Shakti and Zoe. Hikaru felt cool being in the company of two beautiful girls. Shakti and Zoe enjoyed the attention as well. Soon after, Agnes came down the stairs and announced Winston would be arriving in one minute. Everyone got quiet and stood still, waiting to hear him enter.

The roar of the Porsche SUV pulling up into the driveway could be heard, and Winston entered the house. "Hello? Where are my pickneys?"

Some people covered their mouths to not giggle.

"Dad, I'm in the basement. Can you come?" Mark yelled out.

"Mark? Okay son, coming. Why are you in the dark, man?"

Lights flicked on, and everyone yelled, "*Surprise!*"

Winston held his chest and screamed out in genuine startlement. "*Aaahhh*!!" His loud raspy voice made it all the funnier. Everyone cheered in satisfaction of a good surprise.

Agnes came out of the corner and said, "Happy Birthday, honey."

He laughed out and said, "Ohh…you got me good, babe. Wow, that dress is nice!" He picked her up and hugged her. Mark, Zoe, and Mary ran up to him and hugged him too. Winston's eyes glazed over. He addressed the crowd with a huge smile. "Everyone looks so great. I look like a mess, so before I come around and thank everyone individually, I'm going to run upstairs and shower." The crowd laughed and agreed with him. "Be right back!" Winston ran upstairs like an excited boy.

The DJ started at that moment, playing a mix of reggae, soca, and hip hop. This was definitely a crowd with rhythm. Everyone bounced in unison and sang along. Some of the Jamaican songs included shouting words out while raising their hands. Shakti and Hikaru picked up on it quickly. They got clarification on what to shout out from Zoe.

The adults huddled around the food area where it was well lit. Gayatri and Harrison seemed to be having a great time. Shakti looked over at them several times and saw them laughing and talking loudly with hand motions. She was happy for her parents. Hikaru's parents stood with them engaging in conversation, too.

Winston came down after twenty minutes or so. He looked dapper in black dress pants and a black dress shirt with a designer belt and matching shoes. His hair was tied up and wrapped in a cloth. All the adults surrounded him and shook his hands. They were all so loud they could be heard over the music.

While Shakti, Zoe, and Hikaru were preoccupied with watching their parents having a good time, some of Mark's friends asked Zoe and Shakti to dance. Shakti looked like she was about to decline, and Zoe answered for them both, "Sure!" She held Shakti by the hand and pulled her into the dance floor, but not before Shakti pulled Hikaru with them. Both Hikaru and Shakti did not know how to dance to the music. They kept it at a moderate sidestep, left to right.

Mark's friend pulled Shakti in gently to dance closer to him.

"What's your name?" he asked in her ear.

"Shakti. What's your name?" Shakti said loudly over the music to the handsome boy.

"David." He smiled at her. She thought he smelled great. "How old are you?"

"I'm sixteen, and you?" Shakti couldn't stop smiling if she tried.

"Eighteen. Mark's a good friend of mine. We go to Guelph together."

"I see. I'm Zoe's friend. I live next door."

"Oh! Right. Mark told me about you."

"He did? Okay." Shakti was flattered Mark had spoken about her.

While Hikaru danced with an attractive girl, Zoe seemed to be owning the conversation with the boy she was talking to. Eventually, most people were on the dance floor, including the parents.

Winston walked unto the dance floor to a cheering crowd, chanting, "Hey! Hey! Hey!" He performed a reggae dance to a song he liked with people surrounding him, clapping. It was quite a new experience for Shakti and Hikaru. One they vastly enjoyed.

*　*　*

Later into the night, Winston asked to speak to Harrison upstairs for a minute. Harrison followed him.

"Harrison, this is my friend, Garret West," Winston said, holding Garret's shoulder. "Garret, this is my friend and neighbour, Harrison Clairemont."

"It's a pleasure to meet you," Harrison said politely.

"Oh, the pleasure is mine." Garret, a young man in his mid-thirties, looked polished and professional. He wore a crisp white shirt and a custom-tailored jacket with a pocket square.

Winston made light of the introduction. "Garret is the owner and distributor to the largest chain of grocery stores in Canada."

"Wow, that's awesome!" Harrison was genuinely impressed that a young man carried such a distinguished title.

Winston continued, "Harrison is a manufacturer and distributor of fine cooking oils. His products are fantastic quality, all-natural, and the packaging is superb."

"Impressive," Garret said, "I'd love to see it."

"I thought you'd say that, follow me." Winston walked away, and they both followed him into the kitchen. He opened his kitchen pantry and walked in and out quickly. He handed two different products to Garret. "This is just two of his products. We use them to cook."

"You're right," Garret said. "It's a great package, and it's made locally." Garret took a few seconds to read the ingredients.

"Thank you. I have many other products and a variety of packaging available."

"I'd like to see more of what you offer." Garret seemed impressed and handed Harrison his business card. "Let's set up a meeting with my team. Can you do a presentation of all your products?"

"Absolutely. I'll call you on Monday?" Harrison said.

"Yes, I look forward to talking to you," Garret shook his hand again and excused himself.

"Winston! Thank you, man!" Harrison's head was spinning.

"No worries. You have a great product. That's why I introduced you."

"I don't know what to say."

"Don't say anything else. Work on that presentation and get your factory in order. They will do a walkthrough. They don't play."

"For sure! Thanks again." Harrison shook Winston's hand vigorously with his other hand on his chest.

* * *

As the party wound down, the music continued in the basement. After midnight, the caterers set up a coffee and tea bar with biscotti and an elaborate fruit tray. Kate, the baker, hovered over the station, occasionally yelling at the waiters because they were doing it wrong. Her partner, Elise, stopped her, though, so she ended up doing it herself.

Shakti, Zoe, and Hikaru danced with the other kids while the DJ played until the wee hours of the morning. All the adults had left by now, including Shakti and Hikaru's parents. Winston promised the parents Mark and Zoe would walk them to their doors and make sure they went inside safely. As they were about to leave, Shakti took a second to appreciate the night she had. Two guys had given her their phone numbers, including David. Her face had a smile she could not erase.

As they were all saying their goodbyes, Mark got a moment alone with Shakti, "Did you have a good time?"

"Yes, I did. The best." Shakti's face ached.

"I'm happy you did." Mark's good looks were hard to ignore, but it was his humility Shakti found endearing. "You look beautiful tonight." He blushed.

Shakti glanced up, and her smile closed in. "Thank you." Her heart started beating faster and faster. "Thank you for inviting us. My parents had a wonderful time, as well."

"That's good to hear."

Zoe came up to them from behind.

"Hey, let's go," Zoe said.

"Yes, it's super late!" Shakti said, looking at her watch and seeing it was 3:30 am.

Hikaru, Mark, Zoe, and Shakti walked Hikaru home first and then Shakti. As promised, they waited until they went inside and locked the door behind them. Shakti waved goodbye and thanked them once more. She closed the door and watched them leave and enter their house. She took off her shoes, ran up the stairs and into her bedroom. The smile returned, and she clicked her feet together with a jump, "What a night!"

CHAPTER 13

MAY THE BEST NERD WIN

During Christmas break, Shakti and her parents planned to visit the Toronto Christmas market and decorate their house. Harrison closed the factory for two weeks so his employees would have time with their families for the break. The Clairemonts planned to go on their annual visit to a Caribbean island, but they had to cancel because many islands had been battered by a string of hurricanes a few weeks before. Shakti followed the news religiously and took part in a fundraiser to help out.

Hikaru, Zoe, and Shakti hung out most days. They mostly talked about Winston's party and the plans for the vegetable garden. Zoe's Grandma Mae and Aunt Lucy visited from Jamaica. Her grandma was a sweet little lady, no more than five feet tall. She wore glasses and tied her hair up in a cloth. She hugged Hikaru and Shakti tightly upon meeting them. She had a distinct smell of jasmine and baby powder. It was comforting to Shakti. They did not understand a word she said. Hikaru asked Zoe one time if she spoke English.

Grandma Mae loved going for walks in the neighbourhood. She waved at everyone as she passed by. One evening, she got lost. Mark and Winston frantically combed the streets looking for her. When they found her, she was sitting on someone's porch having tea with them. When asked why she didn't call them, she said she knew they would find her. Mark laughed and told that story to all his friends.

Aunt Lucy, on the other hand, was a vibrant, beautiful woman. She wore a lot of makeup and was always dressed in bright colours. She often yelled at Winston for working so much. Aunt Lucy and Zoe got along very well. She made a lot of inappropriate jokes with the kids, but only Zoe and Shakti understood. Shakti jokingly attributed this understanding to her quarter Trini roots.

Aunt Lucy took a liking to Shakti. She would move the hair from Shakti's face, touch her chin and say, "Look how she beautiful." She encouraged her to explore her Caribbean roots through music and food. It got Shakti thinking of her unique lineage.

On Christmas Day, the trio exchanged presents. Shakti had also bought a beautiful glass chess set for Mary. Her face upon receiving the gift was enough to make Shakti happy. It was the one game she enjoyed. Shakti was convinced Mary was gifted in many areas. She thought that Mary would shock everyone when she grew up.

One winter night, during a blizzard after Christmas, Mary came to Shakti in her astral form. Shakti was just about to sleep when Mary appeared through the window. Shakti was delighted to see her. It was their little secret.

"Hi, Shakti," Mary said excitedly.

"Mary! You came to visit me!" Shakti sat up quickly. "You hardly ever come out at night."

"Yes, I have something very special to show you," Mary said proudly.

"Oh yeah? Show me!"

"You have to get dressed and come outside."

"Huh? It's snowing heavily, and it's freezing!" Shakti pulled the blanket up to her nose to protest.

"Come on! You want to see this." Mary was quite convincing.

"Okay fine. Give me a minute to get into some snow clothes over my pyjamas."

Mary followed Shakti down in the dark to the main level and watched her pull on a full snowsuit. Mary gestured to her to go through the back door. Shakti turned on the garden lights, opened the door and slipped her snow boots on. She followed Mary down the patio stairs and into the garden.

Mary turned to her. "Okay, sit right here." She pointed to untouched snow.

"On the ground?" Shakti clarified.

"Yes, right there," Mary instructed. "Now close your eyes and take deep breaths."

Shakti followed Mary's instructions. It was cold and windy. Shakti felt the snow hit her face sharply. She took several deep breaths and started to feel calm. She was no longer shivering.

Mary's light form sat on the snow next to Shakti. "Now, open your eyes."

Shakti opened her eyes and looked at her. Mary was looking forward and smiling. Shakti followed her line of sight. It took a few seconds, but fairies came into focus. They didn't look like the regular fairies. They were dressed differently in little white outfits and were flying around rapidly. Upon seeing this new breed of fairies, Shakti held her hands to her mouth. Then the rest of the fairies came into focus. There were thousands of them flying around playing in the snow.

"Oh my God!" Shakti laughed. "There are so many!"

"I know! They only come out during snowstorms." Mary clapped excitedly.

The snow fairies flew everywhere playfully. They were beautiful and almost didn't notice Shakti sitting there. This Clan of fairies flying around was relaxing to watch.

Shakti turned to Mary, "Mary, thank you for sharing this with me. It is very special, indeed."

"You're welcome, Shakti." Mary smiled. "You better go back to bed. You don't feel it, but you're freezing.

"Yes, you're right." Shakti got up and dusted her pants off and made her way back to the house. Mary followed her closely. Shakti got back into bed, and Mary sat next to her.

"Good night, Shakti. I'm so happy you loved the fairies, too," Mary got up and headed for the window.

"Thank you, Mary! It's one of the nicest presents ever." Shakti was truly grateful. Mary exited through the window, and the room went dark again.

* * *

Other than Shakti's weekly visits to Vidia, the next few months were uneventful. She learnt many new topics and did countless meditations. Winter turned slushy, indicating spring was in the air. Shakti, Hikaru, and Zoe started gathering the supplies for their garden. Mr. Edgar was fully supportive of their venture and provided assistance when needed. By the time the last snow washed away with spring showers, they had outlined the gardening area once more. It was a lot larger than they realized from the drawings. Shakti planned the layout of the produce. Both she and Zoe used wooden pickets and string to keep straight lines before they started digging the ground. Hikaru made drawings of how the rainwater would be collected and diverted to the garden.

Zoe provided large bins for the cafeteria staff to put certain types of perishable foods that would be ideal for compost. It was all coming along nicely; however, it was tiring and time-consuming. They worked on it every day after school. Shakti asked Mr. Edgar to make an announcement at the morning assembly to ask for students to assist with the garden for volunteer hours. They got many people to sign up and brought the garden to life.

By the time it was warm, the garden had bloomed with an array of fruits and vegetables. The produce range was impressive, including strawberries, cabbage, cucumbers, peas, potatoes, and carrots. Also, there would be a lot more to be harvested in the summer months.

All the students and staff involved in the project were excited to see the actual fruits of their labour. Some students even came back to help without needing volunteer hours. Shakti was the only one that could see the elementals hard at work, helping the garden to thrive. She noticed there were a lot more of them than she had ever seen before. The gnomes were even busy caring for the ground vegetables. When a few tools went missing, she looked at them angrily. Sure enough, the tools would turn up the next day in weird places in the garden.

Little rascals, she thought.

Travis and his friends walked by the garden one afternoon. They looked at the trio, working away and snickered out loud, making a scene.

Travis looked at Shakti and Hikaru and said, "It would be a shame if one day your little garden were to...I don't know...burn down." His friends laughed at the comment and pushed each other around.

Shakti got up and snapped back, "It would be a shame if one day your little nose were to...I don't know...break, again." She grinned.

Travis's face changed quickly from amused to serious. "Is that a threat?" His red nose flared as he approached her. He came very close to her in an attempt to intimidate.

Shakti calmly said, "Nope, no threat. I was saying it would be a shame if that happened to you, twice." She picked up her water bottle just then and drank from it. "Ahh...refreshing!"

Hikaru stood up quickly and said, "Travis, you better think before you do anything stupid. We have cameras right around the garden, even on the trees." Hikaru pointed around in no specific direction.

Travis and his friends quickly looked up and around to spot cameras. The other boys hand gestured to Travis to leave it alone, and they walked off.

"What the heck was that about?" Zoe asked while pulling off her gardening gloves.

"Oh, he's the school bully. Long story short, Shakti threw a water bottle at him and broke his nose one time." Hikaru left out the part of the story where he was the victim of Travis's bullying.

"How did I not know about this?" Zoe asked.

Shakti said, "Well, I'm not proud of it, but he pushed it too far, and I reacted. I was a lot younger." Shakti said rapidly, "Karu, when did you install cameras?"

"I didn't." Hikaru laughed wickedly. "But I will now! I have some at home. I'll bring them in tomorrow."

"Good idea. We should have thought about that before." Shakti was worried about Travis vandalizing their project.

Zoe paused and reflected for a moment. "Karu, Shakti, let's take a minute to look at our work. It's incredible. I know you both did this before, but I haven't. I'm so proud of us."

The trio turned around from the far side of the garden and looked at it. Really looked at it. It looked like a well-placed garden, flourishing with fruits and vegetables. They were meticulous with keeping it manicured. There was enough space between rows to walk, and it was evenly spaced. It was functional and most aesthetically pleasing.

"You're right, Zoe. It's awesome. I'm way more pleased about this than our garden in the past." Hikaru placed his hands in his pockets and admired the garden.

"I agree, Karu. Thanks for making us stop for a moment to appreciate it, Zoe," Shakti said.

* * *

The Garden Club filled many baskets with fruits and vegetables to give away. It was a huge success. All three sets of parents stopped by many times to look at their kids' work. They were enormously proud.

The science competition was upon them now. Shakti and Hikaru worked feverishly on their presentation while Zoe worked on the final renderings of the rain collection system and compost. All three documented every step of planting, caring for, and harvesting the garden for the best results. A large part of the project was to ensure the garden would continue for future students.

On the day of the competition, Hikaru, Shakti, and Zoe arrived with their parents and siblings. The trio decided to wear matching green T-shirts with *The Garden Club* written on them. Shakti also invited Vidia and Marty. They showed up like proud aunts and uncles would at a school play.

There were tons of people packed into the auditorium and many elaborate presentations. Most students did a superb job presenting to the judges as they walked around. However, no one wanted to win the competition more than The Garden Club. So much so, Shakti had to excuse herself two times to get her nerves in check. Hikaru paced up and down in front of their garden area, which was linked to the auditorium. Zoe made last-minute adjustments to her drawings as a way to keep busy. On the table were five bowls of fruit and vegetables from their garden. It made the booth colourful and interesting.

Hikaru had come with his dad the day before to set up strings of lights over the garden. Harrison and Winston had dropped off several rustic wooden benches, as per Shakti's instructions. They had placed them around the garden, creating a beautiful, well-lit space, much like Shakti's backyard. It was magical. Everyone who walked by to look at the garden was in awe of it.

They were the last to present because their booth was set up at the furthest door, to be strategically closest to the garden. The judges arrived, looking tired from the numerous presentations. They didn't look excited to be there. This made Shakti, Hikaru, and Zoe nervous from the start. Mr. Edgar accompanied the judges and introduced them.

The three friends did a solid, well-rehearsed presentation. Each was responsible for different parts of the presentation that they delivered nicely. They emphasized the main points of lowering their carbon footprint, educating students on agricultural practices, creating a sustainable garden using rainwater, and reducing waste by making their own compost from the school cafeteria. They also proudly outlined that they provided students and staff with organic fruits and vegetables.

The judges were intrigued, especially the scientist from Environment Canada. However, the points that earned the most praise was that the garden was now a part of the school's identity. Shakti presented the wonderful benefits and durability of having future students take the reins and continue the garden. She showed off their folder of step by step instructions for creating, caring for, and harvesting a successful garden.

Finally, it was time to show the judges the garden. Hikaru asked them to follow them through the door. They walked slowly through the ambient lit garden in silence, often stooping down to read the labels of plants. They looked at each other and smiled, but they gave little away since it was a competition. Shakti, Zoe, and Hikaru stood by watching the judges scrutinize their passion project. It was nerve-wracking. The fifteen minutes they spent in the garden felt like fifteen hours to them.

Mr. Edgar walked up to the trio and whispered, "I'm really proud of you kids. It turned out even better than I imagined."

"Thank you, sir." Shakti, standing in the middle, answered for all of them. "We make a great team." She held Hikaru and Zoe's hands.

"You sure do." Mr. Edgar smiled.

The judges ended the judging session by shaking the friends' hands. They made their way to the stage to deliberate and determine a winner. Everyone was mingling in the auditorium and enjoyed refreshments provided by the school. Vidia and Marty approached the gang and hugged Shakti and Hikaru. Shakti immediately introduced them to Harrison and Gayatri. They were pleased to meet the people their daughter was spending time with weekly. Shakti left them speaking to rejoin her friends.

A Channel 24 news crew was set up on the far side. Shakti wondered why they were here. The science competition was not exactly breaking news.

After a half-hour break, Mr. Edgar took the microphone and announced they had the results of the competition. He asked for all the entrants to gather around close to the stage in their groups and for the rest of the crowd to be silent. The news crew set up on stage, and the judges made their way to the microphone. Mr. Edgar introduced each of them by name, job title, and organization they represented. They were impressive. There was a scientist from Environment Canada, an engineer from the Canadian National Railway, and the chief science officer and CEO of the Ontario Science Centre.

Shakti, Zoe, and Hikaru stood shoulder to shoulder. They held hands and didn't say a word. Nerves ran high, and all the entrants looked stressed out. Shakti scanned the crowd to see her parents. She spotted them close to the front with Hikaru and Zoe's parents. They, too, looked nervous. Harrison had his hands folded, and Gayatri's fingers were clasped together in front of her. Her head was tilted down, and her eyes were closed as if she was saying a prayer. Shakti knew this is what her mother did to centre herself when she was frantic.

Mr. Edgar spoke into the mic again. "I'd like to wish all the entrants to the science competition the best of luck. We had fantastic displays this year, perhaps the most impressive line-up we've seen since the start of the competition. However, there can only be one winner. I'm sure it was difficult to choose just one. Please welcome the judges, Mr. Fiennes, Ms. Samarasekera, and Mr. Hochstein, to present the top three prizes."

The three judges took their positions in front of the mic, and Mr. Hochstein presented. "Thank you, Mr. Edgar. We would like to thank each and every entrant in the competition for putting their heart and soul into their projects and making it the best year of the competition so far. Every year we are impressed by your inventions and creations. However, this year we were blown away by your innovations and commitment to making the world a better place."

Shakti tightened her grip on Hikaru's and Zoe's hands without realizing it. She thought her knees would betray her, and she would fall to the ground.

Hikaru touched her hand and whispered. "Be cool."

Mr. Hochstein continued, "The third prize goes to The Windmill Project." The crowd applauded, and three kids from a nearby school made their way to the stage to collect their prize.

Mr. Hochstein shook their hands along with the other judges and took the mic again. "The second prize goes to The Chemistry Brothers." The crowd cheered loudly as this was a highly favoured project that got a lot of attention. The twin brothers, Sean and Shane Martin, high fived each other and skipped up to the stage. The crowd's cheers lingered with occasional high pitch whistles.

Tension ran high among everyone. The room hummed as the longer than anticipated wait for Mr. Hochstein to come back was creating an unease amongst the crowd. Staff members brought a bouquet of flowers and set up the medals on stage. It looked like the Olympics.

Mr. Hochstein made his way back to the mic. Hikaru looked like he was about to puke on Shakti and Zoe as he leaned over for a second. Mr. Hochstein continued, "The first prize and winner of the annual West Toronto High School Science competition goes to…" he paused for effect, "…The Garden Club!" he shouted.

The crowd erupted! Shakti, Hikaru, and Zoe hugged each other so tight they were shielded from the other entrants tapping them on the back and shaking them. Even the third and second prize winners jumped and cheered for them. Shakti and Zoe's eyes filled with tears and Hikaru covered his face. Mr. Edgar was applauding and whistling. The Garden Club members made their way to stage with loud applause and a path cleared for them. All three kids glanced over to their parents, who were jumping and hugging each other.

They finally made it to the stage, and Mr. Edgar ran ahead of the judges to congratulate the kids. He shook their hands hard enough to shake their entire bodies. They looked out into the crowd in awe and gratitude. Shakti glanced over at all their parents jumping and hugging each other. Winston wiped his eyes.

Mr. Hochstein addressed them with the mic. "This was one of the most impressive projects I've seen in years." The crowd quieted down. "Every science competition produces fantastic innovations with complicated uses of science. It's all impressive. However, what made your entry stand out was your scientific application to a simple agricultural project that would vastly improve the world if applied on a large scale." He turned to the crowd and addressed them. "Everyone with a yard can do this. The Garden Club documented every step in a booklet on how to grow your own garden, build a rainwater collection system, and reuse waste for compost. They shared their produce with the school, and they got students involved in making it a reality." The crowd applauded again. "They did all of this in an eco-friendly way. The world needs more of this, right now. I think this may be the start of an agricultural revolution."

Collective chills ran up and down The Garden Club members' bodies. His comments on the project gave the trio a deep sense of validation. They were instructed to step up to the front of the stage and receive their medals. The bouquet of flowers was handed to Hikaru. Zoe gestured to Shakti to do the acceptance speech. Shakti was hesitant but stepped up anyway.

Shakti held the mic with her hand shaking. "Thank you for this great honour. Winning this competition has been our dream for three years." Shakti wiped her face with her hand. "First, I'd like to thank Mr. Edgar, who recognized our vision and supported us from day one. Secondly, I'd like to thank the staff and students at Swansea District High for rolling up their sleeves and making the garden the success it has been. Without you, none of this would be possible. And last, but definitely not least, I'd like to thank our parents, Mr. and Mrs. Akiyama, Mr. and Mrs. Sutherland, and my parents, Mr. and Mrs. Clairemont. Or as we like to call them, Mom and Dad." The crowd laughed and applauded for their parents. "Without your support, we would not have even made it halfway through the project. You donated your time and money to help us. Thank you."

Shakti felt more relaxed and made her closing statement. "Hikaru and Zoe, you are the best teammates and friends anyone could ask for. The point of this project was to make our school more green and environmentally friendly. We cannot ignore what is happening in the world today. Our oceans are warming rapidly and have become a dumping ground for toxic waste and garbage. As a result, it is killing our marine life at record rates. Due to irresponsible farming and lumber practices, the Amazon Rainforest is burning at a pace that is breaking every record in history. Our air is becoming increasingly unbreathable, and our polar ice caps are a fraction of what they were just ten years ago. Entire ecosystems are collapsing, and hundreds of species are disappearing. Our world leaders are not working fast enough to fix a problem so large that it could be the end of the world as we know it. It is up to us to do what we can to improve the world. Take it upon yourselves to be the change the world needs and apply pressure to your leaders to support a greener way of life."

The crowd was silent. Shakti thought she had gone too far, but they started to clap from one end of the room to the other. The teachers, judges, and principal got up from their seats and cheered loudly. Shakti's message resonated with everyone in the auditorium. They applauded loudly. Shakti looked over at Hikaru and Zoe, and they stared at her with respect and pride.

After the crowd settled down, Shakti gestured to Zoe and Hikaru to join her. They all said, "Thank you," to the crowd in unison and bowed.

They entered their summer vacation on a high. Shakti's speech aired on Channel 24. They received calls from the Ministry of Education and the Ministry of the Environment, inviting them to various events to speak about their project. The idea of an agricultural revolution seemed to catch on quickly. However, all that the friends had on their minds was Paris. The Paris Science Conference was in August, and the Minister of Education asked The Garden Club members to represent the Canadian students with a speech. Many kids from around the world were to attend the conference and represent their respective countries. It was indeed a tremendous honour for them to represent Canada.

CHAPTER 14

THE
HARDER
YOU WORK

*'The beginning is near. When the Earth is ravaged, and
the animals are dying, a new tribe of people shall come unto
the Earth from many colours, classes, creeds, and who by
their actions and deeds shall make the Earth green again.
They will be known as the Warriors of the Rainbow.'*
– Native American Prophecy

Shakti stood next to Vidia, reading this quote mounted on the wall of Bill's impressive penthouse. Bill had invited them over to touch base about Shakti's development. Shakti enjoyed being in the company of her spiritual teachers. She became somewhat of a celebrity within her school after the science competition. Everyone knew Hikaru's, Zoe's, and Shakti's names after the competition, and they received much praise and countless high fives in the hallway that week.

Vidia and Shakti sat in the luxurious nineteenth floor condo, waiting for Bill while he made tea in the kitchen. Vidia spoke about the competition and how proud she was of Shakti. She explained to Shakti that her aura spiked up into the air and fanned out like a rainbow while she made her speech. Shakti was most intrigued by this and wondered what it all meant. Perhaps she was doing exactly what she was meant to do, or it represented her anxiety during the speech. Bill invited them to the breakfast table to sit and talk. Waiting there was a lovely set up of a teapot and a raised platter with muffins and whipped butter.

"So, Shakti," Bill started, "Vidia tells me you and your friends won the science competition at your school. How exciting." He smiled proudly.

"Yes, we did. It was awesome." Shakti sipped her tea slowly as it was still hot.

Vidia quickly said, "You should have seen the garden and presentation they did. Remarkable!"

Shakti blushed. It was all so surreal to her. She never thought gardening would bring her so much fame and admiration. "I find myself worrying about the world sometimes. You hear about all these horrible storms and floods that are wiping out islands all over the world. The seas have risen and are threatening coastal communities. It's too much to process sometimes." Shakti's honesty came through. "Kids don't trust adults anymore to look after their future."

"You're right, Shakti," Bill said. "Kids have every right to be scared. Tell me, how have your meditations been going so far?"

"It's been good. Vidia is a great coach, and I feel more connected to nature and the spirit world." Shakti broke a piece of the muffin off and spread butter on it.

"Have you had any visitors in your meditations?" Bill asked nonchalantly.

Before Shakti could answer, Vidia interjected, "Yes, she's met her spirit guides and guardian angel." She glanced at Shakti and smiled.

Shakti added, "Yes, but I've been to some fantastic places in my meditations."

Bill smiled and asked, "Vidia, haven't you done the pyramid meditation with Shakti?"

"Oh yes, she had a great experience," Vidia said. "That's where she met her guardian angel."

Shakti nodded in agreement with Vidia, swallowed the chewed muffin uncomfortably, as she did not like to tell lies, "Yes, it was wonderful."

"I see," Bill glanced up. "That's great to hear. I'd like to introduce you to a technique that will really help you to connect with your higher self."

Vidia, at attention, leaned on the table, "Oh, what technique?"

"I'd like to do a hypnosis on Shakti," Bill replied.

"Hypnosis?" Shakti asked.

"I don't think that's a good idea, just yet," Vidia said. "It's too soon."

"Why is it too soon? It's for research purposes." Bill defended his position.

"What are you hoping to find? She's already very connected to her guides, and she sees the spirit world," Vidia said sternly.

"Yes, but this will help her immensely." Bill looked a little agitated.

"Bill, I have a lot of respect for your research, but I don't think poking around in Shakti's brain is right for her at the moment. It's invasive, and we should get her parent's permission before we do it." Shakti figured Vidia was not fully speaking her mind. She was protecting Shakti, but from what?

"Vidia, do you blame me for James?" Bill's question surprised both Vidia and Shakti. They both stared at him with open mouths.

"Of course not, Bill. How could you ask that?" Vidia said sharply.

"There is no correlation between James's hypnosis and him taking his life."

"I agree. Nothing to do with it," Vidia said.

"Then why are you stopping me from hypnotizing Shakti?" Bill argued.

Shakti gulped her tea to avoid the awkwardness of the heated exchange. She raised her hand. "Excuse me, folks. I do not want to be hypnotized. I don't feel comfortable with it." She placed her teacup down and looked at them.

"Well, then it's settled," Vidia said.

Bill stared at Shakti and put both hands up. "Okay, it's settled." He backed off. "We will not do anything you're uncomfortable with, Shakti." He forced a smile.

Soon after they finished their tea and exchanged final pleasantries, Shakti and Vidia said their goodbyes to Bill. He spoke nicely, but Shakti could sense the colder undertone. She was also miffed by his lack of aura. Shakti was able to tune into a frequency that would reveal someone's aura and it gave her a sense of understanding about the person. She realized she never saw Bill's aura. As she and Vidia descended in the elevator, they said nothing to each other. They both seemed bothered by the interaction with Bill, especially Vidia.

When they exited the building, Vidia stopped and held Shakti's arm. "Shakti, I'm sorry about that. I know it must have been uncomfortable for you to see us arguing."

"That's okay, Vidia." Shakti touched Vidia's arm. "I trust you completely. If you think it's risky in any way, I'll avoid it."

"It's just that, after James, I don't want to take any unnecessary chances," Vidia said sadly.

"I understand, but," Shakti paused, "I get the feeling you don't trust Bill completely, but your years of friendship cloud your judgement."

I don't know anymore, Shakti." Vidia looked confused. "There was once a time when Marty and I trusted Bill with our lives. But I can't ignore my intuition. Something is just not right this time."

"Vidia, let's keep my meditation classes and development between us. Don't tell anyone else about me. Also, Angel Michael told me the real fight is with humans, not Jinns."

"You're right, Shakti. We need to remain focused. Spirituality is wonderful, but it can take you down a rabbit hole. There is always something to learn. Take your time," Vidia said.

"I'm grateful that I have this gift of Sight, it's worked out great. My mom told me that it was a gift from Angel Gabriel."

"You are truly blessed, my child. Never forget that."

*   *   *

Over the years of Harrison's career, he had enjoyed many successes. He also had a lot to show for forty-four years of life, a beautiful family, a consistently thriving business, and great physical and mental health. However, his business was now about to enter a new phase of success. After Winston introduced him to Mr. West, he made contact with him, and the ball began rolling quickly. He did a presentation for Mr. West's purchasing team, and they loved the products. Harrison's products fit neatly into their company's mission of buying natural products locally. They also did a factory visit and put forward recommendations for improvements. Harrison followed their recommendations and Winston's advice on how to land the account. Sure enough, Harrison received the largest contract in the history of his company.

The new contract called for Harrison to expand his factory and to hire more managers to oversee production and quality. It was a very exciting time at Clairemont's Natural Cooking Oils. Gayatri committed a few hours per week to help out at the factory. Winston stopped by the factory one day. Harrison showed him around like a proud little brother would show off his new toy. Harrison was grateful for Winston's introduction to Mr. West and his advice.

A few days before Shakti and her friends' trip to Paris, Harrison had her over at the factory to show her the new improvements and how they all worked. He told her if she wanted, one day, she would run the business. Shakti was not sure how she felt about it just then, but she thought it was a privilege, nonetheless. She was impressed with the vast operations and stark cleanliness of the factory.

Shakti has been to the factory hundreds of times before, but this was the first time she noticed the intricacies of running a food operation. While she was there, she noticed considerable spiritual activity. A Clan she had never seen before was hard at work. They looked like angels, but they were dressed in similar white work coats and wore hairnets as the employees did. *What peculiar creatures*, she thought. They seemed to imitate the workers. Some looked into the large barrels of oil, some appeared to be doing paperwork, others even stood around the water cooler socializing. She even saw one angel wearing a pair of glasses close to the tip of her nose, flipping through pretend pages. It baffled her.

Shakti wished she had a handbook with all the spiritual creatures and their functions. The factory appeared buzzing with activity. She found a quiet corner in Harrison's office, closed the door and called Vidia. She needed to know exactly what she was looking at. Vidia answered on the first ring, and she told Vidia about what she was seeing. First, Vidia laughed and sounded excited.

"Shakti, those creatures are working angels. I'm guessing there are new developments or perhaps an acquisition at your dad's factory?" Vidia inquired.

"Yes, he got a new contract and has expanded his business," Shakti said.

"Well, that's why they are there. When we progress in our fields, whatever it is, business, career, parenthood, etcetera, we get this feeling of excitement and sheer joy, especially when we worked really hard to get it. Right?"

"Right," Shakti followed.

"Well, that feeling of deep joy and happiness translates into a spike in our energy level, and it can be seen in our auras. It sparkles effervescently. I like to compare it to bubbles rising in a glass of champagne. When the bubbles rise, we attract angels to us. They come around and work with you and the people around you," Vidia explained. "It's that feeling of accomplishment and grit that emboldens them to help us. Have you ever heard the phrase 'The harder I work, the luckier I get'?"

"Yes," Shakti replied.

"Well, it turns out, it's true!" Vidia was fantastic at explaining these spiritual mysteries.

"That's amazing!" Shakti was elated about the angels in her dad's factory. Her eyes welled with joy. She'd never seen her dad so excited about anything in his life.

Vidia continued, "It's also true for students and athletes that work really hard. The angels come around and give them the push and energy to be successful. You've been inspired by the spiritual world time and time again. It's important, you know, nothing beats hard work, Shakti. Nothing."

"Thank you for explaining it to me, Vidia," Shakti said her goodbye and ended the call. She thought, *What a strange and fantastical world we live in.*

*   *   *

Later that day, Shakti made plans with Hikaru and Zoe to go to the school to do some work in the garden. Harrison dropped Shakti off at her school earlier than the planned time. She headed to the back of the school towards the garden. There were students present as summer school was on. A few of them smiled at her and waved. She waved back and remembered a time when she had been invisible to the kids at school. She went into the garden shed on the side of the school and opened the combination lock. Shakti pulled off her runners and replaced them with garden boots. As she turned the corner, she was surprised to see four students already there working in the garden. They were accompanied by the Clans and too busy to notice her.

Shakti opened the makeshift gate and said, "Hi, everyone!"

They all looked up at her and replied out of time, "Hi," with big smiles. Shakti noticed something interesting with this group of students. They all had advanced colourful auras.

"Are we doing a good job?" one of the boys asked her. He looked like he was in grade nine or ten.

"Yes! It looks great," Shakti replied.

"We thought you all would be in Paris by now. That's why we came to take care of the garden." The boy crossed his hands on top of the rake and leaned on it.

"Oh, that's great to hear!" Shakti said, "We leave in three days. But I'm so happy the garden is in good hands." At this time, a few fairies flew up to Shakti, and she tried to ignore them because she was talking to the boy, "I am Shakti. What are your names?"

"I am Peter. This is Laila, Aarti, and Wesley."

"It's really nice to meet you all." The fairies flew around Shakti's hair. She didn't move or acknowledge them in front of the kids, "I will give you the combination to the garden shed, so you can get supplies if needed." Shakti walked around and looked at the garden. She picked up a few dead leaves and old fruits. She felt wonderful that the garden attracted kids to take care of it. The point of the garden was to encourage a sense of community at school.

Out of the corner of her eye, she saw a commotion and heard small grunts. She looked quickly to see two gnomes fighting, rolling on the grass, grabbing each other's red hats while smacking each other with them. Just then, she heard a hefty giggle and looked up to see Peter laughing. He was staring right at them! Shakti got up and continued to look at Peter laugh uncontrollably at the silly gnomes. Aarti and Wesley joined in on the laughing too, and Shakti was deeply shocked that other people saw the Clans. She got up, and then all the laughing came to an abrupt halt.

"You see the gnomes, too, don't you?" Shakti asked. No one answered. In fact, they looked scared. "It's okay. I see them, too."

"You do?" said Aarti.

"Yes, I've been seeing them my whole life," Shakti said.

"Wow, I started seeing them recently," Aarti confessed.

Peter joined in, "I've been seeing them my whole life, too."

"I don't see anything," Laila said sadly. "But Aarti is my best friend, and she told me about them."

"That's okay," Shakti said. "We don't need to see them to believe they are there and to care about the garden."

"That's true. I do love the garden." Laila smiled. "I think your speech at the competition woke something up inside of me, and I wanted to do better and be better to the Earth."

"Then, you are a Rainbow Child." Shakti smiled sweetly. "Being a Rainbow Child means caring about the Earth and taking actions to help it."

Wesley stood quietly in the corner until he said, "I see a lot more than the elementals." He looked bothered.

Shakti turned to him and said, "It's okay. So do I. They can't hurt you. It simply means you see beneath the veil. It's a gift." She was hoping her explanation would soothe Wesley. "I go to meditation classes, and my teacher helps me to cope with the visions."

"Can anyone come to those classes?" Wesley inquired.

"Yes, of course. The class is open to everyone. It's free, and the teacher is absolutely wonderful." Shakti smiled gently. "However, I would keep your gift a secret from anyone who doesn't understand it."

"This is the first time I spoke about it to anyone," Wesley said. "It's been tough, though."

"You just need to meet some more like-minded people. I'll give you a number to make contact with Vidia. Tell her you met me, and I recommended you all to her. She has a lot of answers."

Peter said, "Wesley, you can talk to Aarti, Laila, and me about it. We became friends because of it."

Wesley smiled and looked relieved. "Thank you, Peter."

Shakti felt all kinds of goosebumps. "You do realize that you all were attracted to the garden for the same reason? You're all Rainbow Children!"

The group thought about it for a second. Aarti asked, "Rainbow Children? I guess if being a Rainbow Child means loving Earth and taking care of it, I'm a Rainbow Child."

"Yes, you are. You all can talk to me if you'd like. I've been on this journey for quite some time. It's nice to speak freely about it, too."

Hikaru and Zoe arrived together. They were thrilled to see other students working in the garden. Shakti and the students stopped talking about the elementals and Rainbow Children when they arrived. It bothered Shakti again that she was not including her two best friends in the conversation about Rainbow Children. Hikaru had already been introduced to the topic of her spirituality and attended numerous meditations with her over the months, but she kept him mostly in the dark about the details of her development. She decided during their plane ride to Paris, she would tell them both all about it.

*   *   *

Mr. Edgar called Shakti's house the day before their departure to Paris to wish them farewell and prepare them for what was ahead. He sent all the parents and kids an itinerary of events. Mr. Edgar also sent them the name and contact information for the school's exchange coordinator in Paris. They would have to make contact with her upon their arrival and departure. He explained she would be their point of contact for assistance since there was no chaperone attending.

Mr. Edgar spoke to Shakti about the speech she would deliver on behalf of Canadian students at the conference. He wanted it to be in her own words and be a refined extension of her speech at the science competition. Mr. Edgar told Shakti he was incredibly proud of her, and she, Hikaru, and Zoe were true examples of leaders at school.

Harrison and Gayatri wanted to spend time with Shakti that evening since she was leaving for a long two weeks. With their parents' permission, the trio would spend a total of two weeks in Paris. They decided to extend their trip and sightsee, at their own expense. The Science Conference would only be a total of two days.

They helped her pack, gave her euros to spend and a credit card to use in case of emergencies. They both looked pretty sad sitting on her bed while she ran in and out of her closet. She noticed their long faces and assured them she would be careful. They were deeply happy that Shakti would have such a great experience, but they were going to miss their baby.

Shakti got little sleep that night and got up a few times to make sure she had packed certain items. Finally, she fell asleep and had a strange dream. In her dream, she walked through an ancient forest. The trees were giant and old, in the quiet forest. Vivid green foliage as far as the eye could see. She walked barefoot along a damp natural path and admired the beauty of her surroundings. There seem to be no birds chirping or animals, just deafening silence. As she continued along the path slowly, the sound of running water trickled in. She walked hastily towards that sound. A beautiful crystal-clear stream glistened in the sunlight peeking through the trees. She walked up to it and looked into the water. Grey and brown pebbles could be seen on the edges of the banks. As she looked in, an image of a lady standing over her appeared. Shakti's heart jumped, and she fell back onto the bank of the stream.

There, floating over the water, was a beautiful woman dressed in red, standing on what Shakti somehow knew to be a lotus flower. The lady had four arms, but it looked perfectly normal on her. Two hands were held in different positions in front of her, and the other two held flowers to the side of her. Her long thick black hair was braided and pulled to the front. It ran all the way down past her round hips. She wore a form-fitting red sari, tied in a complicated way that revealed her curvy and ultra-feminine body. Adorned in heavy gold jewellery, a dark green blouse peeked out beneath her sari. A full-bodied gold crown divulged a regal pedigree. Shakti stood in awe. This was unlike anything she had ever witnessed before or could even dream up. The mysterious figure reminded Shakti of her mother for some reason.

She floated upright in the lotus flower staring and smiling warmly at Shakti. She smiled back and became distinctly aware of her apparel. Shakti touched her waist and looked down and admired her clothes, for she too wore a beautiful red sari. It draped over her shoulder, and it fit just right. The weight of the gold bracelets around her wrist felt impeccably rich. She lifted her sari skirt and peered at thick gold anklets. On her hands and feet were strange abstract drawings with dark brown ink. Shakti touched her neck and forehead. It revealed more gold jewellery. She shook her head side to side, and the funny hanging trinket in her forehead swayed, too. Shakti looked up at the beautiful woman and nodded her head as a thank you. She assumed it was a gift.

Just then, Shakti heard her alarm go off. She turned quickly to hit it with one strike and tried to go back to sleep to finish her dream. But it was no use. The dream was gone, and it was time to get dressed for the airport. Again, another vision with a heavenly creature. What did it all mean?

Perhaps she should stop looking for meaning in it all and be grateful instead, she thought.

Her mom came into the room at this time and jumped into bed with her. She hugged and kissed and told her how much she was going to miss her.

CHAPTER 15

PARIS

S hakti, Hikaru, and Zoe's families kissed them farewell. Shinzo loaded up all three suitcases in his SUV and adjusted them to fit. The three friends waved at their families with huge smiles, and off they went to the airport. Their parents watched the car leave the street with a mixture of apprehension and excitement.

Shinzo had a dad talk with the three and warned them to be aware of pickpockets in Paris and to avoid aggressive street vendors. He also warned the girls not to go anywhere alone because he saw a movie about kidnappings in Paris. Hikaru glanced back at Shakti and Zoe and grinned when he said that.

By the time they got to Pearson International Airport, all three teenagers were nervous about being alone for the first time. Shinzo achieved his goal of making them self-aware and responsible for each other. He also told them he had friends in Paris, if they ever needed help. He made Shakti and Zoe save his mobile number on their phones. Shinzo was not the most eloquent man, but he meant well. His natural tone was harsh, but his words and actions showed he cared very much about all three of them.

He held Hikaru's shoulder and told him to take care of himself and his friends and not to do anything stupid. Hikaru smiled and gave his dad a hug and kiss on the cheek. Shakti and Zoe hugged him, too. Shinzo watched from a distance to make sure they got through security. He watched until they collected their belongings and turned the corner. He wiped his eyes quickly and walked back to his car.

The three friends got to sit together on the plane. It was exciting, and they had plans to watch movies and read books. Shakti had something else in mind, though. She wanted to talk to them about the Rainbow Children and her spiritual development. As soon as they took off, within a half-hour, Shakti told them she had to talk to them about something, and they listened attentively.

She told them that it was okay if they didn't believe her, but she wanted to share this with them because they were her best friends. Having been exposed to it earlier, Hikaru was not as surprised as Zoe was. She listened in silence as Shakti told her about her childhood and the Clans. Then the visions she'd had and how Vidia helped her process and make sense of it. The biggest surprise and reaction came from Shakti's story of the Jinns visiting her and how her mother chased them away. Both Hikaru and Zoe looked at each other and gasped. Shakti left Mary out of the story for now, as she was not sure how Zoe would react or if it was her story to tell.

"So, you've been quiet and allowed me to talk," Shakti said. "Thank you for that. What do you think?"

Zoe took a deep breath. "You've never given me a reason not to trust you in the past. So, of course, I believe what you're saying." She hesitated to continue her sentence, but after another deep breath, she said, "I get it now," she glanced up, "why you and Mary love each other so much."

Shakti was surprised by Zoe's intuition. "Yes, I adore Mary. She's extraordinary. Do you know why?"

"Yes," Zoe said. "I do. Mary visits me at night, too." She looked at Shakti to see her reaction. Shakti's jaw dropped.

"You see her as well?" Shakti blurted out. "I'm actually relieved. I didn't know how to tell you."

Hikaru was confused. "Tell her what?"

"Mary is the most gifted kind of Rainbow Child," Shakti said. "In her astral form, she's a wise old soul. She provides me with counsel and warns me about danger."

* * *

Zoe gasped, and her emotions ran over. Her throat tightened while her lower lip involuntarily curled down. She couldn't look at them anymore. She covered her face and wept. Shakti put her arms around her and pulled her into her shoulders to cry. Hikaru touched her arm with one hand and placed a pretzel into his mouth with the other. The crunch from the pretzel made Shakti give him an annoyed look, so he swallowed it hard.

Zoe wept and wept. She was deeply moved that her sister, who appeared limited, was actually a vibrant soul. Mary's paradoxical nature was intense to process. Zoe was happy and sad all at once. She wanted to go back home and hug her sister and tell her she would take care of her forever. Zoe cried for many minutes. She didn't talk to Shakti and Hikaru for almost one hour.

After an hour, the flight attendants came around with lunch. Zoe dried her face and forced a smile. She wanted Shakti to know she was okay and could handle anything she wanted to tell her. Hikaru leaned over and touched Zoe's arm one more time and asked if she was all right. Zoe smiled and shook her head up and down.

The rest of the flight was enjoyable. They watched movies on their individual screens and read books.

* * *

Soon enough, they arrived in Paris. All three felt a surge of excitement. They deplaned and moved through customs quickly. Shakti called the exchange coordinator to let her know they arrived safely. Each of them wanted to have a croissant as the first thing they ate in Paris, so they ran to the closest café in the airport and bought one each. It was as good as they hoped.

The hotel was a Parisian chic boutique-style hotel. They made arrangements to all stay in one room as the girls felt bad to make Hikaru stay by himself. Shakti and Zoe were to share a queen bed, and Hikaru got the sofa bed in their room. The hotel was in the Champs-Élysées district and surrounded by exciting shops and restaurants.

Shakti felt more jet-lagged than Hikaru and Zoe. However, she was aware it was more than that. She felt energy around her more than they did. It was disorienting. She said she wanted to lie down for a bit while they figured out what was around for dinner. Shakti realized this was the price of being more spiritual. She was keenly aware of shifts in energy, and figured she would adjust eventually.

The next morning, Hikaru woke up first, showered, and got dressed. He left the hotel room to go to the lobby to get tickets for the Eiffel Tower and the Louvre. The girls took their time to get dressed and met him in the lobby, where he sat eating a chocolate croissant and drinking tea. He handed them a bag of croissants, and they hurried to the subway, Eiffel Tower bound. The three enjoyed a splendid day in Paris. It was all it was hyped up to be and more. They spent two hours at the Eiffel Tower and then went to the Louvre and walked together for a few hours. Then, they decided to split up to attend their areas of interest.

Zoe was determined to see the Mona Lisa and headed back down to the basement to get into a very confusing queue. It took over an hour, but she made it up to the Denon Wing and marvelled at the Mona Lisa. Hikaru walked appreciatively through the Richelieu Wing. He rented a headset and took in the history of the sculptures. He thought that he could easily spend a week at the Louvre.

Shakti had a very different experience than her friends. The first artifact she walked towards was the Winged Victory of Samothrace, the sculpture that was at the top of her must-see list. It was glorious and enormous. Much bigger than the pictures suggested. She stood from side to side, looking at the asymmetrical statue and the mighty story it told. She was taken away by its raw beauty and significance. The seductive way the cloth draped across the female's body was alluring, revealing a muscular form. Shakti thought that the artist that produced this piece must have been inspired by real angels. In spite of the sculpture's lack of arms and head, the sheer strength and power rang through, much like the heavenly creatures she had met.

Almost half an hour passed of Shakti examining the masterpiece, then something started happening to the surroundings of the great Louvre. Time seem to stop. The hustle of people walking by slowed to a halt. Her ears popped and far and wide, everyone disappeared. Shakti was all alone in the Louvre. Was she about to have a visitor? Now?

The Winged Victory of Samothrace was effectively perched at the top of a grand staircase. She faced it. A horn blew powerfully in the distance, and she turned around slowly following its sweet sound. Shakti looked down the stairs, and there stood a sea of angels facing her direction. They were dressed in white, and they stared forward, but they were not looking at her. Shakti descended the stairs and saw countless more angels, all dressed in white, as far as her eye could see.

As she reached the last step, she felt pulsating footsteps walk towards her from the right. Angel Michael approached.

"Peace be unto you," he said. The hall of the Louvre was high enough to accommodate her favourite giant angel. She strained her neck to look at his face.

"Peace be unto you too, Angel Michael," Shakti said, "Is all this for me?"

"No, Little Warrior." Angel Michael smiled. "You're getting a glimpse into my world. What you are witnessing is my army of angels gathering."

"Why are they gathering?"

"Because the Jinns are winning, Shakti. The humans are failing and sending your world into annihilation." He explained without expression.

"How? Why now?" Shakti asked, terrified.

"Humans are choosing wealth and personal comfort over their loyal planet. Mother Earth is tired. Angels hear her anguished cries from the abuse humans have placed upon her. She can no longer stop the chain of events about to take place. Millions will perish."

"Oh my God!" Shakti clasped her face and then turned to him. "You're a heavenly creature. Can't you stop this?"

"No, I cannot. We have done our part by inspiring and influencing. Humans did not listen. The Jinns will win if this continues. They are close, Shakti. So close they can grasp it. The fall of Earth will happen in phases. Phase one will begin today."

"What can I do?"

"Your pure sincerity has proven to inspire the children who listen. Make your speech at the science conference most impactful. Don't allow politics to sway your message. You will be met with vicious opposition after your speech. Proceed anyway."

"But the conference is not for another week. You said phase one is starting right now." Shakti tried her best to understand the timeline.

"It is too late for those who will be affected by the events already put in motion," Angel Michael said.

"What makes you think I can make a difference?"

"You can, Little Warrior. Trust yourself."

Angel Michael touched her forehead and covered her eyes. He and his angels disappeared. Shakti stood at the bottom of the grand staircase as everyone reappeared, and the hustle and bustle of museum spectators continued. She was numb. She wondered what was about to take place. She looked around, and everyone seemed to be normal, which meant nothing was happening at the moment. She picked up the phone and called her mom.

Gayatri was in her office at the university and answered her phone, excitedly, "Hi, Shaks!"

"Hi, Mom. How are you?"

"I'm great. How are you?" said Gayatri with excitement.

"I'm good. Having a great time with Karu and Zoe." Shakti tried to sound enthusiastic in spite of Angel Michael dropping a bomb on her. "Mom, did you hear anything weird on the news?"

"No, nothing. Did you have a vision or a dream?"

"Umm...Yes, Mom. I did." Shakti did not want to cover it up. "Mom, I think something awful is about to happen."

"Where, honey?"

"I don't know. I just know it's going to."

"Do you want to come home? Or do you want me to come to you?"

"No, Mom. It's probably best we don't get on a plane. Just take care of yourself and Dad. It might be a natural disaster."

"Oh, no." Gayatri sounded scared. "We will. Listen, Shakti. If anything does happen, stay with Zoe and Karu and try your best to get into contact with us."

Shakti felt her eyes filling and the overwhelming pressure of knowing ahead of time. "Mom, I love you. Please tell Dad, I love him, too."

Gayatri said, "Don't worry, Shakti. We will be fine and so will you. I love you."

By the time the conversation ended, Shakti sat on the corner of the stairs to collect herself. She wondered if she should continue her tour of the Louvre or get Hikaru and Zoe and leave. She knew it was probably safer to be there than outside. Then she thought it was absurd of her to worry about their safety because they had no idea where or what was happening. She decided to get up and continue.

After a few hours, the group met up like they said they would in front of the pyramid. Shakti confessed to her friends she'd been feeling weirdly plugged in since they arrived in Paris. Hikaru and Zoe voiced their concern because they noticed she had been different since they landed.

"What exactly do you mean by plugged in?" Hikaru asked.

"The best way I can describe it is, there's a surge of energy that's coursing through this place, and it's been disorienting."

Zoe sat next to Shakti and hugged her. "You are deeply spiritual, Shakti. This means you feel energy more than most people. Is there a way to turn it off or down?"

"I'm sure there is. But I don't know how," Shakti said.

"Call Vidia!" Hikaru whisper-shouted.

"Good idea, Karu," Zoe said.

Hikaru took Shakti's phone and called Vidia. She answered on the first ring, "Shakti, my darling."

"Hi Vidia, it's Karu, Shakti's friend."

"Oh, hi Karu. Is everything okay with Shakti?"

"Oh yes, she's fine. I'm calling because Shakti has been feeling a little off since we got to Paris. We were wondering if there was a way she can turn her receptors down or off?" Hikaru applied scientific terms to everything.

"I see. Yes, there are ways you can do that. But first, what exactly is she feeling?"

"She said she's feeling plugged in."

"Okay, the energy in Paris is very high, like most big cities. Toronto, New York, London, to name a few, have it too, but she's used to it. She lives in Toronto." Vidia wondered out loud. "Ah! Let me speak to her."

"Shakti, Vidia wants to talk to you."

Shakti took the phone and spoke softly, "Hi, Vidia."

"Shakti, what you are experiencing is perfectly normal. Paris is geographically situated on a powerful Ley Line. I'll explain it to you one day."

"Okay, I've been feeling almost electric since we arrived. How do I feel normal again?"

"First, you pull the White Light of Protection around you. Then you meditate. This will help you adjust. It's not about removing the energy from around you because you cannot. It's about adjusting to this higher frequency."

"I see. I can do that," Shakti said. "There something else. I had a vision."

"Oh, you can tell me if you want to," Vidia said.

Shakti got up and walked away from Zoe and Hikaru. "Angel Michael told me something is about to happen that will be devastating to millions of people. He also said the Jinns are winning."

"I see," Vidia said, concerned. "The only thing I could think of is a natural disaster. There is a hurricane forming in the Caribbean Sea right now. I just glanced at the news.

"Can you keep an eye on it?"

"Yes, I will. Shakti, there is nothing you can do about it right now."

"I know, but don't I have a responsibility to tell someone?"

"Honey, no one will believe you. No one."

"Yes, I know." Shakti exhaled, feeling frustrated.

Shakti, Zoe, and Hikaru went for dinner and returned to the hotel. Shakti didn't talk to them much. She wanted to meditate and go to bed. She told Zoe and Hikaru they could get some more sightseeing in without her. Her friends reluctantly left her in the hotel and went for a walk on the Champs-Élysées.

Shakti pulled the White Light of Protection over her and meditated. It helped a lot. She was still exhausted and had an early night.

The next morning, Shakti woke up much earlier than her friends. It was 5:00 am, and she felt much better. She had adjusted well to Paris's enormous energy. She went down to the hotel café in search of breakfast. She exited the elevator and turned left. In the restaurant, there were a few people huddled together. She found a seat by the window. Shakti sat looking outside at a perfect Paris street about to wake up. The ambience was wonderful. She wondered what manner of Clans lived in Paris. She figured she would find a park right after breakfast and take a walk to see what she found.

Shakti waited a few minutes, but no one came to take her order. She got up and walked about looking for a waiter. The few patrons and two waiters were staring at a television that was mounted on the wall. She walked up to them and asked what was going on.

One of the waiters turned and looked at her. He pointed at the screen and said in a French accent, "There is a huge hurricane about to hit the Caribbean Islands, the East Coast of the U.S., and Atlantic Canada." The waiter balanced a tray on one hand. "It's a Category Eight!"

Shakti's eyes went wide, and she sat on a nearby chair quickly. The waiter continued, "There is also a typhoon forming close to Australia! What are the chances of that?"

"That's crazy." That was all that could leave Shakti's lips.

"Yes, it is," the waiter said. "It will make landfall tonight in the Caribbean. It looks like a monster of a storm from the satellite pictures."

Shakti returned to her seat and sat there quietly. She wished she hadn't known ahead of time. It prolonged the stress. By this time, the same waiter came up to her to take her order. She didn't see him, and he got her attention by touching the table.

"Mademoiselle?"

"Oh, sorry! Yes, can I have eggs, over easy with brown toast and an Earl Grey tea?"

"No problem," the waiter was about to walk away but said, "Are you okay?"

"Yes, thank you. I'm fine. I'm sad for the people in the path of the hurricane and typhoon."

"Yes, so am I," he said. Shakti noticed how handsome he was.

"I thought hurricanes only went up to Category Five."

"They do. The news said they had to create a new measuring system for this one."

"I see," Shakti looked down and couldn't talk anymore.

Shakti ate her breakfast, almost mechanically. The news weighed heavily on her. The thought of phase one of a mass extinction was incomprehensible. She glanced at the time, and it was 7:00 am, then looked up to see Hikaru walking into the restaurant. He made eye contact and walked up to the table and sat down. He looked refreshed, and his glasses hung off his front collar.

"What's wrong?" Hikaru asked while adjusting his chair.

Shakti had a blank face. She didn't feel like talking but did anyway. "Did you watch the news?"

"No, what happened? Oh my God, is it a terrorist attack in Paris?" He looked out the window to see evidence of carnage on the street.

"No, Karu, there are two hurricanes happening in the world right now. The one in the Caribbean Sea is a Category Eight and is about to hit the Caribbean, the East Coast of the U.S., and Atlantic Canada."

"A category what?" Hikaru placed his glasses on immediately.

"Category Eight," Shakti glanced up, and tears rolled down her cheeks. "Karu, I knew it was going to happen yesterday. Angel Michael told me. Millions of people are going to die, and all because we have ruined our planet," she whimpered.

"That's messed up." Hikaru's mouth dropped to the sides. "It's too late, then?"

"Yes. It is."

"What about our parents?"

"Toronto should be okay this time. It looks like it will hit the Canadian East Coast." Shakti felt a little selfish feeling relieved. "Karu, we have to get serious about changing children's attitudes. We cannot depend on the adults of the world."

"You're right. They really screwed things up for us in the future." Hikaru's despair started turning into anger. "They should be ashamed."

"I have this platform at the science convention. I intend to use it well." Shakti was in business mode. "Karu, you're going to help me with this speech."

"Of course. We will figure it out together with Zoe," Hikaru's eyes went wide. "Oh, my God!"

"What?" Shakti looked startled.

"Zoe has family in Jamaica! Her grandmother and Aunt Lucy!"

"Oh, no! You're right!" Shakti gasped. "Would she blame me for not giving them a chance to warn them?"

"Shakti, a hurricane does not come without warning. I'm sure they have been warned."

"Yes, you're right." Shakti was relieved that it took some heat off her.

Hikaru finished his savoury breakfast crepe and drank his hot chocolate. The weight of the hurricane was crushing.

Zoe arrived at the restaurant. "Why the long faces?" She plopped herself on one of the chairs at the table and signalled the waiter to come over. She ordered a tea and chocolate croissant and asked, "Seriously, what's wrong with you two?"

Shakti took a deep breath. "There are two major hurricanes in the world right now, one is a Category Eight and about to hit the Caribbean and east coast of North America."

Zoe's face dropped to match her friends. "My grandma and aunt live in Jamaica."

"We know. You should call your dad to ask what's happening with them," Hikaru said.

Zoe stood up next to the table and called her dad. Her breath was short. She held her chest with one hand and the phone with the other. She spoke to her dad for twenty minutes. She paced back and forth and glanced at Karu and Shakti a few times. She wiped her eyes and then ended the call with her dad.

"What did he say?" Hikaru asked.

Zoe covered her eyes and then said, "My dad said he was unable to get Granny and Aunt Lucy out of Jamaica. All flights were overbooked. He was crying on the phone." Zoe took a deep breath. "My dad never cries. It was heartbreaking to hear him like that. This hurricane sounds like a monster."

Shakti and Hikaru leaned over and held her hand on top of the table.

"Just pray," Shakti said. "That's all we can do."

The trio paid for their breakfasts and decided to go for a walk. They were not in a mood to have a tourist day knowing what was going on in the world. They decided they would go to one of the many captivating churches that Paris had to offer. It felt like the right thing to do, although none of them were particularly religious. Hikaru suggested going to the Sacré-Coeur Basilica, an iconic church on Montmartre. Zoe requested an Uber, and they made the trip to the eclectic neighbourhood in the northern section of Paris.

Europe was experiencing the hottest summer in history, as were many parts of the world. It made the climb up the steep mountain that much more difficult. Hikaru insisted they stop for a moment to take pictures on the lookout point before ascending the final steps to the church. No one was in the mood for pictures, but they did it anyway. They were hassled twice by street vendors selling trinkets along the way. One vendor was more persistent than the rest. It resulted in Hikaru swearing at him when he hassled Shakti. The vendor then tried to fight Hikaru, but a police officer was standing nearby and yelled at the vendor. Shakti and Zoe barely noticed the whole incident, as their minds were elsewhere.

There was a long but fast-moving line to get into the church. Upon entering, they were greeted with a blast of cold air from the church's interior. It felt wonderful entering the sacred space. Side by side, they walked quietly through the church, admiring the grandiose architecture. Shakti said she wanted to sit alone for a bit. Zoe and Hikaru continued walking.

Shakti sat in the church in despair and guilt. Her mind quickly shifted to a large number of angels present in the church. They were a lot taller than the people and walked around, sat on pews and prayed as the people did. She thought she would do a brief meditation. Her eyes closed and breaths deep, she escaped quickly. She was still at the church, but there were no people, just angels. Shakti looked up, and the roof of the church was not there, only a vast pink-coloured sky and twinkling stars.

Many angels noticed her right away and smiled at her. One angel, sitting a few pews ahead of her, turned and smiled widely at her. The angel was dressed in a white robe and had a large curly head of hair. She got up and walked to Shakti's pew and sat next to her.

The angel spoke to Shakti in a soothing voice, "There, there. Don't carry the weight of the world on your shoulders, my dear."

Shakti broke down crying. "I don't know how to help the people in the storm's path."

"You can't help those people, Shakti. But you can help others in the future. You know what to do." The angel touched her hand. It felt warm and comforting.

"Why was Angel Michael gathering angels?" Shakti already knew the answer.

"Angels help the souls of the newly departed make their way to heaven. There are about to be a lot of souls entering our realm."

"Please make it easy for them. Especially the grandma and aunt of my friend, Zoe," Shakti pleaded.

"I'll do my best, but making it easy does not mean they will live."

"I know. Whatever their fate, just make it easy," Shakti said. "Thank you."

"You should go now. I love you, Shakti. Remember that the angels love you all. Don't let the Jinns win. Their greatest accomplishment is convincing humans they don't exist."

Shakti was surprised to hear this since she'd seen them many times. "I see. Thank you. I love you all, too."

Shakti returned to consciousness, and Zoe and Hikaru were sitting next to her. They both had their eyes closed and they appeared to be praying. Shakti joined them in prayer. They left the church and returned to the hotel. They decided they would order in for dinner, so they could follow the news.

CHAPTER 16

HURRICANE KALI

T he six-hour time difference made the storm difficult to follow. The friends had their dinner and fell asleep with the news tuned to a channel in English. They tossed and turned and got up intermittently to see its progress. The hurricane, named Kali, would hit the first set of islands overnight. It dominated the news due to its destructive power and enormous cloud cover. News coverage on weather events usually was over-sensationalized. In spite of this, Hurricane Kali was covered in a much more frenetic way. Reporters appeared winded and almost depressed.

At 6:00 am the next morning, Shakti woke up, showered quickly, and ordered room service for all three of them. They had no intention of leaving the room that day because they wanted to follow the news. She thought the people of Europe wouldn't understand how tragic it was to have a catastrophic event happen on her side of the world. She soon realized she was wrong, as on the local news, there were reports of people flocking to churches and mosques. Also, organizing prayer circles to pray for those affected by Hurricane Kali.

Hikaru collected breakfast at the door, and they sat staring at the news to hear about the events. Reporters had nothing new to report. They had not been able to contact the people on the islands affected. They were completely off the grid. No news came out of the entire Northern Caribbean, including Jamaica. Not a word.

This affected Zoe more than it did Hikaru and Shakti. Her heart felt like it was being ripped from her chest. She laid down on the bed with a pillow over her face. Shakti tried to get her to eat, but she was too sad to move. She was very connected to her Grandma Mae and Aunt Lucy, Winston brought them over to Toronto twice a year to spend Christmases and summers together.

Zoe eventually called her dad, but he had heard nothing. The silence was cruel, but it still gave a glimmer of hope. Hours passed with no news. Hurricane Kali was making its way up Florida and the Carolinas. It extended over the entirety of the states it barrelled through.

News started slowly trickling in from Florida. Horrific images of complete and utter destruction. South Florida was submerged in water from the storm surge. Many Florida residents had evacuated. For those who did not, there seemed to be very little hope of survival. Theme parks were flattened, and the idea of a beachfront property was redefined. Ghostly towns, deep in water where once stood mansions and palm trees. A similar story emerged from the Carolinas. Buildings lay on the ground, and bridges collapsed. The hurricane brought a storm surge far and wide across the coastline. The catastrophic event caused a blackout as far as Texas and the rest of central USA. Still, no word from the islands hit by Kali. They remained a mystery, incommunicado. The world followed the news closely.

Kali was reduced to a Category Five by the time it reached New York State, still packing a punch and overwhelming the area. Lower Manhattan was covered in sea water and unrecognizable. By the time Kali reached the New York area, planes were being sent to the islands to assess the damage.

Dismal footage of flattened islands and vast carnage dominated the news, sending Zoe into a tailspin. She became hysterical. Shakti and Hikaru were shaken to their cores watching her scream and tear the room apart. Hikaru confined her to the bed, and Shakti laid on top of her to calm her down. She kept repeating the same words, "My granny, my Lucy, my daddy," over and over again. Shakti reminded her that Winston was safe at home. However, Zoe felt that Shakti didn't understand that she was devastated for her dad. He adored his mother and spoke to her every day. She raised him as a single mother. He sent money to her and got her involved in the Jamaican side of the business. Lucy was his baby sister, and he still treated her as such.

Shakti and Hikaru decided to call Winston and tell him to come to get Zoe. She needed to be with her family. Winston answered the phone, and Shakti told him about Zoe's condition. Agnes grabbed the phone and asked Shakti to tell Zoe that they had not gotten any news from Jamaica yet; therefore, there was still hope. Zoe came on the phone eventually and had a long talk with her mom and dad. It calmed her down, and she decided she would come home if she was allowed to fly, depending on the status of the hurricane.

Hikaru left the room a few times to get food and address complaints by the concierge over the noise Zoe made during her outburst. The hotel staff were deeply sympathetic and sent flowers to the room for her.

News reports continued to cover Hurricane Kali, and it kept getting worse and worse as more information became available. Kali, now a Category Three, struck the east coast of Canada, which sustained much damage, but it paled in comparison to the southeast states and the Caribbean. By midnight in Paris, Zoe had not eaten anything all day and fell asleep on the bed, completely exhausted.

In the morning, Shakti and Hikaru took turns buying delicious food and desserts to cheer Zoe up. But nothing worked. She sat quietly, obsessed with the news, and ate nothing.

"Zoe, look at me," Shakti demanded. Zoe looked up at her, surprised by her tone. "I know you're really going through it. But you need to eat and be strong. You have to be for your dad. You can't fall apart because he needs you right now." A tear escaped Shakti's eye.

Zoe's eyes filled again, and Shakti braced for another meltdown. But Zoe whimpered quietly instead, further breaking Shakti's heart. Zoe whispered, "I know."

Hikaru brought the food over to her and placed it in front of her.

"Hikaru bought some yummy food for you, and a whole box of macaroons for his favourite friends." Shakti tried to cheer her up.

Zoe picked up the fork and ate the pasta slowly. After a few bites, she said she had enough.

There was still no word about Grandma Mae and Aunt Lucy. Agnes booked a ticket for Zoe to return home that day. Shakti and Hikaru packed her suitcase and made sure she had her passport. The trio made their way to the airport with their hearts heavy. They checked her in and took care of everything, including packing snacks for the plane.

Zoe hugged them tightly before leaving and said, thank you. Hikaru stood sadly with his hands in his pockets, watching her leave while Shakti clung to him like a koala on a tree. Zoe was gone, and they had each other to rely on.

Numbers started to pour in about the amount of missing people, and the death toll rose exponentially every day. Hikaru and Shakti still followed the news, as did the rest of the world. The death toll was already over a million. The landscape of Jamaica, Cuba, the Bahamas, and Florida would be forever changed. Large pieces of land eroded away, water infiltrated much of the landmass, and dead bodies overwhelmed local authorities.

Shakti and Hikaru called Zoe a day later, and she told them her dad decided to go to Jamaica on a relief effort to look for his family. She said both Shakti and Hikaru's parents came over every day with food and to see how they could help out. It made them very happy that their parents were such wonderful people.

Shakti's speech was the last thing on her mind at the time. However, it was only two days away, and she wanted to prepare for it. Life continued as usual in Paris. Hikaru and Shakti did a great deal of research for the speech. They both spoke to their parents often to inquire if they heard anything about Zoe's family. However, nothing came up at that time. There was little mention of the typhoon in Australia because the damage was almost nothing compared to Kali.

The death toll for Kali had crossed a staggering two million by that night, and was sure to continue rising. Many places had become uninhabitable and would be abandoned. Water drained slowly back into the sea, taking large amounts of debris, including entire houses, cars and the bodies of people and animals with it.

The world mourned. Countries around the world not only provided billions of dollars in aid, but they had to consider opening immigration for the survivors from the islands. Kali had wiped islands off the map. What once were jewels of the Caribbean Sea were now watery wastelands. A despondent mood swept across the world, causing the suicide rate to skyrocket, and people came to terms with exactly what the words *extreme weather* meant for climate change.

* * *

A few days after Kali made landfall, Winston made the decision to go to Jamaica. After not hearing from his mother and Lucy, he used his connections and influence to secure a coveted spot on a relief plane. This arrangement was made possible because of his generous donation of a twenty-foot container filled with bags of rice to the efforts. He packed only essentials into a large backpack and kissed his family goodbye. Mark dropped him at the airport and hugged his dad with deep sadness in his eyes.

Winston hugged his only boy. "Mark, I love you. Please promise me something." He detangled his hug and held his shoulder and looked him in his eyes.

"Anything, Dad." Mark's mouth inverted in sadness with tears rolling down his face.

"I don't know what the conditions will be down there. Promise me, you will take care of the family if something happens to me."

Winston wiped his eyes and continued, "I need you to be strong, son. Promise me you will finish your education and see to it that Zoe and Mary finish theirs, too."

"Okay, Dad, I promise," Mark said firmly.

"Each one of you has money set aside. Your mom will see to it that it is given to the three of you after you've finished school. Mary has more money set aside for her special needs. Your mom will also have nothing to worry about financially."

"Stop talking like you're not coming back, please," Mark wept. "Please, Dad."

"I am coming back, but every good father needs to put things in place for his family. I had a talk with Mom about how to continue the business. She is to contact Mr. West in my absence. One more thing, I need you to promise me, son," Winston said.

"Yes?"

"Hear me good, boy. Promise me, that if anything happens to me, and down the line your mom finds happiness by moving on, you all will support her. She deserves to be happy." Winston's breaking heart bubbled over in his broken words.

"Dad, I don't think you should worry about that. But I promise. I will support Mom, no matter what. Also, I will make sure Zoe and Mary are good for life," Mark said clearly. "You have my word."

"That's my boy." Winston grabbed Mark by the head and crushed him into his chest.

"Dad, please prepare yourself for Jamaica. You don't know what you're about to face."

"I know, I'll be strong," Winston smiled. "I'm proud of you more than I've ever been in my entire life. Be good, son."

The father and son said their goodbyes, and Winston boarded his flight. Mark drove home thinking of that conversation, replaying Winston's words. He pulled aside into a Timmy's parking lot and wept. He wanted to get it out before he got home.

*   *   *

The plane landed on a makeshift runway at a remote site cleared by local authorities, a few miles from Kingston. The airports were all but destroyed, and relief workers operated on an as-needed basis. There was little to no planning because they never dealt with a complete breakdown of society like they were facing on all the islands hit by Kali.

Winston set off on foot towards Kingston. No clear roads or plans ahead of him. Shades of green and brown dominated the landscape. Fallen trees, toppled homes, and bodies of people and animals laid undignified across the plain. He spoke to a man dressed in a uniform and inquired how he would get to Greenwich Town within Kingston.

Winston's oversized backpack was heavy with two bags of rice he bought for his own purposes from Toronto. Rice was a popular staple in Jamaica. Winston planned on bartering it to get help for his family if needed.

The sight of his beautiful country reduced to ruins took Winston by storm. The area close to the beach had no standing homes or trees. His heart sank, and he started losing hope for his mother and sister. He shook that emotion off quickly. He walked around and spoke to some local survivors. While pointing them in the direction of the relief centre to get food, he inquired about the best way to get to Greenwich Town. Some people told him there was no way to get there, as there were no roads and deep pockets of water to be aware of. Not until Winston came upon a fisherman was a clear plan set into motion. The young fisherman suggested he find a boat and take it out to the sea, then sail around to Greenwich Town since it was close to the coastline.

Determined to get a boat, Winston walked through the water and endless debris talking to people in the village. The weight of the bags of rice in his backpack did not bother him until he felt like there was no hope of getting to Kingston. Then the bags felt like a million pounds on his shoulders. Finally, Winston spoke to an older man looking lost by the bay. He told him to get some food at the relief centre and wait there. Winston asked mechanically if he knew where he could find a boat. The older man said he has one in his garage. If Winston could get it out, he could use it. Winston immediately started clearing a path to the man's garage. The man saw Winston's desperate attempt to get to the boat and helped him with his feeble hands. Winston promised to return the boat to him after he used it.

Finally, the pair freed the boat trapped in the garage. Winston reached in his backpack and gave the older man a bag of rice. The man was as surprised as he was grateful for the sustenance. He walked quickly back into his garage and grabbed a shovel and handed it to Winston. Winston thanked him as he pushed the boat into the water and took off.

Luckily, the boat had gas. Winston was not sure how far he would get but made the decision to paddle if he needed to. He had grown up in Jamaica and knew his way around or at least the right direction to go. He made a moderately long trip and pulled into a safe place to store the boat. He tied it to a pole that had once held a dock.

The area looked like a ghost town with no people or clear structures. Every step Winston took made a loud sound in the eerily quiet coastline. He recognized the roofs of a row of townhomes in the distance that were close to his mom's house and hurried off in that direction, feeling thankful he was a tall man because much of the way was covered in deep pools of water. He crossed carefully with the backpack and shovel over his head. As he went further in, he saw a few people. They looked utterly lost, and many were covered in dried mud, perhaps traumatized after the hurricane.

Winston's focus immediately went to a lady holding the hands of two young children. The sight broke his heart, and he choked up thinking of the future that they had ahead of them. He walked up to them and handed the lady his last bag of rice. She looked at him in disbelief. He told her to find some clean water, boil the rice and feed it to the children, then make their way to a relief centre. She nodded her head in agreement.

Winston carried on in the direction of his mom's house. As he approached the street, his pace quickened along with his heart. His anxiety mounted, and he couldn't control the urge to cry as he ran into the street, jumping over broken trees and marshy puddles. He prayed that the concrete two-story home kept them safe, taking comfort in the thought that Lucy would do anything to save their mom because she was a strong, feisty woman. Winston had promised them he would come looking for them if they didn't get in contact with him.

As he ran along the street and turned the corner, he stopped cold in the middle. Winston covered his mouth upon seeing the horrific sight of his family's home collapsed to one side. The galvanized roof was a mound of splintered wood and rubble. It laid at a forty-five-degree angle with a tree leaning on top. He screeched out loud and couldn't move for a second, "Mama! Lucy!" He screamed at the top of his booming voice. Winston took off in a sprint and leaped over the broken fence.

Adrenaline kicked in as he started from the point of the house he could reach and pulled brick by brick off. He threw debris to the side, made a small entrance and squeezed his way into an open area. He continued to scream, "Lucy! Mama! Knock if you hear me. It's Winston. I came for you!" Winston's words echoed throughout the broken home. He continued to clear bricks and wood away, but there was no sign of them. Winston wondered if they left the house, but he had spoken to them on and off until the phone service went down.

He used the shovel to dig his way to the concrete stairs, which were surprisingly still intact. On the tall wall of the stairs, dangled a painting his mother bought some thirty years ago. He never liked that painting because it looked cheap. The colours of the art, bright yellow, green and orange, were washed off and ran down the wall. While still clearing a path up the stairs, Winston noticed some of the paint colours stained the ceiling above the painting. An eerie realization set in hard. Paint colours on the ceiling meant the house had been entirely underwater at some point. From the smell of the debris and sand in the house, Winston concluded the storm surge poured into the area and overwhelmed their home.

Right there, without another thought, Winston dropped the shovel and climbed the stairs on all fours, making his way to his mother's bedroom. Her door hung halfway off the hinge. He tore it off completely when he forced it open. Winston stood past the door frame with bleeding hands and torn clothes. The sight before him made him drop to his knees and scream with deafening force. His mother and Lucy laid on the floor, slightly bloated. Their feet touched at the toes, and a mattress covered Lucy's face. Winston screamed until nothing came out. He crawled over to Lucy and pushed the mattress off her and pulled her and their mother into his arms. Inconsolable, he rocked them back and forth, washing them with tears. Winston was broken beyond repair. He wished he could have saved them.

He screamed. "Forgive me, Mama. Forgive me, Lucy. I couldn't save you."

*   *   *

On Sunday, Hikaru and Shakti finished writing their speech and had time off to enjoy a day out to explore, one day before the science conference. They took the subway to the Eiffel Tower and had a picnic on the lawn. It was nice to get out since they spent so much time in the hotel room.

"I never thought this trip would have turned out like this," Shakti said.

"I know. It's been crazy since we got here." Hikaru bit into his baguette.

"Tomorrow is the big day." Shakti faced Hikaru. "I feel good about the speech. I was thinking, once we are finished with the two days at the conference, perhaps we should get an earlier flight and return home."

"I was thinking the same thing. We should be with Zoe, and I miss Ki and my grandma," Hikaru admitted. "Zoe's scary reaction to her grandmother in danger made me miss my grandma. I thought of how devastated I would be if I was in Zoe's shoes." He shook his head.

"Agreed, let's talk to our parents about going home early. We really don't need the extra days to explore Paris anymore," Shakti said.

They walked around some more, then got on the subway and returned to the hotel. As they were walking in, Shakti's phone rang. She sat on the bed and answered.

"Hi, Dad!" Shakti said happily.

"Hi, honey. How are you?" Harrison said.

"I'm good. Tomorrow is the big day." Shakti assumed he was calling her to wish her good luck.

"I know. Sweetheart, I have something to tell you." Harrison did not sound like his jovial self. It made Shakti's heart beat faster.

Shakti sat up straight. "Okay. What is it?"

"Is Karu there, too?" Harrison asked.

"Yes, he's right here." Shakti looked at Hikaru, gesturing him to come closer. He sat next to her on the bed.

"Put it on speaker." Harrison's tone was downright dreadful. "Winston found his mother and sister." He paused and took a breath, "They didn't survive the hurricane."

Shakti and Hikaru gasped and covered their mouths.

"Oh no, Dad. That's terrible."

"I know. It's devastating. It looks like they drowned in their home." Harrison choked up. "Winston is the one who discovered them. It seems they were stuck in the house. He's still in Jamaica making arrangements for the burial. Agnes and the kids are a complete mess. Your mother and Karu's parents are there right now."

"How, Dad, how?" Shakti asked fully weeping, completely torn apart for her friend and her family. "We want to come home right after the conference."

"No problem. We will take care of it," Harrison said. "I'm going over to Winston's house right now. Let's talk tomorrow. Best of luck with your speech."

"Thanks, Dad." Shakti sniffed. "Love you."

"I love you, too." Harrison hung up.

Hikaru and Shakti hugged each other tightly. Then they walked away from each other. Shakti went into the washroom, and Hikaru left the hotel room and walked around the floor. They needed to be alone to absorb the news. They imagined the state Zoe and the rest of her family were in. What a horrible way to lose someone you love. Shakti remembered Grandma Mae's warm embrace and her maternal way. She hoped the angel in the church kept her promise of making it easy for them.

Shakti pondered at the number of people affected by Hurricane Kali, and by extension all the families who lived to mourn them. Her consciousness had forcibly expanded to interpret grief.

What right do I have to feel this way? She contemplated. *Does grief only belong to those directly affected by tragedy? Or is it our tellurian consciousness that allows us to share the burden? How will the world receive this colossal loss? History would suggest they will turn their faces away from the house on fire, like they did with so many other atrocities in the past. Would this be the cataclysmic event that would spark a global unity? Or would it just lose its sensational quality before the problem is addressed?* Shakti's head was spinning with questions. She felt more pessimistic than she'd ever felt before. She carried it into bed like a heavy wet blanket over her head. She decided to leave the room and look for Hikaru.

Shakti grabbed her phone and purse and left in a hurry, anything to escape the room of bad news. She walked down the hall towards the elevator. As she touched the down button, Hikaru came around the corner, headed back to the room. His eyes looked puffy, and his nose red.

Shakti pretended not to notice. "I can't stay in that room another minute."

Hikaru forced a smile and said, "Let's get out of here then." He took the lead and held her hand. They walked out of the hotel towards the lively Champs-Élysées.

Clinging to each other, they walked aimlessly down the posh streets of Paris. Hikaru suggested they go into an outdoor café and sit for a while. The fresh air was good for them. They people-watched while sipping drinks made of chocolate and cream. Thoughts of Zoe flew in and out of their minds. They wanted more than anything to call her, but she did not answer any of their texts.

"Let's give her some time before we call," Shakti suggested.

"Would she think we're ignoring her at a crucial time?" Hikaru made a good point.

"You're right. We run the risk of that. That's the last thing we want." Shakti sipped her drink and wondered. "We will call her tonight."

"Okay. You know, we've known Zoe for just under a year, but she feels like she's been here forever." Hikaru surprised Shakti with his sentiment.

"Yes, I know. It feels like we reserved a spot for her in our group." Shakti smiled. "Or maybe we're just too lazy to make new friends, and she moved in next door, and we thought, what the heck!" Shakti threw her hands up in the air.

Hikaru giggled while tapping the table. "That's the more logical reason." He wiped his forehead, "I thought she was so beautiful when I met her, but then I decided not to make a move."

Shakti almost choked on her drink. "Karu, she friend-zoned you faster than that water bottle hit Travis's face!" Shakti flung her head back.

Hikaru chuckled. "You're cruel, but you're not lying."

After a few seconds of laughing, there was silence. They were reminded of Zoe's family and settled into it.

The evening out of the room did wonders for them. They returned to the hotel, and Shakti called Zoe on her phone. She did not answer. They both left messages of love and support for her. Shakti announced that they needed to get into the right headspace for the conference tomorrow. Hikaru agreed, and he quickly researched the route to get there. They prepared their clothes and charged their devices, and off to bed they went. Big day tomorrow.

CHAPTER 17

THE SCIENCE CONFERENCE

onday morning's sunrise met Shakti sitting on the hotel bed, meditating. She wanted to be focused on her speech, after all, she was representing Canadian students. She pulled the White Light of Protection over her and prayed. She felt the warm sunshine's orange light bathe her face. It was truly glorious. She realized since her spiritual transformation, she appreciated these little things more than ever. She asked God to help her make a difference in the world, and most importantly, she asked God to help the people affected by Hurricane Kali.

Hikaru's alarm rang; he didn't notice her sitting on the bed. He went about his business showering and getting ready. Shakti did the same, and the pair picked up their backpacks and headed to the lobby. They bought croissants and tea for the Uber ride to a huge hotel conference centre. The hotel was a sprawling compound with a large main building. They pulled up to the drop-off area and walked inside. The concierge directed them on a map to the large auditorium where the science conference would be held. The lobby was packed with people walking in all different directions. There were a lot of students dressed in school uniforms from all over the world. They walked in their groups. The American and Canadian students dressed casually in jeans and runners.

Hikaru and Shakti expected huge displays of science projects and fantastic models. Upon entering the gigantic hall, there were no such displays. It was set up in a theatre-style layout, and students and adults took seats where available. A lady in a uniform called out to them upon entering and asked for their IDs and tickets for the conference. Hikaru handed her the tickets, and they presented their IDs.

The lady was not very friendly and took it harshly from them without looking up. In a deep French accent, "Shakti Devi Clairemont, you are presenting at 3:00 pm. Please make your way backstage and show your ID at 2:30 pm. Do not be late," she said sternly.

"Okay. Thank you," Shakti said while taking their IDs back.

"Find a seat, and please be respectful. Stay quiet during the speeches." The lady then cracked a smile at them. "Next!" She gestured to Hikaru and Shakti to hurry along.

Shakti and Hikaru made their way to the middle of the seating area and found a pair of chairs together. The hall was packed to the limit. Thousands of people must have been there eagerly paying attention to the speeches given by influential people. They came to the realization that all these students must have won their science competitions and then been chosen to represent their countries. This effectively made them the best high school nerds in the world. Hikaru and Shakti felt right at home.

With all the commotion Hurricane Kali brought to their lives, they forgot how long they had waited for this. This was their moment. However, they couldn't quite get to that high because Zoe's presence was sorely missed. The thought of Grandma Mae and Aunt Lucy could not be ignored. Hikaru and Shakti sat quietly and paid attention to the speeches. Many world-acclaimed science leaders took the stage. Some they knew from reading their published works. Students made speeches about the projects they did and how they would change the world, and some talked about the problems their countries were facing.

At lunchtime, they were funnelled into another hall with tables and chairs. There were many food stations set up to accommodate the enormous crowd. Shakti and Hikaru lined up for the buffet. They took their food to an available table and sat again quietly.

Shakti eventually said, "I miss Zoe."

"Yeah, me, too. But we waited for this for so long. We should try to enjoy it."

"I know, but I can't seem to get there." Shakti pushed around the food on her plate.

"Yeah, me neither," Hikaru sadly noted.

"I can't wait to go home. I wish we were leaving tomorrow instead of Wednesday."

"Yeah, I wonder if your dad already changed the flight?" Hikaru asked, "Let's wait and see."

They ate their lunch and freshened up. Shakti went to the restroom to brush her teeth, and she took out a small makeup bag and applied some makeup. She wanted to feel good about herself before the speech, and she assumed this would help. She applied tinted moisturizer, mascara, blush, and a lightly pigmented lip gloss. Then she brushed her long dark hair and put on a small dangling pair of earrings. Hikaru sat outside the ladies' room, waiting for her. After half an hour, she emerged all dolled up.

He looked at her and said, "Could you have taken any longer?"

"How do I look?" Shakti smiled and flicked her hair behind her.

"Comme ci, comme ça." Hikaru raised his hand with his palm down and floated it.

"That'll do," Shakti said while walking off.

At 2:30 pm on the dot, Shakti made her way backstage. Hikaru told her he was going to record it on his phone, so he would get a seat at the front. Shakti handed in her ID, and they placed her in a seating area in the back. While no one was looking, she took a selfie and sent it on a chat to her parents. They both replied right away with good luck messages and a thousand emojis of love. She took her speech out and read it over. She read somewhere online that she should place a wine cork between her teeth and read the speech before a big presentation. Sure enough, she pulled the wine cork she brought from home, out of her bag and read the speech. She assumed it worked.

Minutes to 3:00 pm, an official-looking man with headphones and clipboard walked up to Shakti and told her to follow him. He instructed her to leave her belongings on the table and stand at the side of the stage. As the last person wrapped up their speech, Shakti closed her eyes and pulled the White Light of Protection around her again. It had a calming effect on her. She took deep breaths and waited patiently.

Whatever it is, it is at this point, she told herself.

The host of the event took the mic and announced, "Please welcome, the Canadian representative, Shakti Devi Clairemont from Swansea District High School in Toronto." The crowd applauded lightly, and Shakti made her way onto stage nervously.

She looked out into the crowd and smiled. Through no effort of her own, she noticed a row of angels standing at the back of the auditorium. They spanned the width of the vast hall, shoulder to shoulder. She didn't understand their presence there and focused on her speech resting on the podium in front of her. She made eye contact with Hikaru, and he gave her a thumbs up with one hand while he set his phone to record with the other.

Shakti felt her stomach tighten and beads of sweat starting to form on her forehead. Shakti wished she could hustle through the speech and leave. "Good afternoon, ladies and gentlemen. I am Shakti Clairemont. Thank you for this opportunity to speak on behalf of Canadian students. It is indeed a great honour to do so. My friends, Hikaru Akiyama, Zoe Sutherland, and I started a club at our school called The Garden Club." She read verbatim what was on the pages. "We did so as an entry into the science competition. We wanted to bring knowledge and hands-on experience in gardening. It would seem to be a simple project, you would think. However, the results were deeply surprising."

Shakti paused for a breath. "We set up a garden on the school grounds, and we brought students together to assist. We built a rain collection system to water the garden and collected perishable waste for compost. The Garden Club members grew significantly." Shakti glanced up at the angels who were still standing there. She took a deep breath and was about to continue reading out of the pages in front of her. However, Zoe and her family entered her mind. It hit her hard on stage, with the lights shining on her. She felt herself getting emotional. *Not now*, she thought. Shakti started breathing hard through her mouth. Hikaru noticed right away and turned to the crowd to see if they noticed the longer than expected pause. They didn't so far. She glanced at him, rubbing the back of her neck and holding back tears. He gestured to her to continue.

Shakti stood looking out at the crowd. "I'm sorry. Give me a moment." She drank a sip of the water they provided at the start of the speech. "I'd love to continue along with my speech, but I'd be remiss not to mention the catastrophic event that took the lives of over two million people and counting. One of my best friends and fellow Garden Club co-founder, Zoe, could not be here today because her grandmother and aunt were killed in that hurricane."

The crowd became silent. Further abandoning the speech in front of her, she looked out into the crowd. "We are a generation that is deeply interested in saving the planet, unlike the generations before us. We do not need to be scientists or climatologists to understand that a Category Eight hurricane is not normal. Natural disasters like hurricanes, typhoons, and rising sea levels are a direct result of warming seas and a warming planet. We know the science behind it. I will not waste my time explaining it to you like you don't already know. Why is it we trust science enough to land a space shuttle on Mars within a fraction of a second? Or build a suspension bridge strong enough to carry thousands of people at a time? Or build the world's largest dam? But we are distrusting of science when it comes to climate change? Tell me, what sense does that make?" The auditorium was painfully silent listening to Shakti. The children's faces were contemplative.

Shakti looked at the audience calmly. "I implore the children of the world to stop depending on adults to save our future. They don't care. They pretend they do, but they really don't. If the Northern Caribbean, Florida, South Carolina, North Carolina, New York, Atlantic Canada, etcetera knew what fate had in store for them, would they have done something differently to prevent a warming planet?" Shakti paused and looked at the crowd, almost waiting for an answer. "The answer is, of course, they would!" The crowd stirred a little, then quieted down.

She continued. "No one has all the answers, but together we can create solutions. My fellow Garden Club members and I have done extensive research into what we can do to help, and one recurring solution is to plant as many trees as we can possibly plant. We need to take steps towards promoting sustainable agricultural practices back into our daily lives." Shakti stared at their faces and pleaded, "Apply pressure to your governments to plant billions of trees around the world. Knock down every barrier that gets in your way, and when they say no, do it anyway!" The school kids in the crowd applauded wholeheartedly. Shakti was on to something. She knew it right away because rainbow auras started popping up around the hall over the students' heads. It shifted the ambience of the auditorium. Something was getting through to them. Shakti managed to awaken a passion within them. She wondered if rainbow auras represented environmental awareness.

Shakti waited for them to stop cheering and continued with final thoughts, "Our previous generations were given a beautiful planet, green and pure. Their greed outweighed their love for us, and they defiled it. They drained fossil fuels from the ground, poisoned the ocean, and cracked our ozone layer. They managed to burn the Amazon, melt the polar ice caps, and kill entire species of animals and ecosystems. Then, if that was not bad enough, they had the audacity to deny that climate change is real!" Shakti's hand motions were on point. "Corrupt politicians and unscrupulous business owners, this is for you. We will never forget that you chose to turn a blind eye when your actions could have made a difference. We will never forget you left it up to your children to save the planet, and we will never forget that you chose to deny the mountains of evidence laid out in front of you. Let Hurricane Kali be a stark reminder that we are in a crisis. For all the climate change deniers out there listening to this, *shame on you* in the eyes of your children, your grandchildren, and every generation that succeeds you. *Shame on you!*" she shouted.

Shakti picked up her papers and left the stage without a smile. The crowd erupted with frantic applause. Kids and adults were off their chairs, on their chairs, and jumping in the air.

"Shame on you! Shame on you! Shame on you!" they chanted. They were fired up. Hikaru jumped up and down, turning his recording phone to the crowd.

Shakti walked backstage into a group of people cheering. She heard many comments, "Go, Canada!" and "The Garden Club!" and "You're a savage!" She didn't have the ego within her to smile. She was angry for some reason. She picked up her stuff and made her way out the door towards Hikaru. She hadn't thought it through, though, because the crowd was still chanting, "Shame on you!" to climate change deniers.

The front row saw her exit the side door into the crowd and started screaming and applauding. Then it spread throughout the crowd like wildfire. She still didn't stop to smile or appreciate the moment. Shakti knew that it didn't belong to her. It belonged to them. She hoped they would go back to their respective countries and make a difference to save the planet.

She walked up to Hikaru, and he hugged her tightly, lifting her off the floor. "What the hell, Shakti! You were incredible! Who are you?" Hikaru shouted in her ear.

"I can't feel my legs. I don't know what came over me," Shakti yelled back while hugging him.

"You totally abandoned the speech," he noted, "But I'm happy you did." Hikaru was beaming with pride for his best friend. The crowd was still cheering loudly around them.

"I'd like to leave," Shakti's nerves were unhinged. Such attention was too much for an introvert's sensibilities.

"You don't want to stay and enjoy this?" Hikaru asked sarcastically.

"Ummm. Nope!"

Shakti and Hikaru made their way through the auditorium through a sea of smiling faces and cheering kids. Hikaru cleared a path like a bouncer leading a celebrity through a club, making sure no one came too close to her. Shakti almost forgot the angels were there, too. As she walked towards the back, she could see them clearly.

The angels were huge and glorious in appearance. They smiled ever so warmly and nodded their heads in approval of her. A few angels stepped backwards and made a path for her to cross. As she walked past them, they all sprinkled a most peculiar sparkling confetti on her. It reminded her of people throwing rice at a wedding. Except this confetti floated down like snow onto her and the crowd. She smiled at them and continued along. Hikaru called an Uber, and they power-walked to the hotel foyer. Some kids followed them. The Uber was already waiting at the door. They jumped into the Mercedes van and took off to their hotel.

The drive to the hotel was a blur. Hikaru spoke excitedly about the speech the entire time. Shakti could only hear her beating heart pounding in her chest. She clutched the collar of her shirt and perspired profusely. Hikaru was caught up on the speech, and Shakti was having a meltdown. She purposely did not think about the aftermath of the speech, although Angel Michael warned her about a backlash from the Jinns. If she considered the consequences of making such a speech, she would have never done it. The speech the group prepared was certainly inclusive of an environmentally forward message. But she abandoned the speech and came out swinging. Shakti spoke loudly and honestly about what the young people of the world were feeling.

They exited the Uber and Shakti walked quickly through the foyer to the elevator. Hikaru called out to her, but she entered the elevator leaving him behind. She took deep breaths and tried to calm her mind. Upon entering the hotel room, she ran into the washroom, started undressing quickly and turned on the shower. Hikaru made it to the hotel room by then and knocked on the washroom door.

"Shakti? Are you okay?" Hikaru's concern could be heard in his voice.

"Yes, I need a few minutes. Can you call my dad and ask them to change the flights for tonight?" Shakti wanted to get home to her parents in a hurry. She needed safety and to be with Zoe over anything right now.

"Sure. I could do that. But are you sure you want to leave tonight?"

"Karu! What the hell is wrong with you?" Shakti screamed, making Hikaru's heart skip a beat, "We need to get home! The speech is made, and our work here is done!" Shakti's voice elevated to a frightening pitch. "Zoe needs us! So could you stop being such a selfish idiot and get us out of here?" Shakti held her head and screamed, "Aahhhhhhh!" She leaned on the shower glass door, slouched down to the floor and rocked back and forth.

Hikaru took a coin out of his pocket and unlocked the washroom door, opening it slowly. Leaned up against the shower door, Shakti sat on the floor halfway undressed. He did not look at her directly. Instead, he pulled the towel from the towel rack and placed it over her. She was still holding her head while tears dripped off her chin. Hikaru sat next to her and pulled her into a tight embrace.

"It's okay, Shakti. It's okay." Hikaru was visibly shaken and his eyes welled. "We will leave tonight. I'll take care of it."

Shakti nodded her head to let him know she understood.

"Shakti, you can't carry this burden alone. Share it with me. It's you and me, forever." He rubbed her palm while talking, "I know you have visions. Let's talk about it and figure it out together."

Shakti sobbed upon hearing such loving words. She was genuinely grateful for Hikaru.

A best friend is a treasure, she thought.

She wiped her face on the towel. "Okay. It's too much, Karu. I don't know what I'm doing anymore. I may have put myself in danger after that speech. The Jinns will come for me. They know for sure who I am now."

"Are you sure they didn't know all along?"

"No. They knew I was a Rainbow Child, but they didn't know I would be the one to deliver the message." Shakti, too, was putting the puzzle together. "Otherwise, they would have tried to stop me before I got here."

"I believe everything you're saying to me, but it all sounds so holier than thou. You're not Jesus!"

"You're right, I'm making it sound like I'm a saviour of sorts," Shakti admitted. "It's not like that. But it is said that a Rainbow Child will deliver a message that will activate the Rainbow Tribe." Shakti adjusted the towel. "I know. I didn't realize it would be so profound."

"We really have to put things into perspective, Shaks. That's why you need to talk to your parents, Vidia, and your friends about this. It will keep you on track. Also, I don't want you seeing things bigger than they are or smaller than they are."

"You're so right, Karu," Shakti said. "I need a team. It's too much to handle on my own."

"Okay, good." Hikaru hugged her again.

"First, you should know that Angel Michael warned me to expect a backlash from the Jinns."

"The Jinns? What can they do?"

"On their own, not much but scare me, I think. Luckily, I don't scare easily. But they can influence humans to try to hurt me or stop me."

"Well, that's terrifying!" Hikaru leaned his head back on the shower door. It was warm. The shower was still running. He got up, turned it off, and made his way into the room. Shakti followed him and wrapped the towel around her.

"Yes, that's partially why I'm crashing," Shakti said as she sat on the bed. She shook her head side to side with her eyes closed. "I saw rainbow auras popping up while I was making the speech, Karu! It's me. I'm the one. The angels were pleased with me at the end of the speech."

"Rightfully so. You were incredible." He glanced up at her and smiled. "Don't worry about the Jinns just yet. We just have to be prepared for them." Hikaru exhaled. "But first, let's get our flights in order and get home."

Hikaru called Harrison. He asked Harrison if the flights were already changed and Harrison indicated he hadn't done it yet. Hikaru assured him that he would take care of it and told him Shakti wanted to come home tonight. Harrison sensed it was urgent and relinquished the responsibility to Hikaru. He even allowed Hikaru to charge his credit card for changes to both flights. Hikaru immediately called the airline and got them on the last flight that night.

Shakti and Hikaru packed up the room in a hurry. A mad rush to the airport, a stop at a bakery to grab goodies for the flight, and a run through security, the pair made it on time. Hikaru tried lightening the mood by making jokes and being extra attentive, but Shakti was still distant. Her thoughts were on Zoe and her family, and then they switched to the Jinns. She couldn't help but think of what they would say to her when she got home.

As the plane took off and they were a few minutes into the flight, Shakti said, "Perhaps I'm looking too much into it. They may just forget about me. The speech is already done."

"Yeah, you're right." Hikaru faked an optimistic response, "They may just move on to the next person to scare."

"I'm so tired, Karu." Shakti looked at him blankly.

"Eat dinner and go to sleep, Shaks. You look terrible."

"I'm not hungry, just tired."

"Okay"

He pulled his sweater out of his backpack and rolled it into a pillow and placed it on the window. Shakti leaned into it, and he picked up her feet and placed them on him

"Sleep, Shaks, everything will work out. Don't worry."

Shakti closed her eyes and fell asleep until they landed in Toronto.

CHAPTER 18

HOME

H arrison waited in arrivals for Shakti and Hikaru. He was excited to see them. This was the longest he'd been away from Shakti. It had been a difficult time apart because of the hurricane and how it affected their friends and the world. He needed to wrap his arms around his kid. Shakti and Hikaru came through the automatic sliding doors slowly. Harrison spotted them and waved them down. Shakti looked up, and they made their way to him. Harrison immediately noticed Shakti was different. She seemed sad from where he was standing. He shook Hikaru's hand and walked up to Shakti, lagging behind.

"Shaks is home!" Harrison picked her up and hugged her with her feet dangling off the ground.

She hugged him back with her eyes closed but no smile. "Hi, Dad."

"Are you okay, sweetheart?" Harrison placed her back on the floor and looked her in her eyes.

She took a deep breath, "I'm okay. I'm so happy to be home. Can we go see Zoe right now?"

"Sure, but it's eight am." Harrison looked at his watch. "Come home, see Mom, shower, eat, and then go to Zoe."

"No, Dad, we see Zoe first," Shakti instructed. Hikaru hung back awkwardly.

"Okay, honey. No problem." He took her luggage, and they followed him to the parking lot.

As they pulled into the street, Shakti and Hikaru glanced at each other. They were happy to be home, but they were not sure what they would say to Zoe. Shakti asked her dad if Winston was back. He told her he had not returned yet. Harrison pulled into the driveway and out ran Gayatri in her housedress. Shakti barely made it out of the car when Gayatri accosted her and pulled Shakti towards her.

"You're home!" Gayatri screeched. "You're okay, and you're home!" Happy tears flowed from her eyes. Shakti was their world after all. "How are you?"

"I'm good. I'm so happy to be home and see you both." Shakti glanced at Harrison. Hikaru was busy taking the luggage out of the trunk of the SUV. "I need to see Zoe before I come in."

"I understand, sweetheart. Go ahead. I'll get breakfast ready for us. Karu, you're joining us for breakfast?" Gayatri said with a smile, glad to have them both back.

"No, thank you, Mrs. Clairemont. I should go see my parents after I see Zoe. They will leave for work soon."

"Ah yes," Gayatri unwrapped her arms from Shakti and allowed them to leave. She and Harrison took the luggage inside.

*　　*　　*

Shakti and Hikaru made their way together to Zoe's house, nervously. Shakti took a deep breath and rang the doorbell. After a few seconds, the door swung open. Standing inside was Zoe, dressed in her pyjamas.

Zoe's eyes went wide and she stepped back. "Shakti? Karu?"

Shakti and Hikaru stepped inside and hugged their friend ever so tightly. Zoe burst out in tears, followed by Shakti and then Hikaru.

Agnes peeked out from the kitchen at the commotion at the front door.

Zoe whispered, "How are you guys here already?"

Shakti wiped her eyes. "We changed our flights to be with you sooner."

"Yeah, we figured you needed your friends," Hikaru said. "I am so sorry to hear about Granny Mae and Aunt Lucy."

"Thank you so much," Zoe sobbed.

"We were heartbroken to hear the news," Shakti said.

Agnes walked up to them. "You left Paris early to be with Zoe?" Her face was blotchy and red.

"Yes, Mrs. Sutherland. We wanted to be here for all of you," Shakti explained.

Agnes hugged them tightly. "You both are so amazing. Zoe is lucky to have you."

"Where is Mary?" Shakti inquired.

"She's upstairs, in the shower. She'll be down for breakfast soon." Agnes smiled.

"When is Mr. Sutherland expected to return?" said Shakti.

"He should be home in a few days," Agnes said. "There is no cell service there, so he called through a satellite phone one day when some soldiers were passing through the area. We can't wait for him to return."

Zoe, finally able to speak again, said, "We have been so worried about him. We just want him home, now. It's been hard not speaking to him. He told us that time we spoke to him, there was nowhere to bury Granny and Aunt Lucy. So, he ended up burying them in their backyard." Zoe's eyes glazed over again. The thought of Winston burying his mom and sister in their backyard made all their hearts sink.

"That's so sad," Hikaru said with a broken voice.

Zoe shook her head in agreement. "Can you imagine the horror?"

"I can't," Shakti said. "I hope he comes home soon. How is he surviving in terms of food and water?"

Agnes replied, "I asked him that, too. He said he found some cans of food in Granny's house. But it was limited." Agnes sat on the sofa close to the front entrance. They were all still close to the front door. "I sit around all day looking at the phone. It's maddening."

Little running footsteps could be heard from upstairs. Mary appeared at the top of the stairs and made eye contact with Shakti. She skipped down the stairs and ran straight into Shakti and wrapped her arms around her waist. Her hair was soaking wet and smelled of flowers.

Shakti hugged her tightly and lifted her off the floor. "Mary! Mary! How are you? I missed you!" Mary gave her an unexplained sense of security and belonging.

"Hi, Shakti! I missed you, too." Mary's smile warmed up the room and lightened the mood.

"Tell me, what's up?" Shakti asked.

"I miss my daddy," Mary said with a smile. Her emotions did not match her expression.

"I'm sure he will be home soon."

Hikaru interrupted the exchange, "I should go home and see my folks before they leave for work. I'll come by later to get my luggage, Shaks."

Zoe hugged Hikaru. "Karu, thank you so much for coming home early to be with me. I love you both so much."

"Anytime, Zoe. We missed you a lot." Hikaru embraced her. "You should know, Shakti rocked the speech."

"You did?" Zoe asked, looking at Shakti.

"I don't want to talk about that right now." Shakti didn't quite understand her aversion to the speech, although, by all accounts, it was a success.

"Don't worry, I recorded it. I'll send it to you," Hikaru whispered in Zoe's ear.

"Okay." Zoe smiled.

Shakti looked at Mary again. "I'll be back. My parents are waiting to have breakfast with me."

"Okay, my darlings. You should both know that your parents were absolutely wonderful. They came every day to check on the kids and me. Shinzo mowed the lawn, and Harrison got groceries for us. Kira and Gayatri coordinated to drop home-cooked food every day."

"I'm so happy to hear that." Shakti glanced at Hikaru. Then she turned her attention to Zoe. "Zoe, please let us know what's happening with your dad when you find out."

"I will." Zoe hugged Shakti again, and they left for their homes.

* * *

Hikaru ran home and rang the doorbell. Shakti could hear his mom's high-pitched voice from her house greeting Hikaru with joy. Everything had happened so fast that they did not know Hikaru was coming home early. Kira and Shinzo hugged their eldest son. Hikaru explained they changed their flights. They were elated to have their child home. The mood of the world felt uncertain after Hurricane Kali. Hikaru ran to the kitchen to see his baby brother. Ki jumped on him and gave him warm kisses. More than anyone, though, Hikaru wanted to see his grandma. She came in through the back door upon hearing the elevated voices inside. Hikaru ran to her and embraced her tiny frame tightly. Unexpectedly, he burst out in tears. His parents looked on.

Grandma Hoshi held Hikaru by his arms and looked at him. She wiped his tears away with her fingers. She told him in Japanese not to worry about her because she was doing very well. She also told him it was okay to feel this way after Zoe lost her grandma. A little embarrassed, Hikaru felt relieved his family understood it was difficult being away from them while the events unfolded. Shinzo and Kira offered to take the day off and stay home with Hikaru. This was a rare offer, Hikaru never remembered them taking any days off to his recollection. He told them he planned on sleeping and spending time with Ki. They both reluctantly left for work late that morning.

* * *

At Shakti's house, Gayatri laid a spread for breakfast. It included cut fruits, eggs benedict, and toast. Shakti sat and told them all about her experience in Paris and explained her vision at the Louvre. Shakti tried to convey how impactful the speech at the science conference had been and how rainbow auras started popping up over the kids in the audience. They listened in awe and silence. Gayatri wept a few times during that breakfast. Shakti promised them to get Hikaru's recording of the speech.

Shakti was honest and raw this time around. She felt she didn't have the energy to hide anything from them or protect them from the truth. She was very clear she was worried about the backlash of the Jinns.

"It disturbs me that I know nothing about this world. How am I supposed to protect you from creatures I can't see?" Harrison said.

"Dad, I know that's hard for you. But there isn't much you can do." Shakti touched his hand.

After two hours at the breakfast table, Shakti excused herself and went into her washroom to shower. She was exhausted mentally and emotionally. She wanted to be alone for a bit. After her shower, Shakti slipped on a light cotton dress and laid on the bed. She had slept well on the plane but thought she could comfortably sleep many more hours right now. Her eyes blinked slowly, and she slipped into a deep sleep.

After a few seconds, she felt boldly awake and light on her feet. *What a strange feeling*, she thought.

She got up off the bed. The room seemed to have a filter over it. Almost hazy. She turned around to straighten the bedspread out to make the bed and screamed in terror. There, she was still lying on the bed, fast asleep. She looked closely at herself, inspecting her face to see if it was really her. Looking at herself, breathing in and out with her mouth slightly open, a surreal feeling flooded her. Immediately, she knew she had managed to astral project. But how? She hadn't tried at all. She walked around the other side of the bed and looked around. Her cell phone was just where she left it, so she knew she was in the present. She looked out the window and leaned forward to see the street. With both hands on the glass to extend her view, Shakti fell right through the window. She screamed again and braced for impact from the ground below. When she opened her eyes, she was floating horizontally right outside the window.

"Oh my God! Oh my God!" she whispered, looking around. She could see a car drive by on the street. "How does Mary do this? Wait, Mary! She could help me with this!" Shakti employed her best swimming moves to move towards the back of the house.

She was able to get into an upright position. It was an odd feeling moving around without gravity. She tried walking, but it didn't exactly work midair the same way or have the same pay off as it did in the awakened world. Another attempt, she tried protruding her body forward from her head first, and to her pleasant surprise, she moved easier. Shakti was able to descend to the lower level, almost touching the stamped stone on the side of the house. She peeked through the window and saw Gayatri busy washing the dishes and Harrison looking for something in the drawers. She wondered if they could see her, but it would be cruel to scare them this way.

Shakti did a few eccentric moves to test her new freedom. She tumbled in thin air and did somersaults. She laughed out loud, as she hadn't been this happy since before Paris. She came up with an excellent idea to visit the Clans in her astral state. "Ah, ha!"

She pushed her way to the backyard and looked around. The vegetable garden was in great shape. It seemed Gayatri and Harrison had spent time on it while she was away. Shakti placed her feet on the ground. It didn't feel quite the same. Instead of soil and grass, she felt an electrical tingle beneath her feet. It tickled at first, but she quickly adjusted. She was preoccupied with this feeling and did not notice the fairies flying up to her. They came in a rush, looking excited to see Shakti in astral form. Shakti assumed they were happy because they flew swiftly around her. Shakti could feel their tiny feet as they landed on her shoulders and arms. The fairies wanted to play and show her around. They moved into the woods, and Shakti followed them fearlessly.

As she stepped off her property and into the woods, a bright golden hue made the forest glow. The gold light emanating from the woods seemed to have a heartbeat, as it pulsed rhythmically. Vivid colours of the Clans appeared more vibrant than ever before. All the Clans were mixed and buzzed around. The leafy green trolls ignored her entirely. They looked like they had places to go as they rushed past her. Shakti noticed they were heavy-footed like men, with rounded shoulders and hunched backs. The gnomes, with their pointed red hats and little boots, paid more attention to her. As she walked next to them, they watched her go by. Until now, she never realized they looked like little jolly men and women with bulbous noses and oversized ears.

Deceptively adorable, she thought.

The fairies were still difficult to see. They never stayed in the same spot long enough for Shakti to get a good look at them. The wings fluttered so fast, they looked invisible.

In astral form, she was able to see details that she could not see before. In her physical form, the spiritual world appeared as if she was looking through the bottom of a drinking glass. However, in astral form, it was clear as day.

Shakti walked through the woods, accompanied by the fairies. The slope of the woods rolled down to Grenadier Pond. It was a beautiful bright day in Toronto. She walked up to the edge of the pond admiring the burbling black water. Looking at the pond, Shakti wondered if she could walk on it. She couldn't possibly drown because she wasn't in human form, she figured. The fairies didn't look at all worried, so Shakti extended her right foot and stepped forward into the water. Her foot did not go past the water's surface. With a broad smile, she continued bravely, feeling a different electrical current of the water. It felt more relaxed than the Earth's surface. Water had a massaging effect, whereas the soil had a charging effect. Shakti had an immediate and distinct understanding that the physical world was presented through the five senses, whereas the spirit world communicated through these senses and electrical charges.

Enjoying this feeling, Shakti took off, running into the water, something one could only do in astral form. She ran, jumped, and played with the fairies without a worry in the world. Each jump higher than the last, revealing gravity was different in this plane. The sun's brilliance seemed to be the one constant between the worlds. She closed her eyes and stood in the middle of the pond, feeling invincible. Shakti was too busy having fun to notice the woods behind her getting thicker. The fairies flew around her as she played on the pond's surface. Suddenly, they stopped flying around and hovered in one spot. Their backs turned to Shakti, and they looked towards the bank behind Shakti's house.

Shakti missed their energetic flight and turned to see where they were. She walked back towards them and looked at their little faces, then followed their line of sight. The pond's bank appeared darker than she remembered. The brilliant yellow glow of the forest turned into a dark mustard tone. She walked towards it to get a clearer picture of what she was looking at. The sight made her worried, and she decided to return to the woods and go home. Off she went in that direction.

The fairies followed her cautiously, but they didn't try to stop her until she reached a few metres away. Into clear view, the darkness took the shape of thousands of Jinns standing in the woods waiting for Shakti. Shakti held her astral stomach and gasped. The fairies came closer to her for protection, it seemed. The Jinns stood tall with a unified shallow sway, back and forth to a silent beat. Black rounded cloaks concealed their faces. Their sight lowered to the ground, and skeletal fingers clasped to the front.

Shakti had a decision to make, either turn around and head towards the other side of the pond to High Park or muster the courage to walk through them as she did before. The latter scared her this time. She felt she wasn't brave like she had been before the speech. But heading too far away from her body seemed risky. So, she took an imaginary breath and walked towards the Jinns.

As Shakti stepped one foot onto the land, the Jinns sway came to an abrupt halt. They then stepped back and created a narrow path for her. So narrow, she rubbed against their chests as she walked by. She peeped at their faces. Unfortunately, they too were clearer than before. Their decrepit skeletal faces were chipped and sharp. The putrid odour of decaying flesh filled the bank. The smell came with an intense spark in her nose, indicative of the offensive stench.

Out of their mouths, the haunting whispers began. "Shakkkktiiii." Her name echoed like a chorus through them. "Shaktiiiii." Over and over again.

Her mind was imploding and hands in fists, she said, "Yes, that's my name. Don't wear it out." Shakti tried to appear her usual rude self, but her fear was transparent this time.

"Shakkkkkktiiiiii," the Jinn to her right called out above the rest. "He's coming."

Shakti's shoulder tilted forward, and her body felt limp. Her core trembled with an urge to scream.

"He's coming for you. He's coming for you. He's coming for you." Their taunts turned into cackling. "He's coming for you. He's coming for you." They laughed in a high-pitched tone.

"Who's coming?" Shakti couldn't help herself. "Who's coming for me?"

"The King," the Jinns whispered and repeated. "The King. The King. He's coming for you."

Shakti's astral knees felt like they would betray her. She wanted to cry and scream. But she stayed frozen instead. *Why would the King come for me?* she thought.

The rancid smell of the demons oozed a greenish-brown cloud that lingered above them. The gnomes looked on from the branches of trees like nosy people walking by a fight, waiting to see what was about to go down. They held each other. Shakti glanced up at them, feeling comforted by their presence. They represented goodness. The fairies hid between the leaves, peeking at her.

Not being able to stomach their stink anymore, Shakti took off with speed and raced up to her bedroom window. She vaulted into the room and dove on top of her sleeping body. Her astral form connected seamlessly with her body, jolting her awake. Her eyes opened, and she popped up, clenching her chest once more.

She whispered to herself, "He's coming!" Rubbing her eyes to wake up fully. "He's coming?"

Shakti's anxiety ripped through her like a knife through butter. It caused physical pain in her chest. She closed her eyes and pulled the White Light of Protection around her. Then she got up and ran downstairs. Her parents were in the family room watching TV, since they took the day off to spend with her. She tiptoed behind them to look out the back door. Sure enough, standing there were hundreds of Jinns watching the house, from a distance. Shakti felt her stomach churn. They were back. This time they were flanked at her doorstep and in vast numbers. She wasn't dreaming, and he was coming. She swallowed that fact like a morsel of nails.

"Shakti?" Harrison said behind her.

"Ahhhgg," Shakti yelped. "Dad! You scared me!"

"By saying your name?"

"You're right. Sorry."

"I thought you were sleeping."

"I can't sleep anymore. I'm just going to hang out with you two."

"Great!" said Harrison. "Want to watch a movie?"

"Okay. It's eleven am, but sure," Shakti said out of breath. She didn't want to be alone anymore. To do anything with them made her happy.

Shakti ran into the hallway credenza and took out a sage incense stick. She found a lighter and lit the stick, then slid the back door open and stretched one foot outside. The other foot was planted firmly inside the house for protection, of course.

Harrison, still looking on, whispered, "Oh brother." Shakti stretched as far as her body could reach and stuck the incense stick in a nearby plant pot with only soil in it, all the while with one foot inside the house. Shakti immediately pulled herself back into the house and closed the back door and locked the two locks.

Shakti spent that day with her parents. They didn't think anything of her being clingy. When it was night, she asked to sleep between them on their king-sized bed. Gayatri happily agreed to have her camp out with them. Shakti slept well that night. However, how long could she go on like this?

CHAPTER 19

EARNING LIGHTS

Hikaru knocked on Shakti's door at 8:00 am the following morning. He had come to collect his luggage. Shakti opened the door cautiously and sighed with relief.

"Wow! You look awful," Hikaru blurted out.

"Get in quickly." Shakti held him by the arm and pulled him inside. She looked around to see if the Jinns were there, but there was no sign of them.

"What's wrong?" Hikaru asked with suspicion.

"I don't think you'd believe me if I told you." Shakti walked to the kitchen with Hikaru trailing her.

"Geez. Just tell me." Hikaru spotted a scone on a saucer with a dollop of clotted cream. He picked it up and bit into it. "Yummy! Okay, now tell me."

"Go ahead. Eat my breakfast. I'll get another one." Shakti was used to Hikaru eating her food. "I don't understand how you're not obese."

"Good genes." Hikaru smiled. "Tell me! Why do you look like death warmed up?"

"Yesterday, I took a nap. I astral projected. Then, I went to the woods to play with the Clans and ran into ten thousand Jinns who taunted me with a 'He's coming' gospel." Shakti's ability to summarize horrific events in one breath was a talent.

Hikaru stopped chewing, swallowed his unchewed bite and started to choke. He picked up a glass from the counter, filled it with water and downed it. After a few seconds of recovery, he said, "What the actual hell? Who is coming?"

"The King! Apparently," Shakti said sarcastically. "You know, I'm making fun of it now because I don't know what emotion to tie to this terrifying information."

"Fear! Unequivocal Fear! Shakti! What the heck is wrong with you?" Hikaru scolded. He went to touch her hand and bring her back to reality and noticed long red scratches on her upper arm. "What's this?"

She glanced down, looking surprised herself. "Oh, yeah. I tend to scratch myself when I feel anxious."

"I remember you doing that when you were a kid, but this looks really bad. You should cut your nails." Hikaru looked more stressed than Shakti.

"That's the least of my problems right now, Karu." She put her head down on the table.

"Seriously, Shakti. What are you going to do?" Hikaru's face changed from frustrated to worried.

"I have no answers, Karu. Nothing."

Shakti's phone rang, making the two of them jump.

"Geez, now I'm giving you mental problems, too." Shakti picked up the phone and read it out loud. "Mr. Edgar?"

"Oh no! He probably thinks we're still in Paris!" Hikaru said. "We didn't tell the exchange coordinator we were leaving!"

"Hello," Shakti answered the phone.

"Hello, my superstar student!" Mr. Edgar's voice was way too upbeat for Shakti's depressed mood.

"Oh hi, Mr. Edgar," Shakti said unamused.

Without getting into exchanging pleasantries. "How are Zoe and her family doing?"

"Oh, they are not doing great. We came back from Paris early to be with her." Shakti slipped that piece of information in assuming he would be mad that they missed the second day of the conference. "How did you find out about Zoe, sir?"

"Oh, from your rock star speech! It was incredible."

"Oh, you saw it?" She put the phone on speaker for Hikaru to hear.

Mr. Edgar paused for a second. "Shakti, when did you return?"

"Yesterday."

"Were you not online or watched the news?" Mr. Edgar asked.

"No, sir. Karu and I travelled for many hours from Paris, then basically spent the day with our parents and Zoe, and slept for the rest of the day. Why?" Shakti touched Hikaru's hand.

"Shakti, umm. You've been all over the news since yesterday. Your speech went viral."

Shakti and Hikaru looked at each other, befuddled. "Can you say that again?"

"Your speech was so good, it made world news! Go turn on the news now. Channel 24 has been talking about it all morning. They're boasting about the Canadian student that said it like it is. *Shame on you* is trending on Twitter, and your face is all over social media. Shakti, I couldn't be prouder to call you my student."

Hikaru ran to Shakti's mounted TV and turned it on Channel 24. Shakti was at a loss for words. "Mr. Edgar, do you mind if I call you back?"

"Sure. Sorry to be the one to break the news to you," Mr. Edgar said happily.

Shakti sat on the distressed leather sofa and watched the news. Nothing came up in five minutes. They both just sat there watching. After a few minutes, the broadcast cut to a casual conversation with three reporters sitting on sofas. They started speaking about the speech at the Paris Science Conference and showed a clip of Shakti making the speech. Shakti placed her hand over her mouth. Hikaru's jaw was on the floor. They used words like *Rockstar Canadian Student* and *Shame on you* hashtags and *Shakti Devi Clairemont*. Shakti wanted to be flattered, but something in her stomach turned, and she reached for her arm and scratched violently.

"Shakti, stop that," Hikaru said sternly.

"Did you see that? I have to call my parents." Shakti called her mom and dad. She instructed them to put Channel 24 on, then call her back.

Hikaru pulled his phone from his front pocket and searched her name up. "Shakti! Your speech has over two million views!" Hikaru was excited.

"Shut the front door!" Shakti yelled.

"I'm texting Zoe," Hikaru said.

Her phone started ringing after a few minutes. It was her mom and dad on a conference call. They were talking over each other rapidly.

"I don't understand what you're saying," Shakti said loudly for them to hear her.

Gayatri won. "Honey, Dad and I just saw the speech. I think I'm having a stroke."

Harrison, not to be outdone, said, "Shaks, my heart is still racing. Your speech is out of this world! What came over you?"

"Thanks, guys. I don't know. I was really feeling Zoe's pain, and I could not let the topic of the hurricane go unacknowledged. All those people lost their lives. It was an unprecedented loss to the world. I thought it should be treated this way."

"You're absolutely right!" Harrison said. "I've never been prouder in my life."

"Me too, honey." Gayatri's broken voice cracked up. "I've been waiting for this moment since you were born."

"Mom, you were? Angel Gabriel told you about it?"

"He didn't tell me exactly what it would be. But he did say your actions will change the world. He also said you would be in danger.

But I haven't really noticed anything crazy, other than the Jinns coming to our house that one time."

"Yes, Mom." Shakti didn't have the heart to tell them about the Jinns this time. She decided to keep that to herself. "Mom, we should all be extra careful. There could be some backlash."

"You're right, Shaks. I want you home for the next few days. See if Zoe and Karu can stay with you," Harrison said.

"Okay, Dad. Karu is here right now," Shakti assured her dad.

"Okay, great," Gayatri said. "I have a class to teach in a few minutes. Love you both."

"Bye. Love you, too." Shakti hung up and turned her attention to Hikaru.

"How did we not see this?" Hikaru said, referring to the enormous attention surrounding the speech. "I know we were travelling, but how did our parents miss it?"

"Because we've all been preoccupied with Zoe's family and taking care of them. Which, by the way, was time well spent."

"Yes, I agree. I'm still in shock. Mr. Edgar sounded particularly impressed with you."

Shakti giggled. "He's funny. I bet he's showing off to all his principal friends."

The doorbell rang, and Hikaru ran to answer it. It was Zoe.

She walked swiftly to where Shakti was sitting. "Shakti! Did you see the news? You're famous!"

Shakti laughed nervously. "Geez, I did not expect this." She scratched her arms again.

Hikaru yelled again, "Stop that! Zoe, look! Look at what Shakti is doing to her skin."

Zoe walked up to Shakti and inspected her arms. Shakti pulled her arm away gently, feeling embarrassed. Zoe bent down and lifted Shakti's loose pyjama pants and revealed long scratches lined with dried up blood on her legs.

Zoe dropped it and covered her eyes. "Shakti!" Then looked at Hikaru, who looked like he was impaled by an imaginary stake. Zoe held Shakti's hand and sat next to her. "You came to take care of me, but it looks like we need to take care of you."

Hikaru sat on the adjacent sofa. "Zoe, you're going through so much, too. I can look out for Shakti."

"Nonsense, you both are my best friends. If Shakti is going through something, I want to know about it and help in any way I can."

"Come with me into the living room. I'll fill you in on everything. It's better Shakti just stays here and relaxes. I don't want her to relive it."

Zoe turned to Shakti and asked, "Is that okay with you?"

Shakti nodded her head, up and down. Her anxiety had become evident to those around her. She was more bothered that she didn't realize it was so bad until she saw it on their faces. Despite being best friends with Hikaru and Zoe, she was still sorely embarrassed. Feeling weak and not able to control herself, she sank into the sofa and pulled a blanket up to her chin. They left the room and whispered through a long conversation.

*   *   *

Hikaru told Zoe everything. Her eyes welled, and she sat down staring at the floor in sadness. She understood that the loss of Grandma Mae and Aunt Lucy triggered Shakti to change the direction of the speech. Shakti's love for her friends poured into the message she gave. Hikaru hugged Zoe, and they wept for a few seconds. Shakti did not even try to eavesdrop. It was okay not knowing what they were saying. Hikaru also told Zoe all about the Jinns and their threats about the King.

After half an hour, Zoe came back to Shakti with a red face and puffy eyes. She knelt beside her and hugged her tightly. Tears flowed from Shakti's eyes but kept a blank look. Zoe and Hikaru were scared for their friend. Shakti didn't feel anything at that moment.

"Where is your nail clipper?" Zoe asked.

"I'll cut my nails. Promise." Shakti smiled.

"Okay, Karu. When Shakti's parents are at work, we will take turns staying with her."

"Yes, good idea," Hikaru said. "School starts in ten days."

"Yes, that's right. That's something to look forward too. Right?" Zoe smiled reassuringly at Shakti.

* * *

In the next eight days, the speech turned into a circus on the news. No one could predict the whirlwind that would follow. It sparked spectacular praise and severe criticism from political pundits and environmentalists. Climate change deniers called her divisive and irresponsible, while others hailed her as a climate change activist. Canadians revered her as their new golden child.

Shakti's parents were bombarded with attention. They tried to shield Shakti from the frenzy, but it was hard to ignore. Young people around the world rallied and protested for climate change reform. It was not clear if Shakti's speech incited this movement, but it seemed to light a fire within them. Shakti's initial call to plant billions of trees around the world seemed to be getting traction. Reporters reached out to Mr. Edgar in a bid to interview Shakti, but her parents turned them down. They thought the only way to protect her would be while she was at home. However, when school started in a few days, she would be easily accessible. Harrison and Gayatri decided to drop and pick her up from school to prevent this. Never did they imagine that Shakti would gain international recognition from one speech.

Hikaru and Zoe kept a close watch on her arms and legs. They made a promise between the two of them that they would tell Shakti's parents if it got any worse. The attention Shakti received from the media and the Jinns sent her spiralling down. The scratches became shorter and more intense. It was not long before Hikaru told Gayatri about it.

At first, both Harrison and Gayatri were deeply heartbroken but pulled it together and made a plan to get counselling.

"What is she going to tell them? The Jinns were bothering her? The King is coming?" Hikaru asked. "I think you should get into contact with Vidia and find a more appropriate solution for her."

Gayatri and Harrison seem to like that idea. Gayatri said, "You're right, Karu. Thank you for looking out for her.

Hikaru and Zoe took turns spending time with Shakti at their various homes. On Friday before school commenced, Agnes came over to Hikaru's house, where Zoe and Shakti were. She excitedly announced that Winston would be home that evening after three weeks in Jamaica. Zoe excused herself and went back with her mom to prepare for his arrival. Shakti texted her parents to tell them the good news. Mark came home from Guelph upon hearing about Winston's arrival. All three houses were on alert, waiting for him.

Harrison was happy to have his friend return, but he thought he would give him space to be with his family. Mark left around 4:00 pm to get his dad from the airport. Zoe and Agnes prepared Winston's favourite vegan dishes. Mary cut flowers from their garden.

Shortly after 6:00 pm, they heard the purr of the Porsche. Harrison sprinted out of the house with Gayatri and Shakti. Agnes, Mary, and Zoe were already outside, waiting for the SUV to park. Hikaru and his parents came out of their home, and each family stood in front of their respective houses. They noticed all the neighbours came out, too. It seemed the news of Winston's relief trip to Jamaica made its way around the neighbourhood.

Mark parked in the driveway, and out stepped a shard of Winston. His tall frame pronounced by a frailer and thinner version of himself. Winston's appearance had been radically altered by his sharply cut off dreadlocks, which had been replaced with short, uneven, dishevelled hair. A pinkish bruised nose and lips, blistered and patchy, revealed a dehydrated state. His right hand wrapped in a makeshift bandage showing apparent signs of injury. Winston stood up with poor posture and limped one step forward.

Agnes stood for a few seconds with a dropped jaw and disbelief in her eyes. She couldn't comprehend what she was looking at. Where were his glorious dreadlocks? They all wondered. Winston's previous healthy face was reduced to sunken cheeks and collapsed under eyes that did not look like him. Undoubtedly, Hurricane Kali claimed another victim. Agnes ran up to him, ahead of Mary and Zoe, and hugged him while crying out loud. He hugged her lightly with little strength to reciprocate. Zoe and Mary tried hugging their dad as well. Zoe cried, and Mary smiled. Mark peeled his mom off Winston to allow him to embrace his daughters. Winston bent down with obvious pain and kissed his girls.

All the neighbours watched the family reunite. Some wiped their eyes, and some stood in sombre silence, even the mean neighbours. Hikaru and his parents decided to give them privacy and went into their house. Harrison resisted the urge to walk over and shake Winston's hand, but he waved at him instead. Winston squinted and waved back with a genuine but weak smile. They understood each other. Harrison gave him time to be with his family and went back inside with Gayatri. Shakti looked past Winston's battered state. Instead, she saw an aura so bright and white, it sent chills down her spine. His light danced around him energetically and trailed behind each limp step he made. She wondered if his aura was the reason for Mary's smile. She had never seen an aura so bright.

What did Winston do in Jamaica to earn these lights? she wondered.

Harrison sat quietly with a distant look on his face. Gayatri reassured him that the most crucial thing was Winston was home safely. Shakti clung to the window, hoping someone would emerge from the house again.

Later that night, Harrison received a worried call from Agnes asking him to accompany her and Mark to the hospital with Winston. Harrison agreed immediately and offered to drive. He got dressed quickly and out the door he went. Zoe and Mary came over, dressed in their pyjamas. Zoe looked nothing short of traumatized.

Rightfully, Agnes became worried about Winston's distressed look. His health seemed in peril as he was not responding the way he should and ran a high fever. Harrison left with them in a hurry.

Gayatri received Zoe and Mary with maternal love. They had not eaten because they were busy taking care of Winston. Gayatri rushed into the kitchen and microwaved leftover dinner for the sisters. Zoe was anxious about Winston's health, but she smiled and spoke gently to Mary. Shakti recognized her worries and held her hand. She turned to Mary to pump her up for their sleepover. Mary laughed and spoke loudly, excited for her first sleepover. Shakti prepared her room with a mattress made nicely on the floor for her and Mary. She gave Zoe her bed.

* * *

The hospital's emergency room was packed. Harrison dropped the three family members at the door and parked. He joined them inside and tried to make Winston comfortable. While Mark and Agnes took care of forms and check-ins, Harrison sat with his friend. He tried not to engage him in conversation in an attempt to save his strength. Harrison inspected Winston's hair, thinking it looked like he cut it off in a hurry with a knife-like object. He missed his dreadlocks. They were a defining feature of Winston's wholesome identity.

Winston's wrecked exterior made Harrison emotional, but he hid it well. He bought a bottle of juice from a nearby vending machine and fed it to him with a straw. A couple of hours later, Winston was set up in a room with an IV. The nurses tended to his multiple wounds and dressed his broken finger in a proper splint. Winston was also severely dehydrated. He sustained many lacerations across his body, but his left leg bore the deepest of all his wounds. It became the source of infection and invited septicemia, causing him to limp as he did.

They stayed with him all night. It was a scary night for Mark and Agnes. They told Harrison he could leave if he wanted, but he wanted to stay with them. They were happy to have him. Agnes instructed Mark not to tell Zoe and Mary about the depth of Winston's condition. It would only worry them. He tried to oblige but told Zoe they were keeping Winston for his wounds and to treat a blood infection.

Winston roughly got through the night. The doctor came in to check on him in the morning and wanted a full report on why he was in the condition he was in. Agnes explained he had gone to Jamaica to save his mom and sister, but he had not been able to, and she too was in the dark about his severe condition. Winston's story touched the doctors and nurses. Harrison walked by the front desk and overheard the doctor telling the staff of Winston's heroism.

CHAPTER 20

WATCH
THIS

Kira, Shinzo, and Hikaru showed up at the hospital early with breakfast for all three and a special vegan meal for Winston. Since they were doctors, Shinzo and Kira spoke to the doctor on duty and got the full report on Winston. Shinzo explained to Harrison they were concerned, as Winston's life was in danger because of the advanced septicemia. Agnes asked Gayatri to bring Mary and Zoe to the hospital to see their dad. Gayatri did this happily. Shakti came along too.

*   *   *

Winston was asleep the entire duration of their visit and they stepped quietly in and out of the room. They all huddled in the hall to discuss Winston's condition. Mary held Shakti's hand the entire time and eventually led Shakti back into the room with Winston. Mary looked at her dad on the bed and slowly closed the door to the private suite. Shakti stood aside and wondered what was going through Mary's mind about her dad.

Does she understand the severity of the condition he's in? she wondered. Mary looked at Winston and held his hand. She then closed her eyes and took deep bated breaths. Shakti couldn't help but follow along, too. It was like involuntarily reciprocating when someone yawns. Shakti took deep breaths matching Mary's pace. She glanced up at the clock. It was 8:55 am. Then the second hand on the clock slowed to a stop. The air became electric, and Mary's astral form popped out of her while she was standing. Shakti gasped.

Was this safe for Mary? she wondered.

Her physical body stood frozen as if she were asleep while standing. However, Shakti had a lot of faith in Mary. Winston's aura reappeared and shone bright, causing Shakti to squint.

Mary's astral form looked at Shakti and smiled warmly. She became the old soul Shakti was familiar with. She turned and said to Shakti, "Watch this."

Mary lifted her little hands over Winston's head. A brilliant emerald-green light appeared at the foot of the bed. Shakti switched her attention to it. Then it beamed to the top, causing the ceiling to disappear. Down floated an angel so pure and radiant, Shakti felt every pore in her body raise. The angel's eyes were sparkling green and full of dancing light energy. Dressed in a long green cape with gold embroidered thread, he smiled at her gloriously while surrounded by a glistening green aura. She held the bed to maintain her stance.

Mary looked up at the luminous being. "Hello, Angel Raphael."

"Peace be unto you, Mary." He beamed at her. "I see your father needs help today." The angel's voice could only be compared to church bells. It was melodious and healing. Shakti couldn't take her eyes off him. Her stress seemed to melt away as she watched his glow.

"Can you help him?" Mary asked sweetly. She looked at Winston with unconditional love as she stroked his aura.

"He's most deserving, and he has yet much to do." Angel Raphael smiled. He raised his hands, closed his eyes, and out beamed an emerald-green light. The green mist-like energy came out of his palms slowly. Shakti and Mary stared at it, spellbound by its luminosity and swirling nature. It encased Winston's body, causing him to levitate. The angel weaved the green light around him by spinning him horizontally. His smaller wounds were exposed, glowed green from within. Out of Winston's stomach, came a single file line of floating black dots. The dots were erratic and disturbing but contained in the line. Angel Raphael redirected the black dots to the ceiling, and out they went. Angel Raphael narrowed his fingers to remove the light and down floated Winston's body in a feather-like fashion. It was magical.

Mary watched with a soft smile. Her poise was otherworldly. Shakti was freaking out in her mind while Mary maintained stellar composure.

Angel Raphael looked at Mary again. "This will help him," he assured her. He then turned to Shakti and nodded his head. "Shakti, your speech brought us jovial tidings." He smiled with an actual twinkle in his eyes. "Don't concede to the Jinn. It is part of their plot. Allow yourself to break down before you breakthrough. Your tribe awaits you." A small spark from his finger leaped a little green light into Shakti's chest. "Meditate, Shakti. It will help you with your angst."

"Thank you, Angel Raphael," Shakti said graciously with a smile and tried to commit his riddle to memory.

"Thank you," Mary said as well.

Angel Raphael lifted off into the ceiling, and the room was normal again.

Mary's astral form re-entered her standing body. She opened her eyes and looked at Shakti and smiled.

Shakti smirked at her and said, "You're a superstar, Mary. You know that, right?"

Mary giggled and turned back to Winston and kissed him on the cheek, "Daddy." Her expression showered him with love. Shakti glanced up at the time, and it was 8:56 am. Time meant something different between the worlds.

Mark walked into the room just then. Shakti gave him a warm hug, and he needed it. He looked at Mary touching Winston's face and smiled.

Mark turned his attention to Shakti again. "Thank you so much. I don't know what we would do without you all. Your parents and Karu's parents are God sent." Mark's eyes filled with tears, and he broke down while cupping his face.

"Don't thank us, Mark. That's what friends are for." Shakti hugged him again. Mary was still focused on Winston, not paying any attention to them.

"I feel like I'm dying inside," Mark whispered, sobbing. "He almost slipped away last night."

"My God." Shakti exhaled. "It's okay to feel this way. You love your dad. But I think he's going to be okay," Shakti said with confidence after witnessing Mary's power to call upon the angels.

"I don't know what I'd do if I lost him. He's the best dad ever." He buried his face in her shoulder. "I think losing Granny and Aunt Lucy broke him." His sobbing made Shakti's throat feel tighter. His pain became hers as she gently rubbed his back.

"You're not going to lose him." She detangled her hug from him and held him by his elbows, then looked into his deep brown eyes, "Trust me, he's going to be okay." She shook him softly for him to really hear what she was saying. Then she glanced at Mary.

Mark nodded his head, "I'm not sure what you are saying or why I believe you. But I do." His sadness seemed to have lifted like a drifting balloon.

Shakti reached into her messenger bag, grabbed a tissue, and handed it to him. He turned away and wiped his face. Shakti said, "I'll leave you both alone to spend time with him."

Mark held her hand before she exited the door, "Thanks again, Shakti." He gratefully smiled. "Can you ask Zoe to join us?"

"Sure." Shakti exited the room and gestured for Zoe to come into the room. "Mark wants you to be with them." She touched Zoe's shoulder as she walked in. Zoe put her hand over Shakti's then entered the room.

CHAPTER 21
MAGICAL MARY

That evening came around quickly at the hospital. There was a lot of fuss around Winston. Shinzo asked a professional favour from the doctor to do extra tests on him. The doctor complied and rushed the test results. Agnes felt her head spin that day, but she remembered to check in with Mary.

Agnes held Mary's hand and led her into the Tim Horton's coffee shop on the main floor. Just the two of them sat for a moment and sipped hot chocolate. Mary seemed in good spirits, making Agnes grateful she lacked awareness. *Or does she?* Agnes wondered, looking at her beautiful daughter. She held Mary's hand and focused her eyes on her.

"Mary, look at Mom," Agnes said softly.

"Mom," Mary replied.

"Are you worried about Dad?" Agnes was not sure what to say or how to say it. She didn't have the strength to find the right words.

"No, Mom." Mary sipped her hot chocolate gleefully. "He's going to be good."

Agnes looked up at Mary, almost surprised. "I hope you're right, baby."

"I am right. Angel Raphael told me so," Mary said with confidence.

Mid-sip, Agnes stopped cold. "What did you say, sweetheart?" Agnes felt her heart pace quicken.

Mary didn't pick up on her mother's shocked tone. She has spoken to her family about fairies and angels before, but this time it was relevant to the situation. Agnes knew from her Catholic upbringing that Angel Raphael was the angel of healing. It made Agnes emotional immediately.

She was aware that Mary was a different kind of child. Over the past years of Mary's life, she displayed spiritual proclivity. It was an unspoken truth in their family. They each saw her visit them at night, her connection to nature and her gentle, loving soul. Agnes didn't press Mary to repeat what she said, she heard her the first time. She noticed Mary looked tired. They finished their drinks and hustled back to Winston's room.

Harrison sat next to Winston, looking at his phone. Gayatri stood by the window, looking out at the busy Toronto street. As Agnes entered with Mary, Harrison got up, offering her the chair to sit. She gestured him to sit back down. Gayatri turned to greet Agnes with a smile.

"Do you mind if Mary stayed with you again tonight?"

"Of course not," she whispered. "All your kids are welcome to stay with us. We have lots of room."

"Thank you, Gayatri." Agnes, still feeling emotional from her conversation with Mary, teared up.

Gayatri pulled her in for a warm hug. "No problem. Would you like me to take Mary home now?"

"Yes. She looks tired. She'll probably go to bed early tonight. Don't be surprised if she goes outside to walk around in the garden." Agnes looked over at Mary touching Winston's face again. Her head was placed on his pillow while she was standing.

"What about Zoe and Mark?" Gayatri asked.

"I'll send Zoe and Mark home later with Harrison, if that's okay."
Harrison said, "No problem."

Agnes added, "Mark will not leave me here alone. So he will probably take a shower and get clothes for me and come back to the hospital."

"Whatever works for you. There is space for everyone. I better be off with Mary and Shakti." Gayatri grabbed her purse and headed for the door. "By the way, where is Shakti?"

"She was just here with Zoe and Karu. They went to the waiting room," Agnes said as she kissed Mary goodbye. Mary kissed her dad two more times on the cheek and left with Gayatri.

*   *   *

On the ride home, Mary was excited once again to have another sleepover at Shakti's house. She was particularly hyper. Winston didn't allow her much sugar or dairy in her diet, so the hot chocolate made her bounce.

Shakti laughed, looking at her. "What's up with you?"

"She's sure full of energy!" Gayatri laughed as well. "Let's put it to good use. How about we go to High Park for an hour. You two can run around for a bit, and then we will go home for dinner."

Shakti looked at Mary sway side to side excitedly. "Yeah, I think it's necessary." Shakti laughed loudly. It felt good to have a normal moment. She adjusted herself to face forward again. "Mom, I'm worried about starting school on Tuesday."

"I know, honey. I thought you'd be," said Gayatri. "Are you worried about all the attention you will get after the speech?"

"Yes, partially that. Also, I'm not sure what the next steps are." Shakti looked worried again. "The news speaks about me like I'm an overnight celebrity. Like I have all the answers. The only suggestion I have is to plant more trees."

"Well, that's good enough for now. I mean, you are an overnight celebrity. You should feel proud of your impassioned speech. But, keep in mind, this can have a dark side. You really have to be careful who you trust. Just as the public reveres celebrities, they are also scrutinized relentlessly. They will not hesitate to enjoy your mistakes, as well."

"I know, Mom. I guess when that bridge comes, I'll cross it."

Shakti couldn't think about it anymore. Mary was singing loudly. It shifted Shakti's thoughts once again to her childlike state. She thought that Mary was good for her soul.

Gayatri pulled the SUV into a parking spot she luckily scored. It was like winning a lottery to get a spot at the beautiful park on a Saturday. All three jumped out and ran towards the south side of the park. It was the most beautiful side. There were huge old trees with a vast shaded area. Many people were playing games, jogging, picnicking, and walking around. Gayatri and Shakti had come to this park several times during Shakti's childhood. It was special to them. Shakti always loved spotting the back of her house from across the pond. It was a game they would play together.

Shakti held Mary's hand and walked over to the water edge. She played the same game with Mary. She told her one of the houses was hers, and she had to guess which one. Mary squinted her eyes and looked intensely. The houses appeared tiny across the pond, but she took some time and seemed to catch her bearings. She then pointed at the right house. Shakti cheered loudly and swung her around.

"You got it!" Shakti yelled. "You're so smart!"

Mary laughed loudly, loving the attention from Shakti.

Gayatri walked over and noticed they played the game. "Mary, you found your home from all the way across the pond?"

"Uh-huh!" Mary laughed, feeling proud of herself. "All by myself!"

"Good for you!" Gayatri double high fived her.

After the excitement, Shakti walked back with Mary to the rolling hills under a shaded area. Gayatri was preoccupied talking to friends from the neighbourhood who she hadn't seen in years. Shakti and Mary sat quietly, looking at the view of their homes. Mary watched the children run around and play. There was a group of kids with disabilities nearby. Some were in wheelchairs, and some were accompanied by adults in uniforms. Mary looked at them with great interest. One boy waved at Mary, and she laughed and waved back at him. He looked no older than fifteen years old.

Mary pointed at another boy in a wheelchair and smiled. Shakti put her hand over Mary's extended arm, bringing it down. She didn't want to appear rude to the caretakers and children that Mary was pointing. But Mary was persistent. She kept pointing.

"Look, Shakti, he's asleep."

"I can see he's asleep, but don't point," Shakti said softly.

"No, look. He's sleeping and playing." Mary showed Shakti again and again. But Shakti did not understand what Mary was trying to say. Mary looked frustrated. "Breathe slow, Shakti."

Shakti then figured it out, although confused. She followed her instructions. Shakti closed her eyes and took deep breaths. Slowly. But she was not working fast enough for Mary's liking. Mary pulled Shakti's ballerina flats off her feet and exposed her bare feet to the grass and soil to ground her to the energy of Earth. Shakti thought this was very odd but didn't fight it. She continued to breathe slowly. Just then, Mary laid backwards on the grass, and out she popped in astral form. By the time, Shakti's eyes opened and could see the spiritual realm, Mary was there waiting for her.

"What took you so long?" Mary joked.

"You were rushing me." Shakti laughed. "What do you want me to see so badly?"

"Look!" Mary pointed once more to the boy sleeping in the wheelchair.

Shakti looked over at him. She gasped upon seeing him run around in astral form playing with fairies. He ran and skipped and jumped. Shakti cupped her cheeks, as she could not believe what she was seeing. A boy restricted by a wheelchair could play unrestrictedly in the spirit world. Shakti tried to make sense of it. The boy spotted Mary in astral form a short distance away. He came running up to her and held her hand. They ran around and played together.

Mary seemed to know the boy well. *But how?* Shakti wondered. She had so many questions. She kept watch of where her mom was, but everyone seemed to be moving slowly. Even the joggers ran slowly. It reminded Shakti that time moved faster in the spirit world. Making it appear that the physical world moved slower.

Mary came back to Shakti and her body a short time after. "That's my friend, George."

"Really?" Shakti asked. "That's great. How do you know him?"

"Oh, we've played together many mornings since I moved here. He lives close by with his friends at a special home. Many of them come out to play in the morning. There's George, Ali, Lexi—"

"Mary, what do you mean they come out to play?" Shakti interrupted her, noting most of them had disabilities that would restrict their movements.

"In astral form, Shakti," Mary said it like it was obvious. "No restrictions there."

"I see. That's amazing!" Shakti smiled. "You better jump back in your body. My mom is done talking to her friends."

She turned to George and yelled, "Bye, George! Meet me in the morning!"

"Sure, Mary! Love you!" George yelled back.

By the time Gayatri made it to them, Mary was awake, and Shakti pretended she hadn't just witnessed the coolest thing in the universe.

"Let's go," Gayatri said, looking at her watch.

Magical moments seem to be a regular part of Mary's life, Shakti thought.

* * *

When the test results arrived, Shinzo took them from the nurse ahead of the doctor on duty. He looked at Winston's bloodwork. His face adjusted with a sigh of relief, revealing favourable results. He removed his glasses and wiped his sweaty forehead.

"The infection has regressed." He glanced at Harrison and Agnes. "His other levels have evened out, too."

"Thank God." Harrison clasped his hands. "The kids are in the room. Let's go tell them."

Shinzo walked into the room with Winston's doctor and shared the news with Agnes, Mark, and Zoe. Their faces lit up with hope that Winston would recover. Winston's doctor did not mind at all that Shinzo took the reins. He spoke to Shinzo with respect as Shinzo had more seniority than him. They discussed the case further with Agnes paying attention carefully.

"Do you know when he will wake up?" Agnes asked.

"He's not in a coma. He's just depleted. The more he sleeps, the better it is for his recovery," the younger doctor said.

"Thank you, both, so much." Agnes felt her tears coming on again. She couldn't say anything else.

Zoe stepped up and said, "Yes, thank you for saving our dad." She embraced her mom.

"My pleasure." The doctor left the room.

Shinzo announced he was leaving. Harrison offered to take the kids home, and they all left. Agnes gathered herself and wiped her eyes. She sat next to Winston and held his hand. They were all alone. She ran her fingers up and down his arm, moving around the bruises. Her stomach churned, thinking of what hell Winston went through in Jamaica to put him in such a weakened state. He was a statuesque man that commanded attention as he entered a room. He wore his dreadlocks like a crown, wrapped precisely on top of his head and banded with a stitched cloth to match his clothes every time. Agnes always admired Winston's ambition and environmental awareness. He represented strength in her mind. Looking at him now made her tremble. His once glorious dreads cut short without care. His body frail and bruised and appeared starved.

Agnes leaned her head down on the bed next to his shoulder and sobbed. She held his fingers with one hand and wrapped her stomach with the other. She wondered if her kids would ever recover from the trauma of seeing their once mighty father fall to this state. She didn't even have the bandwidth to mourn the loss of her amazing mother-in-law and Lucy. She always looked forward to their visits. Granny spoiled her with foods she liked and helped out with the garden. Lucy was her confidante. Lucy's dating life in Jamaica was highly entertaining to Agnes. She also was their children's only aunt, and they loved her deeply.

Deep into her sorrows, Agnes felt Winston's fingers grasp hers. She sat up straight and paid attention to his face. He was coming to. His eyes struggled to open. She rubbed his hands. "Honey, I'm here," she said excitedly but softly. "Take your time. You're in the hospital in Toronto, sweetheart."

Winston peeped through with long slow blinks. His eyes focused, looking forward and then looked over at Agnes. She leaned over and smiled at him.

"Hi. I'm here," Agnes said, smiling and crying at the same time. He tightened his grip on her fingers and managed to smile.

"Hi," Winston whispered. His eyes were now fully awake, and he looked around the room.

"The kids just went home with Harrison and Gayatri." Agnes lifted his hand. "They were here all day."

Winston smiled bigger to show he was happy to be back in Toronto and with his family. "I dreamt Mary."

"You did?" Hearing his voice made Agnes beam from within. "What did you dream?"

"I don't remember, but Mary was there. I think she was taking care of me," Winston tried to recall.

"She's been showering you with kisses while you slept." Agnes laughed. "So, your dream is right."

Winston smiled, thinking of his kids. "Can you tell them to come back?"

"Of course!" Agnes pulled her phone out of her pocket, and speed dialled Mark. He was excited to hear Winston was awake. He said he would bring Zoe and Mary over right away.

After half an hour, the three kids burst into the room. Winston was sitting up and looking a little more himself. He embraced his kids. It was a second reunion, and he was present this time. Winston's health vastly improved over the next few days. He was released from the hospital on Monday. Although still weak, he was on the road to recovery. His wounds healed, all signs of septicemia receded, and his leg did not hurt anymore. Miraculous, indeed. Agnes did not ask him what happened in Jamaica yet. She did not want him to relive the moments. She thought she would get the full story when he was ready.

CHAPTER 22

FIRST DAY, LAST YEAR

The first day of school started with the three friends feeling unprepared. It was their final year of high school, and they took no time to appreciate that a lot would change in the next year. They were all preoccupied with Shakti's struggle with anxiety and Winston's impetuous return. But the day was here, and Harrison and Gayatri were the most worried. They did not want Shakti to be mobbed by cameras and news reporters or anti-climate change protestors. The speech had taken a life of its own. Shakti purposely avoided the frenzy.

Shakti stood at the back door, staring out at the vegetable garden. It was 7:00 am, and her parents were still upstairs, getting dressed for work. She disarmed the alarm, walked out into the backyard and took deep breaths. She wanted to calm her mind. Within seconds, the Clans came into focus. They did their usual routine and bustled about taking care of nature. A few fairies flew around her. She smiled a little with them and continued to look into the forest. The sparkle of the pond could be seen from a distance, and she got lost in it for a minute. She wondered if the Jinns would start coming around her if she stayed out long enough.

Shakti rubbed her arms and legs lightly over her clothes. They burned from a night of anxious scratching. She talked to herself briefly and firmly. "You got this. They want to see the girl who did that speech in Paris. I'll show them." She thought she sounded a little crazy, but it felt good to say it. "My goal is to help save the planet. Planting trees is the way to do it." Shakti closed her eyes and took one more deep breath before returning inside.

Harrison was in the kitchen, cracking eggs. "Hey, Shaks. Good morning."

"Morning, Dad." She closed the back door and walked over to Harrison and semi-hugged him.

"Are you nervous about today?"

Shakti pulled the chair from the table and sat down. "I was. It's all I thought about all night. Now I don't care. Whatever comes my way, I'll deal with it."

"That's all you can do." Harrison wasn't his usual jovial self. "You can call Mom and me at any time, and we will come to school if you need us."

"I know." Shakti smiled to ease the tension. She sensed Harrison had a sleepless night, too. "Don't worry about a thing, Dad. I have Karu and Zoe. They will stay with me the entire time. Karu and I have some classes together. Also, it's our final year, and we have to maintain our grades."

"That's right, school comes first," said Harrison holding her to her promise.

"I know."

The Clairemonts had breakfast, cleaned up the dishes and quickly made their way to school. They arrived early to avoid an awkward entrance. Harrison and Gayatri walked Shakti in and sat in the office until Mr. Edgar had a few minutes to talk to them.

"Good morning, Clairemonts!" Mr. Edgar said. He still looked like he was on a high from Shakti's speech and was way too upbeat for Shakti's mood.

"Good morning, Mr. Edgar," Harrison said. "We know it's the first day of school, so we won't take much time."

"No worries. Tell me, what can I do?"

"We haven't had a moment to talk to you since Shakti made her speech." Harrison smiled.

Mr. Edgar beamed with pride and glanced at Shakti. "Yes, true."

"My wife and I want to be as clear as possible. We do not want anyone outside of the school to approach Shakti for an interview or to talk to her. It doesn't matter if they are from a government institution or environmental organization or from the news. No one is to approach her without our written permission." Harrison's business leadership qualities showed.

"I understand and agree fully. The first priority is the safety of our students. No one outside of school will speak to her without your permission. In fact, I'll inform my staff about it, too."

"Thank you, Mr. Edgar," Gayatri, sitting unusually quiet, finally said. "We appreciate all that you have done to protect Shakti in the last few weeks."

"Ah yes, it was not easy. I got up to fifty calls a day of people trying to reach Shakti," Mr. Edgar said. This information surprised Shakti, but she sat there unfazed.

Harrison and Gayatri finished up the conversation quickly. They exited the office and walked Shakti out to the hall.

Gayatri looked at her watch. "There is still twenty minutes before the bell rings. We will sit with you until Karu or Zoe arrives."

"It's okay, Mom. I'll sit right here and wait for them." Shakti was mindful of her parents having to start their busy days. They said their goodbyes and kissed her forehead.

Shakti watched them leave reluctantly. The sadness in their eyes as they glanced back at her, made Shakti's throat tighten. She could only imagine what was going through their minds. She knew they would be worry-stricken all day, so she decided to send them texts intermittently during the day to assure them she was doing well.

Shakti sat on the bench in the hallway. She wanted to check on the garden but didn't want to go outside the school. The hall was empty and quiet. Kids started trickling in one by one. She didn't make eye contact with anyone to avoid conversations. She kept her eyes on her phone and got lost in it. She felt someone approach and stop in front of her. She looked up with hesitation.

It was an older man. Perhaps a father or teacher. He was stick-figure-looking and had a smirk on his face.

"Well, if it isn't the famous Shakti Devi Clairemont," the man said abhorrently.

"Yes. Do I know you?" Shakti was cautious.

"No, my dear. You don't know me. But you soon will." He walked away in the direction of the office.

Shakti did not understand what that was about. She was already dealing with the day ahead of her and had no time for a rude man. She picked up her backpack and walked to her locker. She passed Mr. Edgar's office and saw the same man speaking to him. It didn't look like a pleasant conversation, as the office staff were on their feet paying close attention to their confrontation.

Shakti continued walking and turned the corner. Leaning on her locker door, with one foot propped up, was Hikaru waiting for her. Butterflies flooded her stomach. Shakti was happier to see him than ever. She must have felt alone and scared if Hikaru could initiate such a reaction. She walked right up to him and hugged him.

He was surprised by her hug, but hugged her back, tapping her back awkwardly. "You okay?"

"Yeah, I'm fine. I'm not looking forward to today."

"The first day back is the hardest. Then everyone will forget you're a celebrity and go back to ignoring you." He meant well, but he was not the smoothest guy.

"That will be best-case scenario," she said. "Let's get to class early to avoid an awkward entrance."

They picked a spot to the front left corner of biology. It was closest to the window and Shakti thought she could easily look outside to avoid stares. Of course, that did not happen. The biology teacher, Mr. Marco, came into class and greeted them. He immediately did a double-take and accosted her.

"Shakti!" he shouted. Hikaru and Shakti were the only ones in the classroom, and they both jumped.

"Hi, Mr. Marco." Shakti forced a big smile.

"I'm thrilled to have you in class. I loved your speech. You are all over the news!" Mr. Marco seemed to have a talent for the obvious. "There's been a lot of talk about your whereabouts."

"I know. I've been at home, avoiding it." Shakti hoped he would take a hint.

"I see." Mr. Marco reeled it in. "Well, it's a pleasure to have you and Hikaru in class." He sat at his table and emptied his briefcase.

As kids started coming into the classroom, Shakti turned her back to them and faced the window. Most didn't notice her, but a few did. There were whispers. It seemed to make Hikaru more uncomfortable than it did Shakti.

At the bell, Mr. Marco got up and introduced himself. As he did the roll call, he got to Shakti's name and skimmed over it, marking her present. Shakti noticed and appreciated his alertness.

Almost three-quarters way into the class, an announcement came over the PA system. It was Mr. Edgar. "Shakti Clairemont please come to the principal's office. Shakti Clairemont please come to the principal's office."

Mr. Marco glanced at Shakti. They made eye contact, and he nodded his head to excuse her. She rose from her seat and gathered her things, amongst many whispers, all eyes on her.

"Do you want me to come with you?" Hikaru asked.

"No, it's okay. Thanks." Shakti glanced at him. "I'll see you in the next class." Then, she left quickly.

Shakti wondered what it was all about. She passed her locker and quickly put her backpack in it, then hustled to the office. She was greeted by the office staff with smiles, except Mrs. Muller, who looked at her with concern. She led her to Mr. Edgar's office and opened the door. She whispered, "Good luck."

It was a full room, including her parents. She walked in slowly and looked around. Sitting at the desk was her parents, Mr. Edgar, the rude gentleman from the morning, and three other people she hadn't seen before. The tension was sharp. The look on her mom's face said she had ripped a few jugulars before Shakti arrived. She knew that look. Harrison smiled, but it was for show.

"Come in, Shakti," Mr. Edgar said. Mrs. Muller closed the door behind her. "Don't worry, Shakti. We called your parents in to discuss a matter brought forward by Mr. Nickels."

Shakti glanced over at the staunch-faced man glaring at her. Gayatri looked like she wanted to decapitate him. Shakti cleared her throat. "Okay."

"Mr. Nickels is a lawyer on the Toronto School Board and a parent of a student in our school." Mr. Edgar glanced down when he said that. "He has brought forward a request to have you suspended for your speech in Paris."

"Suspended?" Shakti blurted out. "Why?"

Gayatri interjected abruptly, "Shakti, don't worry about this ludicrous request. We will get a lawyer and fight Mr. Nickels head-on." If looks could kill, Mr. Nickels would have been dead.

Mr. Nickels, with his legs crossed and his hands clasped on top of them, said. "Your actions have brought immeasurable embarrassment to our school and board," he started. "Did you realize you were representing our school and all Canadian students when you went to Paris?"

"I was very aware of that fact." Shakti felt her anger creeping up. "It's interesting that you see it this way because the rest of Canada and the world for that matter, thought I represented my country in an excellent manner."

"We at the school board were not some of those people," Mr. Nickels snapped back.

"The rest of the school board? Or just you, Alan?" Gayatri growled. "Let's just call this what it is. You are asserting your authority as a means to get back at us."

"Get back at us? Why would he do that, Mom?"

"Oh, yes, I should mention that I am Travis's father. You know, the boy whose nose you broke." Mr. Nickels took a lot of pleasure saying that. The other three people from the school board gasped and stared at Shakti.

Mr. Edgar stood up. "Mr. Nickels, do I need to remind you that your boy, Travis, is a well-documented bully at this school," Mr. Edgar said indignantly. "Travis pushed Shakti's friend, causing him to hit his head on the concrete. Shakti was protecting him. So please, if that is your purpose of bringing this request forward, please leave. I have better things to do on our first day of school."

"That is not the point of this!" Mr. Nickels yelled back. "She is a loose cannon and embarrassed our school." He looked directly at her. "Who do you think you are, young lady? To make such a ridiculous request like planting billions of trees around the world. And speak in such a scolding manner to generations before you. The audacity! You're an embarrassment!"

"Exactly who is embarrassed?" Harrison asked. "Mr. Edgar isn't embarrassed."

"I'm proud, actually," Mr. Edgar added.

"I'd like you to call upon the school board, while we are sitting here, and tell us who is embarrassed." Harrison turned to the woman sitting in the room. "Are you embarrassed by Shakti caring about the future of our children?"

The lady looked up at Harrison and then Mr. Nickels. "Of course not! I really don't know why we are here, Alan."

Mr. Nickels looked furious. "You're here because this kind of behaviour is unacceptable! It will set a dangerous precedent that students can behave in any manner while representing our board."

Seeing Mr. Nickels come undone, Gayatri laughed out loud in an attempt to really ruffle Mr. Nickel's feathers. Then she dropped the coup de grace. "Mr. Nickels, you are a climate change denier. Shame on you!"

Shakti couldn't help it. She burst out in laughter with Mr. Edgar following suit. He stopped himself immediately to be professional. The three other board members looked annoyed by Mr. Nickels wasting their time. They got up and apologized to Mr. Edgar and the Clairemonts and exited without Mr. Nickels.

They hastily opened the door and Mrs. Muller almost stumbled in after being pressed up against it. Mr. Edgar glared at her, unimpressed. She straightened her oversized blouse and exited the room without saying a word. Mrs. Muller peeped at Shakti before she turned the corner and winked at her. Shakti smiled and looked down. While her parents and Mr. Nickels continued to bicker, she took a deep breath feeling relieved. Shakti looked back up at them to refocus on what they were saying. Floating over Mr. Nickels were several Jinns, whispering in his ears. It startled her. Mr. Nickels was being influenced by the Jinns. She remembered Angel Michael telling her that the Jinns will try to get to her through people and organizations.

She had an idea she wanted to test. She interrupted the group discussion. "Mr. Nickels." They all stopped talking. "I would like to apologize to you for breaking Travis's nose."

Harrison, Gayatri, and Mr. Edgar were shocked.

Shakti continued. "I know it was a long time ago, but I owe you and your family an apology. Travis was wrong for bullying my friend, but I should have never thrown that bottle."

Mr. Nickels didn't know what to say. The Jinns above him stopped and hissed at Shakti. She knew she was getting through to Mr. Nickels. The Jinns looked furious! She interrupted their influence on Mr. Nickels. He started to soften up towards her, and by default, stopped listening to them. "Thank you for that," Mr. Nickels said softly.

It seemed to cut the tension. The Jinns started to leave one by one. Shakti felt great about her decision to apologize. She realized Jinns worked on people's vulnerabilities. It takes one person in an argument to be the bigger person and put a stop to it.

Mr. Edgar dismissed the meeting shortly after. To say Mr. Nickels was pleasant after would be a stretch, but there was definitely a change in tone. It seemed he was less mad when he left, but he still swung the door open and left in a hurry to keep up with appearances. Gayatri and Harrison urged Shakti to hurry along to her next class. Shakti waved at them and left. The staff smiled at her for real this time. They already knew the outcome of the meeting, thanks to Mrs. Muller eavesdropping. Mrs. Muller looked particularly pleased.

Shakti couldn't wait to tell Hikaru and Zoe all about her meeting. She hustled to chemistry class on the other side of the school. Hikaru had a chair next to him reserved for her. He asked her what happened, and she gestured that she would tell him during lunch. All the students' attention went to Shakti at first. She was the Speech Girl in school now. They went through all their classes with kids talking about her. But few people approached her to talk about it. She was happy about that.

The rest of the day was uneventful. She told Zoe and Hikaru all about Mr. Nickels. They had a good chuckle and totally missed the point of how Shakti got the Jinns to leave. They were stuck on Shakti's mom calling him a climate change denier.

After school, the trio went to check on their vegetable garden. As always, they were happy to see kids working on it. It looked better than ever. Shakti noticed again the advanced rainbow auras of the kids working in the garden. Something about tending to nature made their auras glow. Some of them spoke to her about the trip to Paris and the speech. It was clear to Shakti and her friends that kids across the world wanted to do better.

A kid leading the conversation asked, "So what are the next steps? How do you plan on planting trees in Canada?"

Shakti contemplated the question and said, "I haven't had a minute to figure it out. But I guess it would involve getting the government involved."

"I can help you with that. My dad works for Environment Canada. He's an engineer," the kid said.

"That would be great. We need to start. Canada should be the country to lead this forward," Shakti said.

"Not really," Aarti said in the background. "India, China, and Ethiopia are leading the way for tree planting."

"Hmm. That's great to hear. We need to catch up then." Shakti shook her head. "Canada has the land. We should be on top of this. It looks like we found our newest project for The Garden Club."

Hikaru smiled. "It looks like we did!"

Zoe added, "I'll get started on it right away. We need a plan on how to execute this." Just like that, Zoe was project managing the tree project.

"We need everyone's help with this. It's a gigantic project," Shakti said, looking at the kids in the garden.

They all looked excited and agreed to help.

CHAPTER 23

FIRST, NOVEMBER

The first week of school stumbled by. Shakti barely got through it emotionally and mentally. There were many long stares and repetitive conversations. However, Shakti had Zoe and Hikaru there to distract her. Reporters and activists made many attempts to approach her. Hikaru was always there to shoo them away. They didn't make it within spitting distance of her before he yelled at them. Shakti noticed that the Jinns also kept a distance when she was at school.

One day, a group of climate change deniers spotted her leaving school alone. They came running towards her with their signs and shouted foul language at her. Hikaru and Zoe came out of the school just then, and Hikaru took off in a sprint towards them, shouting, "I'm calling the police!" They saw him bolting towards them, and they turned around and ran away. Zoe made her way to Shakti and pulled her back into school.

"Are they gone?" Shakti asked Zoe as she looked out the window.

"Yes," Zoe reassured her. "I see Karu standing by the street with his hands on his hips. The only thing he's missing is a broom," Zoe joked. "I'm pretty sure he's swearing at them."

Shakti couldn't help but laugh. "I don't want Karu getting into a fight over me."

"You know how he is." Zoe giggled. "Our dear, Karu."

On many days after school, there would be one persistent journalist who tried to talk to Shakti. Her name was Iris Pavlopoulos. She would not make it within twenty feet of Shakti without Hikaru grunting at her to go away. But she didn't give up. Sometimes she would shout the questions at Shakti, "How do you feel about your speech?" and "Are your parents proud of you?" Shakti would carry on to her parents' vehicles pretending not to hear her. Then she would enter the car and scratch her arms and legs until someone yelled at her. She thought she was doing quite well, considering the attention on her.

Within a few weeks, they already saw the tree project taking shape, thanks to Zoe's managerial skills. Hikaru and Shakti were on the research side of the project. Zoe asked Mr. Edgar for help getting volunteers to assist with the task ahead. They had an excellent reputation at school for pulling off these types of projects. However, Mr. Edgar thought this time they were in over their heads.

Shakti finally reconnected with Vidia and Marty since she returned from Paris. She told them all about the visions and speech. Vidia was enraptured with her story of the rainbow auras popping up. She was used to this world, but she thought this was truly something special.

"I knew it!" Vidia cried out, "It was you all along. I only get guidance for a good reason."

"I suspected," Shakti confessed, "But I only knew for sure after the speech."

"It's a true honour," Vidia said. "Rainbow auras are a sign of enlightenment. The Rainbow Tribe has awoken." Vidia held her chest as tears escaped her eyes. Shakti looked out of the window to avoid intruding on Vidia's epiphany.

"But why me?" Shakti asked, "Why did they choose me to do this?"

"Shakti, the truth is, they chose lots of children to activate the tribe." Vidia paused, not sure if she should say what she was about to. "James was also chosen."

"James?" Shakti said, surprised, "How do you know this?"

"Because Angel Gabriel came to his mother," Vidia confessed.

"What?" Shakti blurted out, "He came to my mom, too. So, he just goes around choosing random pregnant women?"

"No, my dear. It's not like that at all. The saving of the planet is much more important than any one person. Therefore, within the Rainbow Tribe, there would be several kids who would be up to the task. Do remember, Shakti, that no one knew what the task of the Warrior would be."

"But James died for it." Shakti cared about James like she knew him, "Was it worth it?"

"A child taking his life is never worth it, Shakti. His parents are ruined now." Vidia had that look on her face again. It came about whenever she spoke about James, "But it's not just about James. It's about saving the planet for future generations."

Shakti was torn between feeling annoyed by Angel Gabriel misleading her mother into believing that Shakti was the chosen one and feeling appreciative that his method was effective. It certainly took some of the specialness away from her. "I agree, Vidia. I guess it's partly my ego talking. But you're right. It's not about me or James. It's about getting the Rainbow Tribe to make changes to the world. Although, I wish he hadn't misled my mom."

"Judging from the Jinn's hatred of you, I'd say you've been very successful."

Shakti needed to ask, "Do you think they are telling the truth about the King? Or do they just want to scare me?"

Vidia hesitated to answer Shakti. "Who knows?" She seemed to choose a middle ground, neither denial nor full truth. "Shakti, promise me something."

"Okay." Shakti said reluctantly.

"Promise me you will always pull upon the White Light of Protection when needed and you will call upon the Angels if you're ever in trouble."

Shakti sighed, sensing a fear from Vidia she hadn't seen before. "I promise." She smiled. "So you do think he's coming for me?"

"No, Shakti. I just want you to always be prepared. I will always send protection energy, too."

"Thank you, Vidia," Shakti whispered, lost.

*　*　*

Shakti was crystal clear on how to slip in and out of the spiritual world. It only took a few deep breaths, although sometimes she would change frequencies without trying. She mastered navigating the physical world while seeing the spiritual world. She did not like to do it much, as the Jinns still bothered her. She only felt safe in her vegetable garden and the school garden to explore the spiritual world. The promise of the elementals buzzing around her reminded her that she was safe. There she would meditate and sometimes do yoga when at home. As a result, her anxious itching began to lessen. It was never gone completely, but it certainly improved.

The trees behind her house were already putting on a show of colours for fall. They changed the mood of the forest from graceful greens to romantic yellows. Shakti noticed the gnomes' hats would change colours too for fall. They were the only elementals that changed their outfits according to the season: orange for fall, white for winter, green for spring, and red for summer. During winter, the summer fairies would hibernate, and snow fairies would come out. She knew this, thanks to Mary. The trolls didn't have anything interesting about them. They were the same old grumpy trolls all year round. She tried many times over the years to get them to like her, but they usually ignored her. Except for that one time, of course, when the troll warned about the Jinns and called her stupid several times.

A couple of times while sitting on her back porch with her parents, she would look over at the Sutherlands' backyard and see Winston smoking. He looked like his strength was coming back. His short hair changed his appearance completely. Harrison checked on them often but was careful not to smother them. Winston was a lot quieter after Jamaica. He still hadn't talked about what happened, and no one pressed him.

Zoe mentioned here and there to Hikaru and Shakti that she was still worried about her dad. He always seemed to have an underlying sadness in his eyes. Zoe thought in time, it would go away. Agnes accepted the new Winston and was just happy to have her husband home. Winston eventually spoke to her about Jamaica, but told no one else.

By the end of October, The Garden Club recruited scores of students from the school and surrounding schools to help with the tree project. Shakti became used to seeing the dance of rainbow auras from the kids that came forward to help with the project. They used every resource available to them to talk to the right people and ask for help wherever they could.

Shakti was so busy with school and the tree project that she didn't have a care in the world that her seventeenth birthday was fast approaching on November first. Hikaru and Zoe planned on doing something special for her. But they could not figure out what to do. Her birthday also fell midweek, which was an awkward time for a party. They spoke to her parents for suggestions.

"I have a really great idea," Hikaru said to Harrison. "We need a few long extension cords and a ladder."

"I have both," Harrison said excitedly.

Shakti's parents never got to throw Shakti a party since she was painfully introverted growing up. She didn't even want a party for her sweet sixteen. Her parents ended up taking her to the movies instead.

Halloween night, the trio hung out at Shakti's house handing candy out to the neighbourhood kids. Zoe and Hikaru became simultaneously tired and said they were going home to sleep early.

Shakti found it strange that they both were tired early since they both loved staying up late. She didn't think much of it. Gayatri announced she wanted to go to the mall to do some shopping on Halloween. Shakti figured it must be a full moon because everyone was acting weird. She accompanied her anyway to a nearby mall. They sipped their chai lattes and walked about the mall.

"You know what? I'm going to buy you a present since your birthday is tomorrow!" Gayatri announced.

"Oh! Okay. I really wanted these wireless headphones..."

"No!" Gayatri interrupted, "I would like to buy you a dress to wear for your birthday!"

"A dress?" Shakti said, confused. "What are we doing for my birthday? It's on a Wednesday."

"I know, but I realized you don't have many dresses, and Dad and I want to take you for a fancy dinner tomorrow night."

"I can wear pants, Mom."

"Come on, let me buy you a dress." Gayatri was convincing.

They both walked around the mall, and Shakti settled on a trendy sweater dress, perfect for fall. Gayatri also splurged on a beautiful brown leather jacket for Shakti. It matched the above the knee fall boots she was wearing. Shakti left the mall excited about her birthday.

November first started like any other birthday. She woke up between her parents on her bed. Every year, they climbed into her bed early in the morning of her birthday. She loved it. Then two pings to her phone. Hikaru and Zoe texted *Happy Birthday!*

Hikaru and Zoe were all smiles that day for Shakti. They appeared tired, though. Shakti was all about the tree project and the progress they had made.

At 5:00 pm, Harrison picked Gayatri and Shakti up at the house. Shakti took extra time to get ready in her new grey sweater dress, grey quilted stockings, and matching brown leather jacket and boots. She blow-dried her hair and wore makeup. It was her birthday, after all. She stood in front of the mirror, looking at her ensemble, smiling and feeling pretty great.

Harrison made reservations at a gorgeous restaurant in Yorkville. It was a beautiful mild evening in Toronto. Leaves swirled on the fancy lit streets of Yorkville, posh as always. Women dressed stylishly in high heels and huge wraps around their shin-length dresses. It was a workday; therefore, men looked smart in designer suits and shiny shoes. Shakti wondered if she'd live this life in downtown Toronto when she was a young urban professional. Shakti was in the middle of university applications. She knew her grades were high enough to enter any field of profession. She wondered if Zoe and Hikaru would attend the same university or if this would be the end of an era.

"Honey, what would you like to drink?" Gayatri asked, with the waiter standing next to her.

Shakti realized she was lost in thought. "Oh! Sorry. Can I just have a virgin mojito?" Shakti did not want to be lost in racing thoughts all night. She wanted to be present and enjoy this time with her parents.

"Sure." Gayatri made their drink orders, and the waiter left. He returned a few minutes later with their drinks.

Harrison raised his glass of wine. "Happy seventeenth birthday, Shaks. We love you."

Shakti and Gayatri raised their glasses too, and the three enjoyed their dinner. They laughed and talked about many things. Shakti loved spending time with her parents. She wondered if all teenagers felt this way or if she was just one of the lucky ones. Either way, she figured she had the coolest parents in the world.

Harrison paid the bill, and a waiter approached the table with a slice of truffle cake and candle stuck squarely in the middle. Shakti blushed and acted surprised. They did this every year. Gayatri and Harrison sang, "Happy Birthday." Shakti's cheeks became flushed from smiling. The Clairemonts shared the slice of cake, and off they went.

When they arrived home, Gayatri paused and said, "Let's go to the backyard for a bit. It's such a warm, beautiful night for November."

Shakti figured her mom made the suggestion since it was her birthday, and Shakti loved being back there.

"Yeah, sure."

Harrison led the way along the side of the house and entered the backyard. "It's so dark already," he noted. "You're right, G. It's such a beautiful night!" Harrison said out loud while stretching. "Oh my God. What's that?" He pointed into the woods.

Shakti looked quickly thinking it was an animal. "Where?"

"It's there. Look!" Gayatri said.

Shakti was no stranger to seeing odd things in the forest. She was all over it. "I can't see it! What is it?"

"Let's see." Gayatri led the way as they stepped into the forest, just past the backyard.

Shakti followed closely, holding her dad's hand for protection, thinking it might be a wild animal. "I still don't see it. It's pitch black."

They stood twenty feet into the woods, then suddenly lights flicked on in rapid succession.

"Surprise!" a band of people jumped out from behind trees. Hikaru stood in the middle with joined extension cords in his hands, smiling. His face glowed, and Zoe stood closely behind him with her arms in the air.

"Aaahhhggg!" Shakti screamed out loud, frightened out of her skin, and almost fell backwards. Harrison grabbed her hand to make sure she didn't fall. A circle of trees was lit with hundreds of strings of small white lights hanging from the branches and wrapped around the tree trunks. Zoe, Hikaru, Mark, Mary, and a slew of other people stood around laughing at Shakti's response. She focused in to see their faces. It was the kids from The Garden Club and some of Mark's friends. Shakti could not talk. She was in shock, her first surprise party.

The woods were absolutely beautiful. The lights hung down ambiently, creating a whimsical effect on the trees. Like a slow-burning fire, the woods became hauntingly romantic. Shadows cast by the kids on the backdrop of the forest appeared like giant roaming ghosts.

There were a few tables set up with drinks and treats. All thirty-something kids gathered around Shakti to wish her happy birthday and hug her. She was still in a daze, feeling overjoyed and overwhelmed.

"How did you guys pull this off?" Shakti said.

A few kids laughed.

Hikaru pointed behind him. "Everyone here showed up for you, Shaks. The Garden Club came out last night to hang the lights, and Mark and his friends set up the speakers on the trees."

"Speakers? Where?" Shakti said, looking around to spot speakers. She spun around slowly with her head slightly tilted back, taking in the sight of lit trees. "The lights are a dream come true. I always wanted to do something like this."

"I know." Hikaru blushed. "That's why we did it."

This reminded Shakti of how thoughtful and sentimental her best friend really was. He had so much more to him than his sarcastic wit. "It's perfect, Karu. Thank you so much." She hugged him tightly and didn't let go for a few seconds.

"I took care of the cake," Zoe said proudly. "It's Death by Chocolate from Kate's."

"Of course. Who else would make such a big decision?" Shakti laughed as she hugged Zoe. "Thank you so much. You two are the best friends anyone could ask for. How did I miss this?" Then she figured it out. "Ah! That's why you two became spontaneously tired last night," she said with air quotes.

"Yes, the lights took forever. But we all pulled it off." Hikaru felt very pleased with himself. "Thank goodness The Garden Club members showed up."

Shakti turned to the group. "Everyone, thank you so much for this!"

A party for Shakti in the middle of the woods, spoke volumes of her love for the trees. Mary hugged her tightly, understanding better than anyone. Kira, Shinzo, Winston, and Agnes joined the party soon after. They sat in the backyard with Harrison and Gayatri while the teenagers played music and mingled in the woods, a safe distance away.

On a huge rock, some kids sat while others danced. Zoe, Hikaru, and Shakti stood together, watching the party unfold in disbelief.

"Does this mean we're cool now?" Hikaru whispered into Shakti's ear.

"Judging from this party? Definitely!" Shakti laughed. It was just a joke between the two of them. Zoe wouldn't get it because she was actually cool.

Mark and his friends, including Zoe, stood in their circle. Mark glanced at Shakti several times, smiled and looked away. He waited until she was alone to leave his group and made his way to her. Shakti watched him walk slowly towards her, as her heart rate quickened. He stared at her intensely as he walked through the crowd. The lights in the background seem to twinkle to the beat of the music each step he made.

"Hey." Smouldering as ever. "Happy birthday." He smiled, frustratingly handsome under the golden lights. His hair faded to the sides, transitioned seamlessly into a light stubble.

"Thanks." Shakti blushed so hard her cheeks contracted involuntarily.

"I like your jacket. You look beautiful," he said.

She wanted to say that he was the most beautiful thing these woods have ever seen, but instead she said, "Thank you. How come you're not in Guelph?"

"I drove down with my friends, for you." Mark turned up the charm. Shakti's knees shook, and her heart pounded. She was afraid he would hear it.

"I see." She smiled and lowered her gaze. "That's very nice. Thank you. Oh! And thank you for setting up the speakers."

"For you, anytime." Mark touched her cheek lightly and walked away.

Shakti's heart pretty much exploded all over the forest. Was Mark flirting with her?

Aarti was standing close by listening to their conversation. "Hubba hubba!" She squinted naughtily. "Who's that?"

Shakti was surprised that anyone else was within shooting distance. "Oh!" She laughed. "That's Zoe's brother, Mark."

"He's downright dreamy," Aarti said enthusiastically. "Shaks, you need to be all over that!"

"Me? No, no. He's like...Zoe's brother."

"Yeah, you said that already. Everyone is someone's brother. He's into you," Aarti pressed.

"You think?" Shakti had just enough humility to doubt the obvious.

The Garden Club's members particularly enjoyed their time. They rarely sat on the rock, which was all the seating available. They wanted to dance and take advantage of the mid-week party. Shakti was on a natural high all night. Hikaru was her unintentional hype man, getting the party going. Mark played music off his phone that connected to speakers. Everyone danced at some point.

The parents glanced over a few times to make sure no one went too deep into the woods and close to the pond. Shakti wondered if the trolls would be angry that the lights were hanging off the trees. She made a mental note to remove them the next day and clean up the space. After some time, Agnes walked into the woods and took Mary home to sleep. Shakti hugged her goodbye and promised to send her a piece of cake secretly.

Close to 10:00 pm, the parents joined the party and did some odd dance moves, or at least Harrison did. They announced it was time to cut the cake because it was a school night. Zoe clicked her heels and rubbed her palms, excitedly. She ran up to a table and removed a mesh covering and revealed a stunning marble two-tier cake with a topper with the number seventeen. The crowd was wowed by its fancy exterior.

Both Zoe and Hikaru stuck seventeen candles in the cake and proceeded with the birthday chorus. Shakti, feeling shy again, walked up behind the table to face the crowd. As they sang happy birthday to her, she closed her eyes, took deep breaths and made a wish. She wished for her family and friends to be safe. She also wished for the tree project to become a reality. As she opened her eyes, fairies and gnomes came into focus. They lined the branches watching the crowd enthusiastically. Shakti touched her chest, feeling wistful. She was happy her elemental friends showed up to celebrate her, after all, they were her first friends.

Shakti quickly scanned the area for Jinns. None were in sight. She figured her mom had something to do with it. Shakti blew all seventeen candles out in one breath. Her friends and family cheered, concluding a brilliant birthday night. As the parents and a few friends cleaned up the woods and turned off the lights, Shakti could not remove the smile from her face. It was stuck there, causing her cheeks to ache.

Perhaps being social and extending my circle is not such a bad thing, she thought.

CHAPTER 24

RUN,
SHAKTI, RUN

ikaru circled the classroom, thinking. The Garden Clubbers stepped out of his way. His pacing annoyed Shakti, but she said nothing. The Tree Project reached a wall they couldn't seem to overcome. They all did their part in organizing, fundraising, and networking for the cause. When Zoe queried the idea to the environmental board, they said it was not viable. A project of this proportion would cost too much money and would need approval on every level of government. The Garden Clubbers were devastated. What would it take to get the word out? They required public support, and Shakti was their only hope of having an audience.

"I have an idea," Zoe said while she searched for something on her phone.

"Well, spill it." Hikaru stood with both palms out.

"I am going to call Shakti's very own stalker and leverage the crap out of her," Zoe smirked.

"Geez, could you speak English? Who is Shakti's stalker?" Hikaru folded his arms and rolled his eyes.

"I am calling Iris Pavlopoulos." She dialled the number to the network where she worked. "She wants an interview with Shakti, we will give it to her."

"No way! She gives me the creeps!" Shakti said out loud.

Zoe looked up at Shakti indignantly, "Shakti, do you want the Tree Project to become a reality?" Zoe snapped. "Yes or no?"

"Obviously, yes!" Shakti answered assertively as well, startled by her tone.

"Then learn to be stronger," Zoe replied. "And think of the bigger picture here."

Shakti was taken aback by her harshness. Zoe allowed nothing to get in the way of her goals. Shakti glanced at her feet, feeling embarrassed and insulted by Zoe's public scolding.

Hikaru and the rest of the Clubbers looked at each other awkwardly. "Umm…perhaps we should at least hear what she has to say. Remember, the project is bigger than any of us."

Shakti shrugged, feeling hurt still. Zoe left a message for Iris, mentioning that she was a close friend of Shakti's.

Picking up on Shakti's mood, Zoe said, "Shakti, I know it's hard for you to be the centre of attention. But the one thing that stood out to me in your speech was, break every barrier and when they say no, do it anyway."

Shakti immediately softened. "I know. You're right. I'll pull it together to deal with her. I didn't want to talk to anyone from the media or see my face one more time on the news. I hated being picked apart. But this is bigger than me."

"Good job, Shakti." Zoe smiled. "We will all be right there with you. All we want is for a reporter to interview you, and you get a chance to pitch the Tree Project. It's essential that you appeal to the public and government to get on board with this."

Hikaru sat on the table, munching on something, "Yeah, the public has wanted to hear from you since the speech. You've been in hiding. You're the only one in that position here." He swallowed whatever he was eating. "No pressure."

"Listen, I'll do it. We need to come up with a plan. Karu, remember when we pitched the vegetable garden to Mr. Edgar?"

"Yeah."

"You had an aerial image of where the best location for the garden would be based on using land that was unused, and proximity to water, and just the best place for it to thrive."

"Yeah."

"Well, we need to do some research on where it would be ideal to plant billions of trees." She paused, realizing how ridiculous that sounded. "Well, we would need several locations."

Hikaru finally stopped chewing. "That's going to be difficult to assess. I don't think I have the resources for that."

Aarti was standing next to Hikaru. "You don't need to come up with exact locations for the trees, that's not our job. You should come up with a wish list of the ideal types of locations based on the types of trees. Leave that up to the government." Her point made the room buzz. The club members seemed to unanimously agree with Aarti.

"That's a fantastic point, Aarti," Zoe said. "Let's get started on this. I'll deal with Iris and set up an interview. Aarti and Hikaru, can you both deal with figuring out the ideal type of locations?"

"We sure can!" Aarti said with a big smile. She seemed excited to work with Hikaru.

"Shakti, you figure out the most efficient way to plant so many trees." Zoe made notes while she spoke, "She will need help with that. So please step forward if you're interested in assisting."

Zoe was steering the ship. Hikaru and Shakti were happy they did not have to. Also, Zoe's voice projected a lot louder than theirs. Four students walked over to Shakti, willing to help with her part of the project.

Zoe then dismissed the meeting. "See you all next week. Tuesday, same time, same place."

Hikaru, Zoe, and Shakti decided to walk home that day. The trees were almost bare, but it was still quite mild. It was the first time they walked home all semester since Shakti was hounded by the media. They walked slowly and stopped at the park for a few minutes and sat on a bench, watching little kids run around the playground.

The trio left and continued lazily towards their street. They parted ways and entered their homes. Apart from the Tree Project, their work at school was intense, and they had many big decisions to make about their degree choices.

On Tuesdays, Gayatri taught a night class at U of T. She would not be home until later, so Harrison would buy dinner for Shakti and him, so they wouldn't have to deal with the cleanup. After 4:00 pm, Shakti received a worrying call from Harrison.

"Hi, Shaks. I have some bad news."

"Oh! What happened, Dad?" Shakti said quickly.

"There was a fire at the factory. We don't know how it started or why. But thank God, no one was hurt."

"Oh no! That's awful. I'm glad everyone is okay." Shakti was incredibly sad to hear this. "How bad is the damage?"

"The fire trucks came fast, so they were able to contain it quickly. It could have been much worse." Harrison sounded overwhelmed at the thought of his factory on fire.

"It's okay, Dad. You have insurance. It will be rebuilt. No one was hurt. That's all that matters."

"You're right, Shaks. I better go. The firefighters are still here investigating. I won't be home for a few hours. Can you order food?"

"Yes, of course. Don't worry about me. Did you tell Mom?" Shakti asked.

"Yes, I told her as soon as I cleared the factory out. The fire was still raging. I knew that if I didn't tell her right away, I'd have another fire to put out." Harrison giggled.

Shakti chuckled too. "Good call. I love you. See you when you get home."

She put the phone down next to her and took the news in. She was grateful that her dad and the workers were safe. She wondered if the worker angels were still there too and if they ran out because of the fire. Mid-thought, the doorbell rang. She skipped off the sofa, assuming it was Hikaru or Zoe. Without looking through the peephole of the solid oak door, she swung it open.

To Shakti's genuine surprise, it was Bill, "Oh! Bill." She was surprised to see him.

"Hello, my dear!" Bill said jolly as ever, "I'm sorry to show up like this, but it was imperative."

"Oh no, is everything okay with Vidia and Marty?"

"Yes, they're okay. Are your parents home?" Bill glanced in.

"No, but they will be soon," Shakti said cautiously.

"Oh no, I would have preferred if they were home when I came to talk to you. Maybe I'll just come back another time," Bill said, looking disappointed.

"Umm…you can tell me if you'd like." Shakti realized it must have been important for Bill to show up at the house unannounced.

"Are you sure?" Bill asked.

"Yes, sure. Come in." Shakti opened the door wider and allowed Bill to enter. Any friend of Vidia's was a friend of hers, she figured. He came in, removed his shoes, and followed Shakti into the kitchen.

Shakti offered him a drink, and he said he would have tea. She prepared the tea as per his request and plated some cookies. She made herself a peppermint tea. They both sat at the table and exchanged banal pleasantries while waiting for their teas to cool.

"Can I get a napkin?" Bill asked.

"Sure" Shakti walked over to the island and pulled the third drawer open and grabbed the fancier red napkins to give to Bill.

"Thank you, my dear."

Bill somehow didn't seem in a rush to get to the point. Shakti thought this was weird because he had said it was very important. However, she just sipped her tea and continued with the useless banter.

Shakti decided to press him about his mysterious visit. "So, can you tell me what was so importa…"

Shakti's head started to feel weird. She noticed her arms started going numb, and her tongue became heavy. She looked intensely at her hands as she flexed her fingers. Her vision blurred slightly, making her disoriented.

"What's that?" Bill said, sipping his tea.

Shakti slouched over and leaned heavily towards the table, making it shift slightly. She tried to ask Bill for help, but nothing came out of her mouth. Bill continued to sit there and sip his tea. Shakti was still conscious, and a feeling of terror swept over her. Her heart raced, and her forehead started beading sweat. What was happening to her? She cried on the inside.

Bill got up from his chair, and she felt him walk over to her. Her head was laying on the table, and her arms extended to her sides. Shakti lost all control of her limbs while her head felt like it was imploding. She glanced at the teacup right next to her face.

"You stupid, girl." Bill's voice changed from a jolly old man's lilting voice to a nefarious foe. "Didn't your parents teach you not to let strangers into the house?" He enunciated each word with a guttural push, causing Shakti to fade further into her hellish reality.

She whimpered, not being able to say a word.

"Surely, you did not think I showed up today by accident?" Bill laughed out loud, making Shakti go deeper into a calcified state. "Your mom works until 9:00 pm at the St. George Campus, and your dad had an unexplained fire at this factory." He smiled, leaning over right above her. His breath warm on her neck.

She became keenly aware that the fire was no accident, and Bill had everything to do with it. But that was the least of Shakti's problems right now. Why was he confessing this to her? What was he planning to do? She screamed in her head, and tears flowed from her eyes. Shakti was breaking.

Shakti had a choice to make, fall apart and accept what was about to happen or fight to the end. While she contemplated the options in her head, Bill held her hand and dragged her off the chair, knocking down the teacup. She fell foolishly off the chair and hit her shin hard on the solid wood table leg. It hurt, but she couldn't react. He dragged her haphazardly all the way to the sofa and lifted her with one jolt onto a lying position. Bill walked over to the adjacent sofa and sat down.

"Shakti, let me explain something to you." Bill positioned his body to face Shakti while she directly faced the large bay window overlooking the backyard. "First, you should know, my best talent is that I'm able to hide my aura from freaks like you and Vidia. That's why you were not able to see it. I've been playing the long game with those fools for over a decade." He scoffed and turned his nose up. "Vidia and Marty are insufferable. I hate them. Especially that cow, Vidia," He rolled his eyes in disgust. "She handed James to me, and now she handed you to me. I mean, it was too easy." Bill smirked.

Shakti could not believe what she was hearing. What did he do to James?

Bill continued the one-way conversation. "I asked Vidia if I could hypnotize James. Like a fool, she agreed. James was truly impressive, much more special and gifted than you," he snarled. "I implanted a thought in his head that he could never accomplish the task before him. I also implanted that he should take his own life because it was useless."

Shakti's heart rate spiked. She closed her eyes and wept. She took deep breaths over and over again. Soothing her soul as she went deeper into a trance. She felt the energy change rapidly around her, and she flicked her eyes open hoping to see angels. Shakti opened her eyes to a room filled with Jinns. They flew around the ceiling, round and round. They clustered over Bill's head, whispering in his ears. Shakti's heart sank further. The Jinns were heavy. She could easily see their hollow eyes. She wished she could light her sage stick, although that would not get rid of Bill.

"Shakti, here is what I'm going to do with you." He sat up closer to the front of the sofa and rested his elbows on his knees while he rubbed his hands, "I am going to hypnotize you. Don't worry. You won't remember a thing." He smiled like it was a bounty he bestowed upon her. "It's really a favour I'm doing for you." He laughed, then paused and became serious. "Because you see, my King wants you dead. And I am his faithful servant. But I'm no use to him if I'm in jail. Therefore, it's better you do the deed yourself. I'll even make some suggestions for you."

Shakti laid there, staring at the ceiling, petrified beyond reason or words.

Bill got up and walked over to her and slapped her leg. "Are you listening to me?" He looked angry as if she disrespected him. "You unappreciative little fool. It's better for you this way. Otherwise, he will come for you. And that would be far more terrifying."

He bent down over her. "You just had to make that speech, didn't you? Do you have any idea what you did?" he yelled. "You activated the Rainbow Tribe! You fool! The King's Guard has been working for centuries to stop that from happening!" Bill's voice elevated to a frightening pitch. "Do you know how many children lost their lives trying to do the same? You slipped under our radar because your mother knows how to keep a secret."

Bill reached into his pocket and pulled a chain with an odd pendant at the end of it. "This is my most prized possession and the ultimate refuge from being seen by the light side. It was given to me by the King himself." He shook his head up and down as if he was agreeing with himself. "Oh, you should see him. He's glorious and powerful. He trusted me with this task again, and I will not fail him."

Bill got up and stretched his arms in the air. The Jinns circled faster and faster. Creating a storm of dark energy in the family room. Shakti closed her eyes again and pulled the White Light of Protection around her, using only her mind. She opened her eyes, and Bill was standing over her in a trance of sorts. His eyes were closed, and he held the relic close to his heart, invoking a black mass of energy above him. Shakti glanced out the bay window to look at the sky to soothe her soul. To her surprise, she saw three gnomes looking at her. They were standing on the table right outside the window. She was surprised to see them there. They were jumping up and down to get her attention. She focused on them. They gestured with their little arms to come their way. One of the gnomes did the running man motion, gesturing for her to run! But how could she run? She was drugged. They kept telling her to run, Shakti had to try. There was only one man she had to deal with, and he was older. She could probably take him.

Shakti closed her eyes and asked for more than the White Light of Protection. This time, she called upon her guardian angel to release her from this state. Years of Gayatri teaching her to ask for help from her guardian angel flooded her mind. To her immediate surprise, her foot twitched.

That's a good sign, she thought. She willed herself to move her legs again. Bill still stood over her with his eyes rolled back. He was about to start a ritual with Shakti as the centre of it.

Shakti was able to get full motion in her arms and legs. However, the Jinns saw her move and zipped down to Bill to tell him. Bill opened his eyes quickly to check, and Shakti flew up and pushed him with all her might. Bill went tumbling over the coffee table, smashed the glass top, and landed on his head, then rolled over. Shakti could barely run. She dragged her left leg as her right leg was more alert. Shakti looked at Bill, and he was still down, but not out. She aimed for the back door, stumbling and tripping every few seconds. But the more she moved, the more mobility she got. It was like the blood started flowing again in her limbs. Her head was still thumping. She made it to the back door, but her fine motor skills were shot. She tried to unlock the little lock with her fingers.

Bill was getting up and spotted her trying to escape. "Get back here!"

His voice put Shakti into a panic, but she managed to open the lock and used her strength to slide the door open. Shakti stumbled out before Bill could grab her. She spotted the gnomes and followed them down the patio staircase, through the garden and into the woods with Bill close behind. Two of the gnomes saw he was too close to her and stayed behind while the other gnome led the way. As Bill descended the staircase with his round belly, both gnomes held a water hose across the step, sending Bill flipping over it and rolling down the remaining stairs. It wasn't enough to seriously hurt Bill, but it slowed him down. Shakti saw this and took off even faster, feeling the drug wear off slightly the more she ran. The gnome up ahead led her into the area with the largest trees. It was a favourite spot of hers. Standing in the middle was a troll. He usually looked angry, but this time, he looked concerned. He gestured to Shakti to follow him as she could hear Bill enter the woods.

The troll turned around and stopped suddenly, causing Shakti to trip over him, but she braced her fall.

He raised his hands to his mouth and said, "Be quiet, stupid."

Ahh, this guy again, Shakti thought.

The troll spun around once. Then stopped, and did it again. Shakti wondered if she should get up and run because she knew her way around these woods better than anyone. Also, it was getting dark.

The troll raised his hands and tiptoed as high as he could, then sang the most peculiar rhyme.

"My friends, old and wise, awake from your slumber.
It is me, Lorcan, your caretaker. Forgive
my request, I am here to protect,
A Warrior from expiration."

Shakti looked in awe of the troll, Lorcan, as he tapped his feet in a Morse code rhythm. The air became still, meaning time slowed down. The ground shook, and the trees vibrated, causing the few red leaves on the branches to shed. Shakti got up quickly and looked around. As the ground shook, Shakti was still feeling a little uneven from the drug. Suddenly, the largest tree in the area, a statuesque white oak, shook violently and cracked down the middle. It vibrated until the bark split down the centre and opened to reveal an entrance.

Shakti stood with her mouth open. The troll ran up to her. "Go inside, he's coming for you."

Shakti quickly snapped out of the shock and entered the bark of the tree. The tree vibrated again, and the bark closed. Right before it sealed, the troll looked at her and put his finger over his mouth, signalling her to be quiet. Bill was near.

Shakti stood still within the tree. The comforting smell of earth and bark filled the space. She heard Bill's footsteps walk by the tree. The leaves on the ground mapped his path in her mind. Every crunch made her heart sink further, and her chest tightened slowly. He circled the area slowly now. Shakti prayed the Jinns didn't tip him off to her whereabouts.

"Shakti!" he yelled at the top of his voice. "You're a fool! This was a mercy unto you."

Shakti heard him clearly. She closed her eyes as if to protect herself. She raised her hand slowly to cover her mouth in case she felt the urge to scream. Her face was wet with tears and sweat. Her clothes felt damp and clung to her.

"He will come for you!" Bill laughed. "For the first time, he will take care of a Rainbow Child on his own." He turned and walked towards the house. Shakti stood still until she could hear no more footsteps.

Shakti trusted the troll would open the tree when it was safe. She leaned her head on the bark of the tree, accepting its refuge. Fatigue swept over her like a wave. Her legs felt weak again, and her face drooped. She wanted to scream and cry out loud. She couldn't believe this happened to her. But she had to stay focused. A few minutes passed, and the tree vibrated. A crack from the ground grew upward. It opened wide enough to let her out again. She peeped out cautiously and stepped one foot outside. She didn't see the troll or Bill. She walked out, turned around and watched the tree mend itself. Her emotions poured from her eyes. She felt lost in her own neighbourhood. She had so much love for this tree and the elementals.

She bent one knee while facing the tree. "Thank you, beautiful tree." She was grateful beyond words.

A crunched footstep startled her, and she whipped around. It was Lorcan and the three gnomes. Shakti was relieved. She looked at them and bent down further. "Thank you, my friends. You saved my life." They looked at her.

The troll nodded his head and walked away. "Now, go away," he grumbled as he left.

The gnomes stood, watching her and smiling.

Shakti got up and dusted herself off. She wondered if it was safe to go back home. What if Bill was waiting for her? Suddenly, she heard the screech of a car and saw the lights turn into her driveway. Oh no! It was Gayatri. Shakti started to limp towards the house.

"Mom, no! Leave!"

Shakti ran as fast as she could but was still under the influence of the drug. Certainly, everyone would have heard that screech because Shakti was well over seven houses away, all the way at the back.

*   *   *

Gayatri had been warned by Angel Gabriel to rush home. He told her Shakti's life was in danger. As she raced home and made a right-angle turn into her driveway, her tires left skid marks on the road. The smoke of burning tires could be smelled all the way from where Shakti was. Luckily, she wasn't the only one to hear Gayatri coming. Kira and Agnes came running out of their houses alarmed and towards Gayatri.

"Gayatri." Kira sprinted past Agnes's house just as she was coming out. "What happened?"

Gayatri didn't answer and fumbled with her keys to enter.

"What's wrong, Gayatri?" Agnes came up fast behind Kira.

"It's Shakti!" Gayatri started crying. "It's Shakti. She's in trouble."

Gayatri didn't need to say another word. Kira pulled the keys out of Gayatri's trembling hands and opened the door. They entered to a horrifying sight. The chair was turned over, and the coffee table glass was smashed. Clearly, signs of a struggle. Gayatri ran around the house with Kira and Agnes shouting for Shakti, but there was no sign of her.

Kira opened the door to the pantry. Bill was standing there with a long kitchen knife in his hand. He pressed it into her neck just hard enough to not puncture her skin. Kira stood still with her arms in the air, terrified. He gestured for her to back slowly out of the pantry. Kira started sobbing. She backed out of the pantry. Bill did not have time to leave the house. His plan was to wait for Shakti to return and finish the job himself. He was highly agitated. His fear of his King was greater than the fear of going to jail.

As Kira stepped back with the knife at her neck, Gayatri spotted her from the kitchen. She was just about to go outside with Agnes to check the woods for Shakti. She pointed at Kira and gestured to Agnes to hide. Agnes crouched down to the floor and hid behind the large kitchen island. Gayatri ran around the other side and down the hallway before Bill peeped out to see them.

Standing outside of the pantry, in the serving area connecting the dining room and kitchen, Bill shouted out to the women to come forward, or he would hurt the woman under his knife. But before he could, Agnes came swooping around the corner with raised arms and a cast iron frying pan at the end of it. She smacked his head with all her force, causing him to slam to the ground on all fours. Gayatri appeared hurtling around the opposite corner of the dining room with a baseball bat and whacked him on the back. He rolled over to his side, stunned. Kira grabbed the knife and kicked him across the face. Bill laid on the floor in a fetal position. The three women held his arms and dragged him over to the sofa. Seemingly, karma visited this night. They sloppily plopped him on the sofa, and Kira pressed the knife to his neck, much harder than he did to her, causing a line of blood to run down his pressed dress shirt.

With her knee pressed firmly into his stomach, Gayatri did the talking, her voice scarily steady and her eyes, killer locked on to him. "Where is Shakti? What did you do to her?"

Bill was still recovering from the blow to his head. "She's gone."

Wrong thing to say. Gayatri stepped back to allow Agnes enough space. She raised the cast iron pan again to smash his face.

"Wait!" Shakti came through the back door. Gayatri screamed and ran up to her and hugged her tightly.

"You're okay! You're okay!" Gayatri bawled. "What did he do to you?" Her voice screeched to a deafening pitch.

"I'm okay, Mom," Shakti cried. "He tried to make me kill myself!" She pointed at Bill in a childlike way with a curled lip and tears washing her face. Agnes and Kira looked aghast at Bill.

Kira pressed the knife in a little more while Agnes collared him and pulled him up. "What kind of monster are you?"

"Ahhhhgggg," Bill screamed. He seemed to be aching from multiple blows and a stabbing knife in his neck.

"I'm pretty sure if we kill him, we will get away with it," Kira noted.

"He drugged my tea, but I ran away. The Clans helped," Shakti rambled but started to lose consciousness. Gayatri picked her up by holding her under her arms and laid her on the sofa. Shakti came around quickly after lying down.

Kira removed the knife from Bill's neck, but not before shoving it in a bit further. She went over to Shakti and checked her pulse. It was low, and she instructed Agnes to call the police and an ambulance. Bill laid on the sofa. Shakti looked over at him, and their eyes connected.

Shakti looked at Gayatri. "Mom, go into his pocket and get the chain and pendant out of it," Shakti whispered to her mom. "It's a deadly relic."

Without questioning her, Gayatri walked up to Bill, reached into his front pocket and yanked the hypnosis chain and pendant out. She gazed at it, feeling the dark energy. Bill became livid, and he tried to fight her for it. Agnes, still armed with the pan, raised her arms and smashed him again on the head, knocking him out.

"Is he dead?" Agnes asked. "Never mind, he's still breathing."

Everything after that night was a blur to Shakti. Police and paramedics came. Harrison arrived shortly after. She could hear him crying while he kissed her hands and face. She was still out of it. The effect of the drug lingered. The ambulance took Shakti to the hospital with Gayatri and Harrison. No other memories of the night were clear to Shakti. All she knew for sure was Bill was arrested and no longer a threat.

CHAPTER 25

IRIS PAVLOPOULOS

Gayatri and Harrison sat next to Shakti's bed all night. Their friends, the Akiyamas and Sutherlands, stood guard at the hospital room door until the late hours. Gayatri trembled while Harrison wrapped his arms around her to steady her. Shakti would make a full recovery. They managed to flush the drug out of her system. Shakti awoke groggy early the next morning to her parents on each side of her, sleeping in chairs. As soon as she moved her feet, Harrison and Gayatri awoke. They were happy to have her back. This time, Harrison couldn't hold back. He held her arm and leaned into her and wept. He felt powerless. They told her everything that happened. Bill was arrested. They were in the dark about the reason he came in the first place. Shakti shed some light on this for them.

After Shakti gathered her thoughts, she told her parents everything. Every last detail on the fire at the factory, the Jinns taunting her, the Rainbow Tribe, Vidia's connection to Bill, Bill's connection to James, and how the Clans saved her life. Gayatri and Harrison were bewildered. They sat listening to every last detail in horrifying cognizance. Shakti made it clear that it was not Vidia's fault. She too had been fooled by Bill for many years. Vidia taught her many valuable lessons, such as the White Light of Protection and how to ground herself in meditation. She told Gayatri that Angel Gabriel came to many women before her. How he hoped they would groom their children into awakening the Rainbow Tribe, and many Rainbow Tribe hopefuls were killed by the King's Guard when the kids tried to change the world. They were never held responsible because he made it appear to be suicide.

Gayatri covered her eyes and wailed. Her mournful cries came from within. Shakti closed her eyes and took deep breaths. She opened her eyes to a pulsating energy beating from the hunched over Gayatri. Her visceral cry rippled through the room. In a single moment of clarity, Shakti understood. Her mom, her sweet mom. It finally made sense. All those talks about love, changing the world, and guardian angels. The unexplained tears, the weight of raising her, the fear of losing her, and the mysterious visits from Angel Gabriel. It all started to come together.

Shakti told her parents the only reason she was not found out was that Gayatri kept the secret so well. Not even Harrison knew.

There was one more horrifying truth, Shakti needed to share. "He's coming for me."

"The devil?" Harrison asked with a fear that rattled his soul.

"Yes, Dad." Shakti glanced down to avoid seeing their faces. She couldn't bear the heartbreak. "But I'm not afraid anymore."

"How is that, honey? Please tell me, how are you not afraid anymore?" Harrison's voice shook, and tears escaped his eyes.

"Dad, I accomplished so much in the last year. Things I never thought I'd do. Things I couldn't even dream up," she explained. "Somehow, it works out. There is a team of angels, elementals, and guides on my side. They pull me through one way or the other. If the King wants to come for me, let him." Shakti's strength made Harrison's posture change.

"For some reason, I believe you, Shaks."

Gayatri was still deep in her tears, but she listened to every word said.

"We owe our friends an explanation. Agnes and Kira put their lives on the line last night," Harrison said. "We need to come up with a story to explain what this was all about."

"Dad, tell them the truth," Shakti said. "All of it, from the beginning. They deserve to know. However, swear them to secrecy. We can trust them."

"What if they make Karu and Zoe stay away from you?" Harrison asked.

"They wouldn't do that. We're in too deep. Also, Mary is a part of this story, too." Shakti said.

"You're right. They are invested as well. Also, wild dogs couldn't keep Karu away."

Shakti giggled. "You're right. I couldn't get rid of him if I tried."

Gayatri leaned over to the side table and pulled a few tissues. After wiping her face, she said, "We will talk to the parents alone."

"Yes, please. I can't have another conversation like this," Shakti said. "Mom, can you call Vidia? I need to talk to her, but not now. At a later time."

"Of course, sweetie." Gayatri got up from her chair and leaned over the bed and kissed Shakti on the forehead. "I'm taking a sabbatical from January. I want to be home with you for a few months."

"That's great, Mom." Shakti said happily.

Looking at Gayatri, Harrison said, "More time for the daddy, too." He was back. Relentlessly flirting with his wife was a telltale sign of a healthy Harrison.

Shakti rolled her eyes and slipped back into a sleeping position. "Ew. I'm going back to sleep."

Shakti returned home. The fight with Bill affected her more than she knew. She entered her family room and looked around feeling anxious. Harrison had removed the broken coffee table. There was now a bare spot where it once stood. Shakti got over her feelings quickly when she thought about that was ahead of her. She texted Hikaru and Zoe, *Home.*

Within seconds, the doorbell rang. Gayatri shouted from upstairs, "Don't go to the door. I'll get it."

She skipped down the stairs and looked through the peephole and smiled. It was Hikaru and Zoe. They came to see their friend. She let them in and locked the door behind them. Hikaru came with a basket of cupcakes he and Ki made for Shakti. They embraced their friend in one group hug with Shakti in the middle. She felt loved. The trio stood there for a few minutes, saying nothing.

Shakti led the way to the family room. She took a few minutes to catch them up on what happened with Bill. It disturbed them, deeply. Just then, Harrison and Gayatri announced they were going over to Hikaru's house to talk to his and Zoe's parents. Shakti knew they were about to explain everything to their friends, who deserved to know what was going on.

Shakti was thankful she wasn't privy to that conversation. "My parents are about to tell both your parents everything. From the beginning."

"Wow. I'm actually happy about that," Hikaru said. "There were many times I wanted to talk to my mom about what we were going through. But I didn't to protect you."

"Me too," Zoe agreed.

"I know it's all been a huge burden. Being my friend and all." Shakti's sadness showed, despite her efforts to hide it. "But I couldn't have done any of this without you both, and Mary."

"How so?" Zoe asked.

"She opened my eyes to so many possibilities in the spiritual world. About angels, elementals, energy."

"I'm so happy to hear that." Zoe smiled proudly.

"What are you going to do about the King coming for you?" Shakti could feel Hikaru's fear of losing her, even though he didn't like to show emotions.

"I honestly don't know. There is no real way to prepare for it. I'm no longer dreading it for some reason," Shakti contemplated. "You know that feeling when you're so hungry, that you're not hungry anymore?"

"No, no idea what you mean," said Hikaru.

"Okay, you know that feeling when you're so tired and finally you get to your bed, and you can't sleep," Shakti restructured.

"Yes, that I get," Hikaru replied.

"Yes, I know that feeling, too," Zoe said.

"Well, it's like that. I've been so scared since Paris. I scratched my skin off from anxiety. I hated to hear anything about the speech or the conference," Shakti explained. "I feel like I'm now so far past the level of fear that I no longer feel it. It's kind of liberating, actually."

"That's messed up," Hikaru blurted out.

"No, it's good." Shakti pulled her sleeves up. "Look, no marks. I haven't scratched in a long time." Her arms revealed smooth skin with only remnants of scratches. "When Bill came, that was the first time I was scared in weeks."

"Well, your life was in danger," Zoe added. "If you weren't scared then, I'd question your judgement."

Shakti giggled. "You're right. I'm trying to be stronger like you said, Zoe."

"Shakti, you're the strongest person I know. Forgive me for saying that to you. I had no right. Only you knew what you were going through." Zoe's eyes welled over and her lip curled.

"No, please. I needed that. Do you know I wasn't even afraid when you suggested the interview with Iris? I was just in the habit of saying no to everything." Shakti positioned herself to face Zoe directly. "I need my friends to be honest with me. Put me in my place when needed." Shakti noticed Zoe weeping and touched her hand and smiled. "Promise me, you'll always put me in my place when I need it."

Zoe shook her head in agreement and said, "I promise."

Shakti glanced over to where Hikaru was sitting. He was not there anymore. Zoe and Shakti turned to the kitchen and glared at Hikaru, digging in the fridge pulling a cake out.

"I think Karu needs an intervention." Zoe laughed.

"I would agree with you, but he's six feet two and one hundred and sixty pounds soaking wet," Shakti said. "He's a broomstick. I'm guessing all that food goes to height."

"Yeah, when did he get so tall? Why is everyone so tall these days?" Zoe said. "My family in particular, are super tall. But Hikaru's parents are average height, yet Hikaru is tall. Maybe it's the hormones in the food."

"Definitely." Shakti said.

Hikaru was elbow deep in a huge slice of cake and a glass of milk.

*   *   *

Over at the Akiyamas' house, Gayatri and Harrison explained their unique situation to their friends. They prefaced the conversation by saying that they would fully accept and understand if anyone did not believe them. Of course, their friends believed it all. It was a long, difficult and sometimes bewildering conversation. Gayatri mentioned Mary's involvement with them as well. Winston and Agnes were not shocked, but intrigued by Mary's abilities. They were happy that Shakti would be able to give them some insight into their daughter's nature.

Shinzo was concerned about Shakti having to face the King. This was the most difficult part for them all to accept. Harrison and Gayatri could not hide how much it scared them. They both broke down and cried amongst their friends. The Akiyamas and Sutherlands gathered around them and embraced them. They assured them that Shakti was stronger than any of them understood. Kira suggested she try to get in touch with Angel Gabriel again and ask for help. Gayatri thought it was a brilliant idea. She would support Shakti from afar.

After the tears were dried and casual conversation resumed, Winston said, at a later time, when he was ready, he wanted to tell them all about Jamaica. They had all been waiting to hear about it and agreed emphatically. They hung out for a short time again and returned to their homes.

*   *   *

By December, Toronto saw its first snowfall of the season. It was seasonally late, but breathtakingly magical, like most first snowfalls were. Christmas was in the air and brought all the feels with it. School was winding down to the final few days and The Garden Club had a great Christmas party. A true sense of community surrounded the club and it grew exponentially. They stood at over a hundred Garden Club members and three staff members, including Mr. Edgar. All who believed in the cause.

Throughout the world, there were several natural disasters happening on a similar scale to Hurricane Kali. These events took the lives of hundreds of thousands of people. They ranged from severe droughts, sharp storms, biblical floods, disappearing of coastlines, and much more. It seemed to be a way of life now.

Shakti emerged as a leader amongst the group. Zoe, Aarti, and Hikaru handled many of the logistical operations. Shakti, along with a few others, were the researchers. She was also the public face of the group. As promised, Zoe set up an interview with Iris Pavlopoulos. It would be on the last Thursday of school and would include The Garden Club members and Shakti as the main feature. Zoe negotiated with the network to allow Shakti to explain what the Tree Project was about and how the public could assist with it. They agreed to her terms as most networks vied for an interview with Shakti. Harrison and Gayatri reluctantly gave written permission for Shakti to give this interview.

On the Thursday morning of the interview, The Garden Club members showed up in their best casual outfits. They were about to be on local TV. The greater Toronto area was home to over six million people. Therefore, it was an incredibly huge deal to them. Hikaru, Aarti, and Zoe prepared the stage of the auditorium for the interview. They set up chairs in a classroom layout for The Garden Club members to sit and be a part of the interview. Shakti sat in the seats facing the stage with a few students, reviewing and tweaking the pitch for the Tree Project. She asked to be excused after an hour to retreat to one of the classrooms to meditate and ground herself.

Shakti understood all too well that this was their one chance to get the word out about planting trees to help save the planet. She found an empty classroom and closed the door behind her. Wasting no time, she sat and took deep breaths and went into a deep state of meditation.

Iris Pavlopoulos arrived with her crew and began setting up the cameras. She appeared to be an ambitious young journalist. She asked to speak with Shakti ahead of time, but she was in meditation and they could not find her.

Shakti returned after a few minutes and looked from the far side of the auditorium. She slipped into her spiritual state and scanned the room for Jinns. Shakti thought it was worth a try to see if they would influence the interview in any way. She pulled the White Light of Protection over her and made her way down the aisle, then up the stage stairs. Shakti watched as Iris commanded her crew efficiently and rearranged the layout of chairs. Shakti giggled as she saw Hikaru fidget watching them undo the work they did. He seemed to agree in the end that Iris's chair layout was better than theirs.

Before she reached the top of the stage, Iris spotted her. "Shakti!" Iris's voice was loud and boomed across the stage, startling Shakti. "It is a pleasure to meet you." Iris shook Shakti's hand hard, making her upper body shake.

"Thank you. It's a pleasure to meet you." Shakti smiled from ear to ear. "Thank you for coming to our school to talk to us."

"Oh! No problem. I've been wanting to speak to you since your moving speech in Paris!" Iris's blue eyes twinkled when she spoke. "I understand you want to focus mainly on the Tree Project, which by the way, I think is a brilliant idea and way overdue."

"Oh, thank you." Shakti realized her voice sounded low compared to Iris's and cleared her throat to project her voice. "Yes, we have some great ideas for taking the Tree Project to the next level." Hikaru noticed Shakti's attempt to get her voice louder and turned around and walked away, giggling.

"Sounds great. Let's get started!" She clapped her hands together loudly. Everything Iris did seemed to be amplified, even her clap echoed across the large room. "Everyone, take your places!" The crew ran into their stations, and The Garden Clubbers took their seats. Shakti, Zoe, Hikaru, and Aarti took their places in the middle front row. Shakti had a few stapled papers in her hand. They all checked each other to make sure their teeth were clean, their hair was in place, and they looked suitable for the camera.

"This is not a live broadcast, so don't feel nervous," Iris announced.

"And we're rolling," a crew member in the back shouted.

Iris started the interview by introducing herself and the network. She then introduced Hikaru, Aarti, Zoe, and Shakti and members of The Garden Club. They pretended to cut to Shakti's speech, and Iris went into a long-winded explanation on the impact of the speech globally. Shakti felt awkward but had a weird permanent smile on her face.

Iris started by asking Zoe to give a background on The Garden Club. Zoe was stellar and well-rehearsed. She emphasized The Garden Club grew exponentially over the last few months, and they were all willing to roll up their sleeves to plant trees where needed. Iris seemed intrigued by the story and how it spun into a trip to Paris. She asked Zoe about the death of her grandmother and aunt and how it affected her. Zoe didn't look thrilled about the question at first, but answered it with raw honesty and emotions.

Next, Iris moved on to Hikaru. He explained the scientific effects that planting trees would have on the Earth. He, too, was polished and knew his role well. He appealed for governmental support to provide land to plant trees to contribute to better air quality and reduce carbon pollution. He referred to Aarti a few times to explain the ideal types of land that would yield the best results. They were quite the team.

Shakti, for the first time, noticed there was a chemistry between the two of them. What a thing to notice on camera! Finally, Iris got to Shakti. Her body language suggested she was about to aim the bulk of her questions at her. Surprisingly, Shakti was ready for it. She made up her mind that she was going to answer the questions honestly. After all, the King was already coming for her. What else did she have to lose? She might as well make this effective. This new-and-improved Shakti was liberated. It took the edge off, and she appeared relaxed and pleasant. Hikaru noticed her euphoric state.

Iris started with the speech. Shakti explained the details that led up to the speech. How the news of Zoe losing her grandmother and aunt affected her and how she felt she needed to do something to make a difference. Iris seemed satisfied with the answer. Shakti then went on to explain what the Tree Project hoped to accomplish. Their goal was to plant two billion trees across Canada. She referred to the efforts of India and Ethiopia and how they did a superb job planting millions of trees. Therefore, a wealthy country like Canada should have no excuses to falter on their environmental responsibilities.

The Garden Club members were happy with Shakti's performance. Some of them chimed in on the different tree types and landscapes that would be ideal for Canada. Shakti was thrilled to have many members speak about the project with such passion. The collection of rainbow auras across the room was inspiring to her. Iris and her crew's auras seemed to become colourful as well. This was a sign that the interview would be effective to those seeing it.

Hikaru, Zoe, and Shakti made eye contact with each other. Their smiles said it all. *This might actually work.*

The interview aired on Saturday morning. Shakti, Hikaru, Zoe, and their parents met at Shakti's house to watch it. Gayatri and Harrison recorded it. Iris did a fantastic job putting the interview together. Impactful background music, images of destruction caused by Hurricane Kali, and cuts to the speech added up to an effective documentary-style interview. Gayatri and Harrison were high-fiving the kids and each other. It seemed it was a huge success. Shakti reminded them that the success of the interview should be measured by the amount of government support they receive. However, all the parents were thrilled to see their kids on TV.

*   *   *

One evening during the holidays, Shakti made the decision to finally visit Vidia and Marty. She sat with Marty's hot chocolate and had a long, difficult conversation with them.

"I needed time before I could talk to you about this. Not because I was mad, but more because I had to build up the courage to do it," Shakti started.

"Okay," Marty said. "Please, speak freely."

"Bill is a part of the King's Guard." Shakti stared at her cup. "He has been betraying you all this time. He fooled you into believing that he was studying the Rainbow Tribe."

Vidia cupped her mouth and stared at Marty. "How do you know this?"

"When he attacked me, he told me many things," Shakti said. "He didn't think I would remember because he planned on hypnotizing me to forget."

"Oh my God." Marty touched his forehead and leaned back onto the sofa.

Shakti paused. She didn't know how to say what she was about to. "Vidia." Shakti paused again. "Bill is the reason James killed himself."

"No!" Vidia screeched. "No. It can't be." She shook her head side to side.

"He tried to do the same to me through hypnosis," Shakti said while tears escaped her eyes. "I'm sorry, but it's true."

Marty leaned over to Vidia and hugged her tightly. But Vidia seemed to have no peace to salvage. The reality that she was indirectly responsible for James's death, destroyed her. Although Marty comforted her, he too appeared distraught. Shakti had prepared herself for this.

Shakti explained, "Many children before were confronted with the same fate, and you must not blame yourselves."

Vidia lamented over Bill's betrayal. She questioned everything she knew about her intuition.

Shakti assured her, "Bill was a master of deceit. He had a relic that allowed him to hide his true nature. He played you for many years under the guise of studying the Rainbow Tribe. He also had the help of the devil in him."

But it was no use. Shakti watched as Vidia's aura plummeted into a swampy depression. The blood drained away from her face. She would never be the same. Shakti mourned her teacher's loss as she walked slowly down the front stairs. She glanced back at the townhouse, knowing it would be a long time before she came back.

CHAPTER 26

FOLLOW ME

Aarti sent a group text to The Garden Club group chat inviting everyone to her house for a cookie and eggnog party on the eve of Christmas Eve. Most of the kids RSVP'd yes, and so did two members of the staff, including Mr. Edgar. Zoe, Shakti, and Hikaru decided they would go together. It was exciting, after all. They weren't invited to many events outside of their group, or at least Hikaru and Shakti weren't. Aarti sent the address out to the group.

"I hope she has space for everyone because The Garden Club is not small," Hikaru said.

"I was thinking the same thing. There are a lot of us now," Zoe agreed.

Winston dropped them off at the address. They pulled up to a sprawling mansion. Not a mini-mansion, but an actual mansion with electric gates and giant trees that hid the house from the road. The trio was speechless.

"What the actual hell?" Hikaru said, "Aarti's rich!"

"You can say that again." Shakti ogled at the giant posts in front of the house. "And you two were worried about her having enough space!"

"She could host the entire school here!" Zoe added. They looked in awe at the hundreds of trees lit with Christmas lights, lining the driveway.

They rang the doorbell, and the giant door swung open. Aarti stood at the entrance, dressed in a holiday sweater, short flared skirt, and jingle bell tights. She did a little shimmy that made the bells of her tights jingle, and welcomed them cheerfully. Aarti handed them a Santa Claus hat each. She looked beautiful. Her Santa hat matched her red lips perfectly. Hikaru noticed, but he didn't show it.

"Your house is amazing!" Zoe said.

"Thank you. Feel free to look around. Then you can make your way down to the basement. Everyone is there." Aarti embodied Christmas spirit. "I'll be down soon. I want to greet some more people at the door."

"Sure! Thanks, Aarti," Shakti said. They walked around, looking at the interior of the house. It was unlike anything they'd seen before. The main level boasted extra high ceilings and black and white marble everywhere. They stood at the foot of the grand staircase admiring the luxurious décor. In the formal living room stood a small shrine with a flame from a little lit clay bowl. Shakti was drawn to it. She walked away from Hikaru and Zoe, who were talking to someone from school and went over to see the intricately clean prayer area. It appeared Aarti's family were devout Hindus.

Shakti admired the pictures and little statues. One artifact caught her attention immediately. There was a framed picture of the multi-armed woman floating on a lotus from her dream. Shakti blinked and shook her head, then looked again. She went in closer to see it.

"Do you know who that is?" a woman with an Indian accent said from behind Shakti, startling her. The woman smiled warmly and had a remarkable resemblance to Aarti. She was sophisticated and wore a long eggplant-purple Indian-style top with purple pants and purple shoes. Two huge gold bracelets adorned both wrists.

"No, I don't," Shakti replied with a smile.

"That's Mother Lakshmi." The woman approached the shrine as well. "She's very special to us."

"Oh. I see." Shakti looked at the picture again. She was surprised that the picture was so accurate. "I dreamt of her one time."

"You did?" The woman looked surprised. "Yet, you didn't know who she was?"

"I know. Weird, right?"

"Not weird, blessed." She smiled. "Mother Lakshmi only comes to those that need her guidance."

"I see." Shakti looked at her. "I guess she knew I needed her." Shakti recalled she dreamt of Mother Lakshmi the night before she embarked on her trip to Paris. She wondered if Mother Lakshmi came to warn her of what was to come, or if she came to give her strength to complete the task ahead.

The lady looked at Shakti with a confused look. "Are you Indian, my dear?" Shakti knew her mixed-race look could have confused her with most races.

"My mom is Indian and Trinidadian," Shakti explained. "My dad is French-Canadian. I don't know much about any of my backgrounds, though."

"Ahh. I see." She smiled. "Perhaps, Mother Lakshmi came to remind you of your ancestral heritage."

"Perhaps." Shakti liked that idea. "I guess I'll never know for sure."

"I am Aarti's mom, Savi." She smiled warmly. "You can call me Aunty Savi." She laughed.

"I thought so. You are both beautiful."

"I like you." Savi laughed again. "Enjoy your time." She touched Shakti's shoulder and walked away.

"Thank you, Aunty Savi." Shakti watched her glide off gracefully to talk to other guests.

Hikaru, Zoe, and Shakti made their way down to the impressive walkout basement. It was a Christmas Winter Wonderland theme. There were several large and small Christmas trees, tables set up with eggnog fountains. Tables and tables of cookies, brownies, candy canes, and stem glasses of festive drinks. There was also a table of delicious Indian food set up in a buffet.

Hikaru was in heaven. He ran up to the stem glasses and tasted it. "This one is a Shirley Temple." Hikaru double-fisted drinks. "This one is sparkling cranberry ginger ale!"

"Easy on the sugar, Karu," Zoe said. "You're hyper enough."

There was a DJ playing music in the corner. Shakti was pretty sure it was Aarti's brother. The Garden Club members had a great time dancing and overdosing on sugar.

"Starting The Garden Club has improved our social life exponentially," Shakti said to Hikaru.

"Definitely." Hikaru was a little distracted. "Hey. I wanted to ask you something."

"Sure." Shakti sipped her eggnog in a fancy glass.

"Do you think Aarti likes me?"

"Define like." Shakti knew exactly what he meant.

"You know, like, do you think she's interested in me?" Hikaru knew he could depend on Shakti for an honest opinion.

"Karu, she's completely into you," Shakti said.

"Really? Why didn't you tell me before?" Hikaru blushed.

"I only noticed recently," Shakti explained. "I was planning on asking you about it. Sorry I didn't say anything. I meant to."

"That's okay." Hikaru was on cloud nine. "What should I do?"

"You're asking me for dating advice?" Shakti laughed. "That's Zoe's area."

"What's my area?" Zoe approached with a plateful of assorted treats.

"Karu is in love with Aarti, and she loves him back. It's a whole thing," Shakti said without any expression.

"Shakti!" Hikaru said, embarrassed.

"You are?" Zoe said loudly and almost dropped her plate.

"No, it's not like that." Hikaru blushed again. "I want to ask her out. I don't know how to."

Zoe placed her plate on the table. "Karu, Karu. You've come to the right place. Here's what to do." They walked over to the sofa and sat down. Shakti laughed and shook her head. Hikaru appeared stressed out.

After his pep talk from Zoe, Hikaru looked a little more confident. The evening progressed with great fun. Everyone in The Garden Club was friends or friendly with each other. Mr. Edgar showed up and hung out with Aarti's parents. There were even club members from different schools there. Before the night's end, Hikaru asked Aarti to dance. Then, he asked her out on a date. She said yes. Shakti and Zoe hid behind a Christmas tree watching them. They all rejoiced afterwards as friends do. Aarti had a smile on her face for the rest of the night.

Christmas holidays were like most years gone by. Shakti and her parents volunteered at the food drive. Christmas morning, Shakti woke up to her parent's undivided attention. They tried not to spoil Shakti over the years with gifts, but she was an only child, and it made them happy. Shakti sat with them under the tree and unwrapped her presents. This year was a little different. The family room didn't have the same spark it usually did for Christmas. Shakti attributed it to her experience with Bill. She showed appreciation for her gifts and gave her parents their gifts. Her favourite present was from Gayatri, a glossy cherry-red silk pyjama set with a long matching robe. A departure from her animal onesies and flannel pyjamas. These were proper exquisite adult pyjamas. They made her feel grown-up.

Harrison and Shakti cooked Christmas dinner while Gayatri cleaned up. A spectacular spread for their little family. They sat together and enjoyed a beautiful feast. They spoke on world matters, politics, and the Tree Project. Harrison told them about the rebuilding of the burned area of the factory. They had discovered surveillance footage of Bill leaving the factory a few minutes before the alarm went off. Gayatri asked Shakti about how Vidia took the news about Bill's betrayal. Shakti admitted it was one of the hardest conversations she'd ever had. Marty and Vidia's reaction made her emotional every time she thought about it. She pondered how unfair it was for Vidia to carry this burden for the rest of her life. Despite her being such a selfless person, Bill's betrayal seemed to have broken her.

Christmas Day was a success by all accounts. The trio of friends made arrangements to meet the following day to exchange presents. Shakti prepared for bed, kissed her parents good night, and retreated to her bedroom. Shakti showered and slipped into her new favourite pyjama and robe set. She brushed her long hair and admired her grown up nightwear. She remembered she had a new pair of cherry-red socks that would match the set perfectly. Off she went into her walk-in closet to find them. Within a few seconds she pushed her feet into them and ran back out to the mirror to look at the entire ensemble.

"Yes, that's what I'm talking about." Shakti giggled. "Red alert."

Her phone buzzed, and she picked it up and jumped into her bed to read the text. It was Hikaru talking about what he was going to do on his first date with Aarti. Zoe was all over it on their friends' chat. She made several suggestions. Shakti's thoughts were on her new nightwear and how it felt like she was about to slip off the bed in them. She didn't mind, though. They were too pretty to worry about minor things like comfort. She switched the lamp off next to her and turned to her side, reading the exchange between Hikaru and Zoe.

Although it was only 9:00 pm, Shakti's eyes felt heavy, and she slipped into a deep sleep. The house became quiet. Gayatri and Harrison went to bed shortly after as well. Shakti dreamt of random things and events. She must have dreamt about everything that night. Late into the night, Shakti dreamt of the Clans. They played around her as she sat on the rock during a beautiful fall day. She heard her name and turned to see who it was. Standing away from her was Lorcan. The troll stood facing her with a panicked look on his face. He took a deep breath and shouted, "Wake up!"

Shakti's heart skipped a beat, and she sat up quickly. She looked at the time on the phone to see it was 3:00 am on the dot. She laid back down, feeling her heart race.

"Weird dream," Shakti whispered to herself. She closed her eyes again and tried to fall back asleep. Shakti wasn't sure, but she felt her body tremble. Then it stopped. She opened her eyes and figured it was nothing. *Could my stomach be growling?* she thought. Shakti closed her eyes again. This time she felt it again, a little stronger. She knew she felt it this time. But it stopped again. She laid on the bed with her red pyjamas, robe, and matching socks, looking at the ceiling. Still, the vibration returned. This time stronger. This continued for a few seconds, each time stronger and closer until her bed shook. Shakti felt her heart sink and her stress level spike when she realized the vibrations were footsteps. She laid frozen on the bed.

The footsteps came to a halt when the vibrations became unbearably loud.

"I must be dreaming. Wake up!" Shakti whispered.

Shakti noticed a shadow in front of her window. She was too scared to get up to see what it was. But it was there, blocking the light from coming in. Just then, a loud cracking noise started from one end of the room to the other. She screamed in terror watching the roof of her house being ripped off. Shakti stared at the night sky. She continued to scream, knowing for sure that this was no angel entering her space. The sky was black, with only hints of stars twinkling. She looked around at the open space and wondered if her parents were safe. Surely someone else heard this.

Shakti felt her heart rate quicken to a worrisome rate. Her eyes were drawn to an outline of a head in the night sky. She tried to focus on it, but fright made her close her eyes and take deep breaths. Shakti returned her focus to the shadowy outline. It took a few seconds, before the head opened its fiery red eyes. He was here, the King, he had come for her. This realization set in for her. He stared at her, the red in his eyes flared and danced around in place.

He came closer to look at her, lowering his head into the room while Shakti looked on in a catatonic state. His features came into focus as the sharp smell of sulphur filled her room. Her throat went dry, and her stomach felt ill from the toxic stench. He was so big, only his head fit into the room, the rest of him stood outside the house. Shakti's body trembled as she wept, covering her eyes with her hands trying not to look, but he was in her face. The King looked at her and sniffed her, like a beast about to devour a meal. Shakti didn't remember to pull the White Light of Protection over her. She was consumed with the charcoal grey beast invading her personal space. His breath rattled with sparks. He squinted his demon eyes at her angrily. Shakti glared at his most prominent feature, the twin horns on his head, twirled up and outward. The greyish-black scales on his face were shiny and symmetrically arranged.

A beast of such dark energy could only be from hell, Shakti thought.

The devil lifted his head from her room and stood up straight again. He was much taller than the house and stood with his hands propped on his hips, looking down at Shakti. She was still lying on the bed, curled up.

Then, he spoke, "Shakti Devi Clairemont." His voice was the deepest and most terror-inducing sound she had ever heard. It vibrated through her. "Follow me." He waved his hand slowly over the house, and Shakti floated upward. She grabbed for the bed, but it was no use.

Shakti screamed but realized nothing came out. She was mute. He proceeded to do the foulest and most unexpected thing. The devil peeled her astral body out of her physical body. She came screaming out while her physical body fell asleep. Shakti's comatose body levitated horizontally, over the roofless mini-mansion. Her astral body looked at her physical body floating in the red pyjama set like a ghost in the sky. Her hair and robe, loosely floating with her, giving the illusion of full-water immersion.

She felt violated. Her astral form looked up at him. "Put me down, devil." Shakti's voice shook in fear.

"Follow me." Ignoring her demand, he turned and walked away while the sleeping Shakti followed along, tethered to him.

The giant devil walked slowly to the back and between the trees until he reached the pond. His body made creaking sounds as he walked. Shakti's astral form raced after him in midair, trying to protect her sleeping self. He was in control of her body.

Where was he taking her? she wondered. Like always, in her astral form, Shakti felt braver. But seeing her body float towards the devil made her fear for her life.

He stopped for a second on the edge of the water, then continued over the pond. It appeared he could walk on water, too. Shakti still chased after him. Over the pond, the moon shone bright and reflected on the unfrozen black water, showing Shakti the devil in full form. He was barbarous and muscular, having all the traits of an ancient beast. The devil encapsulated the truest form of vulgar dictatorship. Smoke and ash radiated from his body and left a foggy trail of mist behind his giant form.

His long tail moved ergonomically with his giant strides. Shakti couldn't help but notice how unrealistically large his feet were. The devil's entire appearance was grotesquely disproportionate. Yet, she pursued him relentlessly. She had to try to save herself.

He slowed down as he approached the dead centre of Grenadier Pond. Shakti's body slowed down with him. He turned around and looked at her. He waved his hand in a semicircular motion, making Shakti's sleeping body float up next to him and moved from a horizontal position to a vertical crucifix position. Her hair and robe flying about her eerily artful. Again, she looked like she was suspended underwater.

Shakti flew up to him, face to face. "Devil, what do you want with me?"

"Don't ask me foolish questions, little girl." His ghastly voice made her retreat a few steps. "You humans have no respect! I loathe your kind." He spat a giant fireball to the side to show his disdain. Shakti screamed, seeing the fireball hit the water. "Allow me to introduce myself. I am Iblis." His throat rattled like a chain against a metal cage each time he spoke. It was chilling.

Shakti was shocked by his formality. "Iblis, I am Shakti, but you already know that."

"Shakti, I am the ruler of hell and King of the Ifrit Jinn. I was made from the purest form of smokeless fire." He gestured regally in a strangely scripted rant.

Shakti didn't know what to say about that. "What do you want from me, Iblis?" Her voice trembled.

"My Jinns and I were forced into hiding millennials ago. We watched you humans ravage the world. Quickly did we notice, you were a self-destructive species."

"I agree," Shakti said. "So, what does that mean?"

"It would be only a matter of time before you made yourself extinct." Iblis closed his eyes and hummed. Orange-tinted sparks flew out of his mouth. Then he resumed talking. "We watched and waited patiently. The Earth started to respond to your betrayal. Finally, an end was in sight and a new beginning for my reign was imminent." He blinked again slowly, as if talking took much energy.

Shakti listened, knowing full well he spoke of the truth. "We deserve to be saved. Why do you think you should live, and we should die?"

The question made him pause. Then, he became visibly angry. "Your kind does not deserve to live!" he shouted.

"Iblis, you are judging our kind? You are the devil. I see how your Jinns influence humans."

"Influence is right! It is not the same as carrying out the action of destroying the planet!" he persisted. "We whispered into man's ears. We did not force their hand. Free will is their gift and curse."

"That's tricky, devil," Shakti said. "Tricky and cowardly."

Iblis laughed at Shakti's remarks. "You little human fool. Your species have created such doctrines as racism, ethnic cleansing, world wars, holocaust, and slavery." He laughed. "I was impressed by humans' natural state of evil. We may have started the influence, but humans carried out the actions. We are absolved." Iblis bowed his head.

Shakti was taken aback by the devil's logical explanation. She didn't expect that. "We are weak! I get it. But there is a lot more good than bad to our species."

"Good is overrated, Shakti. Look at your mom, for example." He paused again and hummed. It was most bizarre. "She listened blindly to the great Archangel Gabriel." He laughed. "Now, she will find her daughter's body floating, face down, on the Grenadier Pond in the morning."

The devil's words took Shakti's breath away. She felt the pinch in her astral stomach. "No." She shook her head from side to side, devastated.

"You think Angel Gabriel did not know this would happen? He is a farce and trickster." Iblis relished in Shakti's pain. "Humans are fools. Look at your history. The weakest amongst you have become the greatest military leaders."

Still reeling from her impending doom, Shakti, stopped listening. She thought of her parents finding her in the pond. It killed her inside. They would never get over the pain. He might as well drown them all.

She lashed out at him, "It's too late! The Rainbow Tribe has been awoken. There is no point in hurting me now. It changes nothing."

"It changes everything," Iblis said calmly. "Killing you will kill your influence on the Rainbow Tribe."

Shakti thought about that for a few seconds. "Someone else will step up to replace me."

"Then, we will kill them, too." He hummed again with a pleased look on his face.

"You're a coward. Killing children," she cried.

"Am I?" he mocked. "Humans are killing every species in the world, including children, and yet, you call me a coward?" Iblis was as clever as he was evil. His riposte was quick. "They chose great riches over life. That's greed, my favourite of all sins. Humans asserted their power over the poor in fear of losing control. That is being a coward, Shakti."

Shakti found herself breaking, "If you want the Earth so badly, why don't you just take it?" she screamed. "Take it!" Her emotions poured out of her astral mouth and eyes. She paused and quickly came to the realization. "Oh, I get it. You can't. The angels would never allow it." Before he could respond, Shakti noticed far off into the distance a ball of white light rolling towards them.

"Humans are doing a good enough job on their own, getting rid of themselves, like the parasites they are," Iblis noted. "Say goodbye to your physical body now, Shakti. Make your peace and get ready to join the countless bodies this pond has claimed." Iblis became distracted by something behind Shakti.

She turned around quickly to see another ball of light in the opposite direction approaching them. Iblis became furious. A fire lit from one side of his broad shoulders to the other side. He stood up straight and clenched his fist. Several more balls of lights appeared around the pond. Shakti counted them in her head. At least twelve lights approached them.

Iblis's rage grew as he watched it roll closer, making the fire rise above his head and horns. Into sight, small bodies of children appeared in the light. What was this? Shakti tried to see who it was, but instead, she heard a little voice call out her name.

"Shakti!" the brightest of the lights shouted.

Shakti turned swiftly towards the sound and squinted, "Mary?" Shakti asked. "Mary? Is that you?"

"It is me!" Mary smiled.

"How? Who?" Shakti couldn't finish her sentence. "How?"

"These are my friends from the home, George, Ali, Lexi, and the rest of them." Mary pointed at the other balls of light. They glowed brightly in their astral forms.

Iblis broke up their little reunion quickly. "Mary Lucille Sutherland," he snarled. "And her band of misfits." Mary was unbothered by his rude comment. "This is what I mean, Shakti. Good is overrated. A vibrant soul such as Mary, trapped by a limited body. She righteously chose this path, too." He smirked, looking down at Mary.

Shakti whipped around. "Limited? She's the bravest person I know."

By this time, all the children were close enough to be seen. Iblis became agitated and whipped his tail to hit the water below. He howled at them, "You think you dare be a match for the great, Iblis? Made of the purest fire!" The base in his voice elevated and boomed across the open water, causing it to ripple waves

Mary's astral form flew up to Shakti and within the eye line of Iblis. "No," she smirked. "I don't."

Shakti was surprised to hear Mary admit this to Iblis. "What are you doing here, Mary?" Shakti was worried about her and her friends.

Mary glanced at Iblis, then turned to Shakti. Her smile, wide and her light brightened. "Watch this." She closed her eyes and raised her little arms. All the kids floated up to her and did the same. They formed a circle around the now convulsing Iblis, raging in fire and ash. His defensive stance suggested he was about to attack. Shakti and Shakti's sleeping body stood within their circle. The kids joined Mary with their little arms up in the air and their eyes closed shut.

"Oh my God!" Shakti screeched. She knew what came next. Iblis did not. Shakti too followed them and raised her arms and closed her eyes. She immediately tuned into an enormous tornado of energy. Shakti did not know what she was doing, but she knew her energy contributed to the cause. Shakti whispered, "help me, please." A little white light from within their circle shot up into the air. The sky glowed. The pin-drop light expanded widely, casting an indigo circle in the night sky. What Shakti assumed to be heaven opened up, making light flow down over them. It lit the entire pond up like daytime, revealing Iblis's muscular form further.

Down from the sky rapidly descended an army of angels. Among them, the largest angel of all, Archangel Michael. He free-fell to the Earth with divine speed. It was the first time Shakti saw his wings out. It immediately explained the unknown structure behind him every time she saw him. His wingspan could have been a hundred feet wide on each side. He was armed and glorious with a blue-lit sword and a helmet. His angels followed him into battle to take Iblis back to hell. They descended with the force of lightning in a V formation with Archangel Michael at the front and centre. They travelled at a speed so great that if Shakti blinked, she would have missed it.

Iblis became irate. His chest puffed out, smoke swirled from his flared nostrils, and fire blew out of his mouth. With one deep breath, he rolled his eyes shut with his head tilted back. Iblis managed to grow long spikes on his back, screaming loud as they grew. He raised his arms and dropped them suddenly. Out of nowhere, appeared a sea of Jinns standing at ground level as far as the eye could see. Shakti could no longer see the houses around. They were on spiritual territory now. A faint outline of the CN tower could be seen in the smoky distance. Iblis waved his arm one more time, and a giant pitchfork with three-pointed edges appeared in his hand. It was as tall as he was. There was about to be a battle between heaven and hell. Both sides braced for impact.

Shakti yelled at the kids to move out of the way. Iblis bent his knees and projected upwards to meet Angel Michael in the sky. Shakti told Mary to help her move her sleeping body out of harm's way. Mary and the children rushed to help. Just as they approached Shakti's physical form and latched onto her, Iblis and Angel Michael made contact. A nuclear spark lit the Toronto night sky, sending everyone hurling. A crashing sound thundered right after. Shakti and the kids held on to Shakti's body as they tumbled. They tried to protect her from going beneath the water's surface. Mary took control quickly of her, pushing the still floating Shakti over to land and laying her onto the cold ground.

"Shakti, quick, jump back into your body while he's distracted," Mary commanded.

Shakti asked no questions and jumped in. Her body jolted in a seated position and trembled from being exposed. She looked at her arms and legs, shivering beneath her red nightwear. Mary and the kids stood around her protectively. Unexpectedly, several gnomes came jumping out the trees and sat on Shakti's body. She immediately started to warm up, noting a talent of gnomes other than mischief.

Shakti now had a front-row seat to the greatest battle of all time. She watched as Angel Michael and Iblis violently tossed each other around. Both were clearly skilled fighters. Angel Michael anticipated Iblis's moves. Iblis fought dirty, trying to stab Michael with his fork. He missed each time as Michael wielded his sword in fantastic form, creating blue discs of light surrounding him. Iblis's fork was powerful and heavy. Each time their weapons crossed paths, a deafening thunder cracked, followed by a gust of wind.

The army of angels fought the Jinn on the ground level. Shakti watched as they scrapped and fought each other. Angel Michael's side was winning. They were made for battle. It seemed the great Iblis, made of the purest fire, was no match for the greatest soldier in the history of heaven and earth.

While they fought far above the pond, Mary pointed up at the opening in the sky. Way above the battleground, angels descended with their wings expanded. They were different colours and brilliant in appearance. Shakti immediately noticed the green-lit being as Archangel Raphael. There were angels lit in copper, pink, orange, and purple. Perhaps they were all Archangels. She did not know. They floated down to Michael and Iblis.

Michael's elegant war dance ended artfully with a final blow of his giant sword into the belly of the beast. Iblis howled as fire escaped his mouth, and he dropped to his knees. Michael quickly lifted him into the air holding Iblis by the throat, then let him go. Iblis did not fight anymore, he was too weak. Michael placed his well-proportioned feet on Iblis's chest and neck and forced him back down to Earth. Iblis slammed into the energetic surface under Michael's mercy. He held his sword pointed at Iblis's face. The battle was over. Upon seeing Iblis's fall, the Jinns snarled and started fading away in retreat. The army of angels on the ground rejoiced.

A stage was now set with the Archangels standing in a circle around Michael, mounted on Iblis. It seemed they would decide Iblis's fate. They spoke telepathically, looking at each other with soft expressions. It was frustrating to Shakti because she wanted to hear his verdict. Afterall, Iblis did try to kill her a few moments ago.

The gnomes looked on too, highly entertained. Shakti heard the gnomes talk to each other for the first time. But, instead of words, they clicked. She would have been deeply interested in this, any other day, but not today. She raised her finger to her mouth. "Ssshhh."

One of the gnomes looked at her badly and clicked one more time, making the rest of them giggle. Shakti was pretty sure he swore at her. She didn't have time for it and resumed her attention.

All her focus went to Michael perched on Iblis. Shakti wanted this image seared in her memory. It was deeply satisfying. She took a moment to appreciate how brave she was against Iblis. Her greatest fear had come to pass, and she came out the victor. However, the real hero here was Mary. She used her most coveted talent of calling upon the angels to save Shakti's life. Shakti could have wept thinking of her wonderful protector, Mary the Magical.

CHAPTER 27

WHAT LIES
BENEATH

S hakti woke up on her bed on Boxing Day, dressed in her
elaborate silk pyjamas. The last moment she remembered was
sitting on the side of the pond, watching Mary's smiling face.
Then, nothing. The roof of her house was perfectly intact. Both of
her wrists burned a little, and she raised the sleeves to examine them.
There were light purple handprints around her wrist and arms. She
smiled at them, remembering the kids and herself, trying to pull her
body to safety, away from the battleground. She quickly pulled her
red socks off and found the same handprint type marks around her
ankles and legs. She guessed they all held on tightly when they went
tumbling over the water. It should have been a disturbing memory,
but Shakti closed her eyes and felt grateful. It was so much to take in.
She laid in a fetal position and wept.

The worst is over, she thought.

After a few minutes, she skipped out of bed and ran into her
parents' room to check on them. They were fast asleep.

Shakti spent the entire day telling her parents and friends about
what happened the night before. She showed them the marks to prove

it. If it was anyone else, they probably would not have believed her. But Shakti was an honest person. She had built that reputation for herself over the years. The worst was over. This time, it was. It made the experience with Bill seem insignificant.

*   *   *

Harrison and Gayatri took time to process the story. Shakti knew it was a lot. She didn't press the subject. She wanted them to speak to her about it in their own time. Harrison and Gayatri went to separate parts of their home to deal with the magnitude of their daughter's world. Harrison's way of dealing with great stress was retreating to the basement with a beer. He sat on the sizable plush sofa and ran the story over in his head. He took comfort in knowing the devil was defeated. However, he couldn't escape the looming dark reality that his daughter was the centre of a world that was unknown to him. A world that was so dangerous, it would take heaven and hell to decide Shakti's fate. He looked out the walkout basement's back door and caught a glimpse of Grenadier Pond. For the first time, fear washed over him, staring at it. It could have been the end of his only child.

Two floors up, Gayatri had a less fearful reaction to the devil's visit. Feelings of relief made her sob endlessly. She closed her eyes and prayed. Her feelings towards Angel Gabriel were unchanged. Gayatri sat in her master bedroom overlooking the huge pond. That Boxing Day, it was still and deceiving. Like any other pond, it appeared quiet and vast. Few people would ever know the battle that took place over it.

Gayatri's moment alone was cathartic. She had been invested in this story from the very beginning, before Shakti was born, before she even met Harrison. She was preparing, unknowingly, from a tender-aged orphan. Angel Gabriel protected her as a child. He knew it would take great sorrow, grit, and an expanded consciousness to be the mother of the Warrior that would awaken the Rainbow Tribe. She clawed her way through school, overcoming unimaginable circumstances to be the person she was today. Every time she cried as a child because no one wanted to adopt her. Every time she sank into hollow depression as a teenager because no one in school wanted to be friends with the poor orphan girl. She nursed every cold, bruise, and heartbreak by herself. Gayatri sat looking out from her beautiful home, thinking that she had a life worth fighting for. The mother of a Warrior, born from despair. It all made sense. As she stared at a tiny picture of herself at six years old, she wept and rejoiced for the child in her.

* * *

Shakti's conversation with Hikaru and Zoe was very different. They screamed and cheered. Zoe felt she had a celebrity for a sister. She knew in her heart, Mary was unique from the beginning. They hugged Shakti and cried happy tears. Shakti's life was more action-packed than a movie. It reaffirmed their belief that the Tree Project should be their first priority. They couldn't let the Jinns win.

Shakti hugged them again, tighter this time. The trio stood in a circle of embrace, not saying a word to each other. Washed with emotions, Shakti was aware of their priceless contribution to her life.

* * *

SIX MONTHS LATER

Well into spring, the trio of friends were still inseparable. Their minds were made up on their career paths, at least for now. They understood this summer would be time well spent because the group would split up come September. Shakti followed in her mother's footsteps and joined U of T. Her heart was set on becoming an engineer, where she could further her studies in environmental engineering at a later time. Hikaru and Aarti had been dating for many months, but they chose to go their separate ways after Hikaru decided on health sciences at McMaster, and Aarti elected to study political science at U of T. They were most amicable about it and would still be friends. Zoe was thrilled with her decision to pursue a business degree at Ryerson University in downtown Toronto. Perfect for the project manager of the group.

Zoe had been right, as ever, about the interview with Iris. It made all the difference to the exposure and support they received. The Tree Project finally saw significant progress and enthusiasm from the government and the public. Thanks to The Garden Club, Canada committed to planting two billion trees over ten years. Again, Shakti, along with the club members would be celebrated in the media. Of course, there were many naysayers attacking her and the group. But she learnt to deal with criticism a lot better, thanks to Zoe. Hikaru, Zoe and Shakti made The Tree Project a priority. They were determined to save the planet and not let the Jinns win.

The Garden Club was one thousand students strong and a fully functional not-for-profit club. The tech-savvy members of the group created a website to recruit new members to help plant trees, collect funding, and give advice on planting their own gardens. The first goal of The Garden Club was to encourage sustainable agricultural practices. This promoted a new way of thinking, starting in the Greater Toronto Area. Students from all over the megacity started growing vegetable gardens. They even donated produce to charities and events. This, of course, led to better eating habits for children. Soon, Toronto was a leader in health and environmental awareness.

Who knew? Shakti thought. Well, in all fairness, she did. But there was no way anyone expected this to become a movement. It sparked an agricultural revolution for students far and wide.

During a hot summer day in July, Shakti walked through her backyard with a specific goal in mind. Something she'd been meaning to do for many months but had buried it deep in her mind as a means of coping with her trauma. Shakti walked through the trees and made her way down to the water. It was late in the afternoon. Toronto was having a gloriously hot summer. She sat on the ground facing the water, gazing at her surroundings. Her hand dipped into the pocket of her dress and pulled something out of it. She brought her hand up slightly to her face, opened her palm and revealed Bill's relic. The dark metal chain and pendant were weighty. She had not looked at it since Bill invaded her home. Shakti has always been sensitive to energy, and the relic made her lethargic.

She looked at it this time, trying to ignore its lure. For the first time, she realized the pendant was a symbol. She turned it a few times and recognized it was two swirling horns surrounded by a circle. Much like the horns of Iblis. It was nothing special to look at. In fact, it appeared to be an inexpensive piece of jewellery. Perhaps that was its intention, to hide its dark purpose. She pondered at the damage this relic caused and how many lives it destroyed.

Shakti had a plan to get rid of it for good, but she needed help. She placed the relic on the ground next to her and closed her eyes. Pulling the White Light of Protection over her, she opened her eyes and looked around. The Clans were busy doing their work. She looked around for one friend in particular.

She spotted a troll. "Excuse me, Mr. Troll."

The troll paused and looked at her like he was annoyed.

"I'm looking for Lorcan. Can you help me find him?" Shakti was hoping for the best. Although good, trolls were not friendly beings.

The troll looked surprised by her request and turned and walked away.

Shakti was not sure he understood her. She wondered if she should ask the gnomes or fairies to help her instead.

As she was contemplating what to do, Lorcan popped out from behind a tree. "What?"

"Lorcan! Thank you for coming." Shakti was so happy he came. The troll did in fact deliver her message, and quickly.

"What do you want, girl?" Lorcan had places to go from his stance.

"Oh, well, I wanted to talk to you about something of great importance." Shakti was trying to sound respectful.

"Hurry up. I have trees to take care of," Lorcan said abruptly.

"Okay. Okay. I'll be quick." Shakti positioned her body to face him and crisscrossed her legs. She picked up the relic and showed it to him. "This is the property of Iblis. It has a dark purpose."

Lorcan was shocked at what she showed him. His face changed from grumpy to astonished. He walked up to her slowly and stared at it. "This is very evil. Jinns will come for it."

"I know. We must get rid of it," Shakti pleaded. "Where can we hide it where no one will ever find it?"

Lorcan looked up at Shakti's face. "It carries a dark energy that will attract them to it in time." He reached out his hand, and Shakti placed the relic in his palm. "They are probably looking for it right now. They will give it to someone else to work its dark purpose."

"Can you help me destroy or hide it?" Shakti was feeling overwhelmed with the responsibility.

"It cannot be destroyed. For me to hide it, I must cover it with greater good energy. But it is powerful." Lorcan stared at it.

"I don't understand." Shakti prepared for him to call her stupid for not following.

"Dark energy must be balanced with equal or greater good energy," Lorcan explained with a surprising amount of patience. "Only one species on Earth has the energy needed."

"Who has that kind of power?" Shakti was curious about what was so good that it could counteract the evil of a demon relic.

"Why, the trees, of course," Lorcan said. "But, I will need their permission first."

"The trees? Wow."

"The Great White Oak that hid you is old and wise. I will talk to it and find out what to do," Lorcan explained.

"Okay. Thank you, Lorcan." Shakti was relieved to get rid of it. "It's probably best you don't tell me where you hide it."

Lorcan looked at her with concern. "Yes, I will take it now. Trees will decide." Lorcan pulled the chain up and placed the relic in his pocket for safe-keeping. "Most important, it does not get into the hands of humans ever again."

"I agree. We are not strong enough to have that kind of power over people's minds," Shakti said.

Lorcan was confused by her statement. "The relic has more power than your little head will ever understand." He tapped on his left temple.

"Oh." Shakti felt a little foolish. "I can't even imagine."

"Okay, I go now. I must talk to Great White Oak."

"Goodbye, Lorcan. Thank you." Shakti smiled.

He jumped over the large tree root and left. He didn't tell her to go away this time. Shakti saw this as progress in their relationship. She stood up and dusted her dress off.

* * *

On the anniversary of Hurricane Kali, the Sutherlands decided to invite the neighbours over for dinner. Winston played with the idea of hosting a Celebration of Life gathering to commemorate the life of Granny and Aunt Lucy. But it was still too painful. He was not in the mood for a large crowd and opted for a low-key event. The Clairemonts and Akiyamas were instrumental during that time, one year ago. Winston wanted to be surrounded by those people.

Harrison, Gayatri, and Shakti were the first to arrive. They rang the doorbell, and Mark answered the door.

"Clairemonts!" Mark chirped. "Welcome, welcome!"

"Mark! How are you?" Harrison replied.

"I'm great! It's been a while since I saw you all." He looked directly at Shakti, smiling ear to ear.

Harrison whispered, "Oh, brother," at Gayatri. The parents stepped inside and made their way to Agnes and Winston in the kitchen.

Shakti stood at the door. "I know. Where have you been?"

"I'm helping Dad transition the business from imports to exports," Mark said excitedly. "Since Jamaica, there were very few products left to import. So now that they are rebuilding, they need products from here. Same for other Caribbean Islands since Hurricane Kali."

"Yes, I didn't think about how affected your business would have been due to the hurricane." Shakti thought Mark inherited the business brains from his dad as well.

"How are you doing?" Mark smiled, changing gears.

"I'm okay. It has been quite a year. I'm still recovering for the most part." Shakti was surprisingly candid. She didn't care to impress him with wit anymore.

"That incident with Bill was insane." Mark's face was serious now. "I couldn't stop thinking about you. I always asked Zoe about you."

"I know, she told me. Thank you." Shakti shook her head. "It's been rough. To be fair, Mary has been a source of strength for me."

"It seems you know a lot more about Mary that we do." He glanced down.

"I'm sorry. I didn't mean to rub that in your face." Shakti became aware of his drop in mood.

"No, please, no." Mark smiled again. "I love that someone knows her on that level. It's hard for us to imagine her as the hero when she's the baby in our eyes." He smiled.

"Mark, I'd be happy to answer any questions I can about Mary." Shakti moved into the living room and sat on the sofa. "I should warn you, some of it is hard to believe."

"I will one day. Let's go out for dinner, and I will ask you all my questions." His mood shifted again to dashing. He sat next to her. "If you're okay with that, of course."

Shakti's stomach tightened, and her heart raced. "Yes, of course. I'd like that very much." She avoided looking at him in the eyes. "Speaking of Mary, where's that rebel?"

"She's up in her room. I'll go get her." Mark got up and headed for the stairs. "Zoe is in the kitchen."

As Mark bounced up the stairs, skipping two stair treads with each step, Shakti walked into the kitchen. She greeted Agnes and

Winston with a hug. They were happy to see her. Winston looked back to himself now, minus his dreads.

There were two large framed pictures of Grandma Mae and Lucy on easels. A beautiful bouquet of flowers stood between them. Shakti paused for a second to look at it. Zoe sat on the kitchen table on her computer. She gestured to Shakti to join her. She was on the Ryerson University website, checking out activities. They spoke in depth about how excited they were to start university. A sadness was present over Shakti. She was going to miss Hikaru. He was the only one out of them to move to a university residence. At least, Zoe, Aarti, and Shakti would be in Toronto. They could still hang out at parties and study together. But Hikaru would be a few hours away, starting new friendships. It was depressing to think of. Zoe assured Shakti he would be fine. They would see each other on the weekends.

Mary came skipping around the corner. "Shakti!" She laughed.

"My favourite person, ever!" Shakti got up quickly, and they embraced each other. Everyone paused and watched them be silly.

The doorbell rang, and Mary shouted, "I'll get it!" She ran to the front to welcome the Akiyamas. Hikaru came into the kitchen and did a half-wave to greet everyone. He beelined straight to his friends at the table, grabbing a handful of chips set out on the island. Shakti was excited to see him. Agnes announced dinner was ready, and the group made their way to the dining room table. They all sat at the oversized glass table and enjoyed their mostly vegan meal. It was like last year, before Hurricane Kali destroyed more than the lands she hit. It felt pre-trauma. They spoke about all the work that was being done on the various islands to rebuild. Winston was deeply involved in efforts to restore his beautiful island. He was a well-connected businessman; therefore, he used his network well.

Close to the end of dinner, Winston straightened his posture and asked for everyone's attention. "I want to thank you all for coming over to celebrate the life of my mother and sister, Lucy."

Everyone quieted down and listened respectfully.

"When Hurricane Kali made its way through my beloved Jamaica, it erased a piece of me with it. It devastated the island and killed my only two family members there." His eyes became red, but his voice was steady. "Our friends stepped up and came to my aid by making sure Agnes and the kids were all right. I can't thank you enough for that." He smiled, looking at the parents.

He continued, "When I left Toronto, I didn't know if I would return. But I had to go. I had to try to save my mother and sister. Upon arriving there, I faced many obstacles to get to them. But it was no use. They were already gone." Winston's eyes teared up. He picked up a tissue next to him and wiped his face. Agnes touched his hand.

"I thought that was it. I buried them, by myself. I mourned in my backyard, by myself. I thought about all the great memories I had there. How Lucy was my best childhood friend. I thought about how hard my mom worked to bring us up as a single mother. Most of all, I thought about how lucky I was to have these two women in my life. Even if it was short-lived." He paused to wipe his face again.

"I decided to go off to find my neighbours. Maybe someone else needed my help. I thought, I am a strong man, surely I can help." He touched his chest. "I was not prepared to find the entire street was a grave." He paused to take a deep breath. "I found bloated body after bloated body." He closed his eyes and allowed the tears to escape. His voice trembled as he recalled. "Sometimes, I found entire families, huddled together in one room. Little children still pressed against their mother's bosom."

"Oh my God." Kira clasped her hands over her face. The table was quiet as they contemplated the gravity of such natural disasters.

"What did you do?" Harrison broke the silence.

"Well, I lined them up and took pictures of their faces. Then I buried them in their respective yards," he explained. "I took pictures with my phone just in case their families came looking for them. I wrote a note and left it on each person's door, explaining who I buried. Of course, I didn't know each person, so I left a description and an email. I figured, if I could bring even one family member some closure, then I would have done my part." Winston looked at everyone's faces.

"Moving all those bodies and burying so many people took a toll on me. I broke a finger while shovelling the graves, and I got countless cuts about my body digging through the debris. One day I was exhausted and starving, and I tripped over a tire and fell onto a metal sheet. That's how I got the large cut on my leg. It became infected pretty soon after. That's when I started feeling sick and disoriented. One evening I was feeling really terrible, and I found a machete in one of my neighbours' yard." He paused, closed his eyes and shook his head a bit, recalling his deranged state. "I picked it up and cut my dreads off." Everyone gasped. "I know, I must have gone crazy for few minutes. Just as I was prepared to leave. Something very unexpected happened. I came across a little girl...alive." Winston glanced at their surprised faces.

"How did she survive on her own?" Shinto asked.

"That's what I wanted to know! I had not seen anyone alive in days. So, I picked her up, she must have been no more than six years old. I carried her to our house and fed her anything I could find. She was weak and messy. I asked her about her parents. But she didn't know anything besides her name. It was Audrey. After I fed her and cleaned her up, I decided to leave my mother's street. I figured it would be Audrey's best chance of survival." Winston's pace quickened. "I said goodbye, and off we went on the boat back to the landing site. You would not believe what happened." His voice elevated.

"What happened?" Gayatri blurted out for everyone.

Winston spoke excitedly, "When I returned the boat to the owner and carried her back to the base, she shouted, 'Daddy!' It took my breath away."

"Oh my God!" Harrison said.

"Her dad came running over, screaming. He held her and laid on the floor, bawling. They were the only two in their family that survived." Everyone screeched. Some were in tears. "Her dad hugged her and then hugged me and would not let go." He smiled. "Turns out, Audrey was from an entire town away. Somehow, she was washed away and ended up on my street. It was the only moment of hope amongst all that sadness. I gave the man my number and promised to help them out."

"That is incredible, Winston," Harrison said. "You are a hero."

"Thanks, Harry, but there's still much to be done. My Jamaican people are strong and resilient. They are rebuilding slowly but surely," Winston said. It felt like a weight lifted off his shoulders. "Shakti, Zoe, and Karu, I want to thank you for all the work you do to help with climate change. We don't truly understand how important it is until we're faced with it."

The trio looked at him and nodded. They had not understood the depth of loss until they heard Winston's story. No one had.

The dinner party didn't end late that night. Shakti, Hikaru, and Zoe needed to get prepared for the first week of university. They said their goodbyes and made their way home.

CHAPTER 28

YOU AND ME

T he day after dinner with the Sutherlands, Shakti was keenly
aware that Hikaru was leaving for residence at McMaster
that evening. It was a dark rainy day, and it reflected her
mood seamlessly.

Harrison noticed her moping about the house. "He will be back
in a few weeks, Shaks. You start U of T on Tuesday, too! You should
be thrilled!"

"I know! But, it's the end of an era," Shakti said sadly, not wanting
to be bothered by Harrison's chipper mood. "I'm going for a walk."

"It's raining!" Harrison shouted as he made his way upstairs.

"I know! I'll take an umbrella," Shakti shouted back from
downstairs.

Shakti walked down the street and into another wooded area.
Swansea had many little pockets of trees. People loved having access
to nature close to the city, which made Swansea special. She walked
slowly with her rubber rain boots and a clear umbrella. The walk did
wonders for her mood. She was about to make her way back to the
house when the air suddenly went still. She looked around quickly to

see what matter of spiritual being would appear. The air felt light, and the fragrance of lavender was slightly present. The raindrops started falling slowly. So slowly she touched one of the drops midair and watched it burst. It made her smile, and she did it again.

She stood still, waiting for it in the woods. Up above, the tree shade slightly parted and down floated an angel. She'd never seen this beautiful male angel before. He was large, but not quite as big as Angel Michael. He had a beautiful copper-toned aura to match his stunning copper eyes. He landed with a roar, cracking the surface below him. Light spilled out, and he lifted from his landing posture. The angel was gracefully dressed in a white robe held together by a gold rope.

"Peace be on to you, Shakti." He spoke gently.

"Peace be on to you, too." Shakti didn't know who he was, but she was happy to see him.

"I am Angel Gabriel." He smiled.

She did not reciprocate. Her face became serious. "Oh, I see." Shakti didn't know how to feel about him. After all, she assumed he misguided her mother by getting her to agree to a life without telling her the real consequences.

"I know how you feel towards me." Angel Gabriel smiled. "Allow me to explain."

"Please do." Shakti figured she owed him this much, after all he sent her mom to save her in the past.

"Gayatri is an extraordinary human being. She overcame great circumstances in her life. However, those were not the main reasons we chose her. We chose her because she had so much love to give a child," he explained. "We needed the Rainbow Tribe to be activated by great love."

"Great love? I made a speech. That was it," Shakti pointed out.

"Yes, Shakti. Your speech was inspired by the love of your friends and family. Your love runs deep. You tapped into it when you made that speech."

"I see." She never thought about it that way before.

"Your intentions were pure." Angel Gabriel smiled, revealing pearly white teeth. "Love goes beyond your connection to humans. It includes loving the Earth you live on and all the inhabitants of it. This is what generations before you missed."

"You're right about that," Shakti agreed. "They missed a whole lot."

"It's time to look forward, Shakti. Worry only about what you can do."

"I agree." Shakti was not about to let him off the hook. "Why didn't you explain this to my mother? She should have known what she was getting into."

"The full truth was too scary for any human to process, Shakti."

"So, you hid the truth to fool her?" Shakti was appalled.

"No, Shakti, without her involvement, humans would be in line for extinction. Your human minds cannot process the complexity of what was to come."

Shakti felt herself getting less mad, which she didn't want. "I hear what you're saying, but I still think you should have given her some insight into the path she chose."

"It was a strategic decision. It was not meant to mislead. She was a huge part of the divine plan."

"What about James? Was he a pawn in this plan, too?" Shakti asked.

"James chose his path, before birth. His death gave the plan meaning, and it gave you purpose to fight Bill and bring Iblis to you," Gabriel explained.

"Wow. You treat people like they are dispensable." Shakti was not happy with any of these answers. She didn't care anymore about who she was speaking to.

"Quite the opposite. We deeply love humankind. It is the purpose of our existence." Angel Gabriel had a smile on his face the entire time. It unnerved Shakti a bit because she was mad. "We supported you with the right people in your life." He pointed at her. "For you are, in fact, the Warrior."

"What do you mean, the right people? Do you mean Mary?"

"Yes, Mary is your great Protector. We placed her and her family in the house next to you."

"You did that?"

"Of course, she needed to be close to you." He walked over to her. "Mary is your Protector, just as Hikaru is your Gatekeeper." He glowed.

"Karu? Gatekeeper?" Shakti wondered how that made sense. "How?"

"His presence kept bad humans and Jinns away. They could not come close to you when he was around, which is also why no one saw you coming as a Warrior. Think about all the times he stepped forward to shield you."

Angel Gabriel made her contemplate this for a few moments. She flashed back to the science conference after her speech, as he pushed her through the crowd. He shooed away reporters from hounding her outside school. There were countless times he did not let people through to her. It all tracked.

Shakti's mind was blown. "What? Karu?"

"His aura shielded yours. No one came close to you that could have been a threat to you while he was around. The Jinns would only come around in his absence. This was all preordained, Shakti."

"That's incredible!" Shakti held her heart. It solidified her love for Hikaru.

"Shakti, there is one more. You should know as well," Angel Gabriel pre-empted. "Zoe is your Guardian."

"Zoe! My Guardian?" Shakti held her head. "Zoe? It doesn't make sense!"

"Think about it. Who suggested you do the vegetable garden as your project?"

"It was Zoe," Shakti recalled. "This led to us forming The Garden Club."

"Who inspired you to make the speech about climate change with such passion?"

"It was Zoe, losing her grandma and aunt is what took me over the edge," Shakti said, thinking back. "It really upset Karu and me."

"That's right. And who suggested you interview with the reporter? Giving you the much-needed exposure to make the Tree Project come to fruition?"

Shakti held her cheeks and yelled. "Zoe! It was all Zoe's ideas!" Tears rolled down her face. "They all helped me so much, and I didn't get it at the time," Shakti cried.

"That was the point, Shakti. Knowing sometimes spoils the outcome. Like it would have if Gayatri knew the future," Angel Gabriel made his point.

"I see. Well played, Angel Gabriel." Shakti smiled. "I understand now."

Angel Gabriel shook his head, feeling satisfied that Shakti understood him. Shakti was reminded in that moment that she was in the presence of a divine creature. "Forgive me if I appeared less than respectful. I am very protective of my mother."

Angel Gabriel paused. He lifted his hand and placed it on her shoulder. "My child, there is no forgiveness to be had, for there is none needed." He stared straight into her bright brown eyes. "Your ability to think critically and hold those in power accountable is the reason you are the Warrior."

Shakti bowed her head and blushed. She never thought about it that way. She felt satisfied with the resolution he brought to her story. But she had another question. "Angel Gabriel, please tell me what happened to Iblis?"

"I knew you would want to know his fate. Unfortunately, my answer will not give you the consolation you seek." Angel Gabriel looked sad. "The Archangels, myself included, have decided to allow Iblis to return to his abode. You know it as hell."

"What?" Shakti was appalled by this. "You let him go? What if he comes back for me?"

"He is well aware that you are heavily protected," Angel Gabriel assured her. "You will not understand the long contractual relationship we have with him and humankind. It goes far back in our history."

"But he serves no purpose other than to corrupt mankind," Shakti pleaded. She wanted him dead.

"If that were true, Angel Michael would have killed him centuries ago." Angel Gabriel looked disappointed himself. "This is the ultimate price humans must pay for free will, Shakti."

"You're right. I don't understand why angels would allow such a demonic creature to run amok on our beautiful planet."

"Shakti, fear not. We are always watching and waiting." Angel Gabriel stepped back from her. "I must go now, Little Warrior."

Shakti smiled, thinking that Angel Michael called her that in the past. "I wish you could stay. Thank you for coming and explaining your side to me. I know you did not have to do that."

"You've grown so much," Gabriel noted before he prepared his departure.

"Have I?" Shakti asked. "I thought the opposite for the longest time."

"Why is that?" Gabriel seemed surprised. "For you are girl that chased the devil into the night."

"I've noticed everyone around me has matured exponentially. Karu became a leader within our circle. Zoe's entrepreneurial skills have blossomed." She paused and thought how best to articulate what she was about to say. "But I seemed to have cracked under pressure. My anxiety has spiked since Paris. I became more of a recluse. Everything scared me." She sighed. "I know I've accomplished my task of activating the Rainbow Tribe and defeating the devil. For that, I am grateful, but I feel like I'm broken inside. I don't think I'll ever be the same." Shakti glanced into Gabriel's eyes with loss and vulnerability. It was the first time this truth had left her drooping lips.

Gabriel glided over to Shakti, placed his hands on her shoulder and extended his wings. Her eyes weakly looked side to side to see his glorious wingspan. It should have resonated feelings of awe, but Shakti couldn't muster joy from her broken truth. Gabriel stared intensely into Shakti's eyes and elegantly pulled his wings around them, creating a brilliantly lit golden circle. Within that embrace, Shakti was awash with divine love.

Then, Gabriel spoke, "Little Warrior, see yourself through the eyes of an angel." He prefaced. "If love be a force, then I am its messenger. If the sky be your limit, then you, Shakti, fly with angels."

Shakti closed her eyes and allowed his glorious words to sink in, mending her broken soul. Gabriel opened his wings and fastened them behind him. Somehow Shakti felt more whole than she ever had before.

Angel Gabriel stood up straight and flashed his winsome smile at her one more time. "Tell Gayatri, she fulfilled her role. I will be by her side forever." On that beautiful note, Angel Gabriel parted the trees above and lifted with ease into the day sky.

Shakti watched him lift off, and the rain continued to fall rapidly, washing her face as she looked up. "Thank you, Gabriel," she whispered.

She thought about Hikaru that second and ran towards his house to see him. Just as she entered her street, she spotted him knocking on her door.

"Karu!" she shouted.

He turned around and looked at her. "What are you doing?"

"I was just on my way to see you!" Shakti was still shouting as she approached him. "You're leaving today."

"Yes." He looked sad. "I am, that's why I came to see you. I'm just about to leave."

"Let's go inside." Shakti opened the door and let him in. She took off her boots and raincoat.

"You're soaking!" Hikaru said. "I'm hungry."

"I made scones for you." Shakti smiled. "White chocolate raspberry scones."

"You did? Thank you! My favourite," Hikaru said.

"I'll grab some with cream, and let's go up to my room. I need to dry off."

"Sure." Hikaru helped balance the plate of scones, and Shakti picked up a butter knife with clotted cream and a glass of milk for him.

Shakti disappeared into her bathroom to dry her hair and change her clothes. Hikaru destroyed the plate of scones, saving two for her. He was cleaning up the crumbs when she made her way to him. She sat on the bed, while he swung around and around on her desk chair.

"The scones were delicious. Thank you," Hikaru said, overzealous.

"I figured it was the nicest thing I could do for you before you leave, and forget about me," Shakti said, not expecting herself to get emotional.

Hikaru noticed and looked away. "How could I forget about you, Shaks?" He spun faster on the chair.

Shakti couldn't hold it in a second longer. She looked at him and burst out crying, covering her eyes with both hands. "I'm going to miss you so much!"

He quickly placed his feet on the ground and halted the spinning chair, "Stop! You're going to make me cry, too!" He moved over to the bed next to her and hugged her tightly.

Her hands were still over her eyes. She felt quite foolish. "It's the end of an era. We have spent more time together than with our own families. You're my Gatekeeper!" she wailed.

"Your what?" Hikaru said, confused. "It's scary for me, too. Who is going to beat up the bullies now?"

She lowered her hands. "You don't need me anymore. You're a giant."

Hikaru laughed a little. Then he became serious. He touched her hand and wiped her tears. "I'll always need you, Shaks," looking into her eyes. "It's you and me, forever."

Shakti looked at him intensely again. His aura came into focus that minute and flared up into the ceiling. She watched it burn above him. "Forever." She smiled.

Hikaru got up and reached into his pocket and pulled out a little box. He looked at her and handed it to her and sat back down.

"What's this?" Shakti stared at the little green box. "You bought me a present, and I made you scones? How old-fashioned are we?"

"Open it," Hikaru said impatiently.

Shakti took a deep breath and cracked the box open. In it, laid a beautiful gold Tree of Life pendant on a gold chain. She gasped. It was so beautiful that it took her breath away.

"Tree of Life! I love it!" Shakti hugged him tightly. "It's perfect!"

"I thought your life seems to revolve around trees. You're either planting trees or fighting for trees or hiding in them!" Hikaru laughed.

Shakti laughed out, too. "You're right! I love it so much. Thank you, Karu."

Hikaru had one more surprise for her. "Look behind it," Hikaru said excitedly.

Shakti picked up the pendant delicately and looked behind it. Inscribed on the back of the tree was,

S & H, Forever.

Shakti closed her eyes, allowing her tears to escape. He picked up the necklace and placed it on her neck while she lifted her hair.

Shakti let Hikaru go now. They walked out of her house and towards his home.

Just then, Zoe came out of her front door. "About time! I was waiting for you two." She smiled.

"Sorry, I wanted to give Shakti her gift," Hikaru said.

"You're wearing it! Isn't it gorgeous?" Zoe said excitedly.

"I love it!" Shakti touched the pendant.

Hikaru stood watching his friends, smiling. Shinzo came out of his house and gestured at his watch to Hikaru. "I'm coming, Dad." He turned to Zoe and Shakti again. "I have to go."

Shakti took a deep breath, "I know."

Hikaru stepped up to Zoe and hugged her tightly. "Bye, Zoe. Good luck on your first week at Ryerson."

"Thanks, Karu. Best of luck to you, too. We're going to miss you more than you know." Zoe closed her eyes and hugged Hikaru tightly. "Thanks for allowing me into your circle."

"You were the perfect addition." He held her hand one more time. "Thank you for everything."

Hikaru looked down at the pavement and stepped over to Shakti. She leaned in to hug him. She tried to say something to him but struggled to find the right words. Everything that was needed to be said had been said already. Hikaru hugged her silently. His face, buried in her hair. No more words to say. He detangled and looked at her, flashing a smile. She smiled, too. Hikaru turned and walked away. They watched him enter his car and drive away with his parents. Zoe and Shakti stood on the street of The Grand Heights Avenue, waving until they no longer saw him. Shakti and Zoe held each other's hand for a moment, and then walked back to their homes. Shakti felt light as a breeze. She touched her pendant once again. Her sadness departed, and she felt a renewed sense of excitement for her new chapter ahead.

The End

ACKNOWLEDGEMENTS

Thank you to my family, friends, editors, and beta-readers who supported me during this journey.

Beta-Readers

Ryan, Juliet, Savitri, Jada, Daniel, Anusha, Joshua, Philip, Christopher, Nisha, Annilla, Lisana, Isabella, Jolie.

Special Thank You

My husband, Ryan, and children, Jada, Joshua and Jolie.
My mom, Savitri, and sisters Jilian, Judith, Juliet & families.
My dad, Afrok, your presence and inspiration
were felt with every word I wrote.
I love you all.

CONNECT WITH
JANNEL MOHAMMED

To learn about upcoming books,

visit www.jannelmohammed.com

Instagram: @jannelmohammed

Twitter: @jannelmohammed

CPSIA information can be obtained
at www.ICGtesting.com
Printed in the USA
FSHW011346151220
76903FS